The Legend of Joey Trucks

The Accidental Mobster

Craig Daliessio

ISBN: 978-0-9845336-1-9

Craig Daliessio can be reached at craigd2599@gmail
Or at craigdaliessio.com

To Skip D. and To Bingo
Because you need someone who believes in you,
for those times when you don't believe in yourself.

To Leonard Isaacs
"Great stories always happen to great storytellers"
And you're the greatest of them all.

Always, For Morgan

Table of Contents

Prelude   9

1: Meet Joey Trucks   11

2: Make Me an Offer I Can't Refuse   37

3: The End of an Era   71

4: The Long Goodbye   83

5: Time to Go   103

6: Getting My Father's Blessing   129

Book Two: Virginia

7: The Damned Yankee   141

8: Farmer. Joe.   163

9: Nothing But Trouble   187

10: Sleeping With the Seven Fishes   201

11: I Knew it All Along   221

12: La Vigilia   239

13: Burial at Sea   275

14: Chumming for Seagulls   311

15: Two-Flush Tony an the Loan Shark   335

16: Old Hitmen Never Die   355

17: Today I Settled All Family Business   375

Prelude

How am I going to get these people to understand that I'm not in the mob?
I can't believe I was asking myself this. I can't believe these people really believed that about me in the first place. And now here are the FBI standing in my living room, asking me questions about mafia activity. *Mafia activity!* All because of a rumor. A stupid rumor started by my stupid, nosy neighbor...the guy who watched too many mafia shows and had a lot of time on his hands. *I didn't move here for this.* I thought, *I didn't come here to be some pseudo-mob boss. I'm just a dad, for God's sake!*

But now here I am, the victim of gossip, labeled as a Mafia Don and an object of fear to my neighbor, maybe even the whole town for all I knew. Hell, before it was over, the FBI was knocking on my door!

At first I thought the folks down here were just being nice, giving me the best parking spots at the mall, and tipping my daughter ten bucks for a fifty-cent cup of lemonade at her lemonade stand. I didn't think anything of it when they started coming to the house asking for advice, or if I could help settle a dispute with the Homeowners Association. I mean, that's how it was back in Philly where I grew up. People knew my family. They knew we were successful business people. They knew my grandfather and my father and they knew me. I was the third generation owner of a very successful trash hauling company. My grandfather started it with one beat up old truck. My father worked hard with Nonno to keep it alive, and I came back from college, worked with Pop, and made it into something very special.

Now here I am, suspected of being an underworld kingpin by my neighbors, and for all I knew, every family in Forest, Virginia, and all of it based on the idiot across the street and his overtaxed imagination.

I'm *not* in the Mafia. I'm not even *Sicilian* for God's sake! How did it get this far?

It didn't start off like this, moving to Virginia and all. In fact, it started off with a phone call...

1

Meet

Joey Trucks

I wonder what the Old Man is going to say.

Yep. That's the first thing that ran through my mind. Not: "What will I spend the money on?" or "Can I squeeze more out of them?" No, I was worried about how I would tell my father that we had an enormous offer on the table for our family business, and I was going to take it. *How the heck do I tell Pop?* I wondered.

Honestly, it was a good problem to have. Make no mistake, it was very nice being Joe Mezilli. It's not like I was overworked, because to be very honest, I wasn't. In fact I had life by the short hairs and there wasn't much I was lacking by way of material wealth. I was the third generation owner of a small, but successful trash hauling company.

Back home they call the industry "Waste Management" but I call it what it is...trash hauling. I didn't own eighteen "Waste Management Vehicles," they were garbage trucks. But the unions and the political correctness *guastafesta* made it impossible to keep calling them that. My crews weren't garbage men anymore; they were *waste management transportation engineers.* Really? Engineers? What am I, some idiot *scemo*?

Anyway, I saw the writing on the wall. The unions were always calling my guys something new and more important sounding so they could go crossways up my butt with a microscope in their unrelenting effort to unionize my shop, and squeeze more money out of me. It's not that I didn't want to pay my boys good money –in fact I typically overpaid by a few bucks an hour- but the unions kept trying to pressure me. I hate being pressured. I'm Italian, my grandfather was an immigrant. We don't do pressure very well. I knew that one day, they'd force a vote and we'd become a union shop and then it would be all over anyway.

Then there was the mob. Listen, those stories you watch on TV and read in books...they're stories for the most part. But there are –ummm- outside forces, shall we say? I kept them out of my business, mostly because of who my grandfather was, and who my uncle is. But I knew this wouldn't be the case forever. I had a good thing going. Choice routes. Nice township contracts. New trucks. It wouldn't be long before those guys started getting serious about putting the squeeze on, trying to get me to sell...or take them as a partner.

So one day, a lawyer from Waste International called me. Yeah...*Waste International.* You've seen their commercials, about how well they manage landfills and how they've brought science to waste management. It's nonsense if you ask me. But hey, I didn't handle the end product, you know what I mean? I was in the cartage end of the business. You made it, I hauled it. Those guys were the geniuses who figured out how to bury the stuff and not poison the water.

So this lawyer asks can he come see me and discuss business. He says he wants to take me to lunch, and "talk trash." He actually said that to me. "Talk trash." Like I'm some fajut. But I like to eat. And I like to eat on someone else's dime especially, so I said yes.

I arranged to meet him at Felicia's in Philly. It was about a year and a half before they closed. I hate that they're gone. I loved that place. Anyway, this lawyer shows up in a Jaguar and the first thing he does is break the parking valet's stones about the car. He hadn't even given the kid the keys yet and he's yelling at him about some scratch that happened two years before. I could hear him from inside the restaurant. He was obnoxious...a real *boccalone.* He had a damp, unlit cigar in his mouth and thick glasses and a pathetic mustache. The kind that makes you want to ask the guy if he has mirrors in his house. I tried growing a mustache once when I was nineteen. My uncle Tony laughed at me and said "You're trying to grow on your face, what grows wild in the crack of my ass!" It was that bad. This lawyer had the same sad excuse for a mustache growing on his upper lip. I didn't like the guy.

I especially didn't like him after he walked in, sat at the table I had gotten for us, and waved an envelope in front of me. He was huffing and puffing and red in his face. He had a size twenty-three neck and was wearing a size eighteen collar. I thought his head was going to pop. He says to me in his nasally voice: "I am a busy man, as you are Mr. Mezilli. So I'm going to give you this and then I'm leaving. This is our only offer, take it or leave it." Then he stands up, tugs on his strained waistband, like Chris Farley playing Matt Foley the motivational speaker, and tossed the envelope on the table. He spun on his heels and walked out. I thought he was a jerk. I thought he was a fat, bloated *cicciobomba*. More than anything, I thought I was going to run outside and throttle him on the sidewalk because he asked me to lunch at Felicia's and never even ordered. In fact he stuck me with the tab for a lunch that he invited me to. I'm never given to violence, but something about this guy made me want to attack him.

I finished my glass of wine, and signaled for Mario, my waiter. I was going to throw the envelope away without even glancing at it, but something about the porky attorney was interesting. Interesting in an annoying kind of way. So I took the butter knife and slid it along the envelope's edge. I pulled out a notarized letter from Francis Methany, president of Waste International. "Dear Mr. Mezilli...blah blah blah. We would like to expand our presence in your region...blah blah blah. We estimate your business' value at approximately twenty-four million dollars (U.S.) I sat down slowly. *Twenty Four Million?* I said to myself.

Instantly I felt a cynical wave rush over me. He had typed in "U.S." in parentheses. Like I was thinking he was going to pay in what, Kroner? "Lawyers" I thought, "Covering bases that aren't even bases." I folded the envelope and walked outside to my car. I left a hundred dollar bill on the table, a tip of about eighty seven dollars. When I got outside, Mario ran up to me on the street, "Mr. Mezilli!" he said "Mr. Mezilli, you left me a hundred bucks, sir. Don't you want your change?" I turned and smiled at him. "Naah, it's for you Mario. Take Celeste out to dinner tonight. And for God's sake don't take her here because the service is terrible." Mario laughed at my joke, and then he got tears in his eyes. He gave me a hug. I'm Italian, so hugging isn't a big deal for me, I'm used to it. But this was special. Mario didn't say "Ay!" or "Yo!" and he didn't kiss my cheek first. He hugged me like he was genuinely moved. And he was.

There was something about that hug. Something about the wonder in his eyes and the very authentic way he teared up and the lovely warm feeling it gave me to have made his day like that. I knew right then I was selling. I saw this as a chance to do some good while I was young enough to enjoy it.

I got back to my office and shut the door. I didn't tell anyone about the meeting and I locked the letter in my safe. I went home that afternoon like I always did. I ate dinner with my wife and kids and watched the Phillies on TV. Nothing was different, but *everything* was. I was twenty-four million dollars richer. All I had to do was say "yes" to the offer that the fat little lawyer from Waste International had left with me. All I had to do was sign the papers. It was that easy.

16

So naturally I said no. But I did it like an Italian. I went to work the next day and forgot about the envelope. In fact, I didn't think about it the rest of the week. The following Monday I got a phone call from the lawyer. My secretary, Margie, buzzed my office. "Excuse me, Joe; there is a Mr. Donham on the line. He says it's urgent." "Who is he, Margie?" I had a pretty good idea who he was, although to be honest, I couldn't remember the lawyer's name. But I wanted him to think I'd forgotten about him. I wasn't that easy. Margie buzzed me again a minute later.
"He is the attorney for Waste International. He says he met you for lunch last week."

"Bingo!" I thought. "I got him now." I picked up the phone. "This is Joseph Mezilli..." I said. "Mr. Mezilli?" the fat lawyer wheezed, "This is George Donham." I paused a long minute. (I love doing this sort of thing) "Who?" I said. "George Donham" said Chubby, "I met you for lunch last week and gave you our offer." I waited again. I rummaged through some papers. I coughed into the phone...loudly. "Donham...Donham." I offered, "Oh yeah. I didn't recognize the name, especially since you said you were the guy who *met me for lunch.*" I spit those words out slowly and emphatically. Like I was speaking to an idiot. "You mean the guy who skipped out on our lunch meeting and left me with my tab? That guy?"

Donham was quiet for a moment. I had him now and he knew it. For a lawyer, he wasn't that smart, because he followed up my ball-busting with the dumbest thing he could say in a negotiation. He said "So did you consider our offer, Mr. Mezilli?"
No, no, no. It *couldn't* be this easy. See, I have a gift. My sister has it too and it comes in handy. I have a photographic memory. I don't forget anything. Chubby, the corporate

barrister, forgot that when he tossed the envelope on the table at Felicia's the week before; he'd said it was their only offer. In my world that means *only offer*. When you have made your only offer, you don't ask the guy if he had considered it. You say something else. You say "Well I'm calling to find out your answer. Mr. Mezilli" or "Listen, we figured since we hadn't heard from you that you weren't interested and so we've found someone else." Personally, if it were me, I would have said "I just called to inform you that we have cut that offer in half, because you didn't get back to us in a timely manner." But he didn't say anything like that. He just blurted out "So did you consider our offer...?" and instantly admitted that he was ready to up the ante.

The truth is I knew he was going to call. I knew he was going to be open to negotiating the price. I know corporate lawyers. Especially for a company like Waste International. They aren't amateurs. They're thorough. I knew they did their research. I got calls from some friends who informed me that this fat little lawyer had been sniffing around, asking questions, poking and prodding. I knew what he was looking for, and I knew he wasn't going to find it. Not with my company.

The lawyer was performing his due diligence. Big corporations like Waste International do that. They have to. In this business, almost every company has, umm... "Involvements." Most of the guys in this neck of the woods had long ago gotten in bed with the local mob guys. Maybe they'd backed themselves into a corner and needed a loan. Maybe they'd been busted too many times at the weight scales and needed some help getting things straightened out. Maybe they had driver issues. Whatever it was, they found themselves "entangled" as we called it. And they were never going to get untangled. Never.

The mob guys weren't so bad, really. Not in this business. They weren't actually doing anything illegal with the business. What can you do with trash, right? Mostly they used the business to wash their money and to keep a front to cover for the other stuff they were doing. I had plenty of offers to get in bed with them too, but I was careful. My grandfather had started this company with one beat-up old truck that he'd saved for, for about seven years after he arrived here from Montecassino, Italy. My dad started on the trucks when he was in high school. By the time he took over, they had six trucks and eighteen guys. Each truck had a driver and two rollers.

We called them rollers then because they would roll the cans down the street by cocking them on their edge at an angle, and rolling them with their hands. A good roller could steer two cans, one on each side. They dumped the customers' cans into their bigger can and rolled to the next house. Every five or six houses they would dump their big can into the compactor on the truck and roll on up to the next house.

When I turned sixteen, I told my dad I didn't want go into the family business. "The trucks smell, Pop." I'd said. "You gotta get up so early and run all day. I don't want to be a garbage man, I'm better than that." That was the only other time my father ever hit me. He backhanded me across my mouth. For whatever reason, I had my tongue sticking out absentmindedly, and I tasted the back of his hand for a split second before my lip swelled like a hot water bottle. The only time he'd ever hit me other than that, was when I told my mom I didn't want to go to Mass on Sunday morning. She asked me why. I said "Because Father Colangelino's breath smells like Cavallo's butt. And he gets about three inches from my face when he gives us communion. I almost throw up the wafer" (Cavallo was our dog. He was a behemoth and so we gave him his name...which means "horse") WHACK! I didn't even see the old man jump out of his Bark-o-lounger. It was a thing of beauty, one smooth, swift motion. Throw down the newspaper, pull in the footrest with his legs, jump up and backhand me in the pie hole. "You don't talk disrespect about the body of Christ in my house, Joseph!" he bellowed.

Both times the old man got tears in his eyes. He apologized an hour later. I knew he didn't mean to hurt me. He'd told me that when he was really young, his father -my grandpa- would hit him all the time. Pretty hard. Pop excused it, saying he was a smart mouth and deserved it or whatever. But I knew it bothered him, and he swore never to become his father. He loved his dad. He just didn't like him.

Anyway, my dad and I reached a compromise. I would go off to college. I could take anything I wanted to take as a major, so long as I took business for a minor so I could come back and grow the business. My dad has two brothers –my uncle Tony- who wanted nothing to do with the trucks, and Uncle Franny, who fell in love with construction and only worked a couple of years for Grandpa before going off on his own. Uncle Tony was a legend in our neighborhood. He was sort of on the fringe with the local mob guys. He'd grown up with them and they all liked each other. Uncle Tony wasn't in "the family" per se. But he was a Local President for the Cement Finishers union, and he was also a township councilman. So he had choice information. Stuff like the dollar amount on the bids coming in for concrete jobs, and who was going to be getting the next trash contracts for St. Monica's parish, where we lived. Information that makes you invaluable to certain lines of work, shall we say.

Then, there was Uncle Franny. Uncle Franny was a carpenter, and a good one. He went his own way as soon as he left high school. He lives about three blocks from us on a triple-lot, and he grows anything with a seed, in his garden. One time Uncle Franny threw a handful of Cheerios in a corner of his garden. The next morning, hand-to-God, there was a dozen donuts. Franny can grow anything in that garden.

Anyway, neither he, nor Uncle Tony, was going to help my dad with the business, they'd done their time all through high school and didn't see a future in it. So Pop needed me to work with him, and thus he was willing to compromise. So we agreed. I could stay off the smelly trucks and be home every night at five. It was a good deal and I took it.

In June of 1987 I graduated from High School, and in August I went off to college, where I majored in communications and literature, and minored in business. I spent that summer splitting time between the office and the routes, Monday through Friday, and on the weekends I went to the beach. Me, Mark, Tommy Fallone, Skip O'Brien, Mikey Baldino and Joey Fanucci would pile into a couple of cars and head to Wildwood, or Margate, or Ocean City, Maryland, or Dewey Beach, Delaware.

We all had nicknames, because, well...that's what Italian kids do. Even Skip O'Brien had a nickname. He was Irish obviously, but his maternal grandmother was from Naples, and so we let him call himself Italian. Me? Well they called me "Joey Trucks" because I was always talking about not wanting to work on those garbage trucks. Mark was "Monk" and he was my closest friend on earth. I loved him like a brother. Which is good, since my brothers came later in life and we weren't that close. Mark and I did everything together. He spent more time at my house than his own. It was that way all through high school.

Tommy Fallone was "Tommy Felonious." We started calling him that in grade school and as it turns out, it was prescient. Tommy just did fifteen-to-twenty in Holmesburg for robbing an ATM machine. That's always a stupid move because those things are built better than most bank vaults. But what made it even more stupid was that Tommy and his partner, Nicky Farvoli, thought it would be somehow better to knock off an ATM in Atlantic City. Yeah, that ATM heist. You probably read about it.

We went to visit him not long after he was sentenced, and I asked him, "Tommy, stealing an ATM is *stunod* as it is, but you try one at The Sands? You tried picking the mob's pocket for God's sake! What the hell is wrong with you?" Tommy said he and Nicky Farvoli, (whose last name we had mangled into "Farfalle" which is actually bow-tie-shaped macaroni. After a while, we just called him "Nicky Bowties") thought that nobody would suspect the ATM heist in Atlantic City.

They'd posed as repairmen and walked right into the service area behind the big row of ATM's in the lobby of The Sands casino. Nobody asked them a thing, and they might have gotten away with it except that generally, ATM servicemen service the ATM on-site. They don't remove it from the building on a pallet and try getting it into a borrowed U-Haul truck. It was a stupid plan. ATM's weigh like seven thousand pounds and these two mooks were both under 5' 8". The machine tipped over as they were trying to load it into the van, spilling cash everywhere, and nearly killed them. They only made it worse when they ran.   It was a stupid plan, made even more stupid by trying to get away through the lobby of the busiest casino on the boardwalk. The security guys caught them, and made an example of them in between the slot machines. Then the cops got hold of them. Then the mob sent a couple of guys into the jail to let them know they had really screwed up. It was ugly in an ugly kind of way. But they survived it and Tommy got out a few months ago.

Nicky Bowties got out after seven years because he'd rolled over on Tommy and blamed him for the whole thing. I remember telling Tommy to do the exact same thing to Nicky, because I knew Nicky was a weasel, and he was going to take whatever offer the D.A. gave him. The truth is, neither one of them was smart enough to have been the brains of the crew. Heck, the two of them *together* thought it was a smart idea to grab an ATM from a casino in Atlantic City in broad daylight. And that was after talking it out between them for weeks. Neither of them, at any point in time, stopped and said; "Maybe we should pick a different ATM, like a WaWa or an Acme." Somebody actually convinced some grand jury that one of these two morons was the ringleader? That's even scarier than the plan they came up with.

Then there was Skip O'Brien. Skip was one quarter Italian and that was enough for him. He was constantly playing the role of the "South Philly Tony," wearing black turtlenecks and a gold Italian Horn medallion. He worked every summer and every weekend during the school year for his uncle at the Italian Market. His uncle owned a fish stand on Ninth and Passyunk. This was his uncle on his mother's side...the half Italian uncle named Eccole. Eccole was an enormous man with more hair on his back and shoulders than Bigfoot. The family called him "Uncle Squatch" as in "Sasquatch." Skip worked the fish market with his hairy uncle and saved every penny. The summer we graduated he

23

bought himself a year-old Camaro IROCZ. Just like every South Philly Tony in the Tri-State area. Skip always seemed to have money in his pocket. When we were little, we called Skip "The Caviar Kid" for obvious reasons. I asked him if the females ever dumped their eggs on him when he was throwing the fish to his uncle from the back of the truck. I asked him if that's how he'd squirreled away so much money in such a short time, "By selling the fish eggs to Polocks and telling them it was caviar?" My dad overheard me asking Skip this, and he roared with laughter from the next room.

The next time Skip came over, my dad called out to him: "Yo! It's the Caviar Kid!" Skip didn't like it at first, but he liked my dad a lot, and having a nickname given to him by my old man was something special for Skip. His dad had left town when Skip was about two years old. Skip loved my dad and my dad loved Skip. So my dad bestowing a nickname on him made him feel like family. In fact he was. My folks essentially adopted Skip, and he all but lived with us until college. He's a big-time seafood broker back home in Philly. He's a heck of a successful guy. He got married and named his firstborn son after my dad. My dad cried when Skip told him. I did too. I was happy for my dad, plus it got me off the hook of having to do it myself. Let somebody else's kid get teased for being named "Giuseppe IV" It sounds like a frickin' fishing boat. But then "Giuseppe O'Brien isn't much better, now is it?

Mikey Baldino lived next door to my grandfather. My grandfather could have bought himself a new house, years before, but he stayed in the old neighborhood and lived in the same row home. In fact, he and Nonna had the same sofa and living room furniture they'd bought the year I was born. Like all South Philly grandparents, they'd had every stick of furniture in the living room covered in custom made plastic slip covers. Their sofa looked like it was still sitting in the showroom at Levitz. It had endured forty-two years of grandchildren, and dogs, and homemade-wine spills, and it still looked pristine. Those plastic slipcovers played hell on your legs in the summer. I'd go visit Nonna and plop down on her sofa wearing my cutoff jeans. It was hot and humid and she never ran the air conditioner until night time. You'd forget about the humidity and the sweat on the back of your legs and after an hour, you went to stand up and the suction ripped off a layer of skin. "Nonna, Jesus, Mary and Joseph! You gotta turn on the air conditioning down here!"

But she never listened. There was a huge fan in the parlor blowing wet, humid summer air around the house. I tried telling her once that a fan doesn't help with the humidity. Nonna spoke pretty darned good English, except when you wanted to discuss spending money with her. Tell her she needed to turn on the A/C for an hour in the afternoon, or try borrowing her silverware, and you'd think she'd just arrived at Ellis Island after stowing away in steerage on an Italian freighter. Any other time and she'd be correcting *my* English.

Anyway, Mikey Baldino lived next door and I met him when I was little and we lived two doors down from Nonna and Grandpa Guiseppe. We eventually moved a few blocks away, but Mikey and I remained close. When I would spend the weekend at my grandparent's house, he would come over and spend the night with me. We used to take my grandfather's handkerchief and make parachutes for our green plastic army men and dropped them out the second-floor back window.

Mikey was an amazing stickball player. He could hit anything at all. You could shoot BB's at him, at night, and he'd hit eight out of ten. He loved baseball. Loved it. We'd walk over to the Vet with a dollar in our hand and each get a ticket in the seven hundred level. The Phillies were terrible back then and the place was half empty. So after an inning or so, we'd sneak down to the club level and watch the game from seven rows back. The security guys never bothered us, and even if they did, I'd drop my grandfather's name and they'd smile and walk away. A few minutes later the hot dog guys would come by and give us a couple of dogs and Cokes and some peanuts. I'd look up and say "I don't have any money, sir." The guys would smile and say "Naah, you're Giuseppe Mezilli's grandson, you don't pay here. Just make sure you tell your grand pop we took care of ya, okay kid?" "Yes sir." I'd say, and me and Mikey would chow down on Phillies Franks and watch our game and be home by nine PM.

So, Mikey Baldino got his nickname from his love for baseball. His nickname was "Mikey Baseball" as in Mikey Base-Baldino. Mikey loved that name. We used to have this little cheer we'd call out on the little league field: "Here comes Mikey Baldino, the Big Bambino!" Eventually it just stayed *Mikey Baseball.* He went on to play in the Padres farm system for a few years and now he runs an insurance agency in Voorhees N.J. and coaches Little League. He keeps himself in amazing shape and every winter he goes to Florida to a Phillies Fantasy Camp. You know, where old guys spend a week playing baseball against the guys they grew up watching? Mikey takes it very seriously. He works out all year and even had a batting cage installed in his back yard. He went to Florida a couple of years ago and was especially excited when he found out that Curt Schilling was going to be there. He was riding Schilling pretty good at dinner the night before the big scrimmage game that ends the week. Mikey was working on Schilling pretty hard, telling him how he was sure he could hit him. Mikey likes to talk big sometimes. The next morning, Schilling "spun his cap." He hit the bill of Mikey's batting helmet with a fastball at about ninety MPH. Mikey picked himself up off the ground, glared out at the mound and said "Yo Curt! Losing your control, or what?" Schilling paused a long time, stared a hole right through Mikey, and finally said; "I hit just what I was aiming at." Mikey shut up after that.

The last of the guys I grew up with was Joey Fanucci. Now, poor Joey had a double whammy. He had the same first name as me...and as I was the accepted ringleader of our little crew, this was never going to work, so he couldn't use his first name. And his last name was constantly being butchered into a slur. People were always calling him "Joey Fanook." If you don't know what that means, Google it. But suffice it to say it isn't nice. Joey couldn't share my name, (although I hadn't been called "Joey" since the sixth grade) so we called him Domanucce. (You pronounce it "Dom-anootch") His middle name was Dominic. Joseph Dominic Fanucci. So we took his middle name and blended it with his last name, and we got Domanucce.

To say it correctly, you say it fast... "Yo! Domanucce!" Joey loved it. It was very Italian and so was he. His parents were immigrants, the only parents in my circle who were from the old country. The rest of us were second generation American, but Joey was the first in his family born here. His mom and dad were wonderful people. They made me laugh all the time. His mom made homemade wine out of frozen Welch's grape juice and his dad had a cousin with a farm in New Jersey. Mr. Fanucci had a big stake-body truck and he would haul horse manure from his brother's farm to homeowners all over the Philadelphia suburbs. When business was slow with residential customers, he'd haul loads to Kaolyn and Avondale, the two towns west of Philly known as "The Mushroom Capital of the World." He had a full-time job with the township, working for the water department, and the manure hauling business was a side job for him. It's a good thing too, because the way Mrs. Fanucci kept cranking out kids, he needed to sell as much poop as he could.

When Joey and I graduated in 1987, he was the oldest of nine. Three more came before he graduated college. Twelve that made it, plus four or five miscarriages. Mrs. Fanucci always said of the twelve kids who made it into the world that the "Cream, rose-ah to de top!" and she'd brag in Italian about her big family. She was an amazingly good natured lady for being perpetually pregnant for almost 13 years.

That was my "crew". Those were the guys I'd grown up with and that was what I knew I'd be leaving behind that day I decided to sell *Mezilli Trash Hauling and Cartage* and move my still-young family to Forest, Virginia.
And that's where the fun began...

I didn't move to Forest for two years after selling the business. I had agreed to stay on in the transition for one year. After that I had to deal with the never-ending guilt being laid on me, like bricks in a wall, by my grandmother. Like I said before, Nonna spoke darned good English, except when discussing money. The only other time she would lose her ability to speaka-de-English was when she was trying to guilt you into, or out of something. In this case, her first grandchild moving five hours away. The same grandson who just did a business deal that made her a millionaire a couple times over at eighty-six years old. *That* grandson.

She would sit in the living room all day. In the dark. On those sticky plastic slip covers, talking to the picture of the sacred Heart of Mary that hung over the sofa. "Mah-doan"

"Mah-DOAN!" "Mah-DOAN! Why? Why do I'm have such a broken heart? Mother Mary...help-a dis pain!" It was worthy of an Oscar, I swear to God. Finally I said "Nonna, just come with us. You'd love this place. It's near the mountains and it reminds me of the Campania. It's even got vineyards like Campania."

This was a mistake. Because my grandfather was born in Montecassino, which sits right at the south end of the Campania range in Italy. My grandmother's eyes glazed over and she pulled her shawl over her head and started weeping and saying his name over and over. "Giuseppe...Giuseppe! Il mio amore è morto" (*IL mio amore e morto* means "My love is dead.") Now, my grandfather had been gone five years by this point, and when he was alive, he and Nonna would argue a hell of a lot more than they would speak kindly to each other. They were legendary on our block for having screaming matches in the summer with all the windows open. Arguments over things like how my grandfather liked his macaroni cooked. Or why she couldn't "Turn on-ah de air-a condit-chin." If my grandfather had it his way, it would have been cold enough in their living room to hang sides of beef. But Nonna held the purse strings and she lived her whole life like an impoverished immigrant. She never grasped that they had become pretty wealthy, which was true even before I did the deal with Waste International. She'd lived through the Depression and never forgot the growl in her stomach.

So I suggested she move with us and she burst into tears. "Leave dis-a house? Dis-a house that your Nonno built-a with-a his hands? No! Never! I'm-a gonna die here." Then she paused and turned on the eye-faucets and with a hoarse whisper said "I'm-a guess I'm-a gonna die *alone* here." She didn't shoot me the horns, but I saw her right hand twitching nervously...she *wanted* to.

Then she turned to the picture of the Sacred Heart and wailed "Mother of Jesus-a. I'm-a gonna die here of-ah the broken heart. The broken heart like-a the mother of-a Jesus!" I told her I'd pay for those snazzy aluminum awnings she always wanted over each window and she smiled again. I knew my Nonna. She has a price, like everyone else.

So I stayed in Philly for two years. I worked that one final year with Waste International, and then I just piddled for another year. I spent a lot of time down the shore. I hunted and fished, (something I love) I played in the men's hockey league. I took my kids to school every day and eventually...I drove my wife nuts.

Angie looked at me one morning at breakfast after I had rushed her to get done so I could wash the lone dish she was using and I knew I was in trouble. I'd seen that look before. Mostly it was when I came home with a dead deer in the back of her Escalade. "It's a Cadillac, Joseph! You have a truck, but you have to put a dead, bloody deer in the back of my Escalade? I swear if you stain that leathuh!" Angie and I had both been double majors in college and graduated with degrees Communications and English. She enunciated perfectly. But she reverted back to a "Princess of Little Italy" whenever I pissed her off, which thankfully was almost never. She didn't fall back on the street talk very often, but she was a master of the Maloik...*the evil eye.* Her grandmother was even better at it. The Maloik is what Italian women do when they get to a certain age and they realize the power they have. They don't say anything, they just stare at you. They stare the way a butcher stares at a side of beef just before he goes to work filling a freezer order. If they combine this with the "Death Horn" (closing the fist and extending only the first finger and pinky, like a horn) pointed at you, you are pretty much living in your final days.

Anyway, Angie shot me that look. The time I remember seeing that look the longest, was after we had three boys and she decided her life was incomplete without a little girl. Getting her pregnant evolved from something pleasurable that I looked forward to, to a grinding full-time job. "JoZEPH!" She would call upstairs to me. "We are going to have a little Italian princess or die trying!" I was beginning to believe she was hoping for the latter. But in the end, we had our little angel and I was glad she was so adamant about it.

But that morning as I scraped her uneaten scrambled eggs into the disposal she stared a hole through my skull and said "Giuseppe Francesco Mezilli if you don't find something to do and get out of this house, I'm going to turn you into two-hundred pounds of fresh sausage!" Angie had a way with words.

A few days later was Homecoming for my college. I had gone to school in Southern Virginia and always liked the area. We spent the weekend with a friend of mine who lived in Forest, Va. He had a beautiful five-acre spread with a lovely view of the Blue Ridge Mountains. I fell in love with the place. Angie and I stayed a few extra days and met up with a realtor. We wound up putting an offer in on a house in a neighborhood near my college buddy and we also looked at a nice one-hundred acre piece of woodland that bordered Jefferson National Forest. It was perfect for me to build a hunting cabin on. So we planned on making the move the following summer.

I had to endure six months of Nonna's wailing, and calling on the Blessed Mother. Along with this was the back and forth discussions about how much my old man was getting from the Waste International deal. I offered him half. He said it was way too much because I had basically taken over the business for him ten years ago when his sciatica made it hard for him to drive, or sit in the office for more than a few hours. Funny, the captain's chair on that Sea-Ray he bought, never hurt the old sciatica any. He had gotten to the point where he was only coming in Wednesday mornings, through Friday at noon.

But I loved the old man and I figured he'd deserved the break. He'd taken the business from the one crappy truck my grandfather had purchased in 1953 and built it into a going concern. When I graduated from college and came to work for him, the old man had built it into twelve trucks and twenty-eight employees, including two mechanics, and Sylvia who ran the office. Not bad for a guy with a High School education, whose father hardly spoke English, and had backhanded him for pretty much anything.

By my forty-third birthday, I'd grown *Mezilli's Trash Hauling and Cartage* into the biggest independent trash hauler in the Northeast. Everyone else was either a subsidiary of a big company, a three-truck mom-and-pop operation, or so far in bed with the mob that they were only keeping thirty-seven cents on the dollar. I'd steered clear of the syndicate, grew the company slowly and carefully, and thanks in part to Uncle Tony's inside knowledge of Township trash contracts- made us profitable. We had eighteen trucks plus two spares. We had two semis with a pair of fifty-three- foot, open-topped trailers, a huge maintenance building, and forty-six employees. Oh and we owned forty-three percent of the county landfill.

Sylvia retired two years before I did the Waste International deal. She'd been a widow a long time and was starting to suffer from dementia. Sylvia had worked for my dad for as long as I can remember. She was a great old Italian lady with a wisp of a mustache and her clothes always smelled like oregano. Sylvia was a great cook and spent every evening in the kitchen. Bringing us lunch was her great joy. I think it reminded her of making lunch for her late husband Biagio. (Everyone called him Ben) Ben walked a beat for the Philadelphia Police force for thirty-eight years. It took an act of God to get him on the force, because back then, the Irish had pretty much sewn-up the Police force and claimed it as their own. Benny knew a guy from his days in the Army and the guy pulled some strings. To be honest, he was far too sweet a man to be a cop. Had he ever actually apprehended a criminal, Benny would have probably knelt beside them on the sidewalk and prayed the Rosary with them. Then he would have opened his wallet and given them his last twenty bucks. But Benny also was a huge man. So he could afford to be kind. He was still scary and imposing. Everyone in the neighborhood loved Benny and Sylvia.

When she took sick a few years ago, I called her son in Phoenix and told him, "Bobby your momma is starting to really slip. I think you need to consider bringing her out there with you." Bobby got real quiet and started making excuses. He said he would be out at Thanksgiving and take her to her doctor and see what they would do. So me and Angie and my old man watched out for her every day until Thanksgiving. Bobby never flew out, and after a few months I called him again. He made endless excuses, and finally one day Uncle Tony called him for me. I can't repeat what he said, but Uncle Tony cursed a lot. Some in English and some in Italian. A couple of days later, Uncle Tony comes in my

33

office and says "Bobby has gambling issues; he can't take care of Sylvia." "How did you find that out?" I asked him. Uncle Tony usually smiles when he drops references to his mob friends, but this time he looked serious. He wouldn't tell me much except to say "It's not good, nephew. I think you should take care of Sylvia, because that fajut son of hers isn't going to do it."

He told me that Bobby had agreed to give me power of attorney and so I took over Sylvia's affairs. Eventually we put her in St. Rose of Lima's nursing facility. The sisters over there loved Sylvia and Benny too, before he died. They took care of her until she passed away six months ago.   A week after she died, Bobby calls me, real late at night. He starts talking in generalities, but I knew where it was going. I let him squirm until he asked me "So did momma have any assets? Who is in charge of her estate?" I jumped out of my chair and screamed into the phone like he was standing there in my living room with me. I was hot. "Bobby! You haven't been home in seven years. You hadn't seen your mom's face in *five* years, and that was only because we bought her a flight out and back for her birthday. She would come to work some days so lonely you could see it in her eyes and you never even called her!"

I was furious now. My arms were flailing and the spit was flying. I knew I was heading for stupidity with how angry I was, so I gathered my wits and said, "Yeah Bobby. Your mom had some assets. Uncle Tony is holding them. Call him with your questions."

Bobby never called any of us again. The truth was Sylvia was pretty well taken care of. We had a nice retirement plan and I made sure she didn't lack for anything. My dad told me once that Sylvia was as responsible as anyone else for the success of our company. There were days, he'd told me, when she would be doing payroll and notice that there wasn't quite enough money. She would write out her own check but not cash it for three or four weeks, sometimes longer. My dad didn't even discover it for two years. He was having a complete audit done for a business loan we were getting and the accountant came to him quietly and said "You have a real angel working here." My old man said "What do you mean?" The accountant laid some papers on his desk, photocopies of the ledger where Sylvia had waited weeks and sometimes months before cashing her paycheck. It always corresponded to a slow period for our cashflow. Sometimes it was the lag time between hauling contracts or maybe a truck had broken down and needed an unusually large sum to fix it. My dad sat there with his jaw open. He called Sylvia into his office.

The accountant smiled as she walked in but it didn't put her at ease. My dad realized right away she thought she'd done something wrong and so he stood up and walked around from behind his desk and gave her a big hug. "Mr. Robinson here showed me what you've been doing all these years Sylvia...holding your paycheck when times were tough. I never knew. Why would you do that for me?" My dad got teary eyed when he told me this story. He said Sylvia started to get weepy and said how she and Benny always loved our family. Benny's brother Corrado had emigrated here with my grandfather and then he'd brought Benny over a couple of years afterward. The families had remained close and the children and grandchildren had grown up together. At least until that *fannullone* son of hers ran off to Phoenix and abandoned her and Benny.   They'd had a daughter, but she died in the fifties from polio. Bobby was a change of life baby and Sylvia doted on him a bit too much. But it's not her fault he turned out like he did. We were pretty much family to Benny and Sylvia, especially after Benny died. She spent a lot of time with Nonna and with my mom too. And like I said, the old girl could cook. She could throw a shoe and a windshield scraper in a pot and in an hour you'd ask for seconds. Cooking was how she told us she loved us, and she loved us a lot. We loved her back -the whole family did- and she sure wasn't alone in her last years. We made certain of that.   Anyway, I was ready to make the move to Forest and so I had to pin down the Old Man about his share. It was a lot more money than he'd originally thought, and a heck of a lot more than the fat, self-important lawyer from Waste International offered in the first place. That negotiation was a thing of beauty. I had more couth than the Old Man about business dealings, having been to college and all. But sometimes, the old neighborhood just rose up in my soul and I could squeeze a stone with the best of them, and this negotiation was just such a time.

Then too, I didn't need to sell and I didn't particularly *want* to sell. They needed me, I didn't need them. That and they had badly undervalued the business. All of it played into my hands, and I had some fun with it. It was the stuff of legends. The other trash haulers back home still talk about the way I undressed that big prosciutto.
It went like this...

2

Make Me An Offer I Can't Refuse

George Donham called my office about ten days after our very brief meeting at Felicia's. He was wheezing into the phone and I thought he was having a heart attack. I found out later that the pressure was really on this guy to get me to go for the deal. Waste International really needed my routes and my trucks. Everyone else had too much baggage, or was too small a presence in the area for them to buy. They needed Mezilli Trash Hauling and Cartage. The problem for them was that I didn't need or want to sell it. Not even remotely.

So Margie buzzes my office and tells me he is on the phone. I left him dangle for a few minutes and finally I picked up. We exchanged pleasantries and I broke his balls for leaving me at Felicia's the way he did. He was silent for a moment. I recognized this trick. Car dealers use it a lot. You just go silent. Most people are uncomfortable with silence and they'll start talking to fill the vacuum, and usually they'll tell you everything you need to know to get them to buy. But like I said, I was aware of this ploy. So
George Donham says how sorry he was for the "misunderstanding at Felicia's" and did I consider his offer? I said "Yes. I considered it."

That was it. That was all I said. I didn't say another word. I even held the phone six inches from my face after that so he couldn't even hear me breathe. It was silent like a tomb for about two minutes. That sounds like nothing, but time one-hundred-twenty seconds on your watch and imagine that kind of dead air during a business call. I could feel the tubby little lawyer squirming on the other end. I had already decided...if he broke the silence I had him. If not, I would simply hang up. If he called back, I *still* had him. I would tell him I thought he had dropped off the line. Oh and my price would have doubled.

He cleared his throat at the one-minute-forty-five second mark. Finally at two minutes he said "Mr. Mezilli are you there?" He was speaking much softer. I knew he was mine. And he knew it too. And he knew that I knew. For a minute I almost felt sorry for him, but I remembered he was playing with house money here. This wasn't his cash he was flaunting; it was Waste International's, the third largest waste conglomerate in the world and desperate to become number two. Mezilli Trash Hauling and Cartage was a very big part of that plan and I knew it. So did Donham. "Yes I'm here Mr. Donham," I said, wondering if he could *hear* the smile on my face. "I thought maybe you'd hung up. Listen, I have things to do, so what is it you wanted?" He cleared his throat again. "I was wondering if you had considered our offer for your company."

This was way too easy now. But I was at the point where I was ready to talk seriously with pork-chop here and see what he was bringing to the table. So I shot back, "Yes I have considered it, and I consider it well short of where you need to be to make me consider it seriously."

What would happen next was all-important. If he came back with a figure, I knew that was probably his limit. If he said "Well what did you have in mind?" I knew he had a blank check and I could get whatever I wanted as long as it wasn't insane. He paused for a moment, still trying to get me to tip my hand. Finally he said "Well, I have some leeway, do you have a figure in mind?"

Jesus, Mary and Joseph! I couldn't be that easy, could it? Maybe it could. Maybe hard working, third generation, grandsons of immigrants really can make it in the brave new world. I heard an orchestra somewhere. Then I snapped out of it. "Yes," I told him, "Yes I do have a figure in mind." He swallowed hard into the phone and asked me what it was. "It will take a lot more than Twenty-four- million to buy Mezilli and all our assets, Mr. Donham. And it's only negotiable in one direction, if you know what I mean. I don't need to sell and the residuals I get from our share of the landfill alone will pay me more than your offer would over the next twenty years. I'm actually leaving some on the table here, but that's the nature of negotiation, right?"

Donham was silent. I'm not sure, but I swear I heard him loosening his collar. He tried to talk but it sounded like his mouth had run dry. He finally choked out one word: "Residuals?" Oh man. This puffy little muffin was done. Finished. Caput. The hook was in and I had him to the boat. *He didn't know about the residuals.* He didn't know about the landfill. I had him. "The residuals, Mr. Donham. The residuals from Mezilli's ownership in the Delaware County landfill site. We own forty-three percent of the landfill. We get a residual of Three Million dollars a year forever as long as the landfill is in use. You knew about this, right?"

No. He didn't know about it. I'd already established this, but I asked him because I wanted to see if he would try to lie to me and play it off like he knew. Because if he tried to lie I was going to end the deal right there. Nothing good comes from dealings with a liar. But Donham manned up and said "No...No I didn't know about the land deal." *Good boy, George!* I thought to myself, *At least you know when you're beaten and things will go easier from here on out.* I explained the landfill deal to him so he knew why I was asking for almost three times their offer.

"About twenty years ago, the county began making noise about wanting their own landfill instead of shipping trash down to Delaware or up to Philly to the incinerator plant. It was costing them a fortune to dump trash and the residents were getting sick of their trash bills going up every year like clockwork." I relished in telling Donham this story. To me, it showed him the kind of business people he was dealing with. My family knows people. And people are at the bottom of every business deal that ever went down.

"So my Uncle Tony called my dad and I one day, a couple of years after the exploratory committee was formed. A committee he happened to be sitting on." I told Donham. "He told me where the three most likely sites were, and then he gave me all the reasons why it wouldn't be two of them. Uncle Tony was pretty sure it was going to be out by the old Hog Island area near the airport. So the next day my dad and I met with a realtor friend of Uncle Tony's and put a fifty-thousand-dollar deposit down on forty-six-hundred acres of useless swamp land. We signed a private land contract where we held rights for ten years with a yearly renewal fee of twenty-five grand. We didn't even have to take a mortgage. We basically owned the option on this land." I paused here. "Cough, or sneeze, or something Mr. Donham. Let me know I haven't lost you." Donham laughed nervously and said "No...No I'm here. And please, call me George" Perfect! Tubby wanted to be my friend now. I think he saw already that he wasn't dealing with just some stupid garbage man. He respected my business acumen, even if he didn't say so. I continued with my story.

"Anyway, we renewed the option for three years. The fourth year, the county made their decision. It was the Hog Island property. That land that we had one-hundred-twenty-five-thousand invested in, was now worth about one hundred million if you looked at the fifty year life cycle of a landfill."

Donham asked me, "So you sold? I thought you said you had ownership." "We do." I replied. "We negotiated with the county for six months, but they couldn't find enough financing to buy us out. So I went to them with a deal. Pay us ten million dollars over ten years and give us a forty-five percent ownership stake in the landfill. We'll take our money as a residual on profits each year and pay the same fees everyone else pays to dump here." The county came back with forty-three percent. Something about by-laws regarding partnerships and that was their maximum. We took the deal, and we've been collecting ever since. Six years ago the residual hit three million a year and it will go up again next year. There are still about twenty five years left on the projected life cycle of the landfill, so there is a lot of money still out there on that deal."

Donham let out a long breath. He didn't say anything for a few seconds. I could almost hear the numbers running in his head. Finally he spoke up. "I understand your position, Mr. Mezilli. I'll take this information back to the board of directors at Waste International, along with my recommendation that they accept your counteroffer. Will you give me a week to get back to you?

No. No it could not be happening like this. I started to wonder if Donham had ever gotten a speeding ticket and told the cop not to lower the speed. "No office, I really *was* doing Ninety in a Seventy-Five and I'm not taking anything less." He told me he was going to advise them to take my offer. *Why did you tell me that George? Now you can't counter.* I felt like Don Corleone, when Sonny showed his hand about wanting to take the Solazzo deal. And he asked me if I would give him a week. He *asked* me. This guy couldn't negotiate a tip for a shoe shine.

"Sure George," I said..."You take however long you need. You can understand why I'm not in a hurry. I don't need to sell at all." "Oh and George..." I said, "You can call me Joseph."

"Thank you, Joseph." Tubby said, "I'll be back with you in a few days"

Joseph. Nobody has called me Joseph since Sister Joan in seventh grade. I only told him that so that if he asks around about the company, I'll know right away. Everyone he talks to will call me asking who this goo-goots is who calls me Joseph. That'll be worth a laugh by itself.

So all week I get phone calls from the neighborhood wanting to know who this big provolone is who is asking all these questions about me, and why is he calling me "Joseph?" I laughed for the first three days. After that I forwarded all my calls to Margie's line and left my business cell phone in my desk drawer. This guy was like Yukon Cornelius sniffing gold. Except he should have been this diligent when he was actually doing his due diligence. By this point in the negotiations, with no leverage at all, he was merely fact-checking me before facing his bosses and asking for seventy-five Million dollars.

That was my number. I had arrived at it several days before he called me. Now, I knew it was a little high, but I always go in high and come down to where I wanted to be all along. But I didn't tell him this on the phone. What I did next was almost cruel. It was certainly dismissive and to be honest, I regretted it. I'd already broken this Mortodel and I was just picking at scraps. But I figured that when the day came to sign, I'd save his big butt somehow. For today I was having fun.

"George" I said, "I have to leave the office in an hour. I'm taking my boys deep-sea fishing. I'll leave my number in an envelope with Margie and you can drop by and pick it up. If you call back, I'll assume we have a deal. If I don't hear from you, I'll know we don't and I'll understand. And hey, George, even though you stiffed me at Felicia's, it was nice meeting you. Have a good weekend." and I hung up. I never even waited for an answer. If he showed up he was a beggar and the deal was done. I knew he was going to show up. In fact I figured he was jumping in his car right then in an effort to meet me face-to-face. So I wrote my number on a piece of paper and stuck it in a "Mezilli Trash and Cartage" envelope (Putting the entire name of our company on the envelope was a bit too much) and I left it with Margie. I smiled at her and said "When George Donham gets here, give him this. Tell him I don't have my cell phone with me." I said, waving my cell phone at her with a wink, as I left.

I took the boys down to Ocean City, Maryland for a shark fishing tournament and never gave the deal a moment's thought. But George Donham sure did. That poor guy apparently didn't sleep a wink all weekend because he blew up my cell phone with call after call at all hours. Not that I cared. I have a personal cell phone that only my friends and family have access to. I shut off the business cell phone on Fridays. It was a deal I made with Angie years ago.

Playing Hardball

Monday morning I pulled up to my office at seven AM. I was always an early riser and I liked getting to the office early and talking to the guys before they rolled out for their routes. I really liked my guys. All of them. They were quirky and calloused and difficult sometimes, but I also know they were loyal. I paid them well and they would have chewed through a cinder-block wall for me. I paid attention to birthdays and anniversaries. If a guy and his wife had a new baby, I sent Angie shopping with the credit card and orders not to come back with less than five hundred dollars' worth of goodies. You get back what you give out. That's true everywhere but especially in being a boss.

So I pull into my spot and there is the pretentious Jaguar of George Donham. It's 6:47 AM and he's talking to somebody on his cell phone. Loudly. *I just don't like this guy* I thought. Then I thought to myself, *You've broken his stones enough...take him seriously today.* Okay. I will. As soon as he saw me, he shot out of his car like a swarm of bees had just flown in the passenger window. He stuck his hand out and I shook it. It was damp with sweat. Imagine what I was thinking already.

He followed behind me and straight into my office without waiting for me to invite him. *"Take him seriously today..."* I heard my own voice in my head. "Have a seat George." I offered "You want a cup of coffee?" "No thanks" he said impatiently, "I can only drink one cup per day. It upsets my stomach." *"Huh"* I thought, *"Doesn't look like anything else upsets that thing."* I made myself laugh at that, and for a moment I thought I had actually spoken the words out loud. *"Take him seriously today..."* this time it was my grandfather's voice I heard whispering this to me. *"Okay, okay."*

I sat down in my chair and he leaned in closer to my desk. His forehead was sweaty and he was pink around the lips. He seemed pretty nervous. "Joseph, I got your counter on Friday. That's...it's uh...well it's a lot of money." he finally blurted out. "I don't think Waste International will pay this." *Oh dear, George, you just aren't good at this at all.* "So you never presented it to them?" I said, "You're here talking to me on your own?" His puffy face fell. He realized he'd just shown his hand. He was afraid to take my offer to them. Even if they took it, he'd look bad and probably lose his cushy job as a corporate lawyer. And God knows what practicing attorneys are making these days.   "Well you have a problem, George." I smirked. "How are you going to tell them?"

Now, I knew what the guy was hoping I would do. He was hoping I would take far less and make him look like a champ. But I wasn't giving away our company no matter what. So I did what Italian's do best. I made the situation work for me.

"George, who is your boss at Waste International?" I said, phone in hand. "Who is the highest guy you answer to?" He squinted at me and licked his lips like they were going dry on him. He fumbled for words. Then he said "Uh...it's uh...Richard Green. He is CFO and second in command. He oversees all expansion." "Good!" I said, "What is his number?" Donham's face went slack and his jaw dropped a little. "Huh?"   "His number, George! What is Richard Green's cell number?" I bellowed. I thought I sounded a little like Gomez Addams, and that made me laugh.

Donham spit the numbers out like a zombie. I tapped them into my phone and hit the dial button. George swallowed hard. He had no idea what was coming next but at this point, I think he felt like his job was at stake and he was out of options. Richard Green picked up on the second ring. "Mr. Green?" I said, "This is Joe Mezilli." I said nothing more than that. I wanted to see what he said in return. If he pulled the "Mezilli...Mezilli?" and played it off like he didn't know who I was, I'd be a little cold with him. If not, I knew I had a man I could talk to.

"Aah yes, Mr. Mezilli. How nice to speak with you. I assume Mr. Donham is there and provided my cell number?" Okay! This is a straight shooter. I can deal with a guy like this. "Yes he is right here." I answered "He apparently feels like my offer is out of bounds and he wouldn't even take it to you. He's a tough customer, Mr. Green. He's a good negotiator. You better keep him close by or I may hire him away from you." Richard Green laughed loudly into the phone. Great, he has a sense of humor about him! George Donham looked at me like I had just saved his kitten from a tree. I winked at him. I can break balls with the best of them, but I can also shmooze. And I'm not out for anyone's job. Donham will learn the ropes eventually.

Green and I spoke for fifteen minutes. He agreed to meet with me at his office, along with old George here, in an hour. I hung up and looked at George Donham. I thought that he would faint. He looked at me like I'd just shown up in the courtroom with the evidence that kept him from the electric chair. Maybe I had. "I'll follow you over, George. We're meeting with your boss at 8:30." Donham sort of stared at me and his hands moved slowly into his pockets to get his keys. I put my arm around his shoulder. "How old are you George?" He looked at me funny, not expecting kindness in my victory. "I'm thirty-one" He muttered. "Well heck, George, a man doesn't really learn his business until his thirties. You're a good attorney George. Now find some passion to go with it. Skill is just skill until you have passion. Then you have a real career."

I smiled as I said this, a little amazed at my own wisdom on the subject. It was very true. It was passion that gave me the insight to take what Giuseppe and my Old Man had started and made a model for the industry out of it. It wasn't trash removal that was my passion, it was people. I genuinely liked all the guys who worked for me. I really liked being generous and helping people. Angie is the same way. We relished taking care of Sylvia and Nonna and the local kids. We were like the Mayor and First Lady of the neighborhood. I was passionate about where I grew up and the people I grew up with and I felt the same about my children's friends and their families. We had gotten a reputation for being the family that people came to for help, or advice. It's in my nature.

So I follow George Donham over to the regional headquarters of Waste International where his office was, and where his boss was waiting. Richard Green was a nononsense man. I could tell that immediately. But he didn't seem to take himself too seriously. I liked that. He welcomed me into his office and the three of us sat down for a moment at a large conference table. We talked in generalities. Getting to know each other. Finally he says to me, "So what is this offer that apparently I have to refuse?" Oh I liked this guy! He pulled a Godfather quote out of his bag. Granted he'd modified it a bit, but it worked better that way. I liked this move! It told me he was gutsy. He figured out right away that I was not a thin-skinned guy. I could laugh at a Jewish guy making a Godfather joke. Well played Mr. Green.

I pulled the envelope out of my pocket and slid it across the table to him. George Donham swallowed hard and I thought I heard him whimper ever so quietly. *Grow a pair*

George, Jesus, Mary, and Joseph! I said this silently to myself, but I was almost certain that I was so forceful, that he'd heard it anyway. I hoped so.

Green opened it right up. No pause. No drama. More points for the Jewish guy. He read it without expression. Finally he looked up at me with a grin and said "Let's take a walk." He stood up and grabbed a pair of basketball shoes from under his desk and put them on. He had on a really nice pair of Johnston and Murphy's and he slid them neatly into the spot where the Nike's had been. "Nice choice in shoes." I said. He winked and motioned to Donham to follow us.

We walked down a hallway and past a very nice break room. A few steps through a glass door and we were standing in a full sized gym. There was a basketball halfcourt on the far end and Green headed there. He grabbed a few balls from a rack and passed one over to me. "I hate basketball," I said, laughing, "When I jump, you couldn't slip a dime under my shoes." Richard Green bellowed at that. He looked at me and said "Me too. But it helps me think. It's in my blood." "Oh yeah?" I asked "I didn't know basketball was big with Jewish athletes." He roared again. "Yeah...well in my family it was. Eddie Gottleib was a distant uncle or something. They owned one of the earliest teams and formed what became the NBA." "No kidding?" I said, "Well I guess you come by it honestly."

We shot hoops in silence for a few minutes. George Donham was under the backboard, dutifully retrieving balls and throwing them back to us. I felt bad for him. He looked like a chubby valet. I tossed him a ball. "Think fast Georgie!" I said. He caught the ball clumsily. "Show me your jump shot, barrister." George shot Green a quick glance. Green laughed out loud. "Go for it George!" he said. Donham had remarkably good form for a guy who looked like he had a few

50

basketballs stuffed in the backside of his trousers. He made seven of ten from the foul line. I applauded and hooted and hollered like it was Madison Square Garden. Donham smiled like a little kid. Like he'd not heard applause in a long time.

Richard Green dribbled mindlessly for a moment and finally I said, "Listen, boys. I love having male-bonding time with you both, but I have a business to run. Let's talk about what we're here to talk about and then I can get back to my office." Green looked at me and half smiled. "You're that certain I won't take your deal, are you?" Without missing a beat, I shot back, "No, it's just that it takes a few days to arrange a bank transfer for eighty million dollars." Without as much as a blink I turned and shot a perfect free throw. "Swish!" I said with a laugh.

George Donham choked, then he spouted, "But your written offer was seventy-five million!" *"Oh Santino ...Santino..."* I said to myself, *"How many times have I told you. Never tell anyone outside of the family what you're thinking!"*
I shot a knowing look at Green. He smiled slightly. "That's how much his price goes to if we try to counter, George..." He said this to Donham but he was looking at me the whole time. I wisp of a smile played on his lips. "You're no businessman, Green. You're a street thug like me!" I said. Richard Green laughed. "Yeah there are some things they don't teach you at Wharton. I'll tell you what. I'll play you in H-O-R-S-E. If you win I pay the seventy-five million. We'll sign the papers this morning. If I win the price is sixty million. Deal?" "Deal" I said. I didn't really care about the outcome. I actually only wanted sixty million to begin with, but I went in high and figured we'd settle at my number. I'd already won this negotiation. But I'm a competitor.

I beat Richard Green soundly. He got to H-O-R-S-E before I even got to the letter "O". He was not happy about losing the game, but he didn't care at all about the money. I think that was his number all along. He was red faced and a little winded. He shook my hand and said "I'll have George draw up the papers." We can have the money to you by close of business tomorrow. Just give him your attorney's contact information.

"Sixty-five million is a lot of money to have lying around in petty cash" I said. Green looked at me quizzically. "Sixty five?" He shot back. "Yeah. I'm modifying the deal a bit." Green cocked his head slightly and a grin came across his lips. "Nobody leaves ten million on the table Joe. What are you up to?" I laughed and said "You're right, Richard. But here's the thing. My family is beloved in that neighborhood. You aren't just buying my routes and my trucks...and my landfill," I shot a glance at George Donham and smiled a bit. "You're buying my name. People love us because we're one of them. We part of the neighborhood. I'm like the Godfather of garbage. So was the Old Man. You're going to need some good will and a heck of an icebreaker." Richard Green stuck the ball under his arm and got serious. "What do you have in mind?" he asked.   I laid it out for him. It was a great plan and the neighborhood would benefit. In addition, he'd get the goodwill he would need, and I could retire knowing the old block would be well cared for. "You're going to pay me my sixty-five million. Then you and I are going to partner on some charities in the 'hood" I continued, "St. Rose's Assisted Living needs a new wing. You're going to donate two million in the name of Sylvia and Benny Mastofione and the wing will bear their name. Another two million to St. Monica's Church for the charities ministries. And a million for the 'Anthony Mezilli Sportsplex' and ball fields. Uncle Tony will love that." Green was smiling now. I carried on, "You put another five Million in an endowment for the neighborhood, to be administered by the neighbors. Whenever there is a need, they can go there for help. You spend ten million in tax deductable donations, instead of fifteen extra to make our deal fly. You get the tax breaks and the good will with the locals. I leave a legacy behind in the neighborhood. It's good for everyone."

Richard Green put his hand on his chin. He was smiling like a guy who had just seen behind a magician's trick. "You are a master, Joseph Mezilli! A master!" He was laughing hard now. "I should hire you to do all my negotiations from now on!" I smiled and lowered my head. I looked up and winked at George. "Naah...you have Georgie here. He'll be fine. Besides, I know you're going to build it into the deal that I stay on for a year, I'll teach him." Richard Green walked over and shook my hand. He held it for a long time. Then he said to me, "Why?" he paused, "Why leave ten million on the table and instead turn it into ten million for the neighborhood and the church and the nursing home?" He was serious about his question and serious about my answer. I thought for a moment, and then I looked at him and said "Because I never forget where I am from, and because I really, truly, love people." He smiled. It's true. I really do love people. Turns out, that would be the start of all my problems. But that came later.

How do I Tell The Old Man?

The harder business lay ahead. I had to tell the Old Man and Nonna. I had to figure out a way to spread a little of the wealth within the family and still keep everyone's pride intact. People think it's easy becoming a millionaire, but to be honest, sometimes getting the millions is the easiest part. Some people should come with a label: "Instant Jerk...just add dollars"

The first thing I knew I had to do was talk to the Old Man. Now, my dad had given me the green light to complete this deal the day I got the initial offer from George Donham at Felicia's. He said all the usual Italian dad things; "I'm proud of you." "I never thought we'd ever be in this position." and of course... "Jesus Mary and Joseph, did you use a *gun*?" He laughed when he said the last one, because I wound up with about three times what he'd thought we were worth. And that was *before* I negotiated.

Pop never saw the wisdom in the landfill deal. He remembered all the years that Nonno struggled and he was always partial to cash over assets. When the county told us they couldn't raise the funds all at once to buy out our land in Hog Island, he was furious. "Forget the whole thing. We'll sit on that land and let the Airport buy us out someday!"

I had to remind him that the airport was in no hurry to build new runways and cargo warehouses. It took a while but he relented and we did the land deal. Twenty years and a few million dollars later and he forgot his resistance to all that. Now here he was, about to be wealthier than he'd ever dreamed, and certainly beyond what his father ever hoped for.

I called him on my way back to the office and told him the deal was done. "Pop..." I said. "It's done, Pop. The clock is now running on the final year of *Mezilli Trash Hauling and Cartage*." He was almost perturbed. "Joseph I'm fertilizing the tomatoes right now. Can I call you back?" My old man and his tomatoes. Pop had a love – hate relationship with them. He loved to eat them. I mean *loved* to eat them. You want to see a man smile, give him a couple homegrown "Heirlooms" and a salt shaker and it would warm your heart. But he can't grow *anything*. Uncle Franny and I got the green-thumb gene. It skipped my dad. But he tried every year. Every year he planted his tomatoes, watered them, fertilized them, prayed to St. Jerome, said a Novena. Still he got nothing like he'd hoped for. But that didn't stop him.

I knew not to bother him when he was knee-deep in futility. "Pop, let's have dinner tonight. Pagliacci's, on me. Wear your new suit. I'll pick you up at six." The Old Man perked up a bit, "Pagliacci's? What did you do, up the ante on them?" I laughed out loud at this. The Old Man never quite appreciated my skills as a negotiator and always thought I was sticking horse's heads in someone's bed whenever I came away with a win-win. In fairness, Pop never saw things as win-win. If you won anything, you won. If you compromised at all, he saw that as a loss. Not because he was a "black-white" sort of guy, but because he never knew his own value or the value of our company. He saw winning a negotiation as blind ignorance on the other guys' part. If he budged at all he usually wound up feeling so immediately defeated that he gave away the store. He was too emotional when he bargained. Big mistake.

"We did very well today Pop. I'll explain it to you tonight. Six PM sharp. Just you and me, okay. Tell mom we're going to look at a boat or something." I heard the garden hose turn on and water spraying. The Old Man bellowed over the din of the water, "Okay son, see you at six."

I got back to the office and walked in quietly. Margie was there and I could tell she was a bit apprehensive. I hadn't told anyone about the deal, but I knew that people in the neighborhood talked and so I assumed Margie had figured out what was going on. If she did, the guys weren't far behind. So I knew I had work to do right away. I was going to take very good care of my people and I wanted to have a plan. I buzzed Margie into my office. "Margie, put the phone on voice mail and come in here for a minute please." I said to her.

Margie walked into my office sheepishly. She'd come to work for us the year before Sylvia left. She was my mother's sister-in-law's cousin or something like that. That left-handed Italian thing that makes you "family" even though you're no more related than you are to the butcher. Margie was younger than my mom but older than my wife, Angie. I liked this because I never got into that whole "Young hot receptionist" thing. For one thing, it's nothing but trouble in a thousand ways. People don't respect a guy with eye candy answering his phones. The other thing is, my wife is smokin'! I outkicked my coverage when I married Angie...at least I thought so. I love her more every day and I'm not looking to trade in. So why tempt the fates, right?   Anyway, Margie walked into my office and I told her to have a seat. Margie is a "Tab" drinker. She thrives on the stuff. I teased her about her affection for it and even bought her a life-sized cardboard cutout of "Austin Powers" holding a can of Tab and put it behind her desk on her birthday one year. I got her a Tab from the fridge in my office and sat down at my desk. This was not going to be easy.

I decided to just jump right in. "Margie..." I began. She started crying even before I said another word. *Oh Maddon!* "Margie, I'm sure you know what's going on. You're a smart girl. I'm going to tell you some things and I want you to promise to keep it between us until I get the chance to tell the rest of the crew. Okay?" She sniffled and said "Yes Joe." I gave her the basics. We were selling; it was time, better now, than too late to make a profit. Blah blah blah. My grandfather's voice suddenly yelled in my left ear, *Cut the shit Joseph, she wants to know about her job!* Good old Giuseppe...dead for five years and still scaring the crap out of me.

"Margie, listen...one thing you need to know. I have demanded that my staff remains in place. They agreed to it." Margie let out a long breath. "But Margie," I continued, "You won't have to stay here after I leave. Not if you don't want to." She looked at me quizzically, like a puppy trying to comprehend a dog whistle. "I have to work," she said, "The kids are in college for three more years." I smiled at her, "I know, but you're going to be compensated. After I leave, work will be optional for you. That's all I can tell you right now, okay?" She grinned and shook her head. My reputation with my people was stellar. When I said I would take care of someone, it usually went beyond their expectations. Margie wasn't worried anymore. "Margie," I warned, "Not a word of this until I can talk to the boys, right?" "Of course Joe," she said in her Bensalem accent (Margie wasn't from the neighborhood, she was from Northeast Philly) She got up and gave me a hug and said, "You're a good man, Joe. You deserve this. You and your whole family deserve this."

I had work to do. I was sixty- five million dollars richer – besides what we had in savings and assets- and we were here because a lot of good guys worked those five days a week, eight-to-twelve hours a day. I paid them well, but they earned it too. They were good men and hard workers. And they were family. This was their victory as much as mine, and so I knew I was going to share this with them. I buzzed Margie, "Margie, do me a favor. Get me a spreadsheet with every employee and their current salary, and their last three years earnings. Everybody from Tito on down. Even Khalif, whatever we paid him the last three years, include that too." Khalif is the guy who pressure washes and cleans our trucks. He does an amazing job and our rigs always look brand-new. "Can you have it by Four PM?" Margie laughed. She always laughed at me because I always *asked* her for things and never ordered her to do anything. My requests were always preceded by "Can you do me a favor...?" "Sure Joe," she answered, "I'll have it for you in a couple hours." And she did.

I worked the rest of the day on my exit strategy. I was going to have a party, for the guys and their families. That's when I'd tell them the whole story. But I was going to have to tell them about the sale tomorrow. That much I knew. Margie buzzed my office at 12:45PM. "Joe", she said, "I just sent you the spread sheets with the payroll information. I also included each man's 401K information and their Years of Service." That was Margie. No formal training in business or office management, but a head full of common sense. She was way more than just a family member we gave a job to.

I spent the afternoon reviewing each man's earnings, his age, and his years of service with us. I had to do something equitable. I was planning on bonusing everybody in the company and I wanted to be fair about it. I had forty-three employees, including my dad. He was getting a very different kind of bonus so I didn't include him. I worked out some calculations until my watch beeped at 4:45PM. I called Margie into my office.

"Margie, I'm going to dinner with my dad tonight, so I'm going to change here. No more calls this afternoon, okay?" "You bet Joe!" she said. I continued, "Just lock the door when you leave at five, and I'll get the alarm on my way out. And Margie thanks for your help today." Margie smiled. She loved her mani-pedi's and the two-hundred dollar up-do's as much as any woman. But the old girl sure appreciated a complement to go along with it. She turned and went back to her desk.

I have a shower and dressing room in my office. Not because I'm a high roller, but because sometimes the place stinks. Especially in the summer. I have meetings some days and I can't run home. So I had a shower installed and I keep a few suits here. I took a shower and shaved and put on a nice two-piece. Nothing fancy. I try to avoid stereotypes when I can, ya know what I mean? I called the Old Man on my way out. "Pop, you ready?" He was tying his tie. I can always tell because he can't do it right and he asks my mom. Usually he gets so frustrated that he is ready to kill someone. "Yeah, as soon as I tie this damned tie!" He barked. "Pop...just get mom to do it before you get agita and ruin your dinner. It's gonna be a good night, Pop. Don't start it off angry."

"Okay son," he said. "I'll be ready at six." then I heard: "...Annalisa! Help me with this goddamned thing!" That's my dad. He never fought the idea of having a cell phone, he just can't remember to how to end a call. He usually pushes the wrong button and you can hear him talking for another ten seconds after he thinks he hung up.

I set the alarm and locked the door behind me. It occurred to me that my days of doing this routine were numbered

59

now. In a year, there would be a new sign on the door and I would be a very wealthy man, but my family legacy would be ending. I have to admit, it was a little hard.

Exorcising Zippies Ghost

I picked up the old man promptly at Six PM. I pulled up to the house and walked to the front door. My dad is a typical South Philly Italian. He lives in a row home on Wolff Street. The little patch of front yard has long been replaced with concrete. In the middle there is a beautiful marble statue, of a peeing cherub. A gift from my Uncle Tony for my mom and dad's fortieth anniversary. Uncle Tony always gave statuary for important milestones, and they were always peeing cherubs. Sometimes I think it made him happy to make people a tiny bit uncomfortable about the gift.

Uncle Tony was a powerful man, both physically and politically. He was big and tough and larger than life. He was also one of the most kind-hearted people you'd ever met. If he came across someone who needed help, he just helped. No fanfare and usually no recognition. Uncle Tony taught me about loving people.

I rang the bell and walked in. Pop was still fidgeting with his tie and my mother shot me a look that said *Help me. Please help me!* She sighed and said "Joseph fix your father's tie before he chokes himself with it...or I do." I laughed and walked over to my dad. "C'mere Pop, let's see what we have here." My dad was sweating and red faced. The tie was making him angry. "Dad, how did you ever teach me how to tie one of these things when you can't do it yourself?" I said softly as I tried helping him. My dad held up his hands and said "It's the arthritis, Joseph. All those years rolling cans with your Nonno and working on the trucks when they broke down, before we could afford a mechanic. I'm paying for it now." He held his hands up to me. They were huge and slightly disfigured at the knuckles. "They get so stiff some days. Sometimes, son, I can even wipe my own..."

"YO! Pop! Jeez, too much information here!" I cut him off loudly, before he spoiled my dinner with his description. My mother smacked him in the arm. "Giuseppe! For the love of God! Your son needs to hear this? Go get your dinner. You know how you get when you don't eat." My mom planted a little kiss on his cheek. Then on mine. "You boys have fun. I'm going to Aunt Peg's to play Pinochle." "Okay Ma." I said. We'll call you when we're on our way back.

My mom walked out the door and headed over to Uncle Franny's to play Pinochle for a few hours. My dad and I looked at each other for a moment. Here we were, standing in his kitchen, getting ready to plan our exit from the only business our family had ever known. The end-game to grandpop Giuseppe's dream. ""You ready, Pop?" I asked him. "Yeah" he said. "Yeah, let's go." "I handed him his hat. My dad always wore a hat, even now in the early summer when it was getting quite warm out. "Shoot your cuffs, Pop" I told him. He smiled and shot his arms downward in a quick snap, causing the cuffs of his shirt to be exposed perfectly about an inch past the sleeve of his suit jacket. He got teary eyed, which caught me off guard. "I remember teaching you to do that." he whispered. "I'm proud of you, son." He said. Then he put his hat on and spun on his heels, before I could see the tears welling in his eyes, and led me out the front door.

We didn't talk much in my truck on the ride to *Pagliacci's*. *Pagliacci's* is *the* Italian restaurant in Philly. Everyone who is anyone in town eats there. Most of the mob bosses eat there, or they did before the busts, and the breakup of the families. The Zephanelli family has owned the place since 1937. They say Sinatra used to have their Eggplant Parm flown out to Vegas twice a month, on a private plane. It was that good.

My grandfather knew the Zephanellis when they were all kids here in Little Italy. Mario Lanza actually lived next door to the Zephanellis before he got famous. That's why they named the restaurant *Pagliacci's*, because Lanza used to sing *Pagliacci* on warm summer nights on the front stoop before he hit the big time. Once when Lorenzo Zephanelli, the patriarch of the family, was still alive, I asked him why Lanza's picture wasn't on the wall with all the other famous people. I mean, everyone knew he ate there all the time. They used to make jokes that the weight problems Lanza had late in his career were because of all the dinners at *Pagliacci's*.

Mr. Zephanelli smiled proudly and said, in his thick accent: "Because, Mario Lanza is-a my friend! You don't-a put-a the picture of-a your friend on the wall of your biz-aneece. You put-a those pictures in-a your house." He rolled the "R" whenever he said "friend" and he smiled broadly when he spoke of Mario Lanza. When Lanza died in 1959, Lorenzo was beside himself with grief.

My dad and I walked in, and Brian, the headwaiter smiled and waved. "Hey! It's my favorite father and son!' He laughed. "Come on fellas. I have your table" My dad shot me a sideways glance. Nobody gets seated immediately at *Pagliacci's*. "Have we come that far?" he whispered. I grabbed his elbow lightly, "Tonight we have, Pop." I smiled.

Brian pulled out my dad's chair and he sat across from me. "Two anisettes Brian." I said. No sooner had I said this, when a waiter appeared carrying two small aperitif glasses on a tray. He set our anisette in front of us. Brian smiled and said he would send a wine list over in a minute.

My dad and I toasted our good fortune and drank our anisette. Anisette is a tradition to Italians. It warms you up a bit. I love it. The sommelier brought a wine list and I pointed to one particular red. It was a winery from the Montecassino area...Grandpa Giuseppe's hometown. "Very good sir." The wine master said. "I'll send it right out." My dad fidgeted with his fingernails a bit. I knew the Old Man well enough to recognize apprehension. My dad is a complex man for someone in such a rough line of work. I knew that despite our tremendous blessing and good fortune, I had to handle this evening delicately. This was, after all, the business his dad had started from scratch.

I slid the envelope containing the reworked boiler plate of the deal with Waste International across the table to him. I had highlighted the most important items in the agreement, and circled the final number. I know my old man, and he wants to know the bottom line right away. He blinked slowly, his left hand absentmindedly adjusted his necktie and he took a sip of water. His lips puckered in an attempted whistle but no sound came out. Finally he whispered softly: "Joseph, this number here. That's what they gave us? This number circled in red?" I was grinning like a Cheshire cat. "Yeah Pop," I said, "That's what *Mezilli Trash Hauling and Cartage is* worth to the big-time world of Waste Management." My dad tried to whistle again. He settled for a low, baritone, "Maaa-ddon!"

"You did good son. Very good. I never would have dreamed..." Pop's voice trailed off a bit. His eyes grew moist and I knew he was thinking about Nonno. "Zippie would be happy for us, Pop." I said. He smiled. "Zippie..." He chuckled, "I haven't heard him called that name since..." "Since Hank Kroyczek died" I finished the sentence for him. My dad laughed. Mr. Kroyczek was a Polish immigrant who worked on the trucks for my grandfather in the fifties and sixties. He had a thick Polish accent and snow-white hair that he always wore in a crew cut. Mr. K. could never pronounce Nonno's name correctly. He always called him "Zippie." Kroyczek had died a year and a half after Nonno did. They had been friends since they were teenagers working in the textile factories in Chester. Once we got things going with a few trucks, Nonno brought him over as a mechanic and relief driver. They both saw terrible struggles on their way to America, and they'd formed a deep bond.

Mr. K. was probably my grandfather's only close friend. They were fishing buddies on the rare days you could get Giuseppe away from the trucks. He obsessed over making the business work. He'd rolled the dice on that one broken down Ford trash truck he'd bought off the Township in 1953. We called it "The Crusher." Even the grille on the thing looked menacing. My dad had it repainted and we parked it out front of the office and it's a landmark now. It gets a Santa hat at Christmas, flags at Fourth of July and a plastic stork whenever one of the employees' wives has a baby. It's a hulking steel monument to Nonno's determination and grit.

His obsession paid off for his son and grandson. My dad and I were sitting there at *Pagliacci's*, about to decide how to equitably divide sixty million dollars. Giuseppe never saw that coming, I assure you. My dad asked me quietly, "You think he would have been happy with this?" I knew what he meant. Nonno was not happy. Not really. He was not satisfied. Not because he was greedy or materialistic, but because he was afraid. For all his life, no matter how well we did and how much he had, he lived in fear of losing it somehow. Not that he'd blow his money, because Nonno threw nickels around like they were manhole covers. In fact his best friend used to tease my grandfather that he "Wouldn't pay two dollars to see Jesus Christ cross the street on a pogo stick." Nonno was more concerned that something bad would happen. A lot of people who endured the Depression were like that. Especially the ones, like Giuseppe, who immigrated during that time.

"He'd be proud, Pop. I know that much," I told my dad. "But no, I don't think Zippie would have been 'happy'. I don't know that he had that in him, ya know?" My dad smiled softly. He was quiet for a long time. I poured us a couple of glasses of the Montecassino vineyard wine and slid one to him. "To Nonno..." I said, raising my glass toward my dad's. "The Mezilli name was always well represented. Salud" My dad raised his glass and *clinked* mine gently. "Salud" he whispered. His eyes were moist again and he said softly: "Salud, Pappa. Gah-bless." That's how my dad always said "God bless" like it was one word; "Gah-bless" I looked at him a long time. I knew what he was thinking. He was wishing Giuseppe could be here and see this. He'd like to put that money in his hand and see what he would do. My dad lived in his father's shadow his entire life and never heard him say he was proud of him for being a good son, good dad, or good business man. And my dad was all of those.

I broke the silence. This was not a night to be downcast. It was time to exorcise Zippie's ghost. "Pop" I said happily, "Let's talk money." My dad smiled broadly and I knew what was coming next. "Joey, you just give me what you think is fair. This was all your doing, son," He said proudly. I laughed at this. "No Pop, this is our victory, together." I pulled out the paper I had worked on that afternoon. My father and I went over the deal at dinner that night. I explained how the payout to the neighborhood trust would work, who would administer it. I told him about the new wing at the nursing home to honor Benny and Sylvia. He got misty-eyed at that. I told him about the sports complex in Uncle Tony's name. He was thrilled with all of this. Then I tipped over his apple cart a bit.

"Pop," I began, "I'm going to give money to most of the family. Even to the ones who didn't do anything with the company." My father put down his wine. I thought he'd be angry or upset but he wasn't. He leaned forward and asked me directly. "Why, son?" It caught me off guard that he trusted my judgment that much. I told him my reasons, "Because that's the best way to keep the peace, Pop. It's so much money. I don't need all that. I can spread it around a little and that way everyone has something and no excuse to be jealous. I'm not going to give it all away, just a taste to everyone. Full mouths don't complain." My dad roared at that. My grandmother says that all the time. "Okay son, whatever you think is best."

We still hadn't settled on his cut. It was time to nail that down. "Pop, I think we should go fifty-fifty, after we back out the money we give the family. You deserve this as much as I do. Sixty million, after taxes, and the buyouts at the shop, is about forty million. The gifts we give the family come out before the tax hit so that helps a little. Twenty million dollars, Pop...is that fair?"

My dad choked on his wine. His right hand went up toward heaven. He is *such* an Italian.

"No! No son! That's too much. This was your baby. You put us in position where Waste International would want to buy us out. You talked me in to doing the landfill deal. Fifty-fifty isn't fair." Now I was stuck. This isn't a negotiation. Not in the traditional sense. This is egg shells. "Well, what's fair Pop?" I said, "This isn't negotiations here, we're family. Just give me a number." My dad thought for a second. I suspect he realized the nature of this and so he didn't patronize me with a lowball figure that I'd refuse. "How about fifteen million. You take twenty-five million for yourself. You have the family and they're young. You need it more than I do."

I laughed. "Pop, I'm going to need the extra ten million? Really? For what, building a Saturn V rocket so my kid can be a real astronaut? C'mon dad!" But the old man was adamant. Fifteen million it was. "Okay," I said. "You win. I'll call Mark tomorrow and have the money wired to your investment fund. Now promise me you'll take Mom and go meet with him right away and get this money placed where he tells you it needs to be." The Old Man laughed and agreed to call Mark Stimpson, his financial advisor, the next morning.

The rest of the evening was really nice. For the first time in our lives, we were simply father and son, not co-owners of a garbage company. I was glad this happened early enough in our lives that we could have a lot of time together like this. Just hanging out. My dad and I went over the list of family and how much I was giving each one. Of course my brothers and sister would be getting a substantial cut. I gave Uncle Franny a Million and Uncle Tony two Million. My father swallowed hard at that. "Your uncles will not accept this easily, you know. They're proud men, and proud of you and what you made this company. Neither of them wanted to be a part, and neither of them will expect this." He was right, and I'd allowed for that. I explained it to him.

"I'm buying Uncle Franny a tractor, and I'm parking it on the thirty acres I'm buying him in Chester County. I'm just going to give him the deed and a checkbook with the rest of the money in it." My dad laughed loudly at this. "Homer?" he bellowed, "He'll never set foot on it!" My Uncle Franny's nickname is "Homer" because he almost never leaves the house. He likes being in his garden and working on his land. The old guys he hangs with come to the house and play pinochle on the back porch. My cousin Toni lives a mile away and her sister, my other cousin Sissy lives with Franny and Aunt Peg...to keep an eye on them. I told my dad, "I figure he'll get used to the idea. Toni and Nick (Toni's husband) can drive him out there and he can show Pasquale how to drive the tractor. It'll be good for him," Pasquale is my Cousin Toni's son. His name is actually Nick, like his dad, but he was born on St. Patrick's Day and so uncle Franny calls him "Pasquale". It also helps because Uncle Franny has a son also named Nick. At Christmas, when the crowd is in the house, it comes in handy to have little Nick called something else.

My dad bought the idea for the farm. "Maybe he'll go for it. I know he won't take cash, but you can never give him enough dirt." Dad was right about that. We teased Uncle Franny all the time, he doesn't have veins, he has a root system. He was happiest working in the soil.

Uncle Tony was going to be a bigger deal and a harder sell. But I figured my way around this too. I told my dad about it. "Pop, I went to the courthouse yesterday after we finalized the deal. I had Uncle Tony added to the deed for the landfill. Richard Green knows about it and he's going to play along. The day of the actual closing, we're going to call Uncle Tony and tell him he has to come by and pick up his check. The title company will do the calling for us. They'll explain that he was a part owner of the landfill. He'll go for that. He'll never take the money from me, but he'll pick up a check from a lawyer." My dad laughed. "You know your family, Joe. That's for sure." he said. "Okay but you know...Tony will want to do something for you to thank you. And it will be something gaudy. You can expect a pissing cherub within a week." We both laughed at this. "What the heck," I said, "I'd be getting one for my anniversary soon anyhow."

We finished our dinner and talked. We talked about my sons and my daughter and my wife. Was everyone healthy? Were Angie and I happy? The boys are getting big. Was Peter going to play hockey this fall? Is Jack going hunting with us this winter? Was David adjusting to his braces? My dad loved my boys. He doted on my daughter but he loved being with my sons. He'd been so busy when I was their age, and now he was making time to see what he'd missed. It was okay with me, I understood his hard work.

Our waiter brought the check and I left him a $200 tip with a note telling him how I enjoyed his service tonight. People remember things like that. I called my mother and told her we were on our way back. The Old Man and I drove home in silence. We'd talked it all out of us at dinner and now we were really feeling the enormity of what we had done. Yes, we were rich. Fabulously rich beyond what we ever could have dreamed. But as we drove down the streets of Little Italy, past the Italian Ice stands and the Hoagie shops, we felt like the final chapter of a book was closing. Everything that the Mezilli family was known for was going away. It felt odd.

We pulled up in Pop's driveway. We got out and I walked to the door with him, past the peeing cherub, and the concrete front yard. We walked inside and my mom was sitting at the table drinking coffee. My dad sat down next to her and took her hand. He wasn't the tenderest guy to the rest of the world, but he was with my mom.

69

He leaned over and kissed her cheek and showed her the paper we'd been working on at the restaurant. He pointed to the number at the bottom and smiled. "Annalisa, this is what our son has done for us." he said. My mom looked at the paper and her hands started to tremble. She broke down into tears. "Mah-donn!" she whispered. She drew in a deep exaggerated breath, "Guiseppe...this is for us? This is what we're worth?" I paused. "Yeah Ma," I said softly. "And while you're still young enough to enjoy it, ya know?"

My mother came around from the table and hugged me a long time. "My boy...my good boy." she cried. *Oh God...* I thought, *Here it comes. This is where she recounts my birth, second by second and reminds me how the nuns said I'd been born with a "mask" and it meant I was blessed.*
But she didn't do that. She said nothing for a long time. Then she stood away from me and said "My son. What a good, fine man you are."

I have to tell you, I had nothing after that. My dad came over and put his hands on my shoulders and looked me in the eye and said, "Joseph. I'm so proud of you. Not for the money, son. But because you did this whole thing the right way. I'm proud of the man you are." Now I was crying. My dad doesn't say stuff like that. We stood there for a moment and then I kissed my mom on the cheek, turned and left them. It was time to go home and I was worn out from the emotions of the day.

3

The End of
An Era

I awoke the following morning at the same time I always did. I made coffee like I always did and sat at the kitchen table drinking it and mentally reviewing the day's "to-do" list. I did this every day since I can remember. Being the early riser has its advantages and the morning quiet is one of them. Maybe it's my favorite one. Nothing felt different. I didn't have the urge to just blow off the office today and go plan how I would spend my money. I did what I always did. The only thing I did differently was I wore a suit to the office this morning. We were meeting with the attorneys today and signing papers and it was useless to change later in the day.

I pulled up to the office and saw Nonno's old Ford garbage truck had some red roses in the grille. "The Crusher" looked odd with those delicate petals sticking out of that menacing metal scowl. Word was getting out already. Somebody knew what was up and the flowers were a means of portraying sadness. "I had better tell the boys right away." I thought to myself after seeing the roses. "The rumor mill will blow up with this if I don't."

I walked into the office and went to my laptop and sent out an instant email. Now, all our trucks are equipped with a GPS system so we can monitor location, speeds and -in case a new customer is added to a route- directions. I can also send an email alert if a driver is needed and doesn't have his cell phone with him. "IMPORTANT STAFF MEETING THIS AFTERNOON AT 5:30PM. MANDATORY. DON'T CLOCK OUT UNTIL AFTER. FOOD SERVED. CALL YOUR WIVES AND BRING YOUR FAMILIES. JOE"
This was going to be big news for my guys. Life changing news. I wanted their families there if possible.

I called Khalif, our pressure washer / truck detailer. "Khalif," I said, "It's Mister M" Khalif could never say my last name, and his Syrian upbringing wouldn't let him call me by

73

my first name. He was a political refugee. His father was an Orthodox priest and that put him at risk with the new regime. Christians weren't beloved, to say the least. "Come by the shop tonight at 5:30. Bring your family Khalif. I have some news to share with my friends. "I'll be there promptly, Mr. M." he answered. It was 6:45 AM. I laughed into the phone, "Khalif, how many cars have you detailed so far this morning?" If you can hear a smile, it sounds like the voice of Khalif Mousany. "Three already, Mr. M! And four more to go before lunch. The warm weather makes it easy to start early." Khalif worked as hard as Giuseppe did when he first got here. He was going to go far, this kid. I liked him a lot.

I hung up with Khalif and called my wife. "Anj..." I said, "Can you get a party together here at the shop for the boys and their families tonight?" She knew instantly what I had in mind. "Sure babe...what do you want?" I told her not to worry about cost. "Let's do this right," I said "Just run with it, honey. We're looking at 5:30, is that okay?" Anj laughed softly. I love the sound of her laugh. Drives me wild, you know what I mean? "I'll be ready by four, Babe. Love you..." She hung up and I listened to the silence. I am an incredibly blessed guy.

I spent the day writing out letters to each of my guys. I had decided to go above and beyond for each of them. By the end of the next year, they would have the option of retiring, I took each guy's current salary, multiplied it by the years of service, with a minimum of five years and that was going to be their "lifetime performance bonus." The guys who had been with us the longest could easily retire. The guys who had been with us for just a few years could at very least pay off their house or start a business or sock it away for their kids' college. I wanted them to have options beyond the day Waste International took over for good. They'd promised to keep everyone on board, but those agreements are never permanent. I wanted my guys to be secure no matter what happened. They were as responsible as anyone else for our success.

By lunchtime I was done with the letters. The boys weren't getting the money today. I was going to ask them to think about their futures and what they wanted to do. If they decided to leave, I would ask them to hold off for three months to give me time to find and train their replacement. I figured employee decisions would have to be run through Waste International from now on and who knows how long that would take. I didn't want Waste International getting cold feet and letting them go early if they found out what I was doing.

This afternoon, each man would receive an envelope with the amount he would be receiving on a piece of paper inside. The money would be transferred into an interest-bearing, ninety day bond. After that it was out of my hands. I included Khalif in this. He wasn't on our payroll officially, he was a subcontractor. But he was one of us, regardless. I was almost certain that Waste International would either cut back on the frequency of his servicing our trucks, offer him a full-time job at a far reduced rate, or eliminate the position altogether. He's a good kid and deserves a future. After today he'd have one. I made a call to a banker friend of mine and got some information about Khalif I needed. Another call and his part was done.

I had a one-hour meeting with the Waste International lawyers and got back to my office at Two PM. I watched the clock from about two-fifteen until four when Angie showed up. She had boxes of paper plates and plastic forks and knives and napkins in her Escalade. She walked in my office and came over to my desk and sat on my lap, facing me. She put her hands on my cheeks and kissed me and smiled. "You're such a softy, Joseph Mezilli, I love that about you."

Angie is beautiful. No kidding. I'm not saying this because she's my wife or whatever. She's a frickin' gorgeous woman. She's pure Italian like me. Her grandparents had known each other "back on the Boot" and their families came here together. Her maiden name was Amalfitano. She has jet-black hair. So black it looks like it has blue in it. She reminds me of Angie Harmon, with a touch of the old country, like a little Sophia Loren thrown in. She's fiery and intelligent and drop-dead, make-your-eyes-pop-out stunning beautiful. I've known her since the fourth grade, and by the seventh grade, I knew I was gonna marry her. There was never anyone else for me but Angie.

She leaned in and laid her head on my chest. "You okay with this, Chief?" she said. I chuckled. "Yeah, I suppose so, Babe. I don't think I saw this coming. Not this soon anyway. I knew we'd sell someday. God knows our boys don't want to work here and I want them to go their own way and all, but I didn't see it happening like this." I said all this in a sort of wistful, lost-in-the-enormity-of-it way. "Well look at it like this, Joe, you'll be able to be with the kids full-time before your forty-fourth birthday.
Not many men can say that. And you're leaving every person in this company in a position they would never be in without you. I'm very proud of you *Joey Trucks*." Anj was smiling at me and there were tears in her eyes at the corners. Here we were, my wife and I, barely in our forties and in the position to literally do anything we want from now on. I really am blessed.

Margie buzzed my phone. "Joe, the food is here." Angie and I got up and walked out to the lobby. Chris from Di Bruno's was there waiting for us. "Pull around the back,

Chris," I told him, "We have tables set up in the open area. Chris went outside to get in his truck and Angie and I followed behind. As we walked out, Nick Mariello was pulling up in a small box truck. He jumped out and ran over and playfully gave me a hug. Nick and I are old friends and I love the guy like a brother. "You're hand delivering the Pork Italiano these days? Business must be slow." Nick laughed. "No, brother," he laughed "Word is already out what you're doing here." My face fell a little. "Your grandmother told my grandmother at Mass this morning..." Nick said, "Don't worry" he continued, "I put the word out for everyone to keep this stifled until tonight. I wanted to stop by and congratulate you, *mi fratello*. I'm so happy for you. You deserve this, Joe. Seriously." Nick engulfed me in a bear hug and slapped me on the back. Nick Mariello might be the most *Italian* man I have ever met.

My mom and dad pulled in. Margie had called them and told them to come over, because I had forgotten in the emotion of the moment. The Old Man walked over to me and put his arm around my shoulder while Mom went to help Angie finish the last minute decorations. My dad smiled at me. "This is a wonderful thing you're doing Joe. These men will never forget this, not as long as they live." Pop was fighting back tears.

In a few minutes the first of the trucks had started to roll in. The guys were puzzled. It was Wednesday; we didn't usually do this sort of thing until Friday evenings. They parked their rigs in the annex yard and started heading to the locker rooms. Most of the guys showered before heading home anyway. Tonight was no different. The families began showing up not long after. Angie had everything looking beautiful and before long, we were standing by the doorway to the big conference area / meeting hall we had built in the back of our offices when we expanded the building twelve years before. Not many of the wives and children had any real idea why we had asked them to come out for dinner. But impromptu get-togethers were not entirely unheard of for *Mezilli Trash Hauling and Cartage.* Even Giuseppe had softened a bit in his later years. The Old Man and I had built a Bocce court in the back lot for him, and Zippie relished in teaching the game to the children.

By six PM the last of the trucks had been parked and the crew had washed and changed clothes. The families were all there. Khalif had arrived with his wife and two children in tow and his mom and dad along with him. I was glad he'd thought to bring them. I greeted his father with a hug. His dad was a hugger and he fit in the neighborhood like he was born here. His name was "Samir" and I called him "Big Sam." I told him he even had an Italian name and he was welcome here. Big Sam liked that a lot.

I stood on a chair at the front and spoke into a little P.A. system we had installed a few years before. I don't remember why we put it in there but it had come in handy more than a few times.

I cleared my throat. Suddenly it hit me what I was about to say and I got emotional. "Ummm...this is a special day for all of us. Today is a day that I don't think my grandfather Giuseppe would have ever believed would come. My dad certainly didn't expect it. I sort of thought it would come in my life time." I paused here. It felt like I was stalling saying the most important part. In times like this I found it was best to just let it fly.

"Last week we received an impressive offer for Mezilli Trash Hauling and Cartage..." I paused one last time; this was harder than I thought. "We decided it was too good an offer to pass up, and so we took it." My voice choked. It hit me again what I was saying. Then it really hit me how much I loved these people, and how much a family we really were. A loud murmur quickly spread through the group. I needed to reassure them right away. "Listen..." I said clearing my throat again, "Before I give you any details, you need to know that after tonight, you will not have to be concerned about your future, no matter what the new management decides." They grew quickly quiet. I motioned to Angie to hand me my briefcase. She opened it and stood next to me and handed me a few of the envelopes inside. I smiled at her. I was glad she was by my side for this.

"You guys are my family." I continued, "Some of you have been here since Zippie was still coming to the office. More than half of you were hired by my dad." I turned and smiled at the Old Man. He was crying openly, not even trying in the least to hide his tears. "We've been to your weddings, and celebrated the birth of your children..." I sputtered and began to cry. I had to get through this somehow. I lowered the microphone for a second and Angie brought me a shot of anisette. That helped me a bit. I raised my head to look at my guys and now they were crying too. Oh Maddonn, this was going to be tough.

I blew out a long breath and pressed on. "Anyway I have never thought of myself as your boss...we're family. You guys gave us your best, day in and day out and so my dad and I decided that it was only right that you share in the blessings. Because we are very blessed, you guys." I felt better now, maybe because as I was speaking these words, the force of them was warming my soul. I went on, "We have seen dark days and mostly bright ones. We've never had a major injury. Never had a cutback. We haven't had to borrow money from the bank in seventeen years. We've been just a very fortunate group of people, and now it's time for the chapter to close."

I swallowed hard and looked at their faces. I really, truly loved these people. "So here's what we've done. I have taken your current salary and multiplied it by the number of years you've been with us, up to fifteen years. Those of you who have been here less than five years I multiplied it by five anyway. Whatever that number is, each of you will be receiving that amount, in one lump sum, as a bonus." A roar and a cheer went up like Ryan Howard had just hit a Grand Slam. They were laughing and clapping and slapping each other on their backs. It went on like this for a moment. Then the strangest thing happened. One by one, as the reality of what I had just told them was settling on their hearts, they got very quiet, and the cheers turned to sniffles and gentle tears. The truth of what I was telling them started to become reality and they were considering how big a gift this was. They were overwhelmed.

I stepped down from the chair and together with Angie, walked over to stand by my mom and dad. And then they started. To a man, every one of my guys, their wives and their kids came over to us and hugged us. They told us how much they appreciated this, that we didn't have to do this and nobody else would have done this. Our tears mingled with theirs and we smiled and laughed as we cried. After a few minutes I excused myself and stood back on the chair and took the microphone again.

"Hey everyone," I croaked, I want to do one more thing, and then you guys can each come over and get your envelope. There are some papers inside with the specifics of what we're doing here and an agreement for you to sign." I paused and searched the crowd for Khalif. Our eyes locked. "Khalif! Khalif come up here for a minute. Bring your family with you please. You too Big Sam!" Khalif dutifully made his way through the crowd with his young wife and their two daughters. Khalif and his wife stood next to me and I put my arm around his shoulder. "Guys..." I began, "We have all come to love Khalif, you know?"

The guys let out a roar. "Most of you know that Khalif and his wife just gained their citizenship last month after so many years." Again my guys roared in approval. I went on, "Now I don't know if Waste International is going to keep using Khalif for cleaning the rigs or not, so I included him in this celebration tonight and we did something especially for him." Khalif's face went white. He had no idea that he was being included in this. He merely thought he was here for the party. I motioned to Angie and she handed me a large manila envelope and then she came and stood next to Khalif's wife and held her hand.

I looked at Khalif, "You are the hardest working young man I know. You are better at your job than you need to be and we appreciate what you have done for us, Khalif. You're part of this family now." Khalif's eyes grew misty and he smiled sheepishly. I opened the envelope and pulled out a blue-backed bundle of legal papers. I turned to look at him and smiled. "Khalif," I said, "This is the title deed to your house. My dad and I called the mortgage company yesterday and your note is paid in full. It's all yours."

Khalif's hand went to his eyes. His shoulders shook and his wife was sobbing on Angie's shoulder. Big Sam ran to me and gave me a giant hug. My guys roared and clapped. The women cried and so did some of the men. That was always the *Mezilli Way*. We took good care of each other and that was the best way to go out...arm in arm.

We stayed late into the evening. I told the guys not to worry too much about the routes in the morning. "Just get them done and get back here safely." I said. "Life goes on and we still have a service to provide." We stayed a long time. Nobody really wanted to leave. In some ways it felt like once we broke up the party and went home, the life of Mezilli Trash Hauling and Cartage was over forever. Like the scene in *Field of Dreams* when Moonlight Graham crosses the foul line and reverts back into Dr. Graham, never to return. I think in our hearts, every man there wished we could have stayed right there in that moment forever. But we couldn't. Time never stands still.

4

The Long Goodbye

The rest of the week was a blur after that night. Meetings. Planning. Lawyers. Amendments to language. More meetings. More planning. June came and my kids were almost out of school, and I was antsy for this thing to be over with. I called Richard Green and told him what I would like my summer schedule to be. He was fine with what I asked for. I could leave Friday's at noon and take a total of four weeks off before September when the kids went back to school. That was good enough for me. It was hard to accept that I was technically an employee now. I had a contract to fulfill and I was determined to do the very best I could.

I did my job dutifully for the twelve months I was under contract. Angie had bought a big desk-blotter sized calendar and hung it inside the pantry door. Every day she would cross out another day in red marker. The date was circled in blue with stars drawn around it. May fourteenth next year and I would be finished with my lame-duck presidency at Mezilli Trash Hauling and Cartage. I would walk out the door that day with a few cardboard boxes full of mementos from my office and they'd be switching out the signs as I walked past. I imagined a locksmith changing the locks before I even started my truck. The corporate world is not one for emotion or sentiment.

It's funny; you can fall into a series of routines in life and never realize things all around you. Sometime around Christmas that last year I was with our company, we both started noticing things about the neighborhood. It was changing. Crime had never been an issue here. This was "Little Italy" and the neighbors were always watching out for each other and that kept things straight. We had men like Giuseppe and his friends, and then Uncle Tony and the second generation sort of ran things the same way as

Nonno's generation did. But lately -the last five years or so- things were different. It used to be that a kid grew up on the block, and his dream was to buy a house here and stay here and raise his kids the same as he'd been raised. But not anymore. More and more of my friends were leaving and almost all of the kids younger than us were choosing the suburbs. Angie and I couldn't imagine not buying food at Martini's market, hoagies at DiCostanza's or Italian Ice from the Feretti's on the next block.

But it was happening. There was a diaspora of South Philly families, leaving their homeland and venturing to the uncharted adventure of the 'burbs. Anj and I swore we never could do this, but by Christmas of that last year, we were talking about it all the time. Nonna was slowing down and we knew she wouldn't be around forever. The Old Man and my mom were rooted in like an old fig tree and they were never going to leave. Uncle Franny was Homer...no chance he'd ever vacate. Same for Uncle Tony. The neighborhood would always be well represented by the Mezilli's. But Angie and I were growing restless. I wanted my kids to have land and see mountains and breathe fresh air. I wanted some room between me and my next door neighbors. Selling our house and moving away had never even been thought of before. Now we thought about it all the time.

Nothing big happened to make us take the step. None of my kids got sick. Nobody broke into my house. In fact, Anj and I would have been fine there because of who we were and who my family is. But my kids certainly won't be buying a house in the neighborhood and that sort of cemented it for us. If the kids won't be here, I sure won't be retiring here. So Angie and I quietly started thinking about where we might go.

We had been thinking about the South because we knew land was still readily available and reasonably priced. Then too, I didn't want to move more than a day's drive or a couple of hours flying time from home. My folks were in their late sixties –certainly not old, but getting to that point where things start to happen with their health- and so I wanted to be close enough that they would feel okay driving to see us as well.

October of that first year after I sold, I went to homecoming with Angie. The kids went with us because it was a big deal. I attended Liberty University where I played men's hockey. In fact, my freshman year was the very first team we had. The year I sold the business, the Hockey Alumni were holding a special celebration at Homecoming to commemorate twenty-five years of hockey at LU. Angie and I took the kids out of school a day early and drove to Lynchburg where the school is located. We had a lot of friends there and wanted the extra time to visit outside of the scheduled events of Homecoming weekend.

Driving from Philadelphia to Lynchburg Virginia is tedious until you get beyond Washington DC. There is a point on Highway Twenty-Nine South where you round a bend and you get your first glimpse of the Blue Ridge Mountains in the distance. It's a remarkable sight if you aren't familiar with mountains. My kids had never seen mountains at all. We were beach people for vacation and the boys were always so busy with hockey in the winter that we didn't go skiing. When we rounded that bend, and those mountains rose out of the south, contrasting the flatland we'd driven through, my kids were all agape. Emily, my daughter, pointed out the window and said "Daddy, are those real?" I looked at Angie and she smiled her "I just read your mind" smile. "Yeah baby..." I answered Emily, "Those are the Blue Ridge Mountains. They run from here to Tennessee where they become the Smokies." "They're so beautiful daddy." Emily said. She was right.

The Homecoming weekend was such a busy few days that Angie and I didn't have much time to talk about what we were both thinking. I knew she was thinking it, and she knew *I* was thinking it. "What about moving down here?" The kids had a blast in Lynchburg. The boys were fascinated with the "SnowFlex" slopes on Liberty Mountain and Emily loved the art gallery on campus. She is the artist in the family. She sees the beauty in everything and everybody. That weekend was special for her, because there is so much beauty in the Blue Ridge Mountains.

We got back to Philly on Tuesday morning after Homecoming. I went to the office at lunchtime and called a realtor friend of mine in Lynchburg who was the wife of the hockey coach. I told her to start looking for some houses for Angie and I to consider. Yes we were thinking about a move to the area. Yes we were serious. I told her we wanted a fair sized house, maybe five-thousand square feet. A few acres of land. Commuting distance from Lynchburg. She said she'd start on it right away and email us some properties.

After dinner that night, Angie and I sat on our back porch. The boys were doing homework inside and Emmy was drawing pictures at the kitchen table. I could see her framed by the doorway to the porch where Anj and I sat and talked. She handed me a sketch pad. "What's this?" I asked her. "Look through it, Joe." She said. It was Emily's. We'd bought it for her before the Homecoming trip. She'd been drawing in it almost non- stop while we were there. I thumbed through it. It was full. One-hundred sheets, both sides, all pictures of the mountains, the campus, Smith Mountain Lake. The pictures were amazing for a six year old, but what struck me was how this trip affected her. All she could draw for days was mountains. Emily had fallen in love with the place.

"She asked me when I tucked her in last night could we go back there this weekend." Angie told me. "She said she wants to live there." I was surprised. Emily was the one I thought would resist the idea if we decided to move away.
She loved having her Nanna and Nonno three blocks away. My dad doted on Emmy because she was the first granddaughter. My brothers had all boys and I've already explained what Angie and I went through having a girl ourselves. Apparently the Mezilli men have a problem "knocking the nuts off" as my cousin Jimmy likes to say. Eventually my brother Sam and his wife had a little girl, but Emily had already stolen my dad's heart by then. He loved Louise (My niece) but Emmy had her Nonno around her finger. She even has him singing to her. Hand-to-God! The old man has absolutely *no* vocal range. He couldn't hum the theme song from *Jaws*. But Emily taught him "The Wheels on the Bus" when she was in pre-school and she had him sitting cross-legged on the floor singing and going through the hand motions with her. I have it on video somewhere. Thank God for cell-phone cameras, right?

"Well I have Jannie working on it for us, Babe." I told Angie. She looked at me with a smile. "Already?" she said coyly. "Yeah, I called her this morning from the office. She's going to send you stuff through the email. I told her four-to-five-thousand square feet and a few acres. Other than that, it's your call." Angie smirked at me over her coffee cup. "Oh sure, Joseph, heave that decision on my shoulders." She laughed. She knew that I knew that she was the one who had to like the house. All I needed was a basement, a big garage and a place to grow tomatoes. The rest was her domain.

Except for the kitchen. I was a legendary cook in the neighborhood and so was Anj. The kitchen was the one part of the house that we put a lot of cooperative thought into. We worked well together in the kitchen too. We made it fun to prepare for parties, or cook breakfast for the kids. Our friends always said we should have a cooking show together.

Angie and I talked for an hour about moving to Virginia. It felt odd talking about moving away from the homestead. It felt very odd to be speaking of one specific location as if we'd already decided to move there. I stood up and grabbed her coffee mug. "You want a refill?" I asked her. "Of course, babe," She smiled. Then she started to laugh, "You're going to get your legal pad, right?" That's my Angie, she knows me better than I know myself. I am a notorious side-by-side-comparison guy. I'm a big believer in the age-old method of drawing a line down the middle of a legal pad and listing "Pro" on one side and "Con" on the other. Always "Pro" along the left edge...so you see it first. Because I'm an optimist.

"I'll be right back," I laughed. I took her cup into the kitchen, checked on Emmy's drawings at the table and kissed her forehead. She was drawing mountains. In fact she'd drawn "The Bald Spot" on Liberty Mountain. The Bald spot got its name because every spring, lightning would strike up there and burn a few hundred acres. It always looked bald where the fires had been. Eventually the school cleared it out, put down tons of landscape stone and put in a shrubbery monogram. You can see the "LU" from miles away. "It's very good, Emmy" I told her, "It looks just like the Bald Spot!" Emily laughed. I had told her that the students called it that and she thought it was funny. I grabbed a yellow pad from my briefcase and refilled Angie's coffee mug. I grabbed bottled water from the refrigerator and headed back to the porch.

Angie was smiling at me. She'd seen the exchange between Emily and me and it made her feel good. Angie's dad had suffered a stroke when she was only ten years old. Her dad was a sweet, loving man, but not physically able to show it much. Angie told her friends that she thought my abilities as a dad were "hot." whatever that means. I think it helps her when she sees me being loving with the kids, especially with Emmy. It fills the hole her dad's disability left when she was little. Anyway I sat down next to her and dutifully drew the line down the middle of the paper. Angie set her coffee mug on the rattan table and took the legal pad and pen out of my hands. She smiled mischievously behind the pad as she briefly scrawled away. She turned the pad around and handed it to me. Then she stood up and said "I'm going to get Emily ready for bed, babe. This is my input on the matter."

I watched her walk out of the room. My wife is amazing, and I know it. I looked down at the legal pad in my hands and read what she wrote. "We're moving to Lynchburg. You know it and I know it. It's been in your eyes since we got back this morning. Emmy loved it. The boys loved it. Your problem is figuring out how to tell your family!" She drew a smiley face at the end. She was right. We had already made this decision without talking about it. And she was right about the other thing too...telling my dad would be hard. Telling Nonna would be a dramatic event on the scale of a Broadway play. I set the pad down on the table and leaned back into the thick cushions on the loveseat.

The house was quiet except for the sound of the water in the lines as Angie drew Emmy's bath. But the silence of the house was broken by the staccato noises from the highway. I-95 was about three miles away but in the evenings, the sound traveled and you could hear the whirring of the tractor-trailers as they rushed by. Depending on the wind direction, the big airplanes from the Philly airport would approach right over our house. You got used to it because it's all you knew. But the first time you ever really heard silence -like the silence of the Blue Ridge Mountains at evening- you could never be used to it again.

Angie came back downstairs in about a half hour. I looked at her, framed in the doorway with the kitchen light behind her, like an angel. "Do you remember it being this loud back here before?" I asked. She smiled and walked into the porch and sat next to me and laid her head on my chest. "I nailed it, right, about you wanting to move?" she whispered. "Yeah...yeah you did, babe." I answered. "I know you; like I know Me." she said, "For the record, I'm on board with this." I was surprised at that and looked at her directly. "Yeah?" I asked, "Just like that?" "Well we don't have to rush into it, Joey," she said. "And you have six more months left at work. Six months, twenty-three days to be exact." Angie laughed. "I guess we can take our time and pick something nice, huh?" I said wistfully. "How to tell the Old Man, and Nonna. Maddon!"

"I'll go with you when it's time. But I ain't talking." Angie muttered this into my sweatshirt. She was right. Telling my family that we were going to leave was probably going to be the hardest thing I'd ever done. But we had six months before I could even think about that and so Angie and I just sat there for about thirty minutes, listening to the overwhelming noise of the city where we both were born. Noise that we had never really heard before, and now we couldn't quiet down.

Joey Trucks' Last Day

My last day at the office was more emotional than I thought it could possibly be. I didn't sleep all night the night before. Neither did Angie. My dad was hitting that stage of life where he was a night owl and so sometime around two AM I sent him a text message. "YOU AWAKE, POP?"

He called me back in a few minutes. I had been sitting on the back porch, listening to the sounds of the early summer. The Phillies had been in town and had a game against the Braves earlier that night. At one point I heard the roar of the crowd in the distance out toward the stadium. A minute later Peter, my second oldest boy, came running onto the porch to tell me Ryan Howard had just crushed a massive home run. He asked me if I'd come watch the rest of the game with him so I walked out to the living room and sat in my recliner while my boy sat cross legged on the floor, keeping score in an old notebook like I'd taught him.

I sat in silence, watching my son far more than I did the game. This was what we did every summer. If we didn't go to the ballpark, we'd watch it on TV. Citizen's Bank Park is about six blocks from my house. Soon it will be six hours. Am I doing the right thing here? Petey jumped to his feet to watch the final out. The Phillie's pitcher set him down on three strikes and the game was over. Petey grabbed my arm and dragged me out to the back yard. From our house you can see the fireworks they launch after every home victory. He was jabbering as ten-year-olds will do and I just put my hand on his shoulder and listened. "I have such good kids," I thought, "I'm a lucky man."

Petey gave me a hug and said goodnight. He'd be upstairs listening to the postgame on the radio and checking his score

93

sheet against the official line on the internet. He loved the game and he loved scoring it from home. Petey was my biggest sports junkie of my three boys. They all love to play and they play every sport imaginable. But Petey loves it a little more than his brothers do. He's a competitive kid but cerebral as heck.

Angie came in from her aerobics class and asked me if I was okay. I said yes I was and I'd be up to bed in a while. I sat on the porch a while longer and eventually went upstairs and tried to go to sleep. Anj was laying there with her hands behind her head, blinking back tears when I walked into the bedroom. "This is really it, Joseph." she whispered, "Tomorrow morning you clean out your desk and the rest of our lives begins for real." I lay down next to her and she kissed me softly. Her tears dropped gently on my cheek and I didn't move to clear them. We talked for a while and she eventually drifted off to sleep. Angie needed to know I was okay. Then she could be. If I was good with this, she was as well and I had reassured her that I was very good with it.

But at two AM, when I couldn't sleep, it was apparent I was not entirely good with it. Ten minutes later my Old Man shows up at the door with his coffee cup in hand. "Jeez Pop." I said, "You drink that at this time of night you'll be awake for the Second Coming." The old man forced a laugh but I could tell he was edgy. I was worried about him, he was worried about me, and Angie was worried about us both. This was supposed to be the best thing that ever happened to anyone in this neighborhood but instead, it had us all worked up and battling the agita in the middle of the night.

Pop and I sat on the back porch where we could talk without waking the family. We talked about Giuseppe. We talked about "The Crusher" and how we'd held that thing together with baling wire and duct tape for years, while Pop built the business. Every time he thought he could retire the old boy, one of the new trucks would break down or we'd expand to another route and needed to coax another six months out of him. And every time, he'd roar to life and groan his way down the streets, like a steel dinosaur, thundering, and shivering, and looking imposing with that menacing metal scowl of a grille. We talked about Hank Kroyczek, and his wife Helen who was built like a linebacker, and who we'd all joked had played for Joe Paterno at Penn State under an assumed name. We talked about Willie Washington, the guy everyone called "Willie Pickles" because he had a craving for those big deli pickles that they kept in a brine barrel in DiCostanza's hoagie shop. Willie stopped every morning in the summer to buy a pickle before the heat of the day kicked in. Nobody could figure out why he ate them all the time. Turns out he was building up the salt in his body so he didn't sweat it all out. Smart guy that Willie Pickles.

He was the first black man that Giuseppe had ever hired. Not because he was prejudiced but because Giuseppe always hired family first, then friends. Willie was the first black man Nonno had hired but he was also the first employee he'd ever hired using a classified ad. Everyone else had come from word of mouth. Willie was one of Giuseppe's favorite employees. Willie Pickles...we hadn't thought of him in ages. He'd retired to Florida in the mid-seventies and spent his days watching the ponies run at Hialeah. His son Miles had gone to law school and he stayed in touch with us, because he lived in Voorhees. And in return we stayed in touch with Willie through his son. He passed away many years ago but we still exchange Christmas cards with Miles and his family.

So many names and faces. So many memories. You'd think that running a garbage business was just a matter of hauling trash. But these were people. They had families. They *were* family. Everything that Giuseppe and the Old Man and I achieved in this world had come through the efforts of the people who worked for us. And now, those days were done.

The Old Man and I talked until the sun started to break through the dark of early morning. Angie came downstairs at Six AM and made us some coffee. "You guys have been here all night?" she asked me. "Yeah babe," I yawned. "It's a lot to process, and Pop and I were just reminiscing a bit." Angie smiled softly and set two cups of coffee down on the rattan table in front of my dad and me. "It's the end of an era, you know," She said. And she was right. The days of our shiny, unusually clean (thanks to Khalif) trucks running their routes with our name on the side, were coming to the end now. Today I would go to the office, box up my belongings, walk through the shop and say my goodbyes. The guys would pretend not to be emotional. Margie would break down and cry. We'd all promise to remain in touch. We'd mean it too, at first. But eventually the calls will be fewer and farther between, and the family that was Mezilli Trash Hauling and Cartage will be a pleasant, but distant memory.

I took a slightly different route to work that final morning. I drove down a few side streets where our trucks had been running for over fifty years. I know...a sentimental journey in a garbage truck, right? It's funny, it doesn't matter what it is you do, if you love it and you love the people you do it with, it becomes something more than a job.

I was driving the streets slowly, listening to my old friend Angelo Cataldi on the radio. Now, you'll need some background here. Angelo is the morning host on the local sports radio station here in town. In fact, it was the first allsports radio station in the country, and Anj was one of the first hosts. He's been at it a long time, and he is far more than just a radio jock. He is an icon in this city. I've been listening to him since he first came on the air. First I listened in those smelly trucks, and then in the office. About twenty years ago, he and I became friends. The former owner of the Eagles – Norman Braman- had just sold the team to the current regime. Now, I'll be kind and say that nobody really liked Braman, and when he finally sold, we all felt like our beloved *Iggles* had been brought back from exile. So Angelo, never one to hold back his feelings, throws a party. It was a going away party for Braman. I think if I remember correctly, that he called it a "Good Riddance Party."

So anyway, I used to call in from the trucks when I was young and learning the business. My grandfather hated it, when he found out, but my dad always told him it was good advertising. I was still "Joey Trucks" back then and Anj just loves local nicknames.

He gets very excited and animated on-air and he would boom into his microphone: "Joey Trucks is on the line! Our favorite garbage man! What's up Joey T?" And I would go into a rant about the Phillies or the Eagles or the Flyers or the Mummers parade. One time Angelo and I somehow got off course and he asked me what the strangest thing I ever picked up on the routes was. That was a funny discussion, because people will throw away some very odd things and you could make up any kind of story you wanted to about the stuff you found in your crusher.

So anyway, the day of the big "Goodbye Braman" party, I surprised Anj by firing up "The Crusher", my grandfather's first truck, and driving it to the Adam's Mark hotel, downtown. Thankfully I know the cops around here pretty well and they didn't hassle me about bringing that thing to

Center City. I pulled up to the hotel and laid on the old air horn. Angelo and his cohort Al Morganti were doing the show from tables set up near the big picture windows. I managed to get his attention after a few horn blasts and Angelo nearly fell over, when he saw the truck. I went inside and told him I was there to crush Braman in effigy. There was no shortage of Norman Braman figures in the live audience and one of the regulars offered his up as the honorary sacrifice to the frustrations of the long-suffering Eagles fans.

About six guys formed up, three on each side, and solemnly carried the bizzaro-Braman to the back of The Crusher. We threw the stuffed aberration into the compactor and pulled the handle. Somehow the crowd felt like we were exorcising demons and the place went nuts. Now, this was a very visual thing, but Angelo is an amazing radio guy and he did such a great job describing it that it was one of the all-time great bits of his show.

So after the celebration, I parked The Crusher, and went inside and watched the rest of the broadcast. Angelo had never met me face to face and so we grabbed lunch afterward and wound up becoming friends. We have dinner sometimes, with our wives, and I even got him out on my boat once when we had it in Avalon. Away from the radio, Anj is a pretty private guy and that made me treasure our friendship even more.

So I'm driving the streets, that final morning, listening to his opening monologue and it hits me...this is the last time I'll ever hear him on my way to work. Anj has kept me company my entire time. He first came on the air the year I graduated High School, so he's always been a part of my work routine. Every day on those trucks, or in the office. After today, I might not even have a reason to be in my car at this hour. Angelo must have known I was thinking of him because not a few minutes later, he says, on air: "By the way, I want to say a very special congratulations to our old friend Joey Trucks." I smiled to myself; Anj was the last guy to still be calling me that on a regular basis. He always loved that nickname. "Joey is retiring today, Al," Angelo continued, "He sold the business and he's livin' the life!" "Oh yeah?" Morganti responded, "He sold the trash business? To who, Tony Soprano?" Al Morganti is the absolute perfect foil to Angelo and he knows the value of a great line better than most guys. "No Al, you fajoot." Anj feigned his exasperation at his longtime on-air partner, "He took a big buyout. I'm tellin' you, he's got the life. He's young, he's rich now, and his wife...Maddon, Al, have you ever seen his wife?" Angelo was on a roll now. Without waiting for Al to respond, he redirected the question to his other co-host Rhea Hughes. "Rhea, you know beauty. Is Joey Trucks' wife not smokin'?" Rhea was very gracious in her assessment of my bride. Then he sent out the word over the airwaves for me to call in and talk about my last day. "Joey Trucks, give us a call and tell us what it's like to be you, my friend!"

To be honest, this broke me. It's funny, you don't appreciate your routine until it changes, and mine was about to change immensely. I found myself very emotional and had to pull over for a minute. I'd grown to love these guys and even this -something as seemingly innocuous as a radio show- was changing now. I sent Anj a text instead. "Can't call today, Paisan. Too many memories. Too much emotion. But thanks...thanks for everything." Anj understood.

I got to the office at 7:30AM Richard Green's car was there when I pulled up. I pulled into my spot, unfolded my silver dashboard cover and put it in place. I laughed out loud. Written inside the reflector, in red lipstick, visible only from the inside and only after I had unfolded it and placed it on the dash was *"Congratulations Joey...you sexy man. Hurry home to me. The kids are at your parents all night! —A"* Angie always knew when I needed a good laugh and this was exactly that moment. She must have written that last night while she claimed to be upstairs giving Emmy her bath.

Richard Green was still sitting in his Volvo when I got out of my truck. I walked over to his window. "Your key isn't working?" I asked. He smiled. "No my key works fine. But It's your last day here Joe, and I wanted to give you the moment to yourself. It would be tacky for you to walk in and find me in your office, like a vulture. I just came by to wish you well and follow up on a few things." He stepped out of his car and we walked inside together. I noticed that all the trucks were still in the yard. "What the...nobody has left yet? What's going on?" Green spoke up. "I emailed the GPS's last night Joe. I told the guys to wait before rolling this morning. If you don't want to stay all day today I understand and I wanted them to have the chance to say goodbye." I looked at him a little startled. That was a remarkably class move on his part and I appreciated it. "Thank you Richard," I said to him. "That was very nice." Green looked serious for a moment. "You know, I've observed you this entire year, Joe. Your management style is amazing. You know these people like they were your brothers and your sister and they know you as well. Yet you can define the boundaries easily. I have to admit I have implemented some of your policies in other locations since we did this deal. Are you sure I can't bring you on board at the corporate level?" I didn't have to ask him if he was serious because he was. I could tell. But I simply smiled and said "No, I'm finished here. I'm young. I am rich now. And I have a young family that I will get to invest a lot of time in. Corporate life isn't for me."

I walked through those double glass doors for the last time. The guys were all waiting inside the big conference area we'd built. It seemed like just last week I'd called them all together to tell them about this deal. Now here it was, my last day. The guys erupted into a loud, raucous cheer when I walked in. It caught me off guard and I played it off by doing my best "Rocky" impersonation. I shuffled my feet like Muhammad Ali and held my hands over my head in victory. But I felt the tears already starting.

I stood there as one by one the guys all came over to shake my hand, slap me on the back, and even hug me. Khalif was there with his dad, Big Sam. He had a huge grin and he hugged me for a long time. Sam was crying like a baby. Richard Green handed me a microphone and he whispered into my ear, "If you don't say something, they'll stay here all day." he said with a laugh. He was right. This was it. This was the final moment and nobody really wanted it to happen. I stood on a chair, took a breath and said my goodbyes.

"I said my thank yous a year ago. I just wanted to say...You guys were and are my family. We will always love you guys. Thank you again for so many years of hard work, laughter, tears and fun. It's time for me to go. God Bless." The guys started a long, loud, emotional applause. I shook Richard Green's hand and walked back through the double doors without turning around and looking back. It was done.

I had already boxed up my office and the contents were sitting on my desk waiting for me. Margie came in to say goodbye. As expected, she was a sobbing mess. I understood. For the past year we'd all said how we'd stay in touch. How this was just a change at work, but our friendship would endure. But we knew the truth. The sad, unbending truth, that life rolls on and seldom do we keep up with the folks we want to, and even need to keep up with. I knew that for all the good intentions, this was the last day I would see a lot of these people again. Margie gave me a hug and slipped me a card to give to my dad. I hugged her and kissed her cheek and loaded the three cardboard boxes onto a dolly.

Richard Green walked out to the truck with me and helped me load the boxes into the back seat. Another nice gesture. Richard Green was a working man's executive. That was for sure. I felt better and more at ease about the care he would take with our legacy. He shook my hand and asked me one last time if I was sure I wouldn't reconsider and stay on as a senior V.P. I declined. "I have more money than you'll ever pay me. Why would I do that?" I asked. He smiled and shrugged his shoulders. "I envy you, Joe. You're forty-four years old and worth more than you'll ever find the bottom of." I smiled, "It's just money, Richard." I said to him. "Just dollars and cents. My blessings were the memories made here in this building and with these men." Green shook my hand again. "I got more form this endeavor than just a trash hauling business, Joe. I learned a lot from you about how to really be a boss. Thank you." Then Richard Green hugged me. Hand to God. The Jewish guy from Brooklyn with the Wharton School business degree and the four-hundred dollar Johnston and Murphy's hugged me. And I think he was getting tears in his eyes. "I bought a business. I made a friend." He said quietly. And that -as they say- was that.

5

Time to Go

Almost six months had passed since that morning when I said goodbye for the last time, to Mezilli Trash Hauling and Cartage. The first month was fun. It was summer so I slept in, because the kids didn't have to go to school. For the first time in my entire life I didn't have to play "Wake-up Zone" with myself or my children. I had this game...I would walk into their room at six AM sharp, flick the lights and tell them "Okay campers, you are now in the Wake-up Zone!" In a voice that sounded like a camp announcer on a crackling P.A. system. "You have ten minutes to be up and out of bed!"

The rules were simple...you could lay there as long as you wanted but in ten minutes dad was turning the lights on for real and pulling the covers off your bed. I only ever had to do that a few times before the boys got in the habit of just getting out of bed promptly at six. I didn't play the game with Emmy because her school started later than the boys. Usually she heard me getting them up and woke up on her own anyway.

For June, July, and August, I slept until Seven AM, which is like slothfulness for me. We spent almost the entire summer at the beach. We rented a cottage in Margate and essentially lived there for the month of July. June and August we commuted. I went to every Phillies home game with Petey. I planted my tomatoes and helped the Old Man grow some of his own for a change. I worked out every day (which Angie really appreciated) I hung out with Uncle Franny and drove him to his new farm a few times. The kids returned to school in September and so I was driving the car pool in the morning, I puttered around the house, cleaned the kitchen every two hours, washed the dog, detailed the cars, and basically...I started the process of driving Angie nuts.

We were too young to be under each other's feet all day long. Old people can sit in the living room and watch TV in silence, but not a couple in their early forties. I was going nuts without anything to do and you can only vacuum the carpet so many times in a day. I was becoming OCD about cleaning the kitchen and it all came to a head that morning when I reactively scraped Angie's eggs into the sink before she'd even taken a bite, and then started washing the dish. After she threatened to turn me into sausage, she got serious. "Joseph," she said, "It's time for us to move." I sat down at the table across from her. I didn't say a word, I just listened. "You're antsy, Joe." she continued, "You know you want to make this move and yet you keep hesitating. You won't let yourself start the next chapter of your life Babe, and the last chapter ended almost a year ago." Again, Angie knows me. "Babe," she said firmly, "If we're going to make this move, it's time to just make it. You're waiting for the perfect time to tell your dad, right?" I nodded my head, still just listening to her being the wise woman I married. "Joseph there is not going to be a perfect time for him, and if you don't make the move soon, the boys will be in high school and then we'll be stuck here." Angie got up and started making herself another plate of scrambled eggs. Over her shoulder she said, "Homecoming is next month, let's just you and me go this year. And let's come back with a new address." It wasn't a question or a suggestion. It was her statement on the matter.

I got up and kissed her on the cheek and told her I was going for a walk. She looked at me and smiled. "He took Uncle Franny to the farm, Joe. He won't be back until dinner." I smiled at her. My wife, again how she knew me! I was intending on walking over to my dad's house and talking to him about moving. Angie knew it before I even said a word. And she was right; Pop was taking Uncle Franny out to Chester County to the farm. They'd gotten in the habit of this every Wednesday.

"You're right, Anj," I said to her. "It's time." I called Jannie, our realtor friend in Lynchburg, and put her on speaker. Angie and I sat at the kitchen table and talked to her for ten minutes, telling her what we wanted. We'd narrowed it down to Forest, a suburb of Lynchburg where we could still buy a house sitting on a lot that was at least five acres. Jannie said she would email us some more listings. I told her we'd be down the next month for homecoming and we'd be seriously looking. Jannie said she'd get right to work on it and she hung up. I looked at Angie.

"Do you think I should tell the Old Man now or wait until we buy something first?" I said to her. Angie was quiet after that. Thoughtful. She raised her coffee cup to her lips and before she took a sip she said; "Maybe you wait until we buy, Joe. Maybe if the deal is already done when you tell him, he accepts it better, you know?" "Yeah," I shrugged, "I was thinking the same thing. He's going to take this hard, and to be honest, it's going to be hard on me, Anj. Selling the business was the best thing that ever happened to our relationship." Angie stood up and walked over to me and sat down on my lap facing me. She got about three inches from my face and said, "Joseph, we either make this move this fall or we don't move...ever. You hear me? No indecision. You've never been indecisive and you're not going to start now. We go to homecoming, we decide on a house, or we decide to stay. Either way it's done after that, agreed?" That's my Angie. Tough as nails.

The month between this conversation and Homecoming felt like three years. I tried to stay busy outside the house so

I didn't get under Angie's skin. I spent a lot of time with the Old Man and my uncles. Uncle Franny was having some of the boys from the neighborhood come out and help clear some wooded land on the farm. They were the grandsons of the guys he played pinochle with, and some of their friends. It was funny watching Uncle Franny and my Dad work these kids. When I was a kid, my Old Man would put a boot up my rear end without a second thought. "Jeeziz Mary and Joziph!" he'd scream at me, "If you don't step it up, we're gonna have a three-legged race to the hospital!" He said this to me for years until I finally asked him what it meant. He said "It means if you don't work harder (or roll those cans faster, or hose out those dumpsters faster...) I'm gonna stick my foot so far up your ass it will get stuck there and I'll have to hop behind you on one leg, to the hospital, to get it removed!"

I had a work ethic like an ant because of him. Uncle Franny was the same way. Now, these kids who were clearing brush at the farm were in their early twenties. They weren't raised the way I was or the way Uncle Franny raised my cousins. These kids were soft. Seriously. I'm not some old curmudgeon who never thinks "these kids today" stand up to scrutiny when compared to my generation. No, these kids really are soft. It drove Uncle Franny and Pop crazy too. I could always tell when one of them was ready to uncork a stream of profanity on one of these *mooz-ahdells* and plant a boot in their pants. Somehow they both kept each other in check and got the work done. Granted, it took two weeks longer than it should have, but they got it done.

Homecoming was a week away. Angie and I had made arrangements with my folks to watch the kids. The kids weren't very happy about not going with us. It's not that they didn't love spending time with Nonno and Nonna, but they really wanted to go to Lynchburg and see the mountains again. Angie and I almost caved in and took them with us, but we knew we needed to have them stay here so we could leave the emotion out of our decision making. If it was up to the kids, we would have left the furniture and everything and just moved to Virginia the next day. We needed to have a few days alone to look things over and think things through. So we remained firm and we went to Homecoming alone.

Angie and I talked the whole trip down. It occurred to us that this was the first time we'd taken a trip, just the two of us, since before Emily was born. There were always kids, and ball, games, and dance recitals, and family vacations. We had not had a weekend to ourselves in almost seven years. We rounded that bend outside of Culpeper Va. where you can see the mountains for the first time, and we looked at each other, and smiled. There was really no debating this. This trip was a buying excursion, not another fact-finding jaunt.

Pulling into Lynchburg on Thursday afternoon, we checked into our hotel and headed over to Jannie's office. We told her to call her husband Kirk and we would take them to dinner. Jannie said Kirk would be finished with practice at four-thirty, could we meet them at six? It was settled and Angie and I just drove around campus and remarked how the school just kept growing. When I was going to school here, and playing hockey for the men's team, it was so much smaller. We didn't even have a rink on campus. We drove in to Roanoke late at night for practice and games. There was only one floor to the main educational building. There were not nearly as many dorms and they weren't nearly as nice. And of course, there were only about twenty-five hundred kids here when I attended. This year they hit fourteen thousand on campus and another hundred-thousand or so online. Things have changed a lot.

We signed-in for the Homecoming activities at the Welcome Center and walked over to the little prayer chapel on top of the hill. I always loved this little chapel. It had a quaint country feel to it and seemed very sacred in its own way. Angie and I went in and sat down near the front.

Now, you need to know something. We're not Catholic. I mean we are, but we *aren't*. You know what I mean? Angie and I were both raised Catholic, and attended Catholic school from Kindergarten until College. The summer of my junior year in High School, I went to a Fellowship of Christian Athletes camp with some guys from my hockey team and I really liked it. I decided to attend their church as well.

Of course, my Old Man hated the notion and my mother...oh Madonn, my mother thought I'd sold my soul to Beelzebub. "Whadda-you mean you're a *Baptist*?" She hissed at me, "The Pope isn't good enough for you anymore Joseph? Saint Francis isn't good enough for you?" She was losing her grip. "Who do you have to look to for spiritual guidance now Joseph? Huh? Tell me! *We* have the Pope. The Holy Father. Who do you have now?"

My mom was turning green. I knew better than to be a wise guy, not with the Old Man standing there, and his hand twitching like he actually *needed* to belt me one. "Billy Graham, Ma, you like him, right?" I answered. Good God, the only thing my mother hates more than me answering with a smart mouth when she's ranting at me, is me answering with respect and proving her wrong.

She stared at me for a second. Then she cocked her head a little, like a Labrador puppy. "He's a Baptist?" she said, more to herself than to me. "Yeah Ma, he's a Baptist." The

Old Man stepped in and was remarkably calm about the whole thing. "Listen Joey, we're a Catholic family. If you want to go to another church –as long as it's not some cult or some fajoot nonsense- you can go. But you still go to Mass once a week and you make confession too. You understand?" Pop was pretty much laying the law down, but he was calm about it. I thought it was fair enough. "Sure Pop," I said, "That's fair. Listen Ma, I'm not leaving the Holy Church. Just doing both, okay? It's a place to hang out with the guys on the team." My mother accepted the terms reluctantly. When my dad says his piece, it's over. She knows this. They're old-school in that way. But she didn't like it a bit.

To be honest, I pretty much straddled the fence on the matter. I liked the new way of viewing things that my Protestant friends had, but I felt a connection to the liturgy and tradition of The Church of Rome. So I went to Mass on Saturday afternoons with my grandmother and Church on Sunday morning with my FCA friends. Angie had gone with me a few times and decided it was for her as well. In our marriage, we had basically been Baptists, but retained our heritage in Catholicism. It was easier than never seeing our families again, which –believe me- is how it would have played out.

So here we were, sitting in the Prayer Chapel all alone, while fourteen thousand college kids were going about their business down the hill from us, and our kids were back in Philly, being spoiled by their grandparents. Angie took my hand and said, "Joey, let's pray." She's a strong girl, my Angie, and sometimes her strength blows me away. We walked to the front and knelt down by the tiny podium. "I used to come here when I wanted to skip Chapel services" I told her. "We could sit in the back with a textbook and study. It looked like were praying." Angie smacked my arm playfully. "Is that all you did here?" she smiled. The only time Angie and I had ever been apart since seventh grade was the four years I was here in Virginia and she was at West Chester University. I knew what she was getting at, even if she was only teasing. "Oh you know better. There was never anybody for me, but you. These girls can't make gravy like you.

Angie grinned and we were silent for just a few seconds. "I feel like I want to light a candle." She whispered. We both smiled. Angie and I prayed together. Just asking for a little help from above made this decision feel better. So did kneeling next to my wife.

We walked out of the chapel and got in my truck. Jannie had texted us and told us where we'd meet. It was a great little place about five miles from campus. I hadn't seen Jannie and Kirk since last year when we came down for the big hockey celebration. Kirk had played at Liberty a long time after I had been there. He and Jannie are a lot younger than Angie and Me. But we have a common bond with our love for hockey and our school. Kirk is a great coach, and I think he's going to bring us a championship one of these days.

I told Jannie right up front to just go ahead and make this a working dinner. We only have the weekend and we want to see something and make a decision. We're ready to buy. What realtor doesn't like hearing that, right? We ordered an appetizer and Jannie broke out her iPad. Technology is wonderful. I remember when the Old Man and my mom were looking at a beach house in Brigantine. The realtor lugged in those old "MLS" books that were the size of the Manhattan white pages. My mother thumbed through those things for hours looking for a little place "down the shore" as we say in Philly.

Jannie showed us a couple of nice places but nothing grabbed us. She remembered a nice neighborhood out in Forest, where there was still a number of neighborhoods with really big lots. I had told her I wanted two-to-five acres. I wanted a garden and a pool and to still have room for the kids to run around. Jannie showed us one house on a corner lot that backed up to a big section of woodlands. It was "Williamsburg Blue" with big white columns out front. Very Antebellum. Angie squeezed my arm impulsively. That was the one. "Jannie, can we see this one here?" I asked her. Jannie perked up a bit. "Joe, you see the asking price, right?" she said. "That's seven-hundred, thirty-five thousand dollars."

I looked at Angie and laughed a little. If there is a fun thing about being really rich, it's those moments when you realize that nobody knows how much you actually have. I told Angie once that it means we're living right, because we apparently aren't pretentious.

"Yeah I see that, Jannie." I laughed, "If we like it, we'll find a way to make it happen, okay?" Jannie liked that, obviously. Kirk smiled a little and we turned the conversation to the hockey team while Jannie emailed the listing agent. We ordered our dinner while we waited for the other agent to respond. Jannie had taken us to this nice place called *Isabella's*. It was really a first-class restaurant, and I was impressed, which is saying something, considering I'm an Italian from Little Italy in Philly. Angie and I loved the name. We had seriously considered naming Emily, "Isabella" when she was born, but we thought about the teasing she might take being "Izzy Mezzili" and we went with something far less ethnic.

Angie and I had both gone to college away from the city, and when we got back, we were very aware of how

113

stereotypical some of our friends had become. There is nothing wrong with heritage and tradition if that's really you. But some of them had gone to great lengths to cultivate an aura of Italian-American life that really wasn't theirs. Anj and I both decided not to do this. We were proud of where we came from but we weren't trying to live in a time warp.

About fifteen minutes passed and Jannie got an email from the listing agent. We could see the house in the morning if we wanted to. Ten AM. That sounded great to us. We were anxious to actually walk around some houses and come to a decision. Moving your family three hundred miles from the only place they ever called home is something you don't want to drag out forever. My Old Man used to say "If the water's boiling, make the macaroni!" Which was his version of "Strike while the iron is hot." The water was definitely boiling.

Dinner was pleasant and we finished off with coffee and left Kirk and Jannie and headed back to the hotel. Angie and I talked about the old neighborhood. About our families. About the way we were treated back there. We were a little like royalty on Wolff Street. People came to us with questions or for help in a pinch. We liked that role. We all knew each other and most of the people our age and older had grown up in the same neighborhood, sometimes, in the same house. But that was changing, like I said. Angie said' "Better we go now, than five years too late, babe." She would get no argument from me and she knew it. I think she was saying it just to say it out loud and let the words roll around so we could get used to them easier.

"It Reminds Me Of The Campania"

Neither of us slept much that night. It's funny; we both were convinced this was the absolute right move for us and our kids. We both loved it here. We both felt like it was a great place for our family. And yet we both felt like this was the hardest thing we'd ever attempted. Angie drifted off, finally, around midnight. I lay awake watching her sleep and thinking about our life so far. Thinking about our kids. Emily in particular. The night Emmy was born will always go down as one of my favorite fatherhood moments. Watching Angie sleeping next to me reminded me of those nights just before Emily was born, when I would talk to her through the paper-towel tube. Yeah, there's a story there.   The boys were easy for Angie. Bing, Bam, Boom. Just like that, they were out. Now, Angie works out like a pro athlete, and she was blessed with great genetics. She bounced back from each of the boys and looked better than before she had kids. But with Emily it   was   different.   Angie was   battling preeclampsia from about the seventh month on. They had to start giving her Magnesium to stop the contractions. It scared the crap out of me. She was dilating and contracting at the seventh month. It made me nervous to even touch her. I was afraid something would go wrong.

I made the mistake of telling Nonna about Angie's preeclampsia and Maddonn...what I went through! Nonna started to cry. Now, this was nothing new. My grandmother was −like all Italian women of her vintage- a professional wailer. She could turn on the faucets like Tammy Faye at the mere mention of a problem. But when I mentioned Angie's preeclampsia, oh my Lord. She started to cry. Then she genuflected and started calling out to Mary and St. Jude.

Now, I'm no expert on the various saints, but I knew that Jude was the patron saint of lost causes. Holy Mary! I needed this? Nonna was saying the rosary so fast that she sounded like the guy at the end of a car dealership ad, reading the legal section. Then she rounds up every reliquary and lucky amulet in the house. She tried to give me her lock of Giuseppe's hair, that she kept in a little porcelain box next to the votives she had arranged into a grotto in the living room. Yeah...a chunk of my grandfather's hair. I didn't even know she'd taken it when he'd died. Zippie was practically bald as it was, so she must have worked for hours to harvest that sizeable piece that she'd braided and coiled in that box. The old girl was losing it.

I calmed her down and told her, "Nonna...it's okay. The doctors have it under control and Angie is going to be alright. We just have to be careful." Nonna dabbed her eyes with one of Giuseppe's three dollar handkerchiefs that she kept folded up in the sleeve of her dress. Now, there's another contradiction for you. When Nonno was alive, she hated that he carried a handkerchief. "My God!" she would say, with a look of disgust on her face like he'd just farted in front of a priest, "Giuseppe, do you know what kind of germs live on those things? Why can't you carry a little pack of Kleenex like I bought you?" Then Zippie would wave his hand in the air like he was shooing a fly, and curse in Italian, and blow his nose like a trombone into the hanky she hated, and then stuff it back in his pocket. Nonna would look faint after this.

So anyway, she dabs her eyes with the hanky, and she looks at me and puts her hand on my cheek. Now this *always* means trouble. Always. Trouble in the form of a three- minute dramatic performance that would have won her an Oscar had she been doing it in Hollywood, instead of

Shunk Street in South Philly. "Giuseppe..." she said. (She insisted on calling me Giuseppe, even though I hated being called Giuseppe and never ever went by it. I was always called Joe...or Joey. But she was old school and in her world, the oldest boy took the family patriarch's name.) Anyway, Nonna puts her hand on my cheek and says, "Giuseppe, I had a friend who had the preeclampsia." I loved this. It's not "the" preeclampsia. It's just "preeclampsia" but Nonna was from another generation. "I had a friend who had the preeclampsia. Mrs. Tessone, over on Passyunk Avenue. You remember her grandson, Lito? He was the little cross-eyed boy, who started going bald in the third grade."

I had to bite my lip to make myself not laugh at her. Calling attention to his vision problem was bad enough, but I had forgotten about his going bald so early. I swear...hand-to-God, he had a receding hairline in the third grade. We called him "Charlie Brown" because of it. Nonna started tearing up again. "Mrs. Tessone had a daughter who died in seven seconds from the preeclampsia. They found her with the phone still in her hand; she died trying to dial 9-1-1. She only got to "9-1" before she went septic and dropped dead on the floor."   Nice. Thanks grandma! I might as well just take Angie to the hospital tonight and leave her there until Emily is born. "It's going to be fine, Nonna. Trust me." I assured her. But inside I was nervous. This wasn't the first horror story I'd heard about preeclampsia...just the most horrifying. My grandmother had a way of delivering bad news with Shakespearean perfection.

I walked home that night and practically encased Anj in Bubble Wrap. I was afraid to even kiss her for the first three days after talking to Nonna. Now, this is a problem, because pregnant women are, ummm...affectionate, shall we say? Angie was wanting to continue in our marital bliss, and I was afraid I'd put her in labor and be delivering my daughter right there in the bedroom.

Of course, Angie didn't believe me about it being because I was nervous about the preeclampsia. You know how pregnant women get. She got really upset and started saying "You don't even want to touch me...you hate my body!" Two things: I love Angie's body. Maddonn! She has an amazing body, like something Michelangelo carved. That and she never does the drama thing. *Never*. Angie is cooler about stuff like this than most *men*, but the pregnancy hormones combined with her own worries about the early contractions had her pretty edgy.

I always thought it was best to just be direct in times like this, and sometimes try to make her laugh if I can. I told her. "Anj, you know how I can't hardly keep my hands off you. It's always that way. But the doctor said you could go into labor if we aren't careful with this preeclampsia stuff. You really wanna be right in the middle of it and Emily decides to come early?" Angie giggled a little. Then I said "You remember the time the boys walked in on us that afternoon at the beach, when we thought they were on the boardwalk with Pop? Well this would be much worse!" That got her. Angie and I still cringed about that episode at the beach. In the context of this conversation it struck her as hysterical and she burst out laughing until she got tears in her eyes. Then, you know how this goes with pregnant women, she peed herself.

At first I thought her water broke and I panicked. Now she was really laughing. Sitting there on the bed in a puddle, laughing at me until her sides hurt. I calmed down and ran her a nice bath. I sat there on the bathroom floor while she relaxed in the tub and I washed her hair for her. Then I changed the sheets and started the wash with the old ones. I know how to score husband points when I want to. Garbage was *not* thing I was best at.

Later that night, we lay in bed and I grabbed my paper towel tube that I'd saved from the trash about a month before. Each night I did the same thing. I put one end of the tube against Angie's belly and I talked into the other end. "Hello Emily, "I said, "It's your daddy. I love you, and I can't wait to see you!" I did this every night from the time Angie was five months pregnant. That night, after her bath, we lay there and I pressed the tube against Angie's belly. As soon as I said "Hi Emily, it's your daddy." She kicked. She kicked really hard, enough to make a little rustle in the bedsheet. She recognized my voice! Angie and I both burst into tears.

I was trying not to cry as I lay in the hotel bed watching Angie sleep, and remembering that story. I thought about the night, just about six weeks after that night with the paper towel tube, when Emmy came into the world. I had been there for all three of my boys being born but there was something about Emily coming that was extra special. I felt like a first-time dad. We'd gotten Angie all the way through to the 39th week and Dr. Kennedy decided it was time to induce. The preeclampsia was taking its toll on Angie's body, and he didn't want to risk it.

Now when you give someone magnesium supplements for two months and then introduce the hormone pitocin (which induces labor) it causes terrible nausea. Poor Angie was pushing with all her might and in between contractions; she was throwing up into a bed pan. I was holding her hand with one hand, and the bedpan with the other, and also trying to catch glimpses of our daughter being born. At some point, Dr. Kennedy said something about Emily starting to get a little "distressed," whatever that means. He said "I'm going to give her a little help." Okay...now I'm curious. "Help?

Help like what?" I said, nervously. He said "She has crowned, so I'm going to give her a little pull." and he held up a big suction-cup looking thing. I said "Yo! Doc! You pulling some dents here? What is that thing?" Dr. Kennedy laughed. "No, no dents," he said, matter-of-factly "I just attach it to the top of her head and give her a nice gentle pull and help Angie get her the rest of the way out."

I didn't like it at all, but he was the best Ob-Gyn in the city so I trusted him. So he attached this suction cup to her head, and I'm trying my best to comfort Angie as she's pushing, and trying to catch all the puke at the same time. In the middle of this I'm also trying to watch my daughter enter the world. I sneak a peek, and then turn my attention back to Angie and right as I'm looking at her hear this loud "Pop!" and I see out of the corner of my eye, Dr. Kennedy's arm jerk back. For a split second -the longest split second in my entire life- I *swore* Emmy's little head had popped off. Honest-to-God! My face went ashen and my heart topped out at 220.

Dr. Kennedy laughed and held up the dent-puller. "Her head is just fine, Joe, relax." Then he showed me the button on the side that releases the vacuum when he has gotten the baby far enough along. "Here, check her for yourself," he said with a laugh. "Check, her?" I croaked, "Check my *shorts* for God's sake!" Dr. Kennedy bellowed at that one. He always thought I was the funniest husband of any of his patients.

Emily finished the trip in another thirty seconds and we had our little princess. Angie was pretty pooped after the whole affair. Between the contractions, the pushing, and the wretching into that bedpan, she was dehydrated and worn out. So we laid Emmy on her chest for a few minutes, made sure she was able to nurse, and then I took over. I have to tell you, I never loved my wife more, or appreciated what she went through to have our kids, than I did after that last one. And one more thing: my friends were right. Having a little girl...wow was that different from the boys. The boys make a place in your imagination. They cause you to see the generations continuing down the road. But a daughter makes a place in your *heart*. Emily owns me. She really does.

So I'm lying in this hotel bedroom, watching Angie sleep, and thinking about the night our daughter was born, and thinking too, about the road since then. We've been lucky and very blessed. The business has been very good to us, our kids are healthy, our family is close by, and we love each other a lot. So why mess with it, right? That's my nature...over-think everything. Especially the good things. I started to get out of bed at 1:45. Angie stirred lightly and muttered into her pillow: "Joseph Francesco Mezilli. If you are getting out of this bed for any other reason than to go pee, I will kill you in your sleep." I froze. She rolled over and opened her eyes. "Babe, before we left I took the yellow legal pad out of your briefcase. No lists, Joe. We have already decided on this." Then she rolled over and went right back to sleep. I had to put my hand over my mouth to keep from laughing. "What am I worried about here?" I asked myself. "I have more than I will ever need, my wife is on the same side as me, and my family is healthy and happy. What's to worry?" I was right. And I fell quickly to sleep.

Angie and I met Jannie at ten the next morning. Before we even got to the driveway, we loved the place. It was a corner lot with five acres. The house was a nice fifty-nine-hundred square foot colonial with some nice antebellum columns and a semi-circular driveway in the front and another long driveway leading to the enormous detached garage in the back. It turns out it was the builder's personal house while this neighborhood was being built. He had set aside three lots and merged them, and built this house for himself. When the housing market slowed down, he sold this one and moved to Houston to cash in on the growth out there.

Angie loved the colors, she loved the yard, and she loved the bedrooms and the closets. I think we had decided on this place before we got out of the car. We pulled into the half-circle driveway and went inside to meet with Jannie. Angie and Jannie took the lead on the tour. Again, this is where a smart husband stays quiet and let's his wife decide whether "we" love it or not, because to be honest, it would take an awful lot to make me hate this house. Other than bleeding wallpaper, and voices warning us to "Get out *now*," I knew this was the place for me. I let Angie convince me anyway, just to earn some good hubby points for future use.

So Jannie gave us the walking tour and then she and Anj disappeared for a few minutes to look at the size of the closets in the guest room. These things might be stirring and inspirational, but not a deal breaker for me. I slid the patio door open and walked out into the back yard. There was a nice deck and a beautiful view of the Blue Ridge Mountains. Just to the left was the "Peaks of Otter," a favorite sight-seeing location and the first real mountains I had ever hiked in my life. When I was a student at Liberty, we took day trips on Saturdays to hike the trails leading up to the Peaks. The view is breathtaking, especially for a city boy from a very flat South Philadelphia.

The girls came back into the kitchen and slid open the patio door. Angie stopped in her tracks. "Joey...this view!" she said, catching her breath slightly. "I know," I was whispering and I don't know why, except maybe the beauty demanded it. "When Giuseppe used to tell us about Montecassino, and the Campania, I imagined it looking something like this. Jannie had gone to her car to retrieve the sales brochure for the house, but she was really giving us time to talk, just Angie and I. Jannie is smart like that. "I don't even want to haggle with this, Anj. Do you like it?" Angie was ecstatic, but remained cool. "I love this place, babe." She said. "What about you?" I drew a breath. "It's a beautiful home, Anj," I said. If you want it, let's write it up today, and close as fast as we can. We can move at Thanksgiving." Angie looked at me startled. "That soon?" she said, "The kids are in school. You want to move them out in the middle of the semester?"

"I know, babe," I answered, "But they're going to go to the Academy here, not public school so the transition will be easier, and I would really like to be down here for Christmas. The emotions and all, you know?" "Yeah but Joey, it's eight weeks to Thanksgiving. You really think we can do it that fast?" Angie was starting to sound like she was up to the challenge. "If we don't, we won't be moved in until after the Holidays, Anj" I said, "And you know how our families will work on us about this over the Holidays. Better we're gone by then."

Jannie slid open the patio door and walked over to where we were standing. She handed us the ring-bound prospectus on the house. "This won't be necessary, Jannie." I told her. "We would like to put in an offer." Jannie smiled hesitantly, not sure if we were kidding, or maybe just stunod and didn't realize just what this place cost. Lynchburg is an incredibly reasonable place to live and seven-hundred-thirty-five thousand is very high end around here. Back home, it's lower middle range.

Jannie paused and then suggested we go inside and write up an offer sheet. "What are you going to offer, Joe?" Jannie asked, probably expecting us to try to low-ball, since the

123

house was unoccupied and had been vacant for over a year. "The asking price, Jannie," I said, "Providing we can close in ten days." Jannie literally dropped her pen. I picked it up for her and set it on the counter, where she had been preparing to write the offer sheet. "Oh..." she managed, "Well, do you have any special conditions?" "No," I said, "Just the usual stuff. A good home inspection.

We want a home warranty thrown in, and a full survey. Otherwise, just make it happen for us. We can have the money wired tomorrow if the terms can be met before noon. If not, it would be Monday next week because tomorrow is Friday." Jannie was smiling openly now and not even trying a little bit, to hide it. I thought this was great. Realtors are so stuffy. I was really glad we made her day like this. I figured she was too flustered to ask for the earnest money so I brought out my check book. "How much earnest money do you require?" I said off handedly. Jannie said that a thousand would do it. I wrote the check and she finished writing out the contract.

And that was it. The owner was more than willing to drop what he was doing in Houston, find himself an attorney and fill out the contract by fax. I called Mark Stimpson, back home and had him get a wire ready for the next morning, gave him the escrow account numbers for the closing attorney and told him to call me when it was on its way.

Then Angie and I took Jannie to lunch. We chit-chatted a bit, talked about schools, and restaurants and dance schools for Emily. Then she told us she had another appointment and said her goodbye. She'd call us in the morning.

The rest of the day was spent sight-seeing, meeting up with some of my old college friends in the 'Burg, most of whom Angie knew, but a few of whom were first-time acquaintances, and settling into that feeling of having just done something enormous and life changing. Like the way a married couple feels about four days after they get back from their honeymoon and they experience each other's morning-breath for the first time. It's cute, but it feels weird. We drove back to our new house before dinner. I wanted to see the sunset.

Turns out, sunset from our new back yard is breathtaking. It settles down on the little valley to our left and I swear...it looks like the Campania. Angie and I went to Italy once, right before the kids were born. We found some of Nonno's distant relatives and instantly became celebrities. We both loved it, and promised we'd go back someday. Now I guess we were living in our very own Campania range. Sort of. Angie was standing in front of me and I had my arms around her and my hands crossed in front. "Feels a little like Italy, ya think?" I whispered to her. "Yeah," she laughed. "Italy in Central Virginia." "Well we'll bring the old neighborhood down here with us," I smiled. I'll put a Bocce court in the back corner; maybe grow some grapes and figs, and some 'to-may-ter-iz." Angie chuckled at that. Our next door neighbor, Mr. Donello, pronounced "tomatoes" that way. He was originally from Brooklyn, and had that thick New York accent, the one everybody associates with the Mob. Everyone who doesn't know any better that is. He'd stand on a chair and lean over the fence and ask me "Hey Joe, you got a couple-ah to-may-ter-iz I could get from you for my salad?" Every year he tried a garden of his own. Every year he failed at it. The guy probably couldn't even grow a beard.

So that was it. Homecoming went as Homecomings generally do. I played in the alumni hockey game, overdid it a little bit, but survived it for another year; saw a lot of old friends. And my wife and I bought ourselves a house. We were heading for the South, like we'd been talking about.

We'd be driving back home on Monday morning, so we visited with some friends on Sunday afternoon. Anj and I decided to host a little get-together with the people in Lynchburg we were closest to and tell them the news. So we went to the grocery store and bought some food and drinks and what-have you and text messaged the street address to about a half dozen couples in town and had them meet us at our new house. Jannie reminded us this was against protocol since we technically didn't own the place yet, but since the entire purchase price was already sitting in her attorney's escrow account in cash, she could look the other way.

Our friends arrived around Four PM and we were waiting out front for them. They were ecstatic. Leo and his wife Lisa, Cyndi and Jeff, Don and Pam, Jannie and Kirk, Kirk and Robin. It was a small gathering, but it was the people we knew would do the most to make us feel at home and help us settle in quickly. They thought we were kidding at first, but Jannie convinced them that yes, we had actually bought this place. Whooping and hollering ensued.   Our friends headed out around Seven PM and Angie and I were locking the house up and making some notes about carpet colors and wall paint. We walked outside to see another sunset. Neither of us said a word as the sun sank slowly just left of our backyard and turned the entire New River Valley into a brilliant burst of color. "This is amazing" she whispered. She was right. We walked to the front door and locked our way out. It was just getting dark.   "Son of a...!" I said to Angie. "What babe...No! You didn't lock your keys in the house did you?" she asked me. I paused a minute. "No'" I said quietly. "Turn to your left slowly and casually, our neighbor across the street is a peeper." "No he is not!" Angie screeched. "Yeah, he's doing it right now." Now a "peeper" back home, is a nosy neighbor who watches your business through the blinds in his living room. Every block has one back in Philly. Ours was Mrs. Begnetti, the widow who cooked for the parish priests. She did this so she had a reason to be at the rectory every day picking up juicy bits of gossip. Angie turned and saw him. "Good Lord, Joey, he isn't even any good at it. He's got a light on *behind* him. He might as well open the blinds and stare at us with binoculars!" When you are looking out your window and there is a light on behind you, you stand in a huge black silhouette. It's the most amateur thing in the world.

It really irritated me for a minute. What business were we of his? But I decided to let it go for now. I told Angie, "Aaah I'll go say hello when we get back down here. Maybe he's just a bored old guy who hasn't seen a beautiful, exotic, Italian angel in his whole life!" Angie laughed. "Yeah...that has to be it." she said sarcastically. I opened her door and she climbed in. I walked around to my side and paused for a second. It must have been a longer second than I thought because Angie lowered her window and asked me if I was okay.

All the sudden it dawned on me. I looked at Anj and I said "You hear that?" Angie shot me a puzzled look. "Hear what, Joe?" "Nothing," I said, "What you don't hear is *nothing*. It's dead quiet. No trucks on the highway, no kids playing in the street, no next door neighbors. Nothing!" Angie smiled...a beautiful smile that spread itself across her face like an artist's stroke on a canvas. "Yeah, I hear that." She said. "This place is a lot different from home." Boy, was she right.

6

Getting

My Father's

Blessing

We left Lynchburg for home on Monday morning. Angie chattered about the house, making a mental list of draperies and bathroom colors and all the things that a woman does when she goes about making a house into a home. I was more concerned with the garage and the workshop and staking out my garden for the following spring.

We got home at Four PM and went straight to my folk's house to pick up the kids. We walked in to exuberant, gleeful hello from Emily and the usual ho-hum wave of the hand from the boys. And we felt the palpable uneasiness of my mother and father. I had talked to them before the trip and they knew why we were going to Lynchburg. They understood, but they were very upset at the same time. They could see why we wanted to move. They also wished it wasn't going to happen.

We didn't talk about it right then. We gathered up the kids and got them into the truck and I told the Old Man I'd call him later and we'd talk. His face wore a grim, forced smile as he hugged the kids and gave them each a silver dollar. He'd done that every time they visited for as long as they'd been alive. Uncle Tony did that for me when I was little. *Family traditions.* I thought. This was not going to be easy.

The Old Man called me later that night. The kids had wound down and were getting ready for bed and he asked me if he could come over. Now, this was a big deal for Pop, because typically he just showed up. Sometimes, if he was feeling particularly gregarious, he might call on his way over. Usually he did this as he was turning the corner to my street and then I'd hear him cursing at the cell phone, unable to find the "end call" button. But tonight he called from his house. He sounded very subdued on the phone. I figured I knew what was coming tonight. "Sure Pop," I said, "Come on over as soon as you want." "Okay, son," He answered, "I'm just finishing washing the front steps." Yeah...he rinsed off the front steps about three times a week. He said it kept the dust down. Philadelphia streets haven't been dusty in about seventy years, but Pop still washes his steps in response to the dust. I think it's simply him doing what Giuseppe did when Pop was a boy.

He showed up at 7:45 with a bottle of Red wine in one hand, a sack of cold cuts in the other, and a loaf of semolina bread, from Musticelli's bakery, under his chin. Looking like the stereotypical fun-loving Italian, it was hard to not smile at him. I think he was putting forward a good face in front of Anj. We talked for a minute, the three of us, and then he asked me if I'd take a walk with him. I immediately got a lump in my throat. Pop and I hadn't walked the streets together since the night Giuseppe died. He's not an overly emotional guy, unless the Phillies were winning a World Series, so I knew this was going to mean something. I grabbed my keys, gave Angie a peck on the cheek and walked out with the Old Man.

It was early October, but still a little muggy out on the concrete. There were still windows open and Italian Opera was coming from Mrs. Begnetti's living room. Pop and I walked past her house and without looking up, I said, "Buonasera, Senora Begnetti." The curtains ruffled back into place, and the metal venetian blinds clattered as she quickly pulled her fingers back from where they had been holding the slats open, ever so slightly. Mrs. B. tried to duck into what shadows existed in her living room. Her nosiness stopped bothering me years ago. I figured she was a little frightened at being a widow and she was just living like a scared little old lady. I had made an effort in recent years to go check on her every couple of days. I'd check a few windows and make sure her deadbolts were working. I made a big production out of it so she'd feel safe. Anymore, when I saw her peeping I just let her know that I saw her, and figured that might actually make her feel better. God forbid she ever gets the notion to turn off the lights in the room before she spies on the block until midnight...she might actually see something.

"I remember when her husband was alive." My Old Man said, "Best car mechanic in the neighborhood. Couldn't find his way around a diesel engine or Zippie would have hired him." The Old Man sounded wistful. I thought it best to just let him talk. We walked along Fourteenth Street and stopped at Romignoli's for a cup of coffee and a biscotti. Alfonso Romignoli knew the Old Man about as well as he knew his own father. This place was my dad's favorite hangout. They brewed his coffee the way he liked it, which was strong enough to start one of our trash trucks. Pop brewed an equal-parts mixture of Folger's and Medaglia D'oro Espresso. The stuff would literally make your heart race. First time I tried it, the tachycardia was so bad it scared me. "How can you drink that and not stay awake all night?" I asked him. He just smiled and dunked his biscotti. "It's how God made me, son." He said with a shrug, "Caffeine has no effect on me at all."

I knew the Old Man wanted to talk about us leaving. I also knew that he had no real way of dealing with what he was feeling inside, and didn't know how to open the conversation. Men of his generation weren't talkers. I figured I'd let it work itself out for a while before just diving in myself. We sat on a bench outside of Romignoli's for about fifteen minutes, sipping coffee and people-watching, and commenting on the sights and sounds. "These have always been the best biscotti's in the neighborhood, you know?" I said. My dad looked at me and smiled. "They taste like your mother's don't they?" he said. "Yeah, you know they really do, now that you mention it." I was shocked that I had never noticed before. My old man leaned over and, with that tone that parents have when they reveal a family secret, said, "They *are* your mother's biscotti." I looked at him in amazement. "Yeah," he said, "It's true. Mrs. Romignoli could never get the recipe to work. She tried for like, two years when they first opened the shop. One day she's sitting at the house with your mother and she's eating one of Mamma's biscotti and she asks her how she makes them. Your mom made a batch with her, right there in the kitchen. Just pulled out the pans and went to work. And they've been serving them at the cafe ever since." This brought a smile to my face. "I never knew that, Pop."

The Old Man stood up and tossed his cup into the trash and we walked down the street toward St. Monica's. Before I knew it, we were wiping our feet on the doormat and entering the marble and glass foyer. Pop removed his everpresent fedora and dipped his fingers into the Holy Water. He gave me a gentle elbow and whispered, "You still know how to sprinkle?" Of course I did. I just hadn't done it in a while. "What are we doing here, Pop? There's no mass tonight." I asked him. "Yeah I know. Sometimes I come here just to be alone and talk to God. This building...it just *feels* sacred, you know? "I mean, you just feel like you need to whisper and lower your head a little in here. Anyway, it helps me connect."

I knew what the Old Man meant. I was a Baptist in practice since high school, but there is a wonder, and awe, and sense of history and majesty in the old Marble and stained-glass cathedrals and basilicas of my hometown. We walked down to the front of the sanctuary and Pop kept going. We were apparently heading to one of the grottoes to

134

light a candle. "You remember how to say a Novena?" he whispered to me. "Pop, I went to CCD, Catholic School. Mass every week. You think I forget that stuff?" "Good!" the Old Man said, "Then say one with me." "For what, Pop?" I whispered.

"For God's blessing on this new chapter in your life, son." "I turned and looked at him. I realized there would be no talking about this. He was giving me his blessing in this way. I felt tears coming to my eyes and I fought them as best I could. I was never more thankful for the buyout as I was in that moment. If Pop and I had continued on as business partners, he may never have felt like he could show me this side of himself. I wished we had done this years ago.

I knelt next to my Old Man. We prayed a Novena together. At some point he looked at me and I leaned over and said "Charlie." It took him a minute and then a smile crept across his lips. "That's right," he whispered. "Charlie. How long was he missing, a week? Ten days? Then boom! He's back!" "Yeah Pop," I said, "I think that was the last time we prayed a Novena together." Charlie was my mom's cranky old Cocker Spaniel. He was a great dog, but as he got older, he attached himself to my mother and wouldn't really get friendly with any of us. Cockers are known to do that. He got a whiff of a female in heat one day and off he went. He was gone for over a week. Now –truth be told- I didn't like him as much as other dogs we'd had, until he went missing. Then my heart was broken. I was pretty torn up about it and my mother...oh Maddonn, the way she cried! So me and the Old Man spent every evening after school and work walking the neighborhood looking for him. One night we stopped in here at St. Monica's and said a Novena for him. To St. Anthony, the patron Saint of Lost Things, because Charlie was lost. The next morning, the randy old boy was lying on the front

135

porch; sound asleep, like he'd never left. It was a pretty impressive introduction to prayer for an eight year old.

The old man prayed his Novena and then he turned to me. He put his arm around me. Oh God! I was not ready for that. He put his arm around me and said, "You're everything a man could want in a son. God has blessed me and this family. Take that blessing with you when you go, son. And make a new place for the Mezilli name to be counted-on and trusted, and respected." The Old Man was crying.

We walked out a few minutes later. Pop was taking his time now. "I love this neighborhood." He said. "I remember when Zippie bought the old house. It was such a big deal to move from the apartment. All the other immigrant families thought your grandfather had stolen money from someone. Nobody there even knew anyone who *lived* in a house, much less actually bought one." My dad was smiling now. With tears in his eyes. "Zippie was a hard man. Hard to understand sometimes, and hard to please. I think it was the Depression and the poverty and leaving his family so young. Twelve years old is very young to be on your own in a new country."

This was about the most I'd ever heard the Old Man talk about his father. To me, Giuseppe was intimidating. And I had the benefit of the natural barrier that grandchildren have. My father didn't have that. He had been brought up under the constant insufficiency that so many children of self-employed men feel. Their dads were driven by need, and desperation, and they never could understand why their kids didn't feel the same hunger in their belly. It was probably because they were just kids. But Giuseppe always saw it as laziness or slack. He drove my Old Man pretty hard. I have to give my dad credit; he found the balance with me. He didn't force me into the business or make me hate those trash trucks because of the toll they took on him, but he didn't coddle me either.

We walked the block near the Church and he told me about how Giuseppe had bought a truck load of marble for the Cathedral. The parish priests had been asking for donations for the building when it was being constructed. They were trying to raise so much money per truckload of marble. Giuseppe somehow was suspicious of the request, especially since they were instructed to send the money to the Diocese and then the Diocese would handle paying the bills. Giuseppe made some calls, found out what kind of marble they were using, and went to the quarry and paid in cash for a truckload to be delivered to the building site. Father Fizzano called him and asked him what was going on. He said "You asked for money for marble. I just cut out the middle man." I laughed out loud at that. "You never told me that story, Pop." I told my dad. "No? You sure?" he said. "No, dad, I sure would have remembered that story." I told him.

We walked a while longer and eventually found ourselves back at his house. We stood there in silence for a minute; the only sound was the steady tinkle of the peeing cherub in his front yard. Finally I said to him, "You hear all this background noise, Pop? The highway and the neighbors and the airplanes and the sirens? At the new place there's nothing but silence. Silence and stars at night." The Old Man shuffled his feet. "I bet that's beautiful, son. I am really happy for you and Angie. You go. You make this move and I'll stay here and hold down the fort and take care of Nonna. We'll be okay."

Then he hugged me. For maybe the third or fourth time in my life, the Old Man hugged me. It was the closing of a chapter. A passing of a torch someplace in the universe.

After that moment, every day we stayed in the neighborhood felt out of sequence. It was time to go.

So we did.

Book Two

Virginia

7

The

Damned

Yankee

Phil thought he was trouble as soon as he pulled up. Me? I wasn't thinking that at all. But he sure was different. Different from anyone else who moved in here since this neighborhood was built. And I've seen almost all of them come and go.

My name is Hank Milledge. I've been living here in Forest, Virginia for twenty-two years. I was born right up the road in Lynchburg, and we moved here ahead of all the development as the college brought more and more people to the area. It's one of the most beautiful places on God's Earth. My daddy is from around here. My momma was from Madison Heights, just north of the city. My daddy's family originally settled in Georgia, in what became Milledgeville. But they built the insane asylum there and my granddaddy decided he didn't want to live "near them nuts." So they came up here to Lynchburg because the foundry had just opened.

Now, when I say my momma is from just north of "the city" I'm talking about Lynchburg, Va. Not New York, or Philadelphia, or even Washington, D.C. which we are only about three hours from. Lynchburg is all the city I really need. I've been to those other places. Well, I haven't been to Philadelphia, but I've been to New York and to Washington. Nice places. Exciting. But I'm a quasi-country boy. I'm no hick in the sticks. Lynchburg is a big enough town to avoid that. But I like the country. I love the beauty of the Blue Ridge Mountains that encircle this area like a fortress. From three of the four vantage points in my yard, you see mountains. I like that.

Lynchburg used to be a sleepy town. Then Liberty University grew and grew and before you know it, people who came here to go to college fell in love with the place –

for the same reasons I did- and they stayed. They came in droves and they stayed in them too. It's nothing to see the license plates of twenty or thirty different states in one day around here. But that's okay, they don't live out this far. It's a little pricey for a college student to rent something out here, so we only get buyers. Professors at the college mostly. Or retirees. People who want a lot of house for the money, but still have money to spend on a house. Oh and land, they usually want a little land. None of the houses in my neighborhood have postage stamp yards. We have an acre, some have more. It's a great place to live.

There are about one hundred twenty five houses in this community. All of them sit on a slice of heaven. There are no fences to speak of, there's the occasional white picket in the front yard but nothing that screams of "privacy." It's a great place to raise a family. I know all my neighbors. I was here before any of this was developed so I've watched them all come, over the years. They came from a lot of places around the country. My neighbor two doors up is a biology professor at the college. His name is Dr. Jack Ford. He has three kids and a beautiful wife who –if you're asking me- is a little above his abilities. He's not the best looking guy in the world, with that receding hairline and beak-like nose. But he is a sweet man. One of the kindest people I ever met, and they supposedly met in high school and she just thinks the sun rises and sets on this guy.

The house behind me belongs to Larry Erickson and his family. Larry is an insurance agent. He moved here to go to college and fell in love. First he fell in love with the girl who sat beside him in sophomore Music Appreciation class, and then he fell in love with the Blue Ridge Mountains. He almost never goes home. His parents live somewhere in Minnesota and they call him regularly asking him when he's coming to visit. He tells me this all the time. He imitates his mother's voice and her slightly Scandinavian accent.

Both his parents were born in Minnesota, but his grandparents were all Swedish. So his folks have some of the accent remaining. Larry hates the cold. So he never goes back to Minnesota except for a week every summer. He fishes with his dad, and his mother tries teaching his wife how to cook authentic Swedish food. Apparently authentic Swedish food means about ten different kinds of Swedish meatballs, because that's all she ever brings to cookouts or get-togethers. She does a pretty darned good job with them, but it's still a Swedish meatball. This is pretty ironic because he loves meatballs, but not the Swedish ones his wife makes. He loves Italian meatballs. In fact he loves Italian anything. He was immersed in The Sopranos while it was on, and his game room has The Godfather posters throughout. He is fascinated by the mafia. That's why he and Phil hit it off so well.

Phil is my neighbor to the right, Phil Lowery. The Lowery's live between us and the biology professor. Phil grew up in Lynchburg. He's almost my dad's age and he retired from the old foundry years ago. He quit high school to work at the plant after his father died in a car accident. Eventually he got his G.E.D. and then his college degree at the community college. He climbed the ladder at the plant and was running the whole thing the last ten years before he retired. He's a very smart man, that Phil. Wise too. There's a difference.

Phil and I have been here the longest. Usually we stand in my garage, drinking a beer and watching yet another new family unloading the moving van. Phil can size them up remarkably well. He has an insight. Oh and he *loves* Mobster movies. The guy has absolutely no sense of humor at all, so maybe the only entertaining thing he does, besides size up neighbors, and try to fix every outdated appliance in his house, is quote lines from every Mafia movie ever made. The Monday morning after the final episode of "The Sopranos" aired, he was in a funk and didn't speak until Wednesday. When he isn't here in my garage, he and Erickson will be holed-up in Erickson's game room watching The Sopranos on DVD and making mental notes about mob behavior.

We've watched a lot of these folks come here, Phil and me. From all over the country. And he's never been wrong about any of 'em. Never. That's why I'll never forget the day when that Mother-of-Pearl Escalade rolled down the street and pulled into the driveway of the house diagonally across from mine. The big Antebellum with the triple lot. Five acres this fella has. I was hoping that lot would lay untouched for another year. I was going to cash in my 401K after I turned sixty-five and buy it myself. But I never got the chance. Because *he* moved in.

I remember it like yesterday. The Escalade crept down the block, and finally pulled into the driveway. A few minutes later, a beautiful blue Corvette Stingray came around the corner with a growl. I have to admit, I gave him points for not speeding in that thing. I don't think I could have held my foot off the gas. He came down the street with the windows down and Bruce Springsteen playing. Loud enough that I could tell who it was, but not loud enough to be annoying. Okay, more points.

Phil Lowery and I had been tinkering with a vacuum cleaner in my garage and eventually just sat down in some lawn chairs near the workbench and drank a few beers. I sat back with my beer and turned to look at Phil. He had been sitting slumped down in his chair, like a teenaged boy, half asleep. When the Escalade pulled up he looked up and pulled the bill of his Atlanta Braves cap up a bit so he could see better. He didn't say anything.

When the Corvette came down the street, he sat up stiffly. He leaned forward and set his Miller High Life on the concrete floor of my garage. His chin rested in his left hand and he adjusted his sunglasses with his right. The driver of the Corvette got out and walked up to the driver's door of the Escalade and opened it. Out stepped an unspeakably beautiful woman with the blackest hair I ever saw. So black it had blue to it, like an oil slick almost. She was tan and tall and she looked glamorous. As a rule, I don't stare at another man's wife. It says not to do that right there in the Good Book. But I couldn't help it. I caught myself after a long minute. It wasn't lust. I'm a better man than that. It was good, ol' admiration. Like what I felt for his Corvette when I first saw it, except in my loins. Old Boy had outkicked his coverage for sure.

Phil never said a word. He slowly took a swig of his beer, never noticing the eruption of foam when he slammed the bottle down a bit too hard. "Pennsylvania." I said. Phil didn't respond for a long time. He was staring at the guy in the Corvette. I waited and repeated myself "Pennsylvania." I said it a little louder this time. Phil didn't move for the longest time. He was transfixed. I cleared my throat. Finally he looked at me with a worried look on his face. "Huh?" he grunted. "Pennsylvania," I repeated, "...the license plates say 'Pennsylvania." Phil rubbed his eyes. "Yeah." he mumbled. "We ain't had none from Pennsylvania yet." "They look like nice enough folks," I said. "Especially the missus, huh Phil?" I said with a laugh. Phil didn't answer right away. He took another swig from his beer, and turned to me and deadpanned, "They look like trouble to me." With that he stood up and walked over to his house, went inside and shut the door.

If I know Phil, he was probably peeking through his blinds at them right now. Phil does that a lot and we've all accepted it. To be honest, it would be downright creepy except that Phil is so darned bad at it. He'll do it in broad daylight with the sun shining right on him when he splits the blinds to peek out. Or at night he'll do it with a light on behind him, and never, ever realize that he is silhouetting himself in the window. But he's a good man, and it does somehow make us all feel a little more secure knowing Phil has one eye on the street at all times.

Phil went home and I stayed in the garage, back in the shadows a bit, to watch my new neighbors as they arrived. "Pennsylvania," I said to myself. "I wonder if he's a Steelers fan." The three other doors of the Escalade blew open like a tornado had hit them from the inside. Four kids spilled out. Three boys and a little girl. And two dogs. The little girl carried a pet carrier and I figured it must be a cat. The entire family came to a screeching halt in the front yard. They all stared at the peeing angel statue. I had wondered about that thing. A work crew had shown up a week ago, and installed it. It was the most hideous piece of yard art I've ever seen in my life. I've had a lawn jockey or two, and I've had an old wheelbarrow with flowers in it. But this pissing angel was pure ugly.

The guy stood in front of the "Saint Urination" (as we'd all come to call it) shook his head made a call on his cell phone and his hands moved a lot when he was talking to whoever he was talking to. He stood there in front of the peeing angel, pointing at it and talking loudly and waving emphatically while the rest of the family went inside, laughing as they went. The littlest boy was pointing to his crotch, pretending to have his pecker in his hand, and imitating the peeing angel while his brothers laughed at him, which I thought was funny. The guy shook his head, went back to his Corvette, and leaned inside. He was rummaging around in the seat for a second and then I saw him pull his hand back, lift up the tail of his shirt and put a chrome-plated nine millimeter in a hip holster. What the heck was he carrying that around for? *Well he's no college professor.* I thought to myself. *Maybe he's a cop.*

He stood and looked across the street towards Phil's house for a second, shook his head, and went inside, and I went back to finishing this vacuum cleaner so Maryanne would get off my back and we wouldn't go out and by that five-hundred dollar Dyson she wanted. "As long as I have duct tape and a screw driver, we ain't spending five hundred dollars on a vacuum!" I'd told her. I'd managed to squeeze fourteen years out of this Sears unit we had and I wasn't ready to give up on her just yet. "5-4-3-2..." I started counting in my head. My phone rang. I had an extension out in the garage and so I picked up. "Hello Phil" I said. I knew he was going to call me as soon as the guy across the street went inside. I also knew that Phil had been perched inside his living room, right up against the window with a pair of binoculars so powerful that you could probably see the hairs in Teddy Roosevelt's nose on Mt. Rushmore from here.

"Did you see the piece he was carryin'?" Phil asked me, in a slightly high-pitched voice. Phil always gets about a half-octave higher and real nasally when he gets excited or suspicious of someone. And since he is suspicious of almost everyone, this is how he usually talks. You can tell when Phil finally trusts someone and feels comfortable around them, because he goes back to his natural baritone. "What does a man need with a gun like that down here?" Phil hissed. I laughed loudly, "Phil Lowery!" I bellowed, "You have more firepower than the Virginia State Police and you want to know what that man was doing with a nine Millimeter? The bible talks about hypocrites, Phil. You weren't listenin' I guess."

"Weren't no nine Mil. It was a .45 Colt. A 1911 model. And it was stainless steel, not chromed. What's a man need that kind of force for...unless he's afraid of something." Phil answered. "Phil," I said "For the love of God, you haven't even met the man yet. What are you talking about?" Phil grunted into the phone, "I mean the man was carrying a .45 Colt Model 1911 in the console of his *Corvette*. The Corvette with Pennsylvania tags." Phil paused, "You don't find that suspicious?" I was dumbfounded. I literally did not know what to say. "No Phil," I said, clearing my throat, "In fact I'm now suspicious of myself for missing whatever it is you think you saw there."

Phil was getting agitated and it made his voice get higher. "A rich man buys a house,   worth almost a Million dollars, and I heard from Monte Crispin at the county office that he paid in cash. He shows up with a fancy car, and a fancy truck, and a fancy wife, and a pissin' Italian statue in his front yard, and now he has a gun, and you don't see the connection?" I was trying not to laugh, and also worried that Phil was about to make a very bad first impression on our new neighbors. "No Phil," I said, "I don't see the connection. But, did he really pay cash for that house?" Phil whispered into the phone, "I heard he literally brought a satchel full of money to the closing." He paused, I'm going to call my friend Steve at the title company and see if he can tell me for sure. But he pays a Million dollars cash for a house and now he's carrying a gun like that?"

"Phil," I asked him, "How many .45 Colt 1911's do you have?" Phil sputtered and hissed. I had him. "I have three, what does that have to do with it?" Phil was getting angry now. "And the house was only listed for seven-thirty-five Phil. You're going to start rumors before the man has even unpacked a box." "Sure, defend the man." I swear I could *hear* Phil's lips quivering in anger now, "He comes down here paying three quarters of a million dollars in cash for a house and driving at least another hundred thousand dollars in cars and toting a stainless steel Colt. But I'm sure it's all coincidence."

"Phil," I said, trying to reason with him, "You have three Colt 1911's. You also have an AK74, two Weatherby .308's, a snub-nose .38, and at least two dozen decrepit old Claymores that your brother-in-law, the supply sergeant, stole from Fort Benning. You could start World War Three and then supply both sides for a week! And you're criticizing this man for a sidearm?"

My argument made perfect sense, but that only irritated Phil even more. When Phil found someone suspicious, he was seldom ever talked out of it. "Sure," he hissed into his phone, "Side with the mobster. We've been neighbors for twenty years. You and I are the only native Lynchburgers in the neighborhood. But you just go ahead and stick up for our new neighbor. He's probably in the witness protection program, or worse. He's probably coming down here to expand his family's territory."

This was already going too far. I had to reel him in. "Phil," I said, in a calming tone, "The man probably moved here from a city. Maybe he needed a sidearm where he lived. Maybe he is a federal agent or something. Maybe they are carrying a bit of cash...you know, moving and all, and he wanted some protection. My point is, Phil, you can't be sure

151

of nothin' you just said, so why don't you relax a bit until we get to know him?"

Phil was quiet on the other end of the line. I knew he was busy thinking of ways to investigate the new neighbor. "Phil?" I said quietly. No response. "Phil!" I bellowed. "Huh...what?" he chortled, "Yeah. We'll give him a chance. Kick his tires a bit. But I'm going to be watching him. You best believe that." "Of course you are, Phil, you watch everybody." I muttered. "Huh? You say sump'n?" Phil barked. "No, Phil. I just said 'You watch him for everybody else, you're the eldest here, Phil. You keep us aware of this guy, okay?" Phil grunted, like a guinea pig. "Okay Phil, I have to go and finish this vacuum cleaner before Maryanne makes me go out and buy a new one. Keep an eye on the new guy, Phil, just don't overstep your bounds, ya hear?" I hung up the phone and got back to my repairs on the vacuum cleaner motor. But I have to admit, some of what Phil had said was starting to raise questions in my own mind. What if this guy was some sort of trouble? Maybe it was good that Phil was suspicious.

You Can Take The Boy Out of Philly
(But You can't Take Philly Out of The Boy)

We got to Forest just before Thanksgiving. We unpacked over the holiday, going out to eat instead of cooking the traditional turkey, and macaroni, and baked ziti, and antipasta. See, we Italians eat all the things you eat at a traditional Thanksgiving dinner, plus everything we eat on Sundays at Nonna's. That's how we do it in our neighborhood. But with the rush of moving, and settling in, and getting the kids enrolled in school, and buying new furniture, and changing our driver's licenses...you see what I'm saying? Christmas was on us before we knew it.

We decided to go home to Philly that first Christmas. We figured the coast was clear with our families. We had already made the move and so there was no talking us out of it. Our relatives would get another year with us and so we thought that would ease the transition a bit. Plus I was worried about Pop adjusting. He was calling me every single day now, mostly just to chit chat, and I knew he was really struggling to adapt to us not being there.

So we went home. We hadn't sold our house on Shunk Street yet. In fact we hadn't even listed it, and we left all the furniture there and bought new when we moved to Forest. So we just stayed there and it was like we never really left. Anj and I went shopping downtown, took the kids to Wannamaker's to see the lights, and ate Seven Fishes at her parents' house. Christmas morning we opened presents at our house and then went to my mom and dad's for the day, to see my brothers and sister and the kids. It was like every Mezilli Christmas that had come and gone before, except

153

that we'd be leaving to go home when we were done, and home wasn't the next block over anymore.

We got back to Forest just before New Year's. I had a mountain of stuff to tend to. Getting an invisible fence installed for the dogs, Get our heirlooms and antiques shipped down from the house in Philly, and make a good assessment of my hunting camp out in Bedford.

I drove my boys out there at the end of January and we walked it for hours, looking over broken fencing and figuring out where the power lines ran so we could get electricity to the cabin and barn. We figured we'd need to buy a couple of ATV's, which of course, made the boys eyes light up.

Beyond that, it was just another winter. We settled into a routine and got used to where the grocery stores were. I couldn't find an Italian restaurant that was anything like the ones back home. Not that they weren't decent, but they weren't like the ones in South Philly. But then what is? We can cook all the Italian dishes we want, but we can't find a real hoagie or cheese steak here. It's the rolls. You have to use Amorosso's or it's just bread. So of course, I got on the phone and arranged to have two dozen Amorroso's hoagie rolls shipped down here every other week. I pick them up out at the Lynchburg Regional airport.

But that was it. We got cozy with the guy who hooked up our satellite TV and he installed the Philadelphia Sim-card instead of the one for Roanoke / Lynchburg and we could watch the local channels back home. Watching "Action News" with Jim Gardner on my TV in Forest, Virginia was not how I ever saw my forty-fifth year taking shape. But here we were anyway. To make the transition easier, and since our new neighbors were constantly asking us about all the Philly stereotypes, we decided to have a little fun. One Saturday morning in January, I was out front putting up a huge inflatable Santa Claus. I had the thing packed in the garage and we weren't going to put it out until next Christmas, but for about two weeks, every time I saw Phil or Hank across the street, and we got into a conversation about my hometown, they brought up that whole stupid, "Throwing Snowballs at Santa Claus" thing. Every time. That or cheese steaks. We were watching the Eagles on Sunday Night Football one evening in my game room. Of course there were nineteen references to cheese steaks before the first commercial break. Lowery and Milledge kept asking me about them and finally I said, "You know where to get the best cheese steak in Philly? Right next door to Independence Hall...where the friggin Declaration of Independence was signed! My hometown is the birthplace of our nation, and you want to ask me about cheese steaks again?"

Angie got a kick out of that but Phil and Hank didn't get the joke. So anyway, this one Saturday afternoon, I put this big Santa outside. Phil comes sauntering over and asks me why I'm sticking a Santa outside, two weeks after Christmas. I smiled at him. "We have snow coming in tomorrow, Phil." And I walked inside, leaving Phil standing there scratching his head.

The next morning, about five inches of snow had fallen and I kept an eye on Phil's living room blinds. As soon as I saw them move, and knew he was peepin' I marched my three sons out front and we took turns throwing snowballs at the huge inflatable Santa Claus in my yard. I figured, since he was always wondering if we did it, we might as well give him a show.

So, other than that, we made it through our first winter in the mountains of central Virginia without incident.

Honestly, it was no big deal. Winter, back in Philly, is nearly identical. It arrives a couple of weeks earlier back home, but the temperatures are pretty much the same. The biggest difference was that in Forest, we got snow a little more frequently. Otherwise, it was the same sort of winter I'd grown up with. The biggest difference I'd noticed was that fall was a little longer down here and I liked that. Fall in the mountains is beautiful, with the leaves turning. The mountains seem to explode in colors. I also noticed that spring in Virginia arrives a week or two sooner as well. Back home, spring doesn't really get in gear until early April. But here in Virginia, it was warmer and more "spring-like" by early March. I sure liked that.

I had been looking forward to this spring since we moved-in last November. I had this nice big lot, and I was finally going to plant a garden that would rival my Uncle Franny's. There was no way I could grow *anything,* the way he can, but I do okay, because he taught me well. And now I could finally have a garden as big as his. I planned the layout of the garden all winter. I had turned the soil under in December. My neighbor across the street, the peeper, he moseyed over one day asking me about a pump sprayer, and stayed for three hours watching me till my plot where the garden was going. I think he was hoping I would stop and talk. But I seldom do that when I get engrossed in a project.

I have to hand it to the old guy, he wasn't bashful. After he'd grown weary of watching me work, he said, "What the heck are you doing, tilling your land in December?" "I'm getting my garden ready, Phil." I said. He almost swallowed his cud of chewing tobacco, and then he coughed and looked at me wild-eyed. "You're what?" he said. He would have screamed this, I'm sure, except he was choking on green tobacco juice.

156

"I'm tilling for my garden. I need to see how deep the soil is and what kind of acidity it has. Otherwise my tomatoes won't taste right." I said this to Phil, expecting him to think I was nuts. It worked. "You have to have certain soil to grow a tomato?" He asked, incredulously. "A tomato is a tomato; I hate the durned things anyway." I looked him dead in the eye, "A tomato is definitely not a tomato." I thought it would be fun to shoot him the maloik -the "evil eye"- so I did.

That was December. I'd taken a soil sample down to the local Land Extension office and had it tested. It was mostly clay, which, among other things, meant too much iron. Even if I filled the garden with topsoil, it would still leech the iron up through the soil and ruin my tomatoes. Now, we Italians take tomatoes very seriously. I have grown the same strain of heirlooms for nine years. I save the seeds from the dozen biggest producing plants I have and start them in a hothouse. That way I get the same results each year.

I called my Uncle Franny at the end of February to ask his advice on what to do with this lousy soil. "Uncle Franny, I got problems. I began. He chuckled, "Well they aren't money troubles, I know that much. What's wrong?" I said the unthinkable. "I don't know if I can grow tomatoes down here." He laughed, "Well you haven't sold your house up here yet, so you're going to have to move back!" I laughed and then asked him, "Seriously, Uncle Fran, this is like trying to plant in Playdoh. What am I going to do? I can drop some topsoil but that won't change the chemistry of the ground."

Uncle Franny was quick with an answer. "You have to make a base that is going to be deep enough to block the effects of that clay." He said. "Can you get mushroom soil down there?" "I don't know, Uncle Fran," I answered, "I kinda doubt it." Uncle Franny thought for a minute and then said "Call Domanucce and see if his old man knows anyone down there who might have it. Hell if he doesn't, just pay someone to bring you a truckload. It isn't like you can't afford it!" I laughed, but he was right, I had to admit, that was a great idea. "I'll call him when we hang up. Now what do I do with mushroom soil?" Uncle Franny told me to get a piece of paper and he would "Write me a recipe."   "Go ahead Uncle Fran," I said, ready to write. "Okay," he began, "Assuming you get the mushroom soil, you also need about a quarter ton of sand, some compost, and about six bags of lime. I'm assuming you're going to use a truckload of mushroom soil here, maybe seven cubic yards." I could hear the happiness in his voice. Uncle Franny had a knack for growing things, like I said. And he really loved it when someone would ask him about his secrets. Especially when it was family doing the asking.

He continued; "You're going to need a roll of landscaper's burlap, ten feet wide, by probably a hundred feet." He was on a roll now. "Okay, here's the formula. You take a piece of the burlap about ten feet long; lay it out flat on the ground. Then you fill it with about three wheelbarrow loads of mushroom soil. You add to that a half a wheelbarrow of sand, and half a bag of lime and two five-gallon-buckets of compost. Then you roll it up." I was writing as fast as I could. "Hang on a second Franny," I said, "Let me catch up." I finished writing and read back what I'd written thus far. "Good!" He said, "Now, you take this to your plot. You want to use one of these rolls about every twenty square feet. Dig down just enough to bury it, put some more lime on top to start breaking down the hemp in the burlap, then cover it over with some good topsoil and wet it down. Everything in that roll will decompose, it's the perfect ratio of fertilizers

158

and bases, and is full of nutrients for the soil. If you do it this year, it will be ready for next year."

"Wait!" I said, "You mean I have to wait a year for tomatoes?" Franny chuckled. "Yeah, sorry, but it takes a year for the process to take place. You said you have heavy clay there, right?" "Yes." I said feeling a bit defeated. "Well then use a little more lime in the mix. It will cancel out the iron in the soil." He offered. "And don't worry about tomatoes this year. Build some boxes, and fill them with potting soil, about three feet deep. Plant some Bradleys and some Beefsteaks. Give them plenty of sunlight and you'll be able to make it through this summer. Don't waste your good heirloom seeds on bad dirt."

Uncle Franny was right. Tomatoes are like a religion in our house. If I was finally going to have the garden of my dreams I was going to have to do it the right way. Besides, we had a July Fourth trip home planned, and I could raid his garden then, and bring back all the home-growns I wanted. We chatted a few minutes more and then he said he had to go because the pinochle boys were arriving.

My uncle Franny is a legendary pinochle player in the neighborhood. His group of cronies rivals anything you've ever seen in a mafia movie or TV show. If Pinochle was a gang activity, Uncle Franny would have been Don Corleone.

I said my goodbyes and hung up. Searching through my cell phone, I found Joey Fanucci's phone number. He picked up on the third ring. "Yo, Joe!" he said. I paused for a minute. I'd forgotten how that sounded after only four months in Virginia, and I realized I really missed it. "Yo Dom-ah-nootch!" I said heartily. "What's happenin' back home, Cuz?"

Two things you need to know about Philly people. We never say "How ya doin?" that's a New York thing. We greet

159

each other by saying "Yo!" and we call everyone we know "Cuz." It's a term of endearment.

Joey rattled off a list of things that were going on back on the block. Who was leaving, who moved in, who is having another baby, who got divorced. Then he got serious, "Joey, you know Tommy Fallone is getting out in May. You gonna be here for the party?" I'd forgotten that was coming up. I needed to be there for Tommy when he got out, we all did. "Tommy Felonious is finally getting sprung, huh?" I chuckled. "Yeah, of course I'm coming home." I made a mental note of Tommy's release date. I was definitely going to be there for my friend.

But this morning I had a more pressing issue at hand. "Listen, Domanucce, I need you to ask your dad something for me. Ask him if he knows where I can find some mushroom soil down here. I can't grow tomatoes in this clay. I need about ten yards." He told me he'd call his dad right away. "Give him a few days to make some calls, Joe. Pop will find something for you, I'm sure." We talked for a few minutes longer and said our goodbyes.

I went about the next few days buying the stuff I needed for Uncle Franny's "burlap burritos" as I was now calling them. I staked out the garden to allow for the best sunlight and drainage. I went to Lynchburg and bought myself a used Ford pickup truck. I didn't want to use my Tundra, and Angie would have killed me if I used the Escalade, so I bought an old F-150. It was perfect for what I wanted. I also found out that in the South, they have something called a "Co-Op." I think it's short for "Farmer's Cooperative" and you can find almost anything you want there, if growing things in dirt is your passion. They also have "Tractor Supply." Now, I'd seen Tractor Supply's TV commercials during football games, from time to time, so I knew they were out there. But they don't have any in Little Italy, you know what I mean?

I pretty much figured out the difference on the first visit. TSC is where you go if you think you're a farmer. Real farmers go to the Co-Op. Nothing against TSC. But it's not the same. So anyway, I made a few trips to the Co-Op to buy the burlap I needed. The guy asked me if I was a contractor. Apparently a 10x100 roll of burlap is a lot for one man. What the heck do I know? I'm just following orders here. Nobody knew me when I walked in, which apparently is a big deal at the Bedford County Co-op. I walked through the doors and everyone stared. Sheesh, that was something different. In Philly, you know better than stare at anyone. First, it's rude. Second, you're very likely to hear, "Somethin' I can do for you, Cuz?" which is roughly equivalent to "You got a problem we need to discuss?" Besides being that term of endearment, we also use "Cuz" sarcastically sometimes.

But I remembered I wasn't on home turf anymore and I just smiled at the girl at the register. Now, I have very good hearing. Always did. And I swear, I heard my name whispered. Hand-to-God! At the Bedford County Co-Op where I'd never set foot in my life before this very moment, I heard some guy in the seed aisle saying my last name. *We ain't in South Philly anymore, Toto.* I thought.

I asked for the burlap and looked through the seed catalogs. I was standing there looking at dog houses when a guy came up to me, smiling. "Mr. Mezilli?" he said sheepishly. "Yo!" I said, turning to look at him. He stopped in his tracks. Honest to God I thought for just a second that he was afraid of me. I couldn't figure that out. Look, I'm six-foot-four, and I'm a big guy. But I'm not scary. At least I don't think so. I stuck out my hand. "I'm Joe Mezilli. Just call me Joey. And you are...?" The guy stared at my hand for a second. Like he was studying it. He got back on track and shook my hand carefully. "I'm Tim. Tim Peppers. I, uh, I run a landscaping business over by your side of town. I used to take care of the yard for the previous owner. And I was wondering..."

I smiled, "Tim, believe it or not, for a city boy, I like yard work. I'll be doing most of that stuff myself. But we do travel sometimes, and I could use a cut now and then when we're gone." He seemed a bit saddened by the fact that I cut my own grass. I thought I'd throw him a bone. "Hey," I offered, "Do you do irrigation and drainage work?" Tim Peppers lit up. "Oh yessir! I do a real good job to. I could show you some of my work. Why I did the job at the Powell's house. That's two streets from your house. And I designed the..." Now, I have a knack for spotting people who will ramble. I sized Tim Peppers up as a rambler right away. "That's fine Tim," I said, cutting him off before this became a dissertation, "Listen, I am laying out my garden and I will need some irrigation. Can you come by this week and take a look?" Peppers was ecstatic. "Why yessir! How is Monday evening? Around six?" "I smiled, "That'd be fine, Tim. And please call me Joe. Or Joey. Okay?" "Yessir." He answered dutifully.

Man, this was going to take some getting used to.

8

Farmer.

Joe.

I loaded the roll of burlap onto the back of my Ford and set off for the nearest Lowe's store. I still needed about a dozen bags of lime, and some compost, and I also needed a roto-tiller and some lawn tools, since Uncle Franny and I had always shared his tiller back home, and now I was without one. I had decided to just leave my garden tools in my garage when we left. It wasn't worth trifling the movers with.

I drove to the Lowe's and along the way I pulled Tim Pepper's business card from my wallet. I realized that I was going to need a pretty big load of topsoil for the garden, because the soil was so thin and even after I made Uncle Franny's dirt roll-ups, I didn't have enough soil to bury them. I thought maybe ol' Tim could find me some good topsoil and truck it in for me. I called his cell number on the drive over to Lowe's.

Apparently Tim is another guy –like my dad- who can't really work a cell phone correctly. Whereas the Old Man can never quite end the call when he thinks he has, and you hear another five seconds or so before the line disconnects, Tim Peppers is apparently afflicted with the same malady, only in reverse. I don't think Tim realizes that he has already answered the phone when he has, because he picked up after two rings. Over the noise of his truck, and the Country station he was listening to, I heard him say: "Pennsylvania? I don't know nobody from Pennsylvania!" Then I heard another voice say "Well are ya goin' to answer it?"

Apparently Tim decided to take my call because I heard him say "hello" just before the line went dead. He had hung up on me. Since he'd already answered the call, the second time he hit the button –which he thought was the first time- actually ended it. I looked at my watch to see what time it was...and how long it would take for him to decide whether to call me back or not.

Nine minutes later, my phone rang. It was Tim Peppers. "Hello?" he said, "I got a call from this number a minute ago." "A minute?" I thought, "I hope this guy doesn't charge by the hour if that's what his minute is." "Tim, this is Joe Mezilli." I said, "We met this morning at the Co-Op." I thought he was going to wreck his truck, he was that excited. "Oh yessir, Mr. Mezilli! Yessir. How have you been?" "How have I been? It's been 20 minutes, did I look really sick this morning or something?" "I'm fine Tim, listen, I was wondering, can you get good topsoil around here anywhere?" "Oh Yes sir!" He replied, "Yessir I know a few places with good topsoil. Are you needing some?" "No, I just thought I'd ask." I said, Expecting Tim to get the joke. I drastically overestimated the sense of humor here, because Peppers said, "Well we sure do, Mr. Mezilli. You take care now." And then he hung up. For a moment, I seriously considered whether I wanted this guy driving his Bobcat in my yard, but he seemed nice enough so I called him back. "Tim," I said, mystified, "I asked you that question because I need some dirt." Peppers perked up. "Oh, you want me to tell you where to get it?" Wow. Mensa. "Yes. Tim, I need about ten yards. I need it to be really rich and dark." I answered. "Oh and I want it screened, not just plowed up and scooped onto the truck."

"Screened, ya say? Hmmm...Never heard of screened dirt before." Peppers answered, "What do you screen it for...bugs and such?" Tim said. "This guy is a landscaper?" I wondered to myself. "Mostly for sticks and rocks and grubs." I explained, "Clean topsoil is much easier to work with. Can you find me some?" Tim was rustling some papers. "Tim you aren't driving right now are you? I mean, you can get back to me on this." Peppers answered, "Yes sir Mr. Mezilli, I can call my buddy over at Appomattox Farms and see if they have some." "Okay Tim," I said, "Just bring the prices with you when you come to my house on Monday night. I'll see you then."

I rolled into Lowe's parking lot and got my lime and compost. I also bought myself a composter because at nineteen dollars a bag, I was not going to buy this stuff forever. I looked at the bed of my pickup and realized that I still needed a tiller and a composter. So I bought myself a trailer to haul stuff with.

"I'm becoming a real country gentleman." I thought. I instantly laughed at that. I loaded up the lime and the compost bags in the bed of the truck. I put the composter and the tiller in my shiny new trailer, and set off for home. I was pulling out of the parking lot when Joey Fanucci called me. The smile that instantly spread across my face caught me off guard. I was really missing my old paisanos. "Yo! Domanucce!" I said loudly, "Come stai?" Joey was laughing. "It's like you never left, Paisan." "Yeah well, all good things come to an end, right, Mi Fratello?" I snickered. I wanted to stop short of getting wistful again, so I jumped right in. "So Cuz, you found me some mushroom soil?" "Sort of," Joey said, "Pop had to pull some strings, but he found some. It will be delivered this week if you're ready for it. Will ten yards do?" "Perfect!" I said, "You even arranged delivery? Thanks Paisan. What do I owe you guys?" Joey laughed. "Just pay the man when he gets there." He said, "It'll be reasonable. What day do you want it. The weekend works better for this guy." I was elated. "How about Saturday?" I'll be home and I can get right to work on it." "Saturday it is, pal." Joey said. "We'll call you this week to confirm. Say hey to Anj for me." "Domanucce!" I yelled, "you're the best!'

I had my dirt, and my mushroom soil all arranged. Then the thought hit me... "Ten yards is a whole lot of mushroom soil sitting in my driveway. And where am I going to make the dirt rolls?" Angie would kill me for sure if I even considered dumping ten yards of horse poop in the front of our new house. I decided the best plan was to dump it all at my hunting camp and make the rolls there. Then I could bring them back to the house a few at a time. Piece of cake, right?

I drove straight to the hunting camp and unloaded the bags into my barn. I backed the trailer in, unhitched it, and locked it all up. It only takes about twenty minutes for me to get home from the hunting lodge. It was a warm afternoon for late February, and I actually had the window down in the pickup. I turned down my street and as usual, there was Phil Lowery, my neighbor, the peeper, standing inside his garage. He was just inside the shadow lines, where he obviously thought nobody would notice him. The only thing is, he smokes a pipe sometimes and the pipe smoke gives away his presence. I had already begun toying with old Phil whenever I caught him nosing around, so I started beeping and waving at him when he thinks he is being clever. I did it this time and he almost tripped on his own feet as he tried to duck further back into his garage.   Back home, we had a peeper on our block. One day we all decided that the best way to cure the problem was just be rude about it. So we all got our Sunday Inquirer and pasted newspaper over all the downstairs windows. I mean every house on our block, had the windows papered over. Poor Mrs. Begnetti couldn't see a darned thing in any of our houses and her well of gossip dried up.

We knew that she thought we were all busy remodeling, because in South Philly, if you are remodeling, you take down the drapes and cover the windows with newspaper until the job is done. Old Mrs. B. was desperate to find out what we were doing to our houses, but the old bird couldn't ask anybody.

For one thing, every house had paper on the windows so which one would she ask first? Then too, if she asked, she would appear nosy. And, honest-to-God, Mrs. Begnetti never did understand that spying on us all the time from her living room was being nosy.

Not until we told her.

Anyway, Phil was really starting to bug me with his constant staring. And he was still peeping through the blinds at night with the light on behind him, like some stunod stalker. I was sure he was harmless, but still...I have a wife and kids, you know? It was really starting to bother Angie, and to be honest, I was afraid she'd go over and pop the old fart right in his nose one of these days. Angie is all lady, until she feels threatened. Then she'll tear you a new one.

So I parked in the front driveway, and walked across the street to old Phil's house. Now, Phil is not directly across from me, that's Hank Milledge's house. Phil lives next door to Hank, and since we have decent sized lots here, it's about a quarter of a city block to the left of my front door if you were looking out from there. So I couldn't exactly sneak up on ol' Phil. Apparently he still labored under the delusion that he was being stealthy, because I watched him carefully slip back another foot deeper into the shade on his garage. "Seriously, Phil," I thought, "You really think you're invisible?"

"Yo! Philly-boy!" I said loudly. I thought it would be friendly of me to give him his own nickname. "Is that Captain Black you're puffing in that thing?" I was going to go with some version of a "Prince Albert in a can" joke, but thought maybe Phil wouldn't get it. Phil didn't share my affections, apparently. "It's Teender Box" Phil said with a mild snarl. "It's what?" I said. "Teender Box." he replied, not too happily. "What is Teender box?" I asked. Phil pulled the pipe out of his mouth and looked like he was going to try hitting me any minute now. "Teender...Teender!" he said, "Tee-aaah-ayunn-dee-ee-oar. Teender!" For just a second I thought about mimicking his drawl and breaking his balls a little. But Phil is just a curmudgeon and you can't kid with those kinds of guys. "Oh, okay." I said, still not understanding what the heck he was saying. "So whatcha doin' over here Phil? Wife won't let you smoke that thing in the house?" I was trying to strike up a conversation, while letting him know I saw him. "I smoke where I wish to smoke." Phil muttered. Sheesh, what a grouch. I decided that old Phil here just doesn't want to be friendly. I also got the feeling that, while he does try to hide his peeping, and he thinks he's doing a good job of it, the truth is that old Phil doesn't care that you see him. I was pretty sure he sort of liked you knowing he was watching. For some this is creepy. But I sized Phil up as it being more arrogant. Like he was telling me "This is my street and my neighborhood and I'm watching you." I was starting to dislike old Phil a lot.

"I see you got yourself a new truck." Phil said, "Whatcha need a second pickup truck for?" Now that was ballsy. The guy doubles down on his rudeness by asking me why I own a second pickup truck. I was going to ask him what business it was of his, but apparently the answer to that question is that everything in this neighborhood is Phil's business. I decided it was too soon yet for me to get "South Philly" on him. That's what my wife calls it. My brother is worse about it than I am. I never needed the mechanism much. But it's there. Anj calls it "getting South Philly." It's when I become like the men I grew up around.

When pushed, I can become a sarcastic, incredibly acerbic, smart-mouth that dishes out caustic one-liners like a professional. You know the way the guys on The Sopranos talked to each other most of the time? Yeah...like that. But I almost never employ that device. For one thing, as a businessman I couldn't risk getting that reputation. Not if I wanted to be taken seriously. Being Italian from South Philly is an automatic stereotype as it is. On top of that, I was in the "Waste Management" business for my whole adult life. Vito Corleone used "Olive Oil importer" as his cover. Every TV or movie mob boss since then has been in the "Waste Management" field. I tried, for most of my adult life, to put a little distance between myself and "that guy." So instead of saying, "I bought it to haul my equipment over to my still and brew up a little 'shine, Phil. You got a problem wit dat?" (Which is what I wanted to say.) I simply played it close to the vest. I figured that would piss him off plenty. "Aaah you know, Phil. A guy needs to haul things sometimes. Sometimes I need to haul things that might mess up the bed of the Tundra. It's a fifty-thousand dollar truck, you know? And Angie'd kill me if I used the Escalade." I almost said "I don't have her under control like you have Gladys." but I decided against it. Wives are off limits until death is on the line.

"What kinda things you haulin' that you can't clean out with a hose?" He asked. He pulled the pipe from his mouth before asking me this so I knew he was serious. *Good God this guy is like the Inquisizione* I thought. This was my chance to have fun. I knew Phil wanted to know everything I was doing. Every. Single. Thing. But I'd be damned if I'd tell him my business. So I toyed with him. In hindsight, it was a colossal mistake. But I'll get to that. That sunny February afternoon I just wanted to break his balls a little. So I said, "Oh you know Phil, things a man hauls. Stuff you need to get rid of without a lot of mess. Junk you need to dispose of." I actually emphasized "dispose." Boy, was that dumb. Only I didn't know it then.

I saw that attempting conversation with Phil was getting me nowhere. So I figured I'd send one shot across his bow. "Well, I gotta run, Phil. Thanks for keeping an eye on everything. I'm thinking of cancelling my alarm system thanks to you." With that, I turned and walked back toward my house. I don't know how Phil took that comment, I never thought to turn around and look. But knowing what I know now, he didn't like it much.

Mushroom Soil, and Burlap Burritos

Friday night I get a phone call from Joey Fanucci. "The delivery guy will be at the house at 8AM," he said, "Pop said he knows this guy and that you should have coffee for him." That was odd. The guy can't just make some coffee before he drops off my poop? But I figured Joey's dad knew what he was doing here. Maybe the guy takes better care of you if your coffee is fresh, who knows?

Saturday morning, I woke up at 5AM, like always. Even "retired," I still like to be up and moving around before the sun comes up. I made myself a pot of coffee and sat at the kitchen table glancing at the paper. The Lynchburg News and Advance was a whole sight different than the Philadelphia Inquirer. The Inquirer is full of the poison and bite of the city, so to speak. Its editorial page is filled with importance and pith. The News and Advance was more genteel. The people even disagreed casually. I was reading a point-counterpoint about the expansion of Liberty University into the River Ridge Mall when my cell phone rang. It was Joey Fanucci.

"Domanucce!" I said joyously, while trying to keep my voice down. Anj had joined me by now but the kids were still asleep. "Go out on your front porch, the guy says he's on your street right now. You might need to flag him down." Joey said. "Call me back when he gets done, let me know how it went." Click. Joey hung up without a word. Odd, I thought, but I figured maybe he was busy at the moment. I walked to the front door and before I could step onto the porch there was Joey and his Dad, in a very new dump truck I might add, sitting in my driveway with ten yards of horse poop and compost, still steaming in the back.

"Holy shit!" I exclaimed. Angie smacked me on the arm immediately. "Joseph!" She said playfully. I was floored. "What the heck are you guys doing here? You're crazy, both of you!" Joey jumped down from the truck and gave me a huge bear hug and a kiss on the cheek. I returned the affections, and we danced around like we were in high school again. Gosh it was good to see them! Mr. Fanucci took a while to get down from the driver's seat. It was hard seeing him getting so old. He walked over and gave me a much softer hug than his son did. He grabbed my face and kissed my cheek like he was my own father. What a sweet and gentle man this is. He was always like that.

I didn't know where to start. Joey could tell that I was flabbergasted. So he just began by telling me how it was that they were standing in my driveway in Forest, Virginia with a steaming load of horse poop on the back of their truck. "Pop called around a few places. He even had the people out in Avondale at the Mushroom houses call and ask. But nobody even knows what mushroom soil is down here, much less have any." Joey explained. "You can find horse manure all over the place but not the combination, you know." So Dad got the notion to make a road trip of it and come see you. And here we are." Joey was laughing now. His dad had a big grin on his face when I asked him about the new truck.

"Poop must be paying more than ever, mister Fanucci! That's a really nice truck. When did you get this?" Joey's dad had less of the old-world accent than he did when we were growing up, but he still sounded like an immigrant. "The old trucka she fall apart. She runn-ah like-ah the Chitty Chitty Bang-guh, Bang." I looked at Joey and we both burst out in laughter. We had seen "Chitty Chitty Bang Bang" in a suburban drive-in with Joey's parents when we were little kids. His dad thought it was the funniest movie he'd ever seen. Ever. And every time he saw a beat up old car he'd point and laugh and say "Look, boys, it's-ah the Chitty Chitty Bang-guh Bang!" and he'd just laugh himself silly. "Well this one is beautiful, Mr. Fanucci. Really beautiful. Have you let Joey drive it yet?" Joey laughed at that. I knew better. Mr. Fanucci was pretty much married to his dump truck. He only let Joey drive if he was really fatigued. "Pop made it the whole way down here." Joey said, "He was tuckering a bit when we got to Lynchburg but he pushed through." I was amazed. The man is seventy years old. "How long did it take you to make the trip?" I asked Joey. "Oh about six hours." he said "We loaded up at Kaolin last night and drove to Warrenton. That's where we spent the night. We got on the road from there at five AM." "The stuff's still steaming!" I answered Joey, "How'd you manage that?"

"We covered it with thermal tarps, to trap the heat. And Pop ordered this truck with the bed heater like asphalt trucks have. He can deliver year-round now." Joey said. Old Man Fanucci climbed up on the bed of his truck like he was Walenda. "We pulled back the tarps before we got to your neighborhood, Giuseppe," he shouted from the side of his truck. "I wanted your neighbors to enjoy-ah the aroma." He was grinning like a little boy. "Come-ah smell this, Giuseppe. You remember how good this-ah smells?" Mr. Fanucci was the only man on the block who could get by with calling me Giuseppe. He was old world and old school, both, and so I didn't mind. He stood on the tire of the big truck and pulled me up by the arm. Joey climbed up on the other side and we stood there, all three of us, breathing deeply the aroma of real, honest-to-God, Avondale, Pennsylvania mushroom soil.

We jumped down and Angie joined us with coffee for Joe and his dad. I said, "Come on inside, I want to show you guys

175

the house." But Mr. Fanucci grabbed my hand and asked me could we go to the back yard first. "Sure Mr. Fanucci," I said, "But do you need the bathroom, or want to wash up or anything?" He smiled softly, "No," he said, "I wanna go and see those mountains from your back yard. Joey says-ah they look like the Campania." I led Joe and his dad around back and we stood on the deck sipping coffee. Mr. Fanucci was very quiet for a long time. In fact, nobody said anything for a long time.

Finally, he grabbed Angie's hand in his, and with the other, he made a big sweeping arc across the horizon, in the direction of those mountains. Like a painter laying down the base color on a canvas. His voice was full of emotion. "Joey...he was right." He said, holding Angie's hand and looking at Joey and me. "This place, it reminds me of Campania. It reminds me of back home." He was getting teary eyed. Mr. Fanucci had come from a small town in the Campania not too far from my grandfather. In fact, one of the few people that Giuseppe would talk to, besides Mr. Kroyczek, was Joey's dad. Even though there was a pretty sizeable age difference. I think it was because Mr. Fanucci is from the same area in Italy and talking to him reminded Giuseppe of himself at a much younger age.   We drank coffee in silence while Mr. Fanucci got lost in memories of the old country. Eventually, Joey touched his dad on the shoulder and said, "Pop, we gotta dump this load, and we need to see this house of theirs!" The old man turned and smiled. "You're right," he said, then he looked at Angie and said, "Show me your house, Bella." Secretly, I always thought Mr. Fanucci had one of those innocent, old-man crushes on Anj. He held her hand a lot whenever we were around. Angie picked up on it, and used to tease him sometimes, just a little. I never gave it a second thought. Mr.

Fanucci is as good a man as walks this earth. Anyway, we walked inside and gave them the tour. We had another cup of coffee and stepped outside.

"You guys are going to have to follow me. We're going to take this to my hunting camp. I can't have it on the driveway or Angie will divorce me." I said with a smile. Joey and his dad followed me to the hunting camp and we dumped the mushroom soil on some tarps I had out there. I bought the thermal covers off Joey right there in the spot, so it would trap the heat. Mr. Fanucci really liked the hunting camp. There were turkeys feeding as we pulled in. Neither of them had ever seen a wild turkey before. They followed me back to the house and Angie had breakfast ready for us when we arrived. "So, are you guys going to stay the night? We certainly have room for you." Mr. Fanucci smiled and said "No, I have to get back. Mrs. Fanucci, she-ah worry if I don't come right back." I looked at Joey in bewilderment. They had just put six hours on their backsides in that big truck, and now they were getting ready to do the same thing again with only a few hours break.

"Mr. Fanucci," I said, "Please let Joey drive, at least. It's a long trip and you have to be tired." I expected him to protest, but he agreed. "You're right," he said, softly, "I'm getting old, and this driving, it-ah tires me out." Joey shot me subtle glance. It wasn't like his dad to give up the driver's seat so easily. We finished breakfast and talked until Noon. I made them a pot of coffee and filled Mr. Fanucci's thermos for him. "I brewed it like you and my dad like it, Mr. F." I said. "I mixed half Folger's and half Medaglia D'Oro, and double brewed it." He smiled. "I could always drink coffee with your Papa and your Nonno. We old timers like it strong." I handed the thermos to Joey, "Well you could start a car with this. Now you guys drive carefully and call me when you get home tonight so I don't worry and call Nonna." Joey promised he would and gave me a big hug.

"Dominucce...Grazi Paisan. Thank you my friend. I needed this." Joey laughed. "It's just poop, Joe!" I caught myself getting emotional. "No, it's more than that. I needed to see you guys. I needed to hear a voice from back home...you know?" Joey smiled and kissed my cheek. I hugged his dad -after he finished hugging my wife- and told them to be careful. Anj and I waved until they disappeared down the street. I was turning to walk back inside when I noticed the blinds rustle over at Phil Lowery's across the street. Danged peeper.

The following Monday night, old Tim Peppers came over to the house and we walked out back so I could show him where the garden was going to be. "Well this is going to be just about the biggest vegetable garden I think I've ever seen." He said. He instantly acted as if he thought he'd hurt my feelings. "I mean, a big garden is great. It's great! I just ain't never seen one this big." he quickly explained. Tim wouldn't look me in the eye all night. I don't know why he was so intimidated by me, but he was.

I pointed to the lines I had staked out. There were eight lines altogether, ten feet long and each in the middle of a twenty square foot section of my future garden. I turned to Peppers and asked him, "Tim do you have a Bobcat or a small backhoe?" "Oh Yessir!" He said with a bright smile, "Yes sir I do! I'm about the best backhoe man in Bedford County, too Mr. Mezilli." I looked at him eye to eye. "Tim do you want my business?" I asked sternly. "Well...yessir. Of course I do." He said nervously. "Then stop calling me "sir" and "Mr. Mezilli." Call me Joe. Okay?" Tim Peppers swallowed hard. "Yes sir...I mean, yes, Joe. Of course." "Good, now that we have that straightened out, can you dig

178

me a trench on each of these lines, Tim? Just maybe two feet deep, no more. I need you to do that right away. Before you even start the irrigation system for the garden." Peppers shook his head. I can come out tomorrow and dig them if you want."

"Now you're talking, kid!" I thought. "Yes, Tim, let's plan that. It's not supposed to rain all week. I'd like these trenches dug right away so I can bury some things." Peppers looked at me quizzically. "You're what?" he asked, "Nothing, never mind. Bring your rig out here tomorrow and dig these trenches for me. And bring the pricing for the irrigation. Oh and did you find me screened topsoil?" Tim said he had and handed me a slip of paper with a phone number on it. "This here is Earl Davies farm. Old Earl has about the best soil in the county and he told me he screens it. He has about fifty yards over there now so just call him, he'll take real good care of you." I thanked Tim and we walked to the driveway together. "I'll see you tomorrow Tim. Thank you for coming out." I said as I shook his hand. He got in his truck and headed down the street, I was walking in the front door when I noticed he had stopped at Phil Lowery's house and Phil was standing at the curb, leaning in the window of Tim's pickup truck, gesturing frantically as they spoke. I ignored it and went inside.

The next morning I called Tim Peppers as I drove out to the hunting camp. Earl Davies was delivering my topsoil and I needed to meet him at the gate so I told Tim to just go ahead and start the trenches and that I would be back by noon. He was so happy to be using his backhoe on my property that I think I could have asked him to do it for free and he might have agreed. "Don't crack my driveway, Tim, and for God's sake, stay out of Angie's flower bulbs. If you

179

run those things over she'll bury YOU there!" Tim didn't laugh.

Earl Davies looked pretty much exactly as I expected he would. He was a short, chubby, bow-legged man who drove an old Dodge dump truck. I hadn't seen too many of these trucks. Back home everyone drove Chevy or Ford or GMC. Earl's truck was a very faded green, except for the passenger's side door, that was blue. There were peeling letters on the door. The kind you see on mailboxes in trailer parks. "E. DAV_S and S_N." it said. Underneath was his phone number. Earl backed his truck up the long gravel road like he had eyes in back of his head. He was really good at handling that big truck. I was impressed. When he came to a stop and hopped down, I told him so.   "You know Earl, You could have made a lot of money for me back home. You could have been one of my best guys." I said to him cheerfully. Earl smiled and spit some tobacco juice. "Doin' what" he said, pronouncing the soft "H" very emphatically, so it sounded like; "H-what?" "Oh driving for me." He cocked his head a little, "What kinda business did ya have?" he asked. "I was in waste management. I owned trash trucks." Earl just shrugged his shoulders and unchained the gate on his dump bed. I spread out a few big tarps and told him to dump the dirt on them if he could. Earl saw that as some sort of dare.

He walked to the middle of the tarp and reached into his pocket. He pulled out a ten-dollar bill and tore it in half. Handing me one piece he laid the other half on the tarp, as close to the center as a man can be without measuring to be sure. "You just stand aside, Mr. Mezilli" he said. He pronounced the vowel like a long "E", so it came out "Mezeelee." I stood off to the side as he backed his truck into position and raised the bed. The load of soil slid off in one

180

smooth, powerful "Whoosh!" Tim Peppers was right...this was some dark, rich soil. It looked like coffee grounds, and I couldn't see a rock or a twig anywhere.

Davies walked over to me and smiled. He winked as he spoke; "Now when you get all this dirt moved to wherever it is you're moving it to, you'll find the other half of that ten dollar bill...dead in the middle of the pile at the bottom. That's how good I am." He was grinning like a Cheshire cat. "If I'm wrong, you can keep both halves of the Ten. Deal?" This was bold. I like this. "How much do I owe you, Earl?" I asked. "Oh...I charge $295 for a dump load and the extra mileage for delivery out here..." He was figuring in his head. I thought of Jethro D. Bodean doing some "'Cyperhin'. "How's Three-Fifty sound to ya?" he said. I reached into my pocket, "Let's make it Four Hundred." And I'll keep that ten either way. Fair enough?" I said. He stuck out his hand. "Fair enough" he said.

Earl Davies locked up the gate on his dump bed and as he was heading for the cab, he turned and asked, "What is it you're doing with all this dirt?" I didn't feel like explaining what a "dirt roll-up was" so I just said "You don't really want to know." and I headed toward the barn to get my tools. Davis drove down the gravel drive and off toward highway 460. I set out to make my burlap burritos and get them buried by tonight.

Right away I realized I was going to have to make them in the bed of my pickup. There was no way I could make them on the ground, and then lift them by myself. I rolled out about ten feet of burlap in the bed, and cut it off. I filled it with Uncle Franny's recipe. Three wheelbarrows of mushroom soil, one wheelbarrow of topsoil, half a wheelbarrow of sand, a half bag of lime and two bucket loads of compost. I rolled the ends toward the middle and tucked

181

in the sides so it actually looked like a gigantic burlap burrito. I managed to get six of them made before filling the pickup bed to the top. I figured I'd get these buried and come back for the rest. Covering the mushroom soil and topsoil with tarps, I climbed in my truck and headed for home.

When I rounded the corner on our street, I saw Phil Lowery standing on the sidewalk, peering back into my yard, obviously trying to see what Tim Peppers was doing. "Now why doesn't he just walk back there?" I wondered. "I'm never going to figure this guy out." I beeped my horn at Phil, partly to let him know I saw him standing there, but mostly to warn him to get out of my way...I needed to back my truck in right where he was standing. Phil jerked to attention and turned toward his house. By the time I was backing into my driveway, he was back in his house, no doubt peering from behind the blinds again.

I stopped the truck at the far edge of the front driveway, near the gate to the back yard. Walking back to the yard, I saw that ol' Peppers had done a very nice job with the trenches. Turns out he knew his way around a backhoe. I called him over. "Tim, give me a hand will ya?" He followed me to the back of my pickup. When he got to the bed he stopped and stared. "Wh...whatcha got there Mr. Mezilli?" He asked nervously. I shot him a look. "Tim..." "Oh sorry," he said, "Whatcha got there, Joe."

I grabbed the end of one of the burlap rolls and started pulling. "Help me with this." I said. I slid the roll off to the end of the tailgate and Tim grabbed ahold. Hoisting it up to shoulder height, he said, "Oh Lord this is heavy. And it stinks! Whatcha got in here?"

I hate trying to explain things that others will never understand. I also hate talking when I'm working, so I chuckled and said, "Trust me...you don't want to know.

Besides it's a secret." I mean, it was. Uncle Franny guards his soil recipes very closely. This stuff stays in the Mezilli family.

Peppers and I walked the burlap roll over to the garden and walked it back to the farthest trench he had dug. With great relief we dropped it into the hole. We headed back to the driveway to get the next one. I was pulling another burlap roll off the bed when I glanced over toward Phil's house and noticed him in his garage. Like the smart ass I am, I waved at him. He frowned and walked back into the dark of his garage.

Tim and I unloaded the last of the six burlap rolls from my pickup. I told him to go back to digging so he would have the trenches finished tonight. I needed his backhoe out of the way by tomorrow, so I could just pull my pick up all the way back to the garden and not have to hoss these things across the yard. Tim finished up the trenches while I covered the rolls with some lime and then started backfilling them with topsoil. I was pretty deep into my work and hadn't noticed Tim standing there staring at me. He cleared his throat. "Why do those things smell so bad?" he asked me sheepishly. I wasn't in the mood to talk and so I shot him a one-word answer that I figured would stump him and stop any follow-up questions. "Decomposition." I said, turning back to my shovel. *That should do it,* I thought, *why bother explaining the breakdown of the horse manure and compost into nutrients? One word is sufficient.*

I straightened up slowly, and turned toward Tim. "Well, I'm finished here Mr. Mez...Joe." "Okay Tim," I said. "Come on up to the house and I'll give you a check. Unless you'd prefer cash." "Nossir, a check is just fine." He answered. We walked into the kitchen and I wrote him out a check. "You want a glass of tea, Tim?" I asked. "Why yessir...I mean yes,

Joe. That'd be great." he replied. I poured him a glass of tea and he took a huge gulp. Then he made a horrible face like he'd tasted battery acid. "Not very sweet." he managed. I laughed a little. "Oh yeah, I forgot. We don't drink 'sweet tea' back home, Tim. I guess that's a shock to your system growing up down here, huh?" I handed him the sugar and a spoon and he went about mixing enough sugar in the glass to attract hummingbirds.   Angie walked into the kitchen just as I was asking Tim if there were any diabetics in his family. Angie smacked me on the arm. Hard. "Joseph!" she said sternly. Fortunately Tim hadn't heard me, or he hadn't grasped what I was asking him. He finished his tea in what I have to admit was uncomfortable silence. I handed him his check, thinking maybe he just wanted to get home. He took it silently and walked to the front door. "Tim you'll have me a price for the irrigation soon?" I asked. "Sure Joe," he said. I'll call you with it tomorrow afternoon." Great!" I said, "I'll be looking forward to it." Tim walked out the front door and pulled his truck out into the street. He hadn't gotten any further than Phil Lowery's house when his brake lights came on. I shut the door and looked through the sidelight as Tim stopped in front of Phil's house and Phil leaned into the cab of Tim's truck. Phil was gesturing wildly again as I turned to go into the kitchen.

The next morning I drove out to the hunting camp and made up the last eight burlap dirt rolls. I loaded the rest of the lime bags and compost and headed home. This time, because I knew Tim Peppers wasn't going to be there to help me, I backed my pick up all the way to the garden area. But it was still a wrestling match getting those long, bulky burlap rolls off the bed and into position in the trenches, so I yelled up to the house and told Angie to send the boys out to help. Now, the boys couldn't have lifted these things themselves –

they were too heavy and awkward- but they did provide enough help to me to get them in place. We wrestled them off the truck one at a time, the boys wrinkling their noses at the pungent aroma of mushroom soil and compost. "Aww dad!" Said Petey, my oldest, "This stinks something awful!" I smiled at him. "You should have smelled those trash trucks when I'd ride them at your age with Nonno. I smelled ten times worse than this for days afterward." I laughed to myself at how the circle comes back around.

We got the last rolls placed and the boys went inside, except for David. David stayed with me and helped me cover the burlap with the rest of the lime and then – without me asking him- he grabbed the other shovel and assisted me in covering the whole thing with topsoil. It took us about an hour. Afterward, I leaned over to him and said with a wink, "Hey, I'll tell you what, since you've been such a big help, let's you and me ride to town and get a couple of hot dogs at the DQ." David lit up. "Just you and me?" he asked, plaintively. "Yeah. Just you and me, son. Since your brothers didn't want to help out here. You hop in the truck and I'll tell your mom." He was ecstatic. We pulled away from the garden slowly. The late-afternoon sun had warmed the February frost enough that my truck would have dug into the ground pretty good had I goosed her a bit. Then too, I didn't want the other boys to hear us leaving. He had earned this time alone with me, and besides, since we'd moved here, there wasn't any opportunity for our time at the ball park like back home.   As I nosed the truck around the corner of the house and out toward the end of the driveway, I noticed Phil Lowery, scampering across the street with his cell phone in his hand. "What the..." I said under my breath. "This has gone far enough. What's that old man doing spying on us all the time?" I guess I said this louder than I thought, because David asked me "Who, dad?" "Oh Mr. Lowery, son. I think he thinks he needs to know everything we're doing at all hours." "Like Mrs. Begnetti, back home?" David said, "Are you going to put newspaper over the windows down here too?" He was laughing at that. He'd gotten a big kick out of us all playing that prank on Mrs. B. "No son," I said, "That wouldn't work down here with old Phil. I'm going to have to come up with something else I guess." Eventually I would. And that's where the trouble began.

9

I Tell Ya He ain't Nothing But Trouble

I knew this man was in the mafia, I knew it! I tried telling old Hank next-door but he just ain't as suspicious a man as I am. I told him what I seen and I told him what Timmy Peppers told me. I knew he was trouble when I seen that stainless .45 in his hip holster. Driving around in fancy cars and having himself a pretty wife. I knew he weren't no garbage man, nossir!

I called my friend Monte Crispin down at the county records office and he said the man paid cash for a seven hundred thousand dollar house. Cash! Monte said he heard from Susie Travis at the title company he brought it in a suitcase. Seven Hundred Thirty Five Thousand Dollars in a suitcase. Now, tell me what I'm supposed to think about that?

I've been keeping an eye on him. A real close eye. I been here a long time and I know folks. In fact I pretty much know everyone here in Forest and I made sure the word got out; "Ya'll keep an eye on this Mezilli!" Then a week after he gets here I find out he's tellin' folks that he is retired from the waste management industry. Waste Management! And nobody here saw through his disguise? Why, anybody with half a brain knows they all call their business "waste management," it's a cover. It's code. They talk in code, them mafias. They're sneaky. I watched "The Sopranos," I know all about these people.

But I said to myself, "Phil Lowery, if the whole wide world plays stupid to this man, you are gonna be the lone voice of reason! By God you're gonna save this town, even if it means savin' it from itself!" So I've been watchin' him. I watch him all the time. I'm real good at watching folks, I always have been. I'm gatherin' evidence, and when I get what I'm looking for, I'm gonna pounce like a mountain lion. I figure he's either in the witness protection program, or he's come

189

out here to little ol' Forest to expand his mob territory. Either way, he's trouble

I heard he also bought himself a hunting camp out on route 221. What's a city fella need a hunting camp for? What's he ever hunted in his life? I bet I know. I bet nobody here wants to know what goes on out there, but I'm gonna find out. I figured he was doing drug deals out there, or burying bodies. At least that's what I thought until I talked to old Timmy Peppers yesterday. That changed everything.

I seen old Joe Mezilli –if that's even his real name- driving out to the CoOp. I was heading there myself to buy a heat-lamp for my granddaughter's little baby chicks.   I didn't want him seeing me inside the store while he was there, so I went across the street to the Krispy Kreme and had me a cup of coffee, real natural-like. I seen him talking to Tim Peppers on the way out and Peppers handed him his card. Timmy is a real good kid, but he ain't sharp, not like me, he ain't. He ain't suspicious. Or at least he weren't until I straightened him out about ol' Joe Mezilli.

I swung my truck into the parking lot of the CoOp just as soon as Mezilli was out on the road. I seen Tim Peppers over by the Carhart section, buying himself some new coveralls. I walked up to him real casual. Now...Forest has some nosy people and I don't like them knowing my business. So I had me a copy of the Bedford County farm news and I slid up next to Tim Peppers and held that magazine over my mouth when I talked to him...you know the way them football coaches do it so the other team can't read their lips? Same thing here.

I asked Tim, "What'd Mr. Mafia Boss want with your business card, Tim?" Now, old Peppers isn't sharp, like I said. He sorta looked at me like a calf. "Huh?" he muttered. "Mafia who?" "Mezilli!" I half-screamed, "Joe Mezilli, the mafia boss. What'd he want with your business card?" Peppers looked shocked. "Well he, uh.... he wants me to come do some irrigation for him, because he's planting a garden, and he said..." "Irrigation!" I hissed, "What kind of garden needs irrigation? What kind of garden is so special that it needs more water than the Lord can provide with rain?" Peppers apparently fell for Mezilli's smooth talk, because he said, "Tomatoes." "Huh?" I said, "Tomatoes." Peppers repeated, "Mr. Mezil...I mean Joe said he needs his garden irrigated because he grows tomatoes. It's like a family thing or somethin' and..." "Tomatoes!" I said, "He said he needs an entire irrigation system just to grow some tomatoes, and you don't find that suspicious? Huh? And what's with calling him 'Joe'? You boys all chummy all of the sudden?"

Peppers was stuttering now, he does that when he's nervous. "W-w-well No. N-no we ain't chummy, he just likes to be called by his first name." "Well I ain't falling for his act." I told Peppers, "There's something up with that man and I'm gonna figure out what." I had to watch it now because I was raising my voice in the CoOp. I didn't want anyone else getting the drop on me exposing this Mezilli character. "Peppers, when are you going to his house to meet him about this irrigation system?" "Monday evening." Tim said, "Around six." "Okay," I answered, "You stop on by the house after you're done over there. I'll debrief you. We'll put the pieces together for sure." I was watching them Mezilli's for a good hour before Peppers got there. I was standing in my garage with the door up, but I was back in the shadows so he couldn't see me. I'm good at watching folks because I learned how to think like the people I'm watching. I drive past my garage sometimes with the door open and notice where the good hiding spots are, you know...the way a cop will remember places on the side of the road where you can't see his cruiser until it's too late and he's already got you on radar.   Anyway, Peppers was in there for about an hour. He came strolling out of the house with old Joe Corleone over there, smiling and waving goodbye. If I hadn't stepped out to the curb, he'd have forgotten altogether about coming over to talk to me after he was done. Timmy rolled his window down and I stuck my head in the cab. He told me what Joe the "garbage man" was up to. When he got to the part about digging little ditches in his back yard to help with his "garden" I knew I was right about this guy.

"Trenches?" I yelled at Peppers, then I banged my head on the door post, I was so upset. "What's he need trenches for to plant these tomatoes of his? And you say they're how long? About eight feet? Eight feet, Tim. He's diggin' a bunch of trenches eight feet long. I knew it!" Peppers sat there with his jaw slack, as usual. "You knew what, Phil?" I couldn't believe he was this blind. "Trenches, Peppers! He's burying something!" Peppers cocked his head like a puppy. "Yessir, he told me he was burying something. That's why I'm diggin' the trenches." I couldn't take it anymore. "Peppers!" I barked, He's burying something in a trench that's a little bit bigger than a body. Don't you see it Peppers?"

The light came on in old Timmy's head. It was dim, like a flashlight with a weak battery. But it came on nonetheless. "You...you really think so?" He asked. "Well of course, Peppers. What else would he be burying back there?" Peppers eyes narrowed, like he does when he gets suspicious. "You really think so?" he asked. "Of course Peppers. He bought this place as a cover. He ain't planting no garden, he's burying something so nobody else finds it. Peppers drove off with that squinty scowl on his face. I went back to the garage, but not before Mezilli waved at me, like he was keeping his eye on me.

Imagine that. Someone suspicious of me! I went inside and got on the internet and searched his name. The only "Mezilli" I found was that fella what used to play baseball for the Mets. I saw a couple of stories about my neighbor selling his trash hauling company. I think those stories were planted by the FBI to cover his mob activities. But nothing about him being a mob boss. *I knew it!* I thought. *He's in the witness protection program. Or he faked his death and moved here to start him a whole new crew.* They call their gang a "crew." I seen that on "The Sopranos" and on that other show, the documentary about the mob. The one where Shoeless Joe Jackson played Henry Hill, and he married Dr. Malfi.

All the rest of the week I watched those people across the street. I gotta tell you, they're good at pretending to be normal. They'd fool anyone else, I reckon. But not me. Old Phil Lowery has been around and I tell you, I saw through their disguise. Saturday morning I woke up to the sound of a big ol' truck creeping down the street, and it had Pennsylvania tags! I called Hank Milledge, next door. "Hank!" I said, "They's started already. "Started what, Phil?" said Milledge. "What are you talking about?" "They've started invading our neighborhood!" I hissed at him. "There's a big dump truck across the street with Pennsylvania tags!" Hank didn't understand...he just didn't understand! "So? So maybe it's a friend of his coming to visit. Drink your coffee and mind your own business Phil." Milledge said. "Hank!" I shot back, "They'd come to visit in a dump truck?" Hank went silent for a second. I could hear him walking across his bedroom. "Well I'll be, there's a dump truck over there, sure enough." He said.

"Of course there is!" I said, "You think I'd make that up?" Hank didn't answer me. "I'm telling you, this is trouble!" I said to Hank. He cleared his throat and said "You know Phil, I bet there's a reason those folks are here. If it bothers you, just go ask him what's going on. It sure doesn't bother me. I gotto go let the dog out, Phil. I'll call you in a bit." Dang it! I thought, that's just what they want us to believe!

I stuck my head out the front door and walked out to get the paper. I was acting nonchalant and I'm sure my neighbor had no idea I was assessing the situation, but I was. The first thing I noticed was the God-awful stench coming from that dump truck. It smelled like something rotten. That's when it hit me, it was something rotten! That smell was rotting corpses. It had to be. I ain't never smelled nothing so foul in all my days except a rotten corpse. I stumbled across an old hobo once when I was a kid and I was walking the B&O tracks out near Big Island. The old coot had been dead all winter and I found him after he thawed out a bit in March. Well that's what I smelled that morning coming from the back of my neighbor's friend's dump truck. All I needed was a little more proof.

Well it didn't take me long for me to find the proof I was needing. Mezilli left with his buddies in the dump truck. He took his old Ford and they followed him. A few minutes later, Timmy Peppers showed up and pulled his rig into the back yard and started digging those trenches. I knew Peppers couldn't hear me while he was sitting on his backhoe, so I snuck through the woods alongside Mezilli's property and I had me a look. By God, if Peppers wasn't digging graves then I don't know what a grave is! Eight feet long and two feet deep and spaced evenly over the area where my neighbor, "Mr. Waste Management," was claiming to be planting a garden.

What does digging grave-sized rows have to do with growing vegetables? I thought.

I watched for about an hour and then snuck back to my house. I've seen Tim Peppers work his backhoe plenty of times. I didn't need to sit there watching it again. It took half the day, but Mezilli came rolling back down the street with the back end of his Ford dragging from a big load in the bed. I grabbed my binoculars and peered through the venetian blinds. He backed his truck into the driveway and walked into the back yard. A few minutes later, he came back up with Peppers in tow. Then I saw it. I saw the bodies. Why I can't get nobody to believe me I still can't understand, but by God there were bodies in that truck.   The tailgate was down, and Mezilli grabbed ahold of one end of a giant burlap roll. It had the ends tucked in, like a big, old burrito from Manny's lunch wagon down at the foundry where I used to work. It was about six feet long and rolled up tight. Mezilli slid the thing out of the bed of the truck and motioned to Peppers to grab the other end.   Poor Peppers, he ain't suspicious of nobody, and I saw that blank stare on his face. He didn't even think this was odd at all. They wrestled this thing onto their shoulders and walked back into the yard. Dang, thing even sagged in the middle like a body. Whoever this poor old wretch was, he was fixin' to be part of Mezilli's secret burial ground. I figured he was probably some rival gang member or some poor feller that owed Mezilli money. Whoever he was, he was probably some unsavory sort, but dad-gummit he deserved a better final resting place than this.

I grabbed my cell phone and ran across the street and ducked underneath some ewes that ran along the far fenceline of Mezilli's property. I couldn't see real clear...but I seen clear enough! Clear enough to see them dump this poor sucker into one of the trenches that Peppers had dug that morning. Clear enough to watch Mezilli break out a bag of lime and cover the body in the burlap with it! The sick son of a bitch! He even smacked his shovel on the top of the body a few times, because it was sticking up above the edge of the trench a bit!

Next thing you know, Peppers and him were shoveling topsoil on the burlap and covering up the entire crime. I dropped my camera at one point. I was so shocked by what I seen that I forgot to take any pictures at all. I had to sit under that bush for another twenty minutes waiting for them to start burying a few more. Meanwhile, Hank Milledge's dog -the overweight Weimaraner- comes waddling over and pees on the very bush I was hiding under. Dang stupid dog. I hated that dog already. Now I really hate him. So I'm lying there under the bushes with dog pee on my shirt and watching my friend Timmy Peppers help this mobster bury his enemies. Right in his own back yard.

I waited until they were deep into burying their fourth body and I snuck back over to my house. I stood in my favorite hiding spot...in the shadows of my garage where they can't see me...and I snapped some more pictures of them carrying the last few body bags into the back yard. They were getting tired and I seen Mezilli arch his back and stretch himself like he was getting sore. "Serves you right, you heartless animal!" I thought to myself. "I hope you shuffle your spine like a deck of cards!"

I waited in the shadows with my jaw hanging open. I can't believe what I just saw. By God it was just like The Sopranos where they were burying bodies on Tony's uncle Pat's farm. "Cans of peaches" he called them. Like they weren't people they was burying, they was just lumps of dirt. I always knew that show was more truth than fiction. Didn't Rich Little say something about life doing great art imitations, or something like that? Well ol' Rich Little was right.

They finally came back up from burying the last one, and Mezilli put up his tailgate. He shook Pepper's hand and walked back to the burial ground I guess. Peppers rolled his truck and trailer out into the street and I called him on his cell phone. He answered. "Peppers!" I said, "Stop on over in front of my house before you go any further." "Who is this?" Peppers answered. Dear God how does this man walk upright? "It's Phil!" Stop over at my house Tim, right now." I hung up the cell phone and walked to the curb casually. Peppers pulled over to the side and rolled down his passenger window and I stuck my head in.

Peppers wrinkled his nose when I stuck my head in the window. "Phew, Phil, you smell like dog piss" "Peppers!" I barked, cutting him off, "You big dummy! You made yourself an accessory after the fact!" Timmy's jaw dropped open. "A what?" he said, with a look in his eyes like a deer in the headlights. "An accessory after the fact. You're complicitish now!" "What's that mean?" Peppers asked me. Dear God, I thought, This poor boy is just a sheep heading for the shearers. "You're complicitish! You done participated in a crime, Tim! He had you burying those bodies with him and now you're guilty as he is!" I tried not to be too excited but I was losing my patience with Peppers. "What bodies?" Peppers yelped, "What the hell are you talking about, Phil?"

"Them bodies you was burying with Al Capone over there. The ones you dug the holes for, Timmy. You done assisted in the disposal of evidence. I seen this on The Sopranos. I seen this on NCIS. What do you think was in them burlap rolls? Burlap?" Peppers was wide-eyed and he didn't say nothing at all. I think it started to make sense to him. "What did he say was in them rolls, Timmy?" I asked

197

him gently. "Well…" he started, about two minutes later he said, "He told me not to ask." Peppers swallowed hard with this. The light was slowly coming on. "What did they feel like?" I asked. "They were heavy, and bulky. Just dead weight." I waited for this statement to click with him. And when I was done waiting, and nothing clicked, I asked him, "Anything peculiar about them rolls, Tim?" Peppers scratched his head under his John Deere cap. "They smelled real bad," He said, "Like poop, and wet straw."   I banged my head on the doorjamb of his truck. "Poop! Wet Straw? Peppers that's exactly what dead bodies smell like!" I yelled. I hate yelling at Peppers because he's like a child. But the boy done admitted to me that they were burying bodies and he didn't even realize it! Peppers looked like he was going to cry. "Did Mezilli say anything at all about what's in those rolls? I asked him. "Nope," he said, and then his face went white. All he said when I asked him why they smelled, was "decomposition." Hey, Phil, what is decomposition, exactly? Is that the name of a mafia boss? I thought it was when you wrote a paper in high school.

I rubbed my eyes and tried not to laugh. "Yeah, Peppers," I thought to myself, "You ain't never read the papers about "Vinny Decomposition" He's a killer." I waited a second or two then I reached in and swatted him on his head.

"Oh my Lord! You're in danger Timmy!" I said, "The man knows that you know where he done buried them poor souls. Once he don't need you anymore, he's gonna see you as a liability." Peppers swallowed hard and his eyes got glassy. "You don't really think that, do you? I mean he seems like such a nice guy." "Peppers!" I shouted, "Tony Soprano killed his own cousins to cover his crimes! You don't think a mob guy would kill somebody he thought was going to turn him in?"

Peppers rubbed his eyes. "What are we gonna do?" he asked. "We need more proof." I said. "I'm gonna have to keep watching this guy until we can get enough on him to have Sheriff Stevens come out." I leaned back out of the window of his truck. "You leave this to me, Timmy. I'll take care of everything." Peppers looked worried, "What are you gonna do?" he asked, "I'm gonna watch him like a hawk day and night, Timmy. You can be sure of that." "Maybe I shouldn't do that irrigation work for him, huh?" he asked. "No!" I said, "You go on like always with him. Do the job. It will give us a chance to get in that yard." I thought for a moment. "But Timmy," I said, "If you still got your daddy's pistol I'd start keeping it with you when you're around him. Just in case." "Yeah," Peppers whispered solemnly, "I was thinking about that too." "It's gonna be okay Timmy," I said, "We're gonna expose this guy and nail his butt to a tree! Now you do me one favor...keep this quiet. If word gets out about this man, we'll blow our whole operation and he'll just cover his tracks."

Peppers drove on up the street and I snuck back to the hedgerow and hid out while Mezilli buried the rest of them bags. Only this time he used his sons to help him. *His sons!* That murderin' bastard was already training his boys in the art of getting rid of bodies. Hell, they looked they was having fun doing it. Like one big old mobster family. I was sick to my stomach watching it, I tell ya.

I wasn't going to stand for this from this Capo across the street. I'm going to do something about this.

199

10

Sleeping With The Seven Fishes

It got to the point where Tim Peppers was my ears and eyes over at Mezilli the mobster's house. I didn't go over there much because I didn't want him getting suspicious of me. But I watched him. I watched him like a hawk. Like I said, I'm good at it. Nobody suspects that I'm watching them when I watch them. That's the key to it. Don't be suspicious.

But I figured that I'd have to at least be neighborly, otherwise he would get suspicious. Maybe he'd start wondering why I was the only neighbor around here who didn't want to go over and play pool with him in his fancy game room. Or watch the football games on Sundays with him. Or go to a cookout over there. I did those things because there was others involved. I felt safe in numbers. But there were a few things I wouldn't do with old Joe Mezilli. I wouldn't never go out on that big old boat of his. I know all about that little game. That's what they do, them mafias. They take you out on a boat. Way out where nobody can see or hear nothing, and then they shoot you and dump your body overboard with cement shoes on your feet. I ain't stupid.

The other thing I refused to do was take any vegetables from Mezilli's garden. Even Timmy Peppers took some at first. He showed up to cut my grass one afternoon eating a big fat tomato sandwich. I know he ain't never grown a thing in his life except grass, so I asked him where he got the tomatoes from for the sandwich. "Oh Joe give me a big bag full of them." He said, with the mayonnaise running down his chin and a big dumb smile on his face. I stopped dead in my tracks. "You'd eat a tomato from that garden after what we seen him burying back there last year?" I asked. Then I got right in his ear, and whispered, "Does it taste funny, Peppers? Does it taste like a dead man?" I thought Peppers was gonna puke. He spit out the sandwich and started to hunch over on all fours with his stomach convulsing like a dog.

He looked up at me in horror. "Oh lord how did I forget?" he said. I felt like rubbing it in a little, so he'd remember next time. "Was it good Peppers?" I asked him sarcastically. "Well yeah. Actually that was just about the best tomato I ever ate." He said. I smacked him on his head with my hand. "What's wrong with you boy?" Peppers got wide-eyed. "Do you really think those were bodies we buried back there, Phil? Seriously? Because dang, those tomatoes were good. And he gave me cucumbers too. Great big ones. Everything he has back there is huge and delicious. Maybe they weren't bodies at all. Do bodies make good fertilizer Phil?"

I smacked him again, just to get him to stop thinking out loud. It was making me sick. The boy is a wiz at digging with a tractor or a backhoe or cutting grass. But he ain't smart like a scholar, and he ain't naturally suspicious, like me. Timmy Peppers would be best friends with a commie spy and never know the difference. I try to watch out for him, but I can't be everywhere. So he ends up doing things like helping our mob-boss neighbor bury bodies, or eating tomatoes grown on some poor sucker's grave. God only knows where he'd be if I wasn't there to point these things out to him.

That was in July. Peppers told me he went home and was about to throw out all the vegetables Sonny Corleone over there had given him, when he remembered they didn't come from the garden where he buried the bodies at all. "What the hell are you talking about Peppers?" I asked him. He gave me some story about Mezilli not planting in that spot until next season. I told him "better safe than sorry Tim," and made him promise me he'd throw all that stuff out. But who knows with Peppers? The boy likes to eat and I could imagine him digging those big tomatoes out of the garbage two hours later and frying them for another sandwich.

By September, the whole neighborhood was talking about those dang tomatoes and those cucumbers and whatever else he was growing back there. Nobody knew what it was they were really eating. Nobody but me and Peppers. And Peppers kept saying it wasn't the same garden. It was like "Invasion of the Body Snatchers" and I was the only guy who knew what was in them pods.

I tried telling Hank Milledge, one day while we were rebuilding a leaf blower in his garage. But he wouldn't believe me. He'd become chummy with Mezilli and he wasn't going to believe the truth about his new buddy. People are infatuated with the mob. I see it all the time. But they don't understand them the way I do. They haven't studied them. Milledge asked me one time how it is I think I know so much about the mafia when there ain't no mafia around here. "You grew up here in Lynchburg, Phil" he said to me, "You've never even been to New York in your whole life. What the heck do you know about those people?" "Well-sir" I said to him, real matter-of-factly, "I read somewhere that when they did The Godfather, they had to have real mob guys working with the writers, because the mob didn't want too much information coming out. But they wanted it to be true to life." Milledge didn't see the connection. "What's that got to do with anything, Phil?" he asked. "Because, stupid, it means they was telling the truth without revealing the names!" They was showing how the mob works. Don't you see?" Milledge never did agree with me on that.

Meanwhile, Peppers still wasn't sure those were bodies rolled up in that burlap. I kept trying to make him see the truth. The fact is he had really started to like old Mezilli. Mezilli'd been here almost a year and a half now and Timmy was making a lot of money off old Joe. He was clearing parts of his hunting land for him and tending to the yard when they went away. About six months after they buried them bodies, I asked him if he had started on the irrigation system for the garden yet. We were standing in my garage, drinking a beer and tinkering with an old fishing reel I was rebuilding. Peppers told me, "Well it's in and finished and he done paid me for it. But the funny thing is, he ain't used it yet." "What?" I asked him, "What do you mean he ain't used it yet, Peppers? He spent all that money and hasn't used the durned thing yet?" Peppers told me that Mezilli hadn't even tilled that ground yet! He wasn't going to plant anything until the following year because everything in the rolls had to break down and be absorbed.

I threw up in my mouth a little.

"Peppers!" I yelled at him, "What in the sweet name of General Lee takes a year to break down in your garden? A god damned body, that's what! You think old Luca Brazi wants to start tillin' his ground and tear off a body part from one of his rival gangsters he done buried back there? You *still* wonder what it was you was burying in that garden of his? Well there's your proof! He's waiting for the lime to break them down altogether before he tills them under and plants his tomatoes on them."

Peppers just stared at me. "C'mon, Tim," I said, grabbing him by the arm, "We're going down to the CoOp. If you don't believe me, maybe you'll believe Harry Majors." Harry is the soil expert down at the CoOp. If you want to know about growing anything in Bedford County, Virginia, you ask Harry Majors.

We dropped the fishing reel and hopped in my truck. "Now, you let me do the talking, Peppers. I'll ask old Harry without him knowing why we're asking. We don't want anybody getting the jump on us and exposing old Mezilli first. You hear me?" Peppers nodded slowly. He still didn't believe me, I could tell. But this would prove it to him. Harry Majors would prove it to old Tim Peppers and then I'd have me an ally. On the drive over, I asked him about the tomatoes he got from Mezilli. "Peppers, if he ain't even tilled that ground yet, where'd them tomatoes come from?" Peppers answered me; "He planted some tomatoes and cucumbers in big boxes and filled them with somethin' he called mushroom soil. He said it's the secret to big vegetables." "Hmmm, mushroom soil, huh?" I said, mostly to myself, "That must be his code for the buried bodies...like "cans of peaches" was for Tony Soprano."

We walked in to the CoOp and straight back to Harry at the fertilizer section. "Say Harry, what do you know, good?" I asked him casually. Harry smiled. He's a cheerful guy. "Well hello, Phil. Hey Timmy. What are you boys doing here this morning?" he answered. Peppers started to talk, "Oh well we're wonderin..." I elbowed him in the ribs real hard. "Peppers and me have a bet between us and we need you to settle it for us, Harry." I said. "See, I did some fertilizing on a section of my back yard, oh about a year ago, I guess. Now, I read somewheres that you should let the fertilizer set for a while, like maybe for a year, before you till it under and plant your crops. Peppers here says you can plant sooner than that. Which is it?"

Harry scratched his head and leaned on his elbow on the seed counter. "Well..." he began, "What find of fertilizer did you use? Was it just from the bag? 'Cause you could till that under in a week, and plant in two. Now if it was compost maybe you'd need to wait for a couple of months, three at the most. Yessir, compost takes a while to break down." Harry was just getting warmed up. He knows soil like

Einstein knew atoms. "Now if you were trying to change the characteristics of the soil you might let it set longer. What are you trying to grow?"

If I didn't reel ol' Harry back in, he'd ramble on about dirt for a month or so. "Harry," I said, "I dumped a whole lot of umm...natural fertilizer on my patch in the back. At the longest, how long would I have to wait? I can't remember everything in the mix. It was something I came up with off the internet, on one of those organic gardening websites. I can't remember what was in it but it smelled really bad." Harry looked at me like I'd lost my mind. "You put something in your garden and you don't know what it is?" You must be crazy." He was laughing at me. "Okay, worst case scenario, I can't think of a thing we have here that you have to wait more than about three months to till and plant. That good enough for ya?" I looked at Peppers and smiled. "You see..." I whispered, "Those were bodies." We turned and left without telling Harry which of us had won the bet.

On the drive back to my house, Peppers was real quiet. I knew something was troubling him. "What's on your mind, Timmy." I asked him. Peppers was hesitant and looked out the window instead of looking at me when he finally answered. "Oh you know, this business with those bodies in Joe's back yard. I guess if ol' Harry says nothing takes a year to break down, he must be telling the truth. Why would he lie? But dang it, Phil! I just can't believe Joe is a cold-blooded killer who buries bodies in his back yard. I mean I like the man. He's a good daddy to them kids, and he loves his wife and all. Heck I see him at church every Sunday...a Baptist church. Ain't them mafias all Catholics?
We must be wrong about this."

If I wasn't rounding the curve at Peelers Bend and needed both hands on the wheel I'd have reached across and smacked Peppers in the head again. "Peppers you're going soft on me! The man buried things in his garden and you helped him, remember? Those things were about six feet long; they were heavy enough that it took both of you to carry them. They were wrapped in burlap. They smelled like rotten flesh, remember? And he covered them in lime, Peppers! What else could they be? And as for him being a good daddy, well hell, son, Paul Potts doted on his kids too but he was still a ruthless dictator" Peppers looked at me like a puppy, "Who was Paul Potts?" he asked. "Peppers! Dear God in heaven did you not pay attention to history class at all? Paul Potts was the feller in Cambodia that killed a couple million of his own folks. You don't remember "The Killing Fields?"

Peppers leaned back against the window and looked out at the passing landscape. "I don't know, Phil." He said softly. "Heck I never did see inside any of them burlap bundles. How do we really know they was bodies?" Then he paused and whispered, "I never said they smelled like rotten flesh..."

I slammed on the brakes, and pulled off the road in a cloud of dust and gravel. "For the love of Stonewall Jackson! Boy what the hell is wrong with you? What more proof do you need, Timmy? You want them bodies to just get themselves up out of Mezilli's garden and come over to your house, all rotten and decayed, and start telling you how he killed them...like that movie theater scene in American Werewolf in London? You need me to go to Quantico and get the FBI cadaver dogs and root around in his garden? What's wrong with you, Peppers, have you gone crazy?"

Hell, I guess the whole dang world's gone crazy...

The Last Ride for Nonna

We'd been in Forest for almost a year. That first Christmas came and went pretty quickly because we'd moved-in over Thanksgiving, and by the time we'd gotten unpacked and the house in order, Christmas was about a week away. We'd barely had time to decorate and put up a tree and all that. So we'd decided to go home, like I told you before.

Now, my family does Christmas like few others. Between the Christmas lights, and the food, and the music, and the relatives, we really make a month-long celebration out of the holidays. Yet for all the effort we put into it back home, I never had the room to do it up the way I'd always dreamed. The house in South Philly was narrow and tall, as all city houses are. It was hard to decorate the upper portions, and we had essentially no front yard. This year...this year I was going to really put on a show. While the kids were still young.

The other thing we didn't get to do last year was host our annual "Feast of Seven Fishes" dinner on Christmas Eve. Now, you have to understand, this is a very big deal. *Festa dei sette pesci* is an Italian-American tradition with roots in the old country. Like most of the holiday traditions that aren't directly linked to the Church, there is no official guideline for the celebration. So depending on whose house you were visiting on Christmas Eve, the table would vary in content.

At our house, the rules are relatively simple: Seven fish entrees, three of them have to be baccala, which is salted cod. The rest can be any kind of seafood. We always open with Uncle Franny's renowned baccala stew, which is very much like Manhattan clam chowder, only with chunks of baccala instead of clams. From there we have macaroni and gravy with any combination of calamari, crab, shrimp, and sometimes plain macaroni with anchovies fried in olive oil and garlic. We usually have baked baccala, fried baccala, always some smelts, and my cousin tries to find one unique fish we've never tasted before to top off the menu.

We eat like kings, and we talk loud, and laugh even louder. There are always guests at the table and nobody is a stranger. Sinatra and Dean Martin sing Christmas songs in the background. We're big Christmas music people, us Mezilli's, and usually it's the classics we're listening to as we keep "la vigilia." Dinner lasts until around eight PM when Uncle Franny leaves to go home and get ready for midnight Mass. The rest of us will hang around a few minutes longer, but we filter out a few at a time until the last ones are gone.

Angie and I really missed hosting the dinner last year, but with the move and all, it was really hard to try putting it together, and then too, convincing my family to come to Virginia for Christmas was essentially impossible. So we flew home a few days before Christmas and spent the holiday in Philly. This year, however, Anj and I had decided we were going to have it here. I also decided I was going to have as many of my family come in as I could, no matter the expense. I knew Nonna wouldn't fly. Heck I didn't know if I could convince her to come at all. She was eightyseven years old now, and had never spent Christmas Eve anywhere except Naples and South Philly.

I called my dad in October and ran the idea by him. "Pop," I said, "I know Nonna won't fly. And I don't want you and mom driving down here with her wanting to stop every seventeen minutes to take a picture or use the bathroom again." My dad laughed, "Oh God no!" He said. It would be like the Sea Isle Affair except it would take two days!"

The Sea-Isle Affair

The Sea Isle Affair is a legend in our family; you'll need a little background.

See, Pop owned a beach house in Sea Isle City, New Jersey. This was his first beach house, a little cottage about six blocks from the ocean. He sold it when he bought the SeaRay, and later he bought a place in Avalon. Anyway, he decided to take Nonna to the Sea Isle house the summer after Giuseppe died. It was one of the biggest mistakes he ever made. Ever.

Nonna never did like to ride in a car. I have fuzzy memories of my grandfather driving us to Philadelphia Park to watch the horses race, and she would be in the front seat, yelling at him in Italian, pumping an imaginary brake pedal on her side of the car, and waving her hands every five minutes like we were going to crash. Making all of this exponentially more frightening for me, was that Nonno drove a 1962 Cadillac Sedan De Ville. It had bench seats and I was sitting in between them both on the front seat while my grandfather smoked a smelly El Producto, and my grandmother gave him the maloik and screamed Italian profanities and prayers to every Saint in the heavens.

The other thing she did was make him stop about every ten minutes. Apparently Nonna was born with a bladder the size of a shot glass because the woman can't hold her water in the car at all. Philadelphia Park is a thirty minute drive from South Philly. Our trip took two and a half hours. So the day that my Old Man decided to drive Nonna to Sea Isle was a legendary mistake. It's an hour and a half trip. Two hours at the most. It's a nice drive once you get outside of Philadelphia, and you can breeze along with the music playing and be there in no time at all...if you aren't riding with Nonna. Nonna had never been over the Walt Whitman Bridge before. Come to think of it, she probably had never been over any bridge before. She was whiteknuckling the armrest at the toll booth, and literally crying and calling the Virgin Mary the very second she felt the car start to climb the grade toward the middle of the span. She hyperventilated. She spit and coughed and clutched her heart. She crossed herself and started praying the Rosary. "Days-a no bridge!" she kept saying. "Days-a no bridge!" She grabbed my father's arm while he was driving and she screamed "Giuseppe! Days-a no bridge! Look!" Then she finally fainted.

My mom was fanning her from the front seat. Pop had bought himself a nice Cadillac too, just like Nonno, except the STS model has bucket seats and Nonna was in the back. Pop thought she'd be more comfortable with the extra room. The problem was, Nonna couldn't see very far up the road ahead from that back seat. As they climbed the grade toward the top of the bridge, she couldn't see that the bridge deck continued on to the other side. From her vantage point, it looked like the whole bridge just stopped in the middle. The poor old girl was looking out the window and seeing impending death staring her in the face in the form of a two hundred foot plunge into the Delaware River. That's what she kept screaming "Days-a no bridge!" She was warning Pop, "There's no bridge..." only he didn't realize it until they got to Sea Isle.

Nonna woke up after about a minute. By that time they were down the other side and had pulled off into a service lane. From there the trip is flat and uneventful, unless Nonna is going along for the ride. She had to stop to pee every mile or so. The only thing in the whole world that pees more than my grandmother on a road trip is that marble cherub in my front yard. It would help if she didn't drink a gallon and a half of coffee every morning. And by coffee, I mean coffee. Coffee the way Italian men like it.

Apparently my great grandfather, her dad, had died at age sixty three but continued to walk the Earth another thirty years. His heart kept beating as a result of the caffeine buzz provided by the rocket fuel he brewed every morning in that old silver percolator. Nonna told me she'd started drinking coffee with her papa by the time she was seven or eight years old. I simply cannot imagine a child buzzing around on that stuff. I bet her parents were hitting the whiskey by nine AM.

Anyway, it took Pop almost four hours to get her to Sea Isle. Four hours. To go about sixty miles. The poor man called me and asked me if I would come out and drive them home. He was absolutely certain that if he had to drive her, he would either kill his own mother in cold blood and dump her in the Pine Barrens, or just hang a hard left on top of the Walt Whitman and end the whole affair for both of them. Angie and I drove down the following Sunday in her Escalade. Other than the drive, Nonna had herself a marvelous time down the shore. She was tanned and smiling when we got there, and protested loudly that she didn't really want to leave. At one point she grabbed my arm plaintively and asked me "Giuseppe, are we gonna have to drive over that-ah big-ah breedge?" It was pathetic. She looked like a little puppy, scared by the traffic and trying to cross the highway. I put my arm around her and said, "No, Nonna. I found a different way to go home. No bridges, okay?" She blew out her breath and sat back in her chaise lounge on the front porch. "Giuseppe," she said to me, "Look-ah at the Ocean. It's so beautiful, no?" I think the thought of crossing that bridge had been on her mind all week and she only just now permitted herself to enjoy this view.

Anj and I had cooked up a plan. Now, Nonna is pretty much a prude where vices are concerned. She never touched a cigarette, although she tolerated Giuseppe's stogies, and she never touched liquor. Well, almost never. The old gal had a weakness for anisette. Break out the 'bucca after dinner and she'd be dancing one of those whirling Mediterranean dances and singing in Italian in the living room. So Anj and I called Mr. Tripoletti at the drug store on Passyunk Avenue and asked him for a few spare Xanax. Of course he grilled us about this. But as soon as I told him it was for Nonna and she was taking a ride in the car, he said "Come on over." Mr. Tripoletti could have caught a lot of flak for giving us that stuff without a prescription, but he knew my grandmother.

That Sunday evening, after dinner, we ground up a Xanax and put it in her shot glass and we drank a few rounds of anisette. She was laughing like a school girl in about a half hour, and passed out in the back seat of Angie's Escalade by 7PM. I had to carry her inside her house. She woke up on her couch at 10:15 and called me up, asking how she got there. She had nothing but fond memories of the trip home. And *that* is the Sea Isle Affair.

So you can understand why the Old Man won't drive her down here, and she won't fly, so I had to come up with a viable solution. It took a little creativity but I got the problem solved. First, I called a friend from the neighborhood, Jimmy DiNardi. Jimmy and his dad owned a limousine service, City-Line Livery, and they had some really nice vehicles. I figured we'd need an Escalade or a Suburban to get three adults and their luggage comfortably to Virginia. Jimmy said that he would love to provide a car and a driver, but it was Christmas and it would be hard to get a driver to commit to making that trip twice during the holidays.

I had asked him about driving them down around the twenty-second of December, and picking them up and taking them back on the twenty-seventh. Jimmy said he'd put the word out to his guys, but that he thought it would be hard. He said he'd call me the next day. So I went about procuring airline tickets for everyone else in the family. Uncle Tony was a lifelong bachelor and had no reason not to come, so he said yes. My cousins, Angie's cousins, Angie's mom and dad would come but her brothers and sisters all did Seven Fishes with their in-laws. I understood completely.

I had all the arrangements made except for the driver and car for my mom and dad and grandmother. Jimmy DiNardo called me just as I was heading out to my garage to order a batting cage for Petey. It was late afternoon and he was home from school and I didn't want him to hear me talking to the guy at the company who makes them. I ordered him a really nice, professional sized batting cage with pitching machine. Petey was becoming a very good baseball player and this would give him a jump on the pitchers next spring.

I gave the guy my credit card number and wrote down the delivery date and shipping info and was just hanging up when Jimmy DiNardo buzzed in on the call-waiting.   "Yo Joey!" he said cheerfully. "Yo Jim," I returned, "What's the good word?" Jimmy was apologetic. "Chiedo scusa, paisan. I can't find a driver to make this run for me being so close to Christmas. I could find you another company, Joey, but I'm afraid you'd run into the same problem no matter where you go." Jimmy sounded forlorn. "Aaah it's okay Cuz," I said, "I understand." Jimmy asked me why I needed this car for the trip. "It's my Old Man and my mom. They are fine and they might even be convinced to fly, but they're going to bring Nonna." Jimmy laughed, "Sea Isle." he said. *Boy, word gets around in South Philly I thought.* "Yeah," I replied, "Sea Isle. Anyway, I need to have them driven down here without my dad doing the driving. Nonna behaves herself much better when a stranger is around." Jimmy apologized again and told me that if there was anything else he could do, just ask.

I hung up and thought about it a bit. Then I got a brainstorm: Tommy Felonious!
Tommy had no family left now that his dad had remarried and his stepmother didn't want him around. He was still a parolee but at a much reduced level and he'd gotten his license back. He'd probably love coming down here for Seven Fishes. I called Tommy right away.

The phone was ringing when I noticed someone coming down the driveway from the house to the garage where I was standing. It was Phil Lowery, carrying my leaf blower that he'd borrowed. He'd been tinkering with his own blower in Hank Milledge's garage for weeks and the leaves kept piling up in his yard. I sent Petey over there at one point to offer to rake them for him and he said "No thanks, I'll get that leaf blower working this week for sure." The following week, when the leaf blower had apparently gotten the best of him, I gave mine to Milledge after a game of pool in my house. I told him, "Just give it to him and tell him you borrowed it. For some reason, Phil doesn't like coming over here, unless you or Erickson or one of the others are here too. I don't think Phil cares for me too much." Milledge tried convincing me otherwise, '"Oh no, Joe it's not like that at all," He protested, "Phil is just shy, that's all. I think he likes you just fine." *Shy, Huh?* I thought, *He's not too shy to be watching me at 11PM through those metal venetian blinds with a light on in the room behind him.*

Anyway, Milledge took my leaf blower to him and he got his yard straightened up. And now here he was, early December, three weeks after the rest of us had already bagged our leaves, finally returning my blower. Oh well, I thought to myself, It gives him an excuse to come over without anyone else holding his hand. Maybe we can finally chat.

Tommy Fallone picked up on the third ring. "Yo! Tommy Felonious! Come stai?" I yelled loudly. Phil was still a long way up the driveway when Tommy answered. Phil walks really slowly, like pages-of-a-calendar slowly. I waved to him to let him know I saw him coming, and to come on in the garage. I continued my conversation with Tommy while Lowery trudged down the driveway.

"Yo Tommy!" I said loudly, "I got a job for you, if you're interested. It'll get you off the fish trucks for a few days and you can spend Christmas with my family down here. You game?" I could almost hear Tommy smiling. I guess he was figuring he'd be spending Christmas alone. "Sure" he said, "Tell me what's going on. I smiled at Phil Lowery, who had just entered the garage. I held up my finger to Phil, signifying "Just give me one minute Phil." I grabbed him a Dr. Pepper out of the fridge and set it on the workbench. He took a seat on a stool and wiped the bottle feverishly before he took a sip. I continued with Tommy.

"Listen, Tommy, your probation is light enough now that you can drive out of state, right?" I realized that, even though Phil didn't know Tommy, this was personal. So I slowly meandered to the far side of the garage where I figured Phil couldn't hear me as well. "Okay Paisan, this Christmas might be my Nonna's last, you know what I mean? She's eighty-

218

seven years old. So I've been thinking about Seven Fishes. I think I want to do it down here instead of back in Philly. But I need to get them here to do it, Nonna, my Old Man, and my mom. Pop can't drive her, so I was wondering if you'd do the job for me?"

Phil coughed suddenly. "Hang on Tommy..." I said into my phone. "Phil...You okay? Dr. Pepper go down the wrong pipe?" Lowery looked at me wide eyed. He nodded his head and set his bottle on the bench and cleared his throat a few times. I went back to Tommy. "You know how Nonna is, Tommy. She still pushes the Old Man around and she has to stop every fifteen minutes if he's driving. But she behaves when she's around strangers." Tommy chuckled on his end. "What do you want me to do, Joe?" he said.   "Here's the plan," I said. "I'm going to rent an Escalade, or a Suburban...black, so it looks like a limo. She hasn't seen you since you went away to Holmesburg, so she won't recognize you. We're not telling her where they're going, just that me and Anj and the kids will be there. She'll figure you for a professional driver. You get them here, we do Feast of Seven Fishes, and you stay with us for a few days after Christmas and head on home. Bip Bop Boop...the job is done!" Tommy laughed, "Just like that? You really think she'll go for it?" "Oh yeah," I told him. "Like I said, she hasn't seen you in ten years Tommy, she'll never suspect anything. If she asks any questions, just make up a name or something." We both laughed at that.

"What do you say, Tommy" Will you do the job? I'll talk to Skip and get him to loan you to me for a week so he doesn't think I'm muscling in. He'll be okay with it." Tommy agreed. "It would be nice to be around family for Christmas, the first one since I got back and all. Yeah sure." He said. "Excellent!" I yelled in excitement. Hey tomorrow when you see Skip tell him to call me. I need to make arrangements and have a shipment delivered down here by the twenty-third." Tommy said he'd do it first thing in the morning. "Thanks Joe," he said. "It's going to be great to see you all. Let me know when you arrange the car for the trip. Tell Anj I said hey." I hung up with a smile on my face. I turned back towards Phil, but he was gone. I glanced up the driveway and there he went, almost running.

"That's odd." I thought. "That old bird doesn't run for anybody. I hope he's alright."

I made a list of the fish I was going to order from Skip O'Brien in the morning, turned out the garage lights and walked back to the house. As I walked in the side door, I saw Phil in his living room, silhouetted by a light from his kitchen, pacing back and forth and talking on the phone, very animated.

11

I
Knew It
All Along

"Milledge!" I yelled into my phone, "Milledge get over here right now!" I was so upset I barely remember Hank's number when I dialed it. It took me three tries. He whined about me calling him at "this hour." "For God's sake, Hank it's seven forty-five, and you're watching Deadliest Catch reruns until ten. Now get over here!" Milledge still didn't want to leave his recliner. "Come on Phil," he said, "Can't this wait?" "No!" I barked. It cannot wait. It's life and death!" "Okay..." he said, "I'm on my way."

Milledge knocked on my front door about ten minutes later. I opened it carefully, grabbed him by the arm and yanked him inside. Once he was in the living room, I locked the door, threw the deadbolt and fastened the security chain. "What in the name of...?" Milledge sputtered, "What is going on, Phil?" "I told you! I told you!" It's all I could spit out. I was so angry, so upset, and to be honest, a little scared. "I told you he was a murderer!"

Milledge sat down on the couch. "Who, Phil? Who the heck are you talking about?"

"Mezilli!" I yelled, "You're dear pool-playing buddy Joe Mezilli. He's a cold blooded, ruthless killer!" "What?" Hank said incredulously. "Spit it out, Phil." "I was just over there. I was in his garage and he was arranging a hit!" Hank laughed, "C'mon, Phil," he said. "Your imagination is working overtime again."

"I'm telling you I heard him. I heard him making the arrangements." "Arrangements?" Hank asked, "What kind of Arrangements, Phil?" "I tried to explain it the best way I could, but it was a lot of information and I worried that Hank might not grasp it all. "He called it the 'Feet's and Seven Fishes.' And my guess is it's something worse than old Tataglia done to Luca Brazi. Milledge cocked his head like a dog. "Who?" "Luca Brazi!" I barked, "Remember in The

223

Godfather when they sent that Sicilian Message and there was a fish inside Luca's flak jacket? It meant he was going to sleep with the fishes. It means they killed him, Hank. Killed him dead and dumped his body in the ocean." Milledge scratched his head under his ball cap. "Phil are you certain? I mean The Godfather was a great movie, but it was a movie. How do you know for sure that means what you say it means?" I was so mad I was quivering. "Because Hank," I started, "They done the same thing in The Sopranos! Big Pussy!" Milledge jumped up off the couch, "Phil I really don't appreciate you calling me names like that just because I don't understand what you're getting at. I mean...maybe I ain't as wise about the mafia as you are, but you ain't gotta call me...call me..." I was dumbstruck. "Milledge!" I yelled, "I ain't calling you no Big Pussy I'm talking about the big fella on The Sopranos. His name was Big Pussy and they shot him up on a boat and then wrapped him in a bodybag and dumped him overboard." Milledge sat down slowly. "So...so you weren't calling me a...you know a big..." "Oh for God's sake NO, Hank! I was telling you about another fella who slept with the fishes. Just like your pal Joe Barzini across the street is going to do. Apparently he's planning on killin' seven of them at once. That's why he called it 'Feets and Seven Fishes' I reckon it means seven poor bastards are gonna have cement shoes on their feet and then sleep with the fishes!" Milledge let out a long, low whistle. "And you know what?" I continued, "You know who one of his victims is going to be? His own grandmother!"

Hank snapped to attention. "Phil I've never seen you this worked up. Are you sure you heard this? His own grandmother?" "Am I sure? Am I sure?" I was almost biting my tongue off. "I'm so sure, that I'm calling the sheriff in the morning. I got him! I got that phony waste managing mafia sombitch! I got him!" Hank stood up and walked over to me. "Slow down, Phil, tell me what you heard." I took a breath. "I was returning the leaf blower, and he was on the phone with some guy named Tommy. Tommy who apparently had been in jail! Yeah, he did a stretch in Holmesburg!" Hank was silent, I continued. "I heard him say he was going to have seven of them sleep with the fishes! Seven! That heartless, no good rotten bastard! One of them was his grandmother and two more were his own mother and father! And to make it worse, he's going to do the job on Christmas Eve. Christmas Eve! What kind of cruel, cold hearted sombitch could kill his own parents and his grandmother, on Christmas Eve to boot? I'm tellin' ya Hank, he's a mafia and I know it! His parents are too dang old to make the journey down here and his grandmother doesn't like driving at all. He even told this Tommy fella to drug her if he needed to. He mentioned about how they done it to her years ago. He even laughed about it! Anyway he was gonna rent a Suburban so his grandmother thinks it's a real limosine company coming to driver her down here. Then when he gets her here, she's gonna sleep, feet-first, with the fishes. Along with his momma and daddy and four other folks. I'm thinking the other four must be locals. This ain't good Milledge...this ain't good!"

"You sure about this?" Milledge asked, "This is a big accusation Phil." I laughed at him for even doubting me. "I'm as sure as I'm standing here. This is it. I have him now! The game, as Inspector Cluseau said, is on foot!"

Buying off the Cops

Phil Lowery is no stranger to my office. We used to get calls from him about once a week when he first moved out there to the Meadows. He'd call us complaining about a neighbor parking two feet into his property. He'd call about kids launching fireworks on Fourth of July. He'd call about strange lights in the sky. But he's never actually come down to my office to personally file a complaint. This was a first. Stevens is my name. Stan Stevens. I'm the Bedford County Sherriff. To be truthful, I'm also Phil Lowery's wife's cousin. Gladys and me was real close growin' up. Our whole family was. Phil was not one of the people we all ran with back then. He came from up in Lynchburg and his daddy was a coker at the foundry and they didn't have a lot of money. Neither did we, but they were really poor. We accepted him anyway because Gladys fell in love with him, and our family has never been the kind to split over things like that. But Phil came closer than anyone ever had to testing that rule. He was definitely different from the rest of us.

If there was a strange noise in the swamp, Phil heard it. If there was a series of sonic booms, they always seem to break Phil's windows. If aliens ever came to Bedford County to conduct weird experiments on one of the residents...they'd have probably picked old Phil. God help them if they didn't, because if anyone around here gets the chance to outdo Phil in the tall-tale category, he gets downright bent about it. Phil has done it all. If Phil hasn't done it, then it shouldn't have ever been done by a human being in the first place.

But Phil has never looked as upset, or seemed as sincere, as he was when he walked into my office the first week in November, last year. Lord he was trembling! Wait, did I just use "sincere" and "Phil Lowery" in the same sentence? There, ya see? That's how serious he was. He came in to my office and shut the door behind him. That door don't ever get shut. I told him so, but he just shut it anyway, then came over to my desk and leaned in until his face was about six inches from mine and he scowled. "You just never mind about that door, Stanley. We got a real problem and I don't want nobody else hearing us talking about it. Them mafias infiltrate everywhere. Even the sheriff's office.

I set my coffee cup down on my desk. "Them what?" I asked him. "The mafias. The mafias, Stan. We got 'em right here in Forest, yessir. Heck we got 'em on my street!" he hissed. "What..." I said slowly, standing to my feet, "...In God's green earth are you talking about?" Phil started explaining, "The mafia, Stan! The mafia is right across the street from my house. I seen him burying bodies last year, and just this week he was on the phone, talking about having his own grandmother, his father, and his momma, wearing concrete shoes on their feet, and sleeping with the fishes, along with four other poor souls. Seven of them Stan! Seven people are gonna be sleeping with the fishes. And do you know when? Christmas Eve!"

Phil was lathered up real good now. He pounded his fist on my desk and kept going. His voice was about as high as it's ever been. He gets that way when he's upset. "Some excon hit-man named 'Tommy' is coming down here from Philadelphia to do the job. I heard that part too. He's driving them down here in a rented Suburban, to make them old folks think they's coming here to spend the Holidays. Then the guy's gonna whack them. In cold blood. Why I bet he's gonna wrap them in burlap, and bury them in his garden like them other poor saps." Phil was wildeyed now. "You gotta

227

stop him Stanley. He's a sick, deranged sociopath!" He was serious. He never calls me Stanley.

"Phil, slow down, now. Who are you talking about?" "Mezilli! Mezilli! Joe Mezilli, my neighbor, dang it! He's one of them mafias, Stan, I'm telling you! You have to go and get him before he kills off his own family. He's gonna kill his own mother, Stan! What's that remind you of?" Phil sputtered. "Oedipus?" I asked. "No wait. Oedipus killed his father. I don't know, Phil, none of my acquaintances ever killed their mothers." Phil had no idea who Oedipus was. I hadn't really expected him to. "Tony Soprano! Tony Soprano!" Cousin Phil yelped. "Tony was going to kill his own mother in the hospital with a pillow! Don't you see? He's a mafia." I took a sip of coffee. "Phil," I said quietly, trying to soothe him a little, "The Sopranos was a TV...never mind." I didn't want to have this conversation with him about the reality of TV shows. Not again. I tried a diversionary tactic instead. "You have all six seasons on Blu-Ray now, Phil?" This ploy didn't work. "Yes I do. And what difference does it make. The man is a killer!" Phil took a breath, because he was just getting warmed up.

"Besides that, there are the drug deals I told you about." "What drug deals, Phil?" I asked. Phil's head almost popped. "The drug deals. He goes to the airport in Lynchburg every week and comes back with a package. Every Wednesday, like clockwork. The man is retired. What's he having flown in here every week Stanley?" He stood up again. "And what about this!" he said. He pulled out his cell phone and started scrolling through the pictures. "Why is Hank Milledge's dog peeing on you in the bushes, Phil?" Phil sputtered and coughed and scrolled to the next picture. "He's peeing on the bush, you moron. He didn't see me! I was hiding. Hiding so I could take these pictures!" He scrolled to the next one and showed me a grainy picture of two very blurry figures carrying a blurry brown object.

I was getting nowhere with Phil. Instead, I thought I'd appease him. I figured I'd drive out there and introduce myself, get to the bottom of this whole affair. Besides, this was an election year coming up, I could use another vote.

So I set out to meet Mr. Joe Mezilli, the big-shot mafia don. ...according to my cousin-in-law, the idiot.

The Way To A Sherriffs Heart

I sure wasn't expecting to see the sheriff at my front door. At first I thought maybe one of the boys hit a baseball through the neighbor's window or something. But then I realized that my neighbors are all about four hundred feet away and my boys can't hit a ball that far. Not yet anyway.   He was nice enough. Really gentlemanly. *Stan Stevens*, I said to myself, *I am really going to have to get used to these vanilla names.* I invited him in. The boys were out back playing *Rough Touch* which is the Philadelphia area version of touch football. If you've seen the movie, "Invinicible" those guys playing that brutal football game in the empty lot...that was the *Delco Rough Touch League*, and yeah...they really do play that hard.

Anyway, the boys were all outside, and Anj was in the kitchen with Emmy. Anj had decided it was time to teach Emmy how to make cannoli in time to help with the Christmas cooking. They were mixing up the sweetened ricotta, and talking about going to look at horses. Now, they've seen plenty of horses before. We weren't that cityslick. Angie had decided that Emily should take riding lessons and it turns out Emmy was a natural. So in reality,

229

they weren't going looking at horses...they were buying one. We'd board the horse at a stable until Emmy was older and knew how to take care of one. Then maybe we'd keep some at the hunting camp.

Anyway, Stan Stevens came calling on a Saturday morning, in mid-November. I asked him to come in and have a seat. "Stan, can I get you a cup of coffee?" I offered. "Why that'd be great." he replied. He was an immediately friendly guy. I liked that. He is also a pretty stocky fellow. Pretty much like you'd figure from a southern, small-town sheriff. At least the way the movies and TV always portrayed them. He had a very genuine smile. I'd come to appreciate a genuine smile in a neighborhood where everyone seems to be smiling on the outside but inside not so much. Stan was large in the shoulders, and equally large in the belly. He wore a Stetson and carried a revolver, not a semi-auto. I don't know why, but I kind of liked that. He reminded me a lot of Benny Mastofione, whose wife worked for my dad all those years..

Stan sat down on the couch, and I walked into the kitchen to get him a cup of coffee. "What do you take in your coffee, Stan?" I asked him. The kitchen is open right into the living room so Stan was only in another room, technically. "Oh, cream and sugar. Thank you sir." "Sheriff," I said, "We're gonna have to start this relationship out on the right foot. Now unless you want me spitting in your coffee, you just decide right now to call me 'Joe,' okay?" Stan chuckled. "I deeply respect and appreciate the manners down here, sheriff, but it just feels like I'll never get to know anybody very well, with all the 'sirs' and 'ma'am's' and 'Mr. Mezilli's' I keep hearing. Please...I'm Joe and this is my wife Angie, and our daughter Emmy." Emmy got up and shook Sheriff Steven's hand, just as bold as life.

230

Stan Stevens laughed deeply at that. I liked him already. He stood up and walked into the kitchen and took the coffee cup from the counter. He walked over to Anj and Emmy and asked, "Whatcha making over here, ladies? He asked. Emmy answered him, "My mom is teaching me to make cannolis." Stan smiled, and turned to me. "You know, I've heard that word for years. I mean everybody quotes 'Leave the gun, take the cannolis' from The Godfather, but I never knew what they were." "They're a pastry, Stan." Angie answered him, "They're a thin, crisp shell, fried and dusted in powdered sugar and filled with sweetened ricotta cheese and chocolate chips. I like to use candied fruit sometimes too. If you stick around, you can try the first batch."

Before long, Anj had Sheriff Stevens rolling out the next batch of cannoli shells and helping Emmy fill them with the pastry bag. The first time he tried one was magical. I thought he was going to start crying, right there in my kitchen. He had filled about a dozen shells and then he looks at Emily and says, "Well...how'd I do?" Emmy put her hands on her hips and cocked her head a little and said, "Well I think you did okay, but this is my first time. My Mom is the expert. Ask her!" Angie piped right in, "You did great, Stan. You ready to try one?"

I thought, for a minute, that I might have to call an ambulance. Sheriff Stevens almost fell over right in my living room. The look on his face when he tasted that cannoli for the first time was something I'll never forget. I instantly spotted him as a guy who likes to eat. Now, he is a pretty rotund fellow, and it was easy to see that he liked eating. But his reaction to the cannoli told me he really liked great food. "Stan, you're going to have to stay for lunch," I told him. "I made gravy yesterday and we were going to have some ziti and meatballs after the cannoli were done. "Like sawmill gravy?" he asked. "What's a ziti?' Now that made me laugh. "No," I said. "You'd probably call it 'spaghetti sauce.' we call it 'red gravy' if we make it with meat. If we don't, it's sauce. Marinara is sauce. And ziti is macaroni shaped like a tube. Trust me, you'll love it."

Sheriff Stevens laughed and joked his way through the filling of about fifty cannoli. He ate two, and would have eaten more except I reminded him that we were having lunch soon. Anj put the finishing touches on the last cannoli while I made the ziti and fried the meatballs. "Come over here Stan," I said, "let me teach you how to make a real meatball. The kind Nonna makes." "Who?" he asked. "Nonna," I answered, "It's the Italian word we use for our grandmothers. Nonno is our grandfather. You know, back home they have a saying: 'Nobody can claim to cook Italian who didn't learn in Nonna's kitchen.' Anj and I both learned the same way, from our grandmothers." Stan smiled.

"So, which of you is the better cook, then?" Angie laughed, "Well you know how to divide a family, sheriff." She smiled, "It's really a tie," she said, "Both our grandmothers are great cooks. It's like a contest with no losers." That's my Angie. The cannoli were all done and Emmy helped her mom clean up while I had sheriff Stevens standing at the kitchen island, shirtsleeves rolled up, teaching him how to roll meatballs. "Not too firm, but not too loose, either." I told him. "My meatballs are famous in Philly. Once you get them rolled and stacked on your plate here, we fry them in olive oil until the outsides are just a little crispy."

Stevens was literally smiling like a kid. The smells in our kitchen were driving him nuts. We had the meatballs frying, and the kettle boiling and ready for the ziti, and the gravy simmering on the stove. "Come over here and taste this, Stan." I said to him. I grabbed a spoon from the drawer and dipped some gravy from the pot. Stevens approached it like the Holy Grail. "You know," he said, "The only Italian food we have around here is Olive Garden. We have to drive in to Lynchburg to get anything better than that."

"I'll try to forget you said that name in my house." I laughed, as I handed him the spoon. "Now you try this and tell me again about 'Olive Garden." Stan Stevens almost cried. I mean, he caught his breath, stared at the spoon like maybe Jesus Himself had once used it, and literally stood there with his jaw open. "Dear Lord!" he said slowly, "I mean...that was...I've never had anything like that. That was amazing." I'd won over yet another newbie to the magic of Nonna Mezilli's gravy.

"What's your secret, Joe?" he asked. "Stan," I smiled, "You'd need a subpoena to get that out of me." Lunch was a typical Mezilli family affair. The boys ate their way through two pounds of Ziti and about six meatballs each. Between the adults and Emmy, we used another pound-and-a-half, and another dozen meatballs. Stan had little beads of sweat on his forehead, and not because I make my gravy particularly spicy. It was because he was working over that ziti, and those meatballs, and the Amoroso's rolls we have flown in every Wednesday.

"I've never had bread like this, Joe." he gasped in between bites. "And this gravy is just the best thing I've ever put in my mouth!" he said, smiling. Then he patted his belly and laughed, "And I've put a whole lot in my mouth, as you can see." We ate and joked and he asked my kids questions, and we swapped stories about our families. Suddenly, as if a bolt of lightning hit me, it dawned on me that the Sheriff of Bedford County was sitting at my kitchen table eating my Nonna's gravy and laughing with my kids and my wife. And I had no idea why. Be subtle. I thought to myself.

233

"So Sheriff, other than the time Frank Rizzo came by my grandparents' house to sample Nonno's homemade wine, I've never had dinner with the local law enforcement." I smiled, "What brought you out here today...rumors of my cooking?" Stevens smiled and took a sip of his tea. "Frank Rizzo drank homemade wine with your grandfather...the Frank Rizzo?" He laughed. "Sure," I said, "Giuseppe and Rizz went way back. You here because you heard rumors about Frank Rizzo at my house, eating gravy?"

"No, rumors of your garden." Stevens answered. I laughed out loud at that. "Really?" I asked, "My garden?" "Yeah, no kidding." he said. "I've heard about those tomatoes you grow back there. And the cucumbers and zucchini. Nobody can grow that stuff around these mountains. Why I even heard you imported your own soil last year. I didn't believe it, myself. I mean that's a lot of work for tomatoes."

"You're in my wheelhouse now, Sherriff." I said coyly. "Tomatoes are sacred to the Mezilli family. I had some special ingredients shipped down here, that much is true. It's a family secret though, Stan. I'd be in a lot of hot water if I told you." I was joking around, but Stevens seemed a little serious when I said that. "Did I break some kind of law, or something, Sheriff? Having soil trucked down here, I mean?" Sheriff Stevens was silent for a long moment. Then he slapped his hand on his knee and laughed.

"Oh heck no, Joe!" he bellowed. "If your tomatoes are as good as this meal was, I might be having you bury some of that secret recipe in my garden next year." "Well Sheriff," I answered, "how about if I just give you some tomatoes from time to time instead. I can only tend one garden, these days." "That's a deal." he said, "Now I think I'd better get going. The other reason I came out, Joe —besides wanting to finally meet you and all- is that, well...the election is coming up next year. I'd sure like to think I could count on your vote. You and Angie." He stuck out a beefy hand and I shook it with a smile. "Sure thing Stan. Anything I can do to help your campaign, you just say the word, okay?"

Stan was putting on his jacket when Angie walked in with two paper grocery bags filled with food. "Stan, you take this home to your wife." She instructed him. "There's a box of macaroni in there. It's San Giorgio, the kind we get back home. And two quarts of gravy and some meatballs. And this box has six cannoli in it." Stan smiled widely at Anj's hospitality. "Now, don't you eat those cannoli on the way home. You share them with your missus!" Angie joked. Stan laughed and thanked us both and I walked out the door with him.

"Let me help you with the car door, Stan." I said. We walked to the driver's side of his Ford. "That's a real sweet family you got yourself there, Joe." He said. "I'm glad I stopped out to meet you today. Shaking my hand again, he said, "Really happy to have you as a neighbor, Joe. Real happy." I held the bags as he got in his car. "Drive carefully Sheriff!" I said as he backed out of my circle. He tooted the horn as he drove off. I turned to walk inside.

Son of a... I started to say to myself. Phil Lowery was peering through the venetian blinds again. And not even trying to hide it.

The Last Smart Man in Forest

"Dang it! Dang it, dang it dang it!" I yelled. "Dang that Joe Mezilli! And dang that spineless cousin of yours...the sheriff!" I guess I shouldn't have blamed Gladys for her cousin being sucked in by Joe Mezilli's charm, and I didn't feel any shame for it, he's her family, not mine. Gladys answered, "What on earth are you talking about Phil? What's Stan got to do with the Mezilli's?" "Well he's over there right now, supposed to be checking them out. But he just came out of the house and Mezilli handed him two grocery bags...probably full of money to keep him quiet and buy his favor!"

Gladys looked completely baffled. "Quiet about what, Phil?" "Quiet about the bodies!" I hissed. "What bodies? What does Stan have to do with them?" I was steaming. "What's he got to do with them? I'll tell you what he has to do with them, Gladys. I'll tell you." I grabbed my phone and scrolled through the pictures. I started showing her the pictures I took of Mezilli carrying bodies to his garden. "Why did you take a picture of Milledge's dog peeing in the bushes, Phil?" She asked.

"Oh...fiddlesticks! Forget about the dog for a minute, Gladys. Look at this one." I scrolled to the next picture. "That's Mezilli, and that there is Timmy Peppers, and they're carrying a body. A body wrapped in burlap!" Gladys looked a long time at my picture. Then she handed me the phone and said, real meekly, "I can't tell what that is, Phil. It's so blurry. I think you're just stirring up imaginary trouble again. Besides, I like Angie and Joe. I think they're sweet folks, and good neighbors, and this wild obsession of yours with the mafia is gonna get you in trouble."

I couldn't stand arguing with Gladys so I slunk out to the garage and stood in the back with the lights off, just watching the Mezilli house and planning on how I was gonna expose this Yankee mobster once and for all. *Mezilli...you ruthless scoundrel,* I thought to myself in disbelief, *you even got to my wife.* Then I stiffened up and whispered, "This is war."

I had to come up with a plan. I usually do my best thinking when I'm working with my hands. So I went out to the garage to try fixing the leaf blower again. Dang thing just won't start and when it does, it won't stay running. I like to make lists when I think. It helps me think. So as I saw it, I had two problems. One was that by Christmas morning, there'd be seven people sleeping with the fishes and I was the only one who cared enough to be upset about it. The other was that my neighbor was a mafia and nobody seemed to care much about that, neither. I had to solve the one problem immediately and then hope that I could solve the other one soon after that. After a few hours tinkering on the leaf blower I come up with a plan. It was a darned fine one too, I might add. Gladys and me was going to Mezill's Christmas Eve party!

12

La

Vigilia

Christmas came at last. I spent the month of December hanging lights on every square inch of the house, and most of the five acres. I had a cousin who lived in the suburbs of Philly and he had enough yard to make a Christmas display so big that people came from miles around just to see it. I always wanted to do that, because it felt like you were giving the Christmas spirit to the whole world, you know? I had every inflatable Christmas item I could find. I literally had seven miles of strings lights. I had a giant manger scene, Santa sliding down the chimney, angels, and reindeer. Man, it was fun.

Angie took care of the inside of the house. She has wonderful style, my wife. Every room but the laundry room had some sort of Christmas tree in it. Each bedroom, the guest rooms, the dining room, all of them. The crowning glory, of course, was the giant twelve foot Douglas Fir we bought for the great room. That was the only room with ceilings high enough for a tree that tall, something we never had in Philly. There were wreaths, and garland, and lights and, of course, a leg lamp in the picture window.   I had arranged flights for as many of my family as wanted to come, and I rented the Suburban for Tommy Fallone to drive my mom and dad and Nonna down. Nonna was only told that "Joey was sending a car and a driver to bring them to his house for Christmas." When she protested, my Old Man simply said, "We're doing Seven Fishes with Joseph this Christmas, momma. If you don't come, you'll be alone here." Nonna finally relented, and the trip was scheduled for December Twenty-First. I figured I'd give them two full days, in case Nonna and her bladder needed the extra time.

I wired Tommy five thousand bucks. Actually, I wired it to my cousin Arty and had him give it to Tommy in cash, because the Feds were still watching his checking account for any illicit activity. The poor kid was probably going to have to live with that for the rest of his life. I called Tommy a week before the trip. "Tommy," I said, "Take the money I sent over with Arty. Use it to buy yourself a nice suit. Black. Don't skimp either. You go to old Mr. Lagolo's shop and have him tailor a nice suit for you." Tommy was a little baffled at this. "Why, Joe?" he asked me, "Is Seven Fishes a formal affair down there in Virginia?" I laughed at that. "Seven Fishes is no affair at all in Virginia, Tommy. As far as I know, we might be the only family in this part of the state having *La Vigilia*."

"Then why the monkey-suit?" he asked. I explained: "Because Nonna will be on her best behavior only if she believes you are a professional driver. If she thinks you're Tommy Felonius from Shunk Street, she'll be peeing at every exit and taking pictures of every road-marker between Philly and Forest, and the trip will take three days. Now, if you want that..." "No!" Tommy said with a laugh, "No, No, No. I am well aware of Nonna Mezilli's road trip habits. I'll get the suit." "Good" I said, "Now...that suit should set you back a grand or so, since Mr. Lagolo isn't cheap. So you get yourself a few more nice changes of clothes, and you do some Christmas shopping for your family before you leave town. I sent my credit card with Arty as well...you put the expenses for the trip on that, don't use your own money. Anything else you need, you call me. Capicse?"

"I got it, Cuz." he said emphatically. He was silent for a minute, then he said softly, "Hey Joe...thanks for letting me do this. My first Christmas out and all. It's gonna be nice to be with some family again for the Holidays. Christmas sucked in Holmesburg." Tommy was pretty emotional when he said this. "Yo Cuz!" I said, trying to lighten his mood a bit. "What's Christmas without uncle Franny's baccala stew...Huh? Besides, you might not be thanking me after driving my folks and my grandmother down here." Tommy laughed. "Now, you get that suit and some clothes. Oh, and buy yourself a nice piece of luggage for the trip. You show up with your clothes in a garbage bag and I'm shipping you home on a Greyhound!" "Naaah, no Polish luggage." he said. "I'll get myself a nice suitcase. Thanks again Joe. I mean it. I'm really looking forward to this trip." "Me too, Paisan," I said, "We lost a lot of time, pal. This will be a good chance to just hang out."

Tommy said goodbye and hung up. I was thinking about how long he was away. The best part of his life. He was almost thirty-one when he and Nicky Bowties tried knocking off that ATM. He did thirteen years. By the time I was thirty-one, I had three boys and we were working on that little girl. I had a house. I'd been married for eleven years. I had weekend cookouts with my friends and beach trips and weddings and celebrated the births of friends' children. All those christenings, and birthday parties for our children, and the general feeling of growing up, Tommy'd missed that. He went in when all his friends were just getting started. He came out forty-three years old and way behind everyone else.

I missed Tommy when he was away. I wrote, and we visited every month. I put money on his commissary card so he could buy things. I sent him pictures of the family and the families of the kids we grew up with. I did what I could to help him pass the years. But he still lost a lot, and now he was a convicted felon, and if it hadn't been for Skip O'Brien being successful and giving him a decent job at the fish market, Tommy might be bagging groceries at the Acme, and living in a flop house somewhere. Usually, a guy with no prospects and no support system ends up back in the can because he gets desperate and does something stupid again. We were all determined not to let that happen to Tommy.

I was talking to Angie at breakfast one morning, in mid-December. "Anj" I began, "I've been thinking about Tommy Fallone." "Yeah?" she said, "Thinking about knocking off a bank?" Angie laughed at this. She loved Tommy as much as I did. She was friends with his sister Maria, and she knew Tommy was really just a dumb kid when he did what he did. But she has the same acerbic wit I have, and she likes to bust 'em now and then.

"No," I chuckled, "Thinking about helping him really rebuild his life. He's got the job with Skip, and he's living in our apartment on Oregon Avenue, but he's fourty-four now, he needs to feel like he's accomplished something in his life. He needs some success, at something he's good at." "Oh jeez, Joe," Angie laughed, "You're gonna get Stan Stevens to let him get away with knocking off an ATM? Help him deal with his unfinished business? Is this about closure, Joe?"

I literally shot coffee out of my nose. Angie could be the funniest person in the world when she was on a roll. When I stopped laughing, I said, "No Babe. Mikey Baldino told me that when Tommy was inside, he got a job in the woodshop. Turns out he's a heck of a carpenter. He'd get old house project magazines and he could duplicate the stuff like it was nothing. They eventually made him a crew leader on grounds maintenance." Anj shifted forward in her seat and got real close to me. She was smiling coyly. "What do you have in mind, Cuz?" she asked.

"Well," I continued, "I was thinking about buying some investment properties over by the college. I'd like to make them as cheap to rent as possible. Maybe find out from the school which students are from real hardship situations and give them their rent at a discount. Maybe free to the right ones...you know?" "Where does Tommy come in with this idea?" she asked. "Well, I was thinking I could bankroll him in his own business. He could get his contractor's license and do the work on the properties for us. Maybe buy a few to flip, as well. Let him get creative and do the work and put the profits in his own pocket. I think it would be good for him. He'd get away from the old element, and he'd be someplace where nobody knows his history but us, and he could make something for himself, instead of feeling like he owes Skip and us for what little he has."

Angie sat back and sipped her coffee. "It's a good idea, babe. I think he could use the fresh start. You'll maybe let me do the interior designs, hmm?" I had her now. Anj loves designing a home. We'd be great partners in this, and Tommy would have a real second chance at life. "Yeah, babe." I said, "You and me and Tommy Felonius, building our empire. I'll talk to him over Christmas. Okay, I gotta get going. I'm having the boat winterized today. I'll be back at dinner.

I walked out into the bright winter sunrise. In a few days, my entire family would be here, all of them seeing this place for the first time. I was looking forward to this like maybe no other Christmas before. It was going to be wonderful. I had invited the neighbors to drop by on Christmas Eve as well. I wanted to show them a really good time...Philly style. The Milledge's said they were coming. The Erickson's. Even though Larry Erickson likes to pretend he's in the mob every single time he sees me and he talks to me like I'm "Vinny the Goombah," and it irritates me like nothing else. Larry is laboring under the delusion that, simply because I'm Italian, I am mobbed up, have people's legs broken, settle arguments with a gun, and arrange people's deaths. To be honest, it gets on my nerves and I'm often tempted to just play to it and throw a scare into him. But he's a good guy at heart and so I try to tolerate it.

All the neighbors had responded and most said they were coming. All except Phil. Now to be honest, part of me was glad he hadn't gotten back and I was thinking of quietly ignoring it so he wouldn't show up. But we're gonna be neighbors for a long time and so I thought I'd reach out to him once again. When I walked outside to leave for the marina, Phil was in his driveway, picking up his newspaper.

"Yo! Phil!" I yelled, walking toward him across the street. I walked over to him and said "Good Morning." He muttered a greeting and I figured he just wasn't a morning guy. "So Phil, listen, everyone else is coming on Christmas Eve, but we haven't heard from you and Gladys. You coming over for Seven Fishes, or what?" I was pretty cheerful about this, but Phil went white. It's hard to tell with Phil, because other than Larry Erickson, Phil is the whitest human being in the world. Erickson is Swedish, so he has an excuse.

"Well...Uh...I haven't really talked to Gladys about it yet." Phil stammered, "I'll, uh, I'll discuss it with her today. I'll have her call your wife either way...'kay?" "Sure Phil," I said politely, "but try to stop by for a little bit at least. I'd hate for you to miss it. I'd love you to meet my folks, and my grandmother. They won't be around forever...ya 'know?" Phil started coughing like he was having a heart attack. "Jeez, Phil...You okay?" He coughed for a long minute and looked up at me with watery eyes. "I'll see what we can do." he said. He sort of snarled when he said it and I wondered what the problem was. "Well...okay, Phil. I have to run. Let Angie know, okay?"

I drove out to Smith Mountain Lake and the marina where my boat was being stored. Now, my boat is too big for the lake. It's a fifty-four foot Hatteras with twin Cummins diesels. It's a straight-up, deep-sea rig. But the only marina in the area that was equipped to winterize her was at the lake, so I had her delivered there. In the spring, I'm taking her over to Hampton, to a slip I leased on the James River side that opens out into the Chesapeake Bay.

It was a longer drive to get to her than when we kept her at Fortesque, NJ, but it's a straight shot on highway 64 and still only about two hours. Angie and I had decided to buy a smaller boat for the lake. Smith Mountain Lake is only thirty minutes from my house, and we realized that in the long run, we'd be spending more time there than on the big boat at the beach.

On my way out, I called Skip O'Brien, to discuss the idea I had about Tommy. "Yo! The Caviar Kid! What's up Paisan?" Skip is always up early to meet the trucks at his warehouse to oversee the off-loading. He has an eye for anything that looks bad. Bad fish would ruin his reputation. Skip worked very hard for that rep of his. Every fish man in the Italian Market buys from him, as do most of the seafood restaurants. Skip is obsessed with perfection where his business is concerned. "What's happening down there, Joey Trucks?" I laughed out loud. "Maddonn, Skip, you know when was the last time anybody called me that?" Skip chuckled, "Well don't blame me, you're the one who moved to Mayberry."

There comes a point in your time as a South Philly guy that you shed the nickname. You keep it all through your childhood, then usually when you get married, and your pals get married, they stop using nicknames for a while. Then sometimes in your mid-thirties, you start reminiscing about the old days and start calling each other by the nicknames again. It's comforting. But for some reason...maybe the position I had in the neighborhood and with the business and all, they never resumed calling me "Joey Trucks" In fact the only people who still called me that were Skip and the guys, and Angelo Cataldi. It was actually really great hearing it again.

"Skip," I said, "Let's talk about Tommy." Skip got serious. "Yeah, that's a good idea," he said, "I was going to call you about him anyway. I think Tommy is getting restless working with me. He's a great worker, you know? He appreciates everything you and I have done for him. But as it turns out, he's a creative guy and a heck of a carpenter. I had him build a deck for me at my beach place...you should see it, Joey. It looks like something Bob Vila created." "So I heard." I said to Skip. "Mikey Baseball told me about it. He told me about Tommy rising to the top when he was inside at Holmesburg, because he was such a good carpenter. That's what I want to talk to you about."   I laid out my plan for Skip. I told him about buying investment properties and getting Tommy his license and his own crew of guys. Skip agreed it was a great idea. "But Skip," I said to him, "I don't want to take him from you if he's a great worker. But you're telling me he doesn't seem happy and if he doesn't have a real future with you -and you're okay with it- then we'll do it." Skip assured me that he was all for the idea. "Listen, Cuz, Tommy's one of us. So that means he has a job with me as long as he needs it. But I want the guy to be happy. He still has half a life left, you know? So whatever you'se decide...it's good with me.
Absolutely."

"Okay Skip, I'm gonna talk to him about it when he drives my folks down here at Christmas. Speaking of which...you got my fish ready to send down?" Skip laughed, "You better believe it. I'm heading over to get the dry ice tomorrow and shipping it Wednesday. You'll be looking at a garage full of baccala and a crate of smelts and calamari. Anything else you're gonna need?" I thought for a moment, "Can you get us some good blue claw crabs this time of year?" Skip laughed, then in a playful, smug tone he said, "Joey Trucks...I'm the Caviar Kid, remember? Uncle Squatch can get you a mermaid and the Loch Ness monster if you have the cash!" Then he said, "I'll call my guy down in the Gulf, They bring in crabs all year long. Six dozen be enough?" "Yeah that'd be great, Skip," I told him. "Really great. Call me with the final number and I'll give you my card. Thanks pal. I'll talk to you again before Christmas. Say hello to Joanne and the kids."

I clicked off the phone just as I was pulling into the St. Georges Marina at Smith Mountain Lake. I drove around to the storage yard and there she sat...my pride and joy. Fifty-four feet of fish-chasing beauty. The Emily A. I named her after the two best girls in my life...my daughter and her beautiful momma. They were just putting on the shrink-wrap around the hull when I pulled up.

The yard is owned by Pat Sylvester and his family. Pat grew up here at the lake and his father is a tremendous marine mechanic. They were the only people with the facilities capable of winterizing such a big boat. I rolled up to where she was sitting in the trailer and hopped out. "How's she coming Patrick?" I asked. Pat leaned over the rail and waved. "Hey Joe." He said, "Just about finished up. The fuel is stabilized, batteries are inside in storage with chargers on them. We painted the hull and detailed the cabins and staterooms. Once she's wrapped, she'll be good until you ship her to Hampton. She's a beautiful boat, by the way. I've always been partial to Hatteras, myself." He climbed down the ladder and we walked into his office.

"You know, you could just keep her here," he laughed. "Smith Mountain Lake is plenty deep enough and I could sell you a slip at a good price." I smiled at the notion. "Yeah but the lake isn't big enough. I could never open her up." "True...true." Pat responded. I got you the brochures on the houseboats and the runabouts that you asked for. You just let me know what you want to look at and I'll call the rep and find where they have some nearby." Pat is a responsive, conscientious businessman. He knows what boat owners like. I appreciated that. I'd only been out here a few times but I'd really been impressed with him and his father, both.

"You have a bill ready for me, Pat?" I asked. "Yep, right here. Now you're going to store until mid-March?" "Yes," I told him, "That's my plan. Then we'll have her trucked over to Hampton and she'll stay there." Pat handed me the bill and I wrote him a check. I picked up my copy and headed out to my truck. On the way home, I called Jannie, our realtor. I figured I'd have her check on the "fixer-upper" market. I asked her to be watching out for the availability of something we could rent out, and a few we could flip. She said she would, and that she and Kirk and the kids would be over for Christmas Eve.

That was settled for now. In a week, Tommy would be here with my folks and Nonna and we'd discuss what he was going to do for the second half of his life. The house was ready, the food was being shipped, and my family was on their way. This was going to be the best Christmas in a long time.

Over the River and Through the Woods

Christmas was only three days away. I called Tommy and made sure the final details had been worked out for the trip down. I called Mr. Tripoletti at the pharmacy on Shunk and asked him to send a couple of Xanax over to my dad. If worse came to worse, he could drug the old girl again and get her down here. Tommy called me on the twenty-first of December. They were loading up and heading out. So he tells me they were on their way. If all went well, they would be here by dinner. I knew better than think all would go "well." Not with Nonna in the car. I told Tommy to take Eighty-One South and avoid the whole D.C. corridor traffic jam. That way he wouldn't be paralyzing the old girl with the Baltimore tunnel. The only bridge on this trip would be the Tidings bridge at Havre de Grace. It's straight and flat, so she won't ever lose sight of the road. He did as he was told, but she still had to pee every forty-seven seconds or so. Then, once they hit Nelson County, she saw the signs for "The Walton's" museum and made Tommy stop, under the guise of another pee break.

Nonna loved The Waltons. So much so, that when we were kids, my friends and I had a game where we made up Italian names to replace the characters on the show. We called it, *If The Waltons had Been Italian...* We had characters like Poppa and Mamma of course. Nonna and Nonno, obviously. But the kid's names were classics. Elizabeth was "Elisabeta" Jim-Bob was Jimmy-Roberto (There's no real Italian version of "James") Ben was "Biaggio" a little side note on this one...Nicky Bowties once cracked that "Biaggio" on the Waltons was the result of an illicit affair between John Walton Sr. and Sylvia Mastofione, my dad's office manager. The group of us went silent for a second and then I threw a pretty bad beating on him for it. I never liked Nicky after that and he felt that same way. I always suspected that he'd rolled over on Tommy because of my cleaning his clock that day. I can never be sure, but you didn't disrespect Sylvia and Benny. Not when I was around.

Anyway, next was Mary Ellen, who we named "Maria Elaina," then Jason, whom we simply called Lenti, derived from the Italian word for freckles, Lentiggini, because he had 'em, I had to ask Nonna what the word was. Of course the star of the show was John-boy. At first we called him "Giovanni-boy" which wasn't very funny. The Italian word for boy is "ragazzo" and "Giovanni-Raggazo" is too cumbersome to be funny. So –being twelve and thinking this is hysterical- we called him "Johnny Rags." Sort of an amalgam of the Italian and the American. I made the mistake once while watching the show with Nonna, of saying outloud, "Hey look, it's Johnny Rags!" I had to cook up some elaborate story about that one or she'd have figured out the game my friends and I were playing.

So now you can understand how enamored she was to have stopped at the Walton's Museum on Nelson County, Va, and why it made the trip last almost nine hours.

By the time she finally said goodnight to John-boy, it was 7PM, and they still had about 90 minutes left to go. Tommy called me again at 9PM. They were turning down my street, he said. "Get out here!" he said as he hung up. Angie and I and the kids were waiting on the porch when the black Suburban rolled up the circular driveway. Tommy came to a stop and jumped out to open the doors. He was shaking his head and looked pale around the lips. Pop hopped out and helped my mom out of the truck. Then he opened the door and started to get Nonna. I stepped in and said, "I got her,

Pop, you take momma inside. We have food in the oven for you."

My dad looked relieved. I'm guessing Nonna drove him nuts. I helped Nonna from the car and she gave me a kiss on the cheek. The kids came over and hugged her dutifully...all except Emily, who hugged her like she was a long lost puppy. Emmy loved Nonna, and had a different relationship with her than the boys did.

Emmy walked her into the house and I helped Tommy with the bags. "You look good in that suit, Tommy." I said, punching him in the arm. "Yeah, well it's okay I guess," He said. "But this trip...Maddonn this trip!" I laughed and asked him, "What happened, the old girl's dam break?" "No, no water damage." he said, "But somewhere around Harper's Ferry, she remembered who I am." Tommy told me how it went down. "Oh you're Rose Fallone's boy Thomas, aren't you?' she said, "the one who went to Holmesburg for robbing a bank." Tommy was trying not to laugh at himself. He does a great impersonation of my grandmother.

"I swear, from that moment on, she was calling the shots, Joe." Tommy shook his head. "Stop here, Thomas. Stop there Thomas. Thomas I'm hungry, do they have wedding soup here, Thomas? I want some wedding soup." When I tried telling her that we needed to hurry and get here, she'd start with the guilt-trip. 'Oh!' she'd say, 'Oh how your momma cried when you went away, Thomas. Every day she'd go to mass and say prayers for you. The other people in the neighborhood would mutter under their breath when she walked in, but I stayed with her. She was a wonderful mother, Thomas.' Maddonn, Joey...I wanted to slit my wrists!" Tommy was laughing about it now, but I imagined it was very awkward for him at the time.

I put an arm around his shoulder. "Tommy...you're a champ. C'mon inside, Anj made Osso Buco for you, special." This made Tommy smile. He loved Osso, and Anj made it better than anyone. We carried the luggage to the guest rooms and sat down to dinner.

Tommy was having his first Christmas with anything like a family since he was 31. It was a time for celebrating. Christmas Eve was only a couple of days away now and with it would come Dei Festa, de Sette Pesci. The Holy Feast of Seven Fishes. My family was either here already, or on their way.

All was right with the world.

The Christmas Eve Massacre
(Joey Trucks Makes His Move)

"Gladys, get over here!" I whispered. Gladys came from the kitchen. As she entered the living room, where I was standing, she turned on the light. "Why are you sitting in the dark, Phil?" She said. "And why are you whispering?" I tried not to punch myself in the face. "Gladys!" I whispered loudly, "Turn off that infernal light, and lower for voice, for the love of God!" Gladys stood there, like a deer in the headlights for about 3 seconds. Then she turned off the light and walked over to where I was standing near the sofa in our living room, looking between the blinds at my murderous, mobster, neighbor.

"Phil," she asked again, "Why are you whispering?" "Why am I whispering? Because I don't want Mezilli to know I'm watching him, that's why!" How can this woman be so thick? "Phil, he's across the street and it's December 21. The windows are closed. You think he can hear us?" She made a good point. "Gladys listen to me...I just saw him deliver three of the seven victims." Gladys cocked her head like a Labrador again. "What victims, Phil?" She was sounding sarcastic. "The victims, Gladys. The victims. The seven people who are going to sleep with the fishes on Christmas Eve. I saw them. Here have a look." Gladys looked through the slit in the blinds.

"You see that young fella there in the suit? He drove the Suburban, so I'm guessing that's his paisano." Gladys said, "What's a paisano?" I shook my head. "Gladys, did you not pay attention to Goodfellas or The Sopranos or The Godfather, at all?" Paisano is what them mafias call their friends." I explained. "That one wearing the suit is the guy

255

our murderin' neighbor arranged to kill his parents and his grandmother. His grandmother." I hissed. "That heartless, ruthless animal has four more coming, I 'spect. And they're gonna all get whacked on Christmas Eve."

"He's going to hit them? Like a pinata?" Gladys questioned. "What on earth are you talking about, Gladys?" I said, trying hard not to start smacking my head against the wall. "Well, you said he was going to 'whack' them. Like whacking a baseball? Or playing 'Whack-a-Mole?'" How our kids survived childhood with this woman is amazing. "Gladys, how did you ever figure out how to boil water? When them mafias are gonna kill somebody they use a code word. They say "whack." He's gonna whack seven people on Christmas Eve and make them sleep with the fishes." I explained. Then –because I knew it was coming anyway- I explained what "sleep with the fishes" means.   "So he's gonna kill these people on Christmas Eve? Gladys asked. "Yes," I said, exhausted from the amount of thought power I had to expend here. Gladys was quiet for a minute. Then she asked me, "But he's having an open house Christmas party that night. Their house will be full of people from about 7PM until midnight. When's he gonna kill them all?" "I don't know, Gladys!" How the heck am I supposed to know? I'm doing my best to expose this killer as it is, I can't think of everything! Maybe the party will be his alibi somehow."

Then it hit me. The party. We'll go to that party –as much as I don't want to go- and I'll keep real close to them poor souls he plans on whacking. I'll saved their durned lives, that's what I'll do. That's just what I'll do! "Gladys!" I said emphatically, "Tomorrow, you call Mrs. Mezilli and you inform her that we'll be coming to that 'Christmas Party' they're going to be throwing. You tell her we'll be there. I'll get my proof at the party, that's for sure!"

Gladys told me she would tell Angie Mezilli the next morning that we were coming to the party. "Heck," I said, "I should just walk over there right now and tell him myself" Gladys looked at the clock and said "Phil you can't go over there now...it's ten-thirty!" I know that Gladys, but heck, Joe and his hitman friend from Philadelphia are still standing out there on the porch. In fact they're looking right over here at us. Good thing I'm so good at this or he'd see me. Look at them over there...drinking coffee and smoking big cigars like Tony Soprano himself. Nobody but them mafias do that" "Nobody but mobsters smoke cigars and drink coffee Phil?" I heard in a whisper over my shoulder. I turned to look at Gladys, "You tell her we'll be there. I'm gonna get my proof at that party."

The Redemption of Tommy Felonious

"You had one of these since you've been out?" I asked Tommy as I lit the Presidente. We were sitting on my front porch, catching up after Tommy feasted on his absolute favorite dish in the world. "No, Skip doesn't smoke 'em. And I haven't felt right about spending the money on something for myself since...you know." I felt Tommy's embarrassment. I needed to put his mind at rest. "Tommy...listen. Nobody who loves you holds that stuff against you. You got that, Cuz? That was a one-time mistake. It was a big stupid one, I'll give you that. But that was over twenty years ago. You more than paid your debt. Everyone else has let it go. So it's okay for you to do the same."

Tommy was quiet. His voice broke as he turned to look at me. "Thanks Joey. Thanks a lot. That means the world to me. It's hard...ya know? I mean I was gone during the best times

257

of a man's life. The years when you become something." Tommy paused, took a deep breath, and stared at the glowing ash of his cigar. "Look at me, Joe. I'm forty-four years old. I'm a convicted felon. I've been in a federal pen a third of my life. What the heck am I going to become?"

I wanted to handle this delicately. I didn't want Tommy to think I was giving him charity. That would suck whatever remained of his pride right out of him. "You aren't happy working for Caviar?" I asked. Tommy took a pull on the Presidente, paused, blew it out slowly and said. "Skip? I love Skip. He's one of us, ya know? But c'mon...there's no future for me on the docks and in his warehouse. Skip has kids. He's gonna set up a dynasty with his boys. He keeps his Uncle around but other than that, his goal is to have all four of the boys running the show by the time he turns sixty.

"Squatch still works with Skip?" I said, a little surprised. "I didn't know that. I figured him to be retired in Avalon NJ, by now." "No, he still works with Skip." Tommy answered, "Skip says the Squatch knows shellfish better than anyone alive. So he lets him do the purchasing for that. Plus the old guys who buy from Skip remember him from the Italian Market days. He's an icon in that industry." I chuckled. "Still hairy as Chewbacca?" I said, smiling around my cigar. "Oh yeah," Tommy replied. "And he's taken to wearing those tank-tees in the summer. He gets sweaty and the shirt sticks to him and he looks like a beaver pelt wrapped in a shower curtain." We both had a long laugh at that.

After a minute of laughter, and another of silence. I looked over at Tommy and nudged him a little. "This is nice, eh Cuz?" Tommy smiled sweetly. He always had a sweet smile. "Yeah...yeah it is." I was really enjoying the moment when I glanced across the street and saw the kitchen light playing Phil Lowery's silhouette against his living room blinds, again. "Son of a...I swear I am going to really start to hate that guy!" Tommy look startled. "You don't hate anybody, Cuz. What the heck are you talking about?" "Tommy," I said. "Real slow and natural, take a look across the street, diagonal to my house. You see the guy peeping?"

Tommy casually looked over at Phil's house. "Ha!" he laughed, "You brought Mrs. Begnetti down with you?" I smiled at that. "No, paisan. This guy's worse than old Mrs. B ever was. His name is Phil Lowery, and for whatever reason, he has seen to it that I don't do anything over here without him peeping. If he's not peeping, he's snooping around in my garage when I'm back there." "You mean he hides and spies on you?" Tommy asked. "No, not quite." I answered. "But he'll return a piece of lawn equipment or a tool and then linger around, listening to conversations. He drives me nuts. I've reached out to the guy as much as I can figure out how to. I think he just thinks he's some sort of private eye."

Tommy smiled wistfully. "You gonna cover the windows with newspaper?" "You remember that, huh?" I said. Tommy nodded. "Yeah, that was the summer that...you know. Nicky and me." I felt a wave of sadness roll over me. I knew what Tommy meant. The summer we decided to teach Mrs. B. her lesson about peeping was the same summer Tommy and Nicky tried knocking off the ATM. That was the last summer he was on the block until he got out. In fact, the whole newspaper affair happened only about a week before his arrest. That was Tommy's last freedom and he was only thirty-one at the time. Now here he was, fifteen years later, smoking a cigar with me on my front porch in Virginia.

"That was a long time ago, Tommy." Tommy stared at his feet, and he was slow to answer. "Yeah. It was. Half a lifetime. The good half, ya know?" I thought for a few seconds before asking him the next question. "Tommy," I

259

began, "One thing I never asked you. Not in all this time." Tommy knew what was coming. "Why?" he said, "hell I don't know, Cuz. Seriously. I thought about it a million times while I was inside. Why the hell did I let Nicky Bowties talk me into this? Why did I have to try the endaround and hit an ATM?" I let Tommy talk this out. I think he was still trying to reason it within himself.

"I guess," Tommy continued, "I guess it was just watching you guys all become successful. Becoming grownups and all. Something inside me felt like I was never going to get anywhere. I mean, you had the trash trucks. And even thought you really didn't want to join in the business with Giuseppe and your dad, it was obvious that you were going to do really well for yourself. Plus you had Angie and, to be honest...god damn Cuz! You hit the lottery with that girl." Tommy blushed immediately. But he knew I wouldn't be offended.

Tommy went on, "Skip was already brokering with his uncle Squatch and he'd gone to college. Mikey had gotten his insurance license, Dominucce had his job as a teacher. My crew was growing up and moving on. I guess I felt like youse were all gonna grow up without me." I didn't know whether to speak or not. I sat there silently for a few long minutes while Tommy turned this stuff over in his head. "I guess I just wanted to do something big. I don't remember if I ever even considered whether I'd get away with it. I guess maybe just the thought of trying...you know?"

Tommy took a sip of his coffee. He stared down at the ground and poked the concrete on my front steps with a little piece of a stick. "I don't know, Joey," he said, "I was scared. I was scared I was never going to be anything more than Tommy Fallone Jr. Some mook from the neighborhood that everyone called 'Tommy Felonious', who never amounted to what his friends did. Maybe get a job driving a delivery truck like the old man, or work down at the Navy yard like everyone else's father did. I was thirty-one, I'd never done anything at all with my life, and Nicky Bowties made it sound like a good idea."

I let a few long minutes pass. Tommy seemed to be sorting this out in his own soul for the first time. Finally I asked him, "Tommy, why did you not speak up to the D.A? Why did you just let Nicky roll over on you like that and not give your side of things? Didn't they offer you a deal too?" Tommy looked at the ash on the end of his cigar for a long time. Then he looked at me. "You remember when they booked us and you and Anj came to the Roundhouse to see me and check on making bail for me?" I told him I did. "Well," he said, "I was so embarrassed when I saw you and your wife coming in to sign papers to bail me out. Angie was pregnant with Petey and came to the jail anyway. I knew what they set bond at and how much that cost you. I was pretty low at that point. I guess I felt like I deserved prison. So I got silent and took my lumps."

I didn't say anything. I couldn't understand Tommy's reasoning for that, except that, to be honest, I'd never felt like a failure to that degree in my whole life. I'd swung and missed more than a few times – we all have. But I have never been humiliated at my own reflection. Tommy had been, by that point. While I didn't comprehend it or understand it, I somehow grasped the pain it made him feel.

"Well, listen, Paisan," I said, finally breaking the silence. I have an idea that you might like. Tomorrow, on the drive to the airport to pick up everyone else, we'll discuss it. But we'd better get inside and get some rest. The plane arrives in Roanoke at 10 AM. We need to leave here at 8:45." Tommy stood up and without a hint of warning, gave me a big hug. "It feels like Christmas again, Cuz." He said.

And it did.

Ala Familia!

The next morning, Tommy and I were up early and getting ready for the drive in to Roanoke to pick up my cousins. We were sitting in the kitchen, me, Angie, and Tommy, drinking coffee when my father came downstairs.

"You're up early, Pop." I said, "Momma snoring again?" The Old Man laughed and reached for a coffee cup. "Naah." he said. "Just felt like getting an early jump on the day. There's lots to see around here. We got in so late last night I really didn't get the walking tour."

I filled his cup and handed him some of Angie's homemade biscotti. "Well Tommy and I are driving out to Roanoke to pick up everyone else at the airport. Once we get back, we'll give you the tour, Pop." My dad was already giving Anj a hug and a peck on the cheek and he smiled, "I'm sure my beautiful daughter in law can show us around, son." My dad, the ladies' man. "Just the same," I said, "We'll take a ride out to the hunting lodge this afternoon after every one is here and settled in. I want to show you around out there, Pop. It's the most beautiful place you ever saw."

Tommy and I grabbed refills and headed for the door. "The plane lands at ten A.M." I called back to the Old Man, "We should be back here by around one, Pop. Then we'll have lunch and go for a ride." We climbed into the Suburban and headed out for Roanoke. From my house in Forest, it's about an hour to the Roanoke airport. Tommy and I would have time to discuss his future.

We rode along in silence for a few minutes until we reached the interstate, and headed for Roanoke. Then I gave Tommy the thumbnail on my idea about the construction business. "Listen, Tommy...I wanna run something by you." I began. Tommy turned toward me and was listening intently from the beginning. "I know you aren't particularly thrilled working for Skip. And I know you became quite a carpenter when you were inside." Tommy smiled shyly. It must have been awkward for him to be receiving a compliment after all he'd done and seen.   "Well, here's my idea." I started to lay out the plan for him. "Angie and I were thinking about buying some rental properties up in Lynchburg, by the school. It would be a good opportunity for me to help out some students by keeping the rent low, and I thought you could manage them for me. Do the renovations, take care of them once they're rented. You know." Tommy was quiet and attentive. This instantly struck a chord in him. "I also want to maybe buy a few properties to flip. Angie needs a creative outlet, you know how talented she is in interior design, and I thought we'd make you a partner on the properties." Tommy shifted in his seat. "Joe, that takes money. I don't have anything, you know that." I smiled at Tommy. "I know, Cuz. Anj and I figured you could invest some sweat equity into the properties. We figured you give us a price on the work, and maybe we knock ten percent off each job and you hold ten percent interest instead. It wouldn't take more than a few before you're a full partner, Tommy. And no handouts. It's something you really earn yourself. I know that matters to you."

Tommy's voice broke a little. "You'd do that for me Cuz? I mean, you and Anj don't need the extra money that investment properties would bring you. Essentially you're staking me to a business. Why would you do that, Joe?" I knew I couldn't fool Tommy. What he lacked in business acumen or common sense, he made up for in transparency. "You're right, Tommy," I said. "I don't really need to do this...but I want to. It helps you, but it's not a handout. It helps some college students, and it gives Anj a chance to get creative again. This isn't a freebie, Cuz. This is business." Tommy blew out a breath. "Man. I'd love to have my own truck and my own tools and a real crew. I've been reading home improvement magazines every night since I've been home. There's a thousand ideas I have." He paused, "Yeah Joey...I'd love this chance."

I smiled at Tommy as we turned off 460 onto the airport access road. "I already talked to Skip. He's all for the idea if you want to do it. I think the first thing we need to do is get you set up down here in a place of your own and then we can go looking for property. The apartment over our garage is huge, Cuz, and it's empty. I don't want you down here alone. You can move in there right away."

We pulled up to the arriving passenger gates and my Cousin Toni and her husband and my cousin George were there. Uncle Franny and Uncle Tony came along. I wondered until the very minute they walked out the doors if they'd actually make the trip. Various other cousins were in tow and a few more were driving down today as well. We piled them all in the big Suburban and headed for home.   The trip home was loud with laughter and jokes. We arrived back at the house with my favorite Sinatra Christmas record playing and my family singing along. Angie and the kids came out and met everyone on the porch while Tommy and Nick and I carried the luggage inside. I was walking in with the last suitcase when I looked across the street and saw Phil Lowery standing in his garage, back in the shadows where he always stands, watching my family coming for a visit. I'd had about enough of this guy.

I walked in the front door and called out to Angie, "Anj! Yo Anj, did the Lowery's ever get with you? Are they coming for Christmas Eve?" Anj could tell I was upset. "Yeah Babe, why, what's wrong?" she asked. "I'm just tired of looking across the street and seeing Phil Lowery peeping and thinking nobody sees him peeping. It's moved from annoying to downright obnoxious and I've had about enough." Of course my cousin George only needed to hear that someone was messing with our family and he was ready to go knock on his door. "Yo, Joe!" He said, "Let's go see this guy right now..." I had to stop him from putting his jacket back on and marching across the street. George is probably my closest male cousin, and more like a brother to me than anything else. He is the most fearsome defender of our family and it's something I love him for dearly.

"No, Cuz, I can't do down here like we would do back home," I said, "It's different." I decided to find a better way to send my message to Phil Lowery. But I had to think of something that would do the job, but still be innocent enough to not harm anyone. I didn't want to make an enemy, just lose a peeper. That would come later. I decided that the best thing I could do was watch him closely at the Christmas party. See what his likes and dislikes were. Maybe I could find something in there to make my point about his incessant peeping. I had to make sure he came to the party.

The rest of the day was spent hanging out with my family, showing them the house, and taking the men to the hunting camp. That turned into a friendly shooting contest between my father, his brothers, (both of whom had military experience) and me and my cousins. We had a blast. Literally. I hadn't spent that sort of time with my uncles and my dad maybe in my whole life. Turns out George is a heck of a shot. We got caught up in the moment and started a little campfire and spent time just talking and reminiscing. Before long, it was dinner time and we headed for home. My dad was riding along in the back and I heard him bragging to my uncles about the hunting land and the house, and how well I'd done for them all in business. It was the first time I'd ever heard him brag to his brothers about me. I knew he'd done it before, but I'd never heard it.

I caught his eye in my rear view mirror and he winked at me. A big show of emotion for the Old Man.

We pulled into the driveway at 6PM. Emily came outside with Nonna in tow, covered in flour, and telling us about how they were making cookies. We walked inside and the house smelled great. Angie had been making sausage and peppers and meatballs and the house smelled like Nonna's house always did. I imagine it was because the old girl had lent plenty of her influence to the evening's meal.

We had a big feast and then we sat around by the fireplace and told my children and their cousin Nicky great stories about how it was when we were growing up in Philly. We told them all about the nicknames we'd given each other, and the funny games we'd invented. We told them embarrassing stories about their grandparents and their great uncles. Toward the end of the night, I broke out the Anisette and Uncle Tony picked up one of my guitars and started playing old Italian songs very quietly. Then, Nonna did something I hadn't heard her do since I was a little boy. She sang.

She sang in Italian to my daughter. It was a song I remember her singing when I was very little. Younger than Emmy is now. It was about her hometown and the smell of the flowers in the springtime. Uncle Tony had tears in his eyes when she was done. So did Nonna. It was a very special night and I was really glad we'd made arranged for her to be there with us for Christmas.

Phil Lowery Saves Christmas

"Gladys if you don't hurry up, we'll be late for the party!" I said. I say this all the time, except it's not usually a party we're late for. Usually its church, or dinner, or going to a Hillcats game. We don't go to parties much, Gladys and me. We stay put most of the time, but whenever we do go someplace, well, you can count on us being late.

Most time I just deal with it. I sit in the car and honk every ten minutes or so while I listen to Rush Limbaugh, but tonight...tonight we just can't be late. Not when there's lives depending on it. We had to be over at the Mezilli's house promptly at 7PM when the party started. Every minute we were late was a chance for that ruthless killer and his prison buddy to do their evil deeds and make them seven folks sleep with the fishes. I still can't even bring myself to think about it. How can a man kill his own kin...on Christmas Eve? But then I seen enough of *The Sopranos* to know how cold blooded them mafias really are. Plenty cold blooded.

Gladys was finally ready at 7PM. "Dear God in heaven, woman, can't you ever be on time?" I barked. Gladys looked like she'd hit me if she hadn't known her place in the home. I'm the man, and when I say we're gonna be someplace at a certain time, Gladys knows she needs to hop to it. It's just that she forgets sometimes. Anyways, we finally made it across the street and to the Mezilli's. The front door was open and there was a note on the glass storm door. "Come on in!" it said. We rang the doorbell dutifully. "Phil," Gladys whispered, "The note says to just go on in, and I..." "Gladys!" I snapped, "We knock. We ain't a friendly basis with these folks yet and I don't walk into a man's house uninvited under any circumstances. I was raised right!" "But Phil," Gladys whispered, "We...were invited."

Joe Mezilli opened the door with a smile. "Phil!" he said, "You didn't have to ring that bell! Come on in. Buon Natale!" "Bone *who*?" I asked him. "Buon Natale, it means Merry Christmas in Italian." Mezilli explained. "Oh, well Buon Natale, to you too." I was trying to be cordial and pleasant so he wouldn't suspect I was really here to thwart his evil plot. Joe took our coats and escorted us into the dining room.

He made his way around the room, introducing us to his family. "Phil and Gladys Lowery live across the street," he said. "He's the guy who reminds me of Mrs. Begnetti." I don't know who Mrs. Begnetti is, but it must be good to be compared to her because all of Joe's family laughed and smiled and shook their heads. Whoever she is, they must really think she's a hoot. *That's good,* I thought, *I put them at ease.* Joe continued; "Phil, Gladys, this is my Mom and Dad, Giuseppe and Annalisa Mezilli." I shook hands with the soon-to-be-deceased parents of my neighbor, Al Nitti Jr. "And this," Joe said, walking me over to an old lady sitting in a chair, with Joe's little daughter on her knee, "Is my Nonna...Sussana Marie Mezilli, the matriarch of our familia." The way he said it, acting like he loved her and all, it just broke my heart. Here she was, holding his daughter on her lap and before the clock struck midnight she'd be sleeping with the fishes. Feet first. Her and six other poor bastards. She seemed like such a sweet old lady, why would he want to whack her. *Well she's the matriarch*, I thought, he even said so. *Maybe he can't rise to power in his family until she's dead.* I was caught up in these thoughts while Joe introduced us to the rest of his family and guests. His family, Angie's family. There was a whole lot of mobster types in that living room on Christmas Eve. It always baffled me how they could be such religious, family oriented people and be killers at the same time. *Well your cover ain't foolin' me, Mezilli,* I thought to myself. *I'm here to make sure your family lives to see another day.* I spent the next few hours practically standing next to Joe's mother and father and grandmother. I didn't let them out of my sight for a minute, just in case Joe was trying to lure them away and do the whackin'. I stood vigil next to them like the palace guard. Old Man Mezilli is actually a nice fella, and it troubled me that I knew his fate and he didn't. *This poor man is gonna be dead in a few hours, unless I can stop it,* I thought. *How am I going to do that?* The evening actually went pretty well. The neighbors all came at various points in the night. Larry Erickson brought that hideous lutefisk he always tries pawning off on us every Christmas. I don't know how anyone can eat that stuff. I reckon you gotta get a little drunk first and then close your eyes and just swallow it down. Joe was telling me about the different dishes they had and what it meant to eat *baccala*. "You ever had baccala, Phil?" He asked me. "Baccala...ain't he that feller on The Sopranos? The one who played with the trains and married Tony's sister?" It seems nobody else in the room thought that was a fair question, because they seemed to go silent and look at me funny.

"The Sopranos was a TV show, Phil," Mezilli said, "Baccala is salted Cod. We eat a lot of it but especially on Christmas Eve. It's essential to Seven Fishes." There it was. That code again. I can't believe he just says it out loud like nobody would know. This fella has some nerve, I'll tell you. It's bad enough to plan on killing your family on Christmas Eve but to say it right in front of them...that takes some brass nuggets. *Funny,* I thought, *nobody seemed to notice, and if they did, they don't seem to care.*

Then it hit me...they're all in on it! *Oh Lord!'* I thought, *they all know about the killin! All of them except the victims obviously. They're all in on it!* Now I had to watch them all. *Where the hell is Peppers?* I thought, *Peppers can watch a few of them, and Hank Milledge. I need Hank.* Joe handed me a plate and we walked through the food line as he told me what each dish was. Spaghetti, spaghetti, spaghetti! Spaghetti and shrimp, spaghetti and crab, spaghetti and calamari. They had three different kinds of cod, and they had a huge bowl of shrimp cooling on the table with a big ice sculpture in the middle. They had crabs too, but they weren't them *Deadliest Catch* kind. They was different. They was smaller and they had blue to them. Joe asked me if I had ever had Blue-claw crabs before.

"Well, no, Joe...no I haven't. I've had me some of them big old crab legs at Red Lobster though. Are they the same?" A couple of his guests snickered, which I thought was rude, but I let it go. Mezilli teased me a bit; "Now Phil how can you have lived your whole life an hour and a half from the Chesapeake Bay and never had blue-claw crabs?" he asked me, "Here, try these. They get messy but they're worth it." Joe peeled a crab for me and gave me something he called special sauce. His cousin, the one they introduced as "George" asked him, "Hey Cuz, is that *the* special sauce?" Joe smiled real big, "Yep, Billy DiNardo made it himself. He said it was the first time he ever made it for anyone outside of his restaurant. I paid him $100 for a gallon and he still won't tell me what's in it!" The room laughed at a joke I obviously didn't understand. "Here, Phil," Mezilli explained, "Get a big chunk of crab meat from the claw here and dip it in this sauce. It's the best thing you've ever had."

I was hesitant at first but I seen old Joe eating some so I figured it wasn't poison. I tasted it and by God, it was about the best thing I'd ever put in my mouth!

Before I knew it, I'd pulled up a chair next to Joe's daddy at the big table and we were hammering crab claws and eating spaghetti four different ways from Sunday. I'd forgotten all about the evil in Joe Mezilli's heart. Suddenly I remember what this "Seven Fishes" business really was all about. I looked around the room and everyone seemed to be safe for the time being. Joe's daddy and momma were right there by me and his grandmother hadn't let go of the little girl all night. Surely he wasn't going to kill the old lady while his daughter was sitting right on her lap.

We was having a high old time, and I nearly dropped my guard. But at one point I cornered Hank and Timmy Peppers and I reminded them of my suspicions and told them to keep an eye out. "Suppose you're right, Phil," Milledge asked me. "How do you plan on stopping it? If these guys are professionals as you say." "I don't know," I replied, "You two just keep your eyes on them poor old folks and I'll come up with something.

About thirty minutes later I was enjoying some shrimp with my crabs and Joe walked up to me looking concerned. *I bet he's on to me, me being on to him and all...* I thought. "Phil, are you feeling okay?" I heard him say it, but it sounded funny. It sounded like one of them laughing boxes when the battery runs low. "I feel grapes," I said. "Just grapes. How about some more of that Bobby Baccala." Suddenly the room was spinning and I felt my face swell. My lips felt like I was sucking an air hose down at the Gulf station. My heart started to race. *Oh my God...he's poisoning*

271

me! I thought. I felt my chest tighten and my skin got really cold. The last thing I heard clearly was Gladys saying "Phil...oh Lord...Phil are you okay?" Then I heard Mezilli say "It's anaphylaxes, he's going into shock. *Anaphylaxes,* I thought to myself. *He poisoned me with anaphylaxes! What the hell is anaphylaxes?* Right then, the room went black and I fell down face-first in a bowl of mussels.

Ms. Anna Phylaxis

Peppers was standing next to my bed. Hank Milledge was out in the hallway talking to Gladys and a doctor. "Where am I?" I asked. "Lynchburg Baptist," Peppers answered, "You was out cold for the entire ride." My heart was racing and doctors was coming and going. "Mr. Lowery?" the one doc said. "You're a lucky man. If your neighbor hadn't known what was going on, you'd have never survived to make it here."

"Wha...who? What neighbor?" "Mr. Mezilli," the doctor answered, "He saved your life."

The doctor explained. "Mr. Mezilli recognized that you were going into anaphylactic shock. He stuck coffee grounds under your tongue and got help as fast as he could. I don't think you'd have made it without him, sir."

I was stunned. "You're a lucky man," the doctor said as he turned to walk out the door. "Anaphylactic shock?" I mumbled. Peppers leaned in. "Phil," He asked, "was this your plan? Your plan to stop that sleeping with the seven fishes business and save Joe Mezilli's family?" I'd forgotten all about that for a moment. Peppers, apparently, had not. "Is this how you did it, Phil? By eating them shellfish even though you knew you was allergic?" I was still cloudy from the medicine they gave me. "What Peppers? What the hell are you talking about?"

"You had an allergic reaction to shellfish, Phil, That's why you went into shock and how you ended up here. I'll tell ya, that was one hell of a plan, Phil. You sure brought the law to their house in a hurry. Of course, Stan Stevens was already there, 'cause he was invited, so it might have been hard for Joe to kill his folks anyway. But then the ambulance came, and three more sheriffs, it was quite a sight! That was some good plan Phil!" "Peppers..." I groaned. "Shut the hell up."

Hank came in the room, leaving Gladys in the hall, talking to the hospital folks. "Well, you saved the day for sure, Phil." Hank said with a belly laugh. "Yes sir, there won't be any whacking at the Mezilli household tonight, not with half the first responders in Bedford county over there eating Mezilli's seafood. Nice going there, *Agent Lowery.*
"That ain't funny Hank," I said, "it ain't funny at all. Now that I thwarted his plan, Mezilli will be out for my head, you watch!" Milledge stuck his hands in his front pockets of his jeans. He does that whenever he gets angry. "Now look here, Phil," he began, "The man saved your life tonight! The rest of us were sitting there watching your head blow up like a beach ball and wondering what the hell was going on. Hell I thought an alien was going to pop out of your chest, the way you was turning blue and writhing. If Mezilli wanted you dead, he sure could have just sat there and watched it happen like the rest of us were doing. Now I think this game of yours has gone on long enough. He's a good man and that's a good family. He ain't no mobster. Now let it go!"

Milledge turned and walked out the door. "C'mon Peppers!" he barked on his way out. "Let's go back to Mezilli's before the *shellfish* is all gone!" He said the word with a snarl. *Nobody believes me*, I thought. *Nobody understands.*

13

Burial

At Sea

Another summer was fast approaching in our new home. We'd really settled in here. The kids were making friends and I finally convinced my parents, and even my grandmother, to start taking the train down here for long weekend visits. The train had food and a bathroom for Nonna's microscopic bladder, and she never feared the tracks would suddenly end over a body of water. They actually fell in love with the train rides, and were talking, from time to time, of moving down here.

One evening in late May, my mom, the Old Man and Nonna were sitting out on our deck in the backyard. Angie and I had gotten the kids squared away inside and we were all just sitting around sipping some wine we'd found at a local vineyard nearby. My grandmother started getting very wistful watching the sun set behind the mountains to the south and west of our home. She never drinks, but tonight we'd convinced her to have a glass with us. I guess it loosened her up a bit. She got teary-eyed, and started telling us about her courtship with Nonno. "This sunset on the mountains...it looks like back home." She whispered. "Your grandpa, he was from a little village about halfway up Montecassino, and I lived down in the town below. His father, your great-grandfather, was a cobbler up there. They lived on a little patch of land and had a couple of cows and some chickens and a goat. Giuseppe would ride into town on his bicycle when he was just eight or nine years old and he'd make deliveries for his Poppa. That's how we met.   I leaned forward on my chair. It was getting a little chilly and I wrapped a thin little blanket around Nonna's shoulders, and she smiled and patted my hand. "I never knew that Nonna. How did you fall in love?"

She continued; "Giuseppe, he never did want to be a cobbler like his Poppa. He always said he wanted to go to

277

America. He came to our house once to deliver a pair of shoes to my mother and when I answered the door...the lightning bolt! I was only ten years old, but I knew I was going to marry this boy one day."

She let out a little laugh, "Just like you and Angie, Giuseppe. I remember you walking home from Mass one Saturday night and your Nonno asked you why that little girl made you smile so much when we were walking out. That was you, Angie." She said, nodding at my wife. I looked at Anj and she was crying softly. I felt her grip my arm tightly.

Nonna put her hand gently on Angie's cheek. "It's true," She whispered. My Giuseppe asked Joey why he was smiling so much and what your name was and when Joey answered; "Her name is Angie, Nonno." It was the biggest smile I ever saw on Giuseppe's face. Giuseppe told him how he met me when he was eleven and I was ten and he was delivering shoes for his father. Joey do you remember?" I was surprised to find myself blinking back a few tears. Typically Nonno didn't elicit warm emotions. But this time was different.

"Yes I do, Nonna," I answered, "I remember we stopped at D'itillio's and had Water Ice and he told me about how he thought you were so beautiful the first time he saw you. How he would talk his dad into doing extra deliveries in your town so he could ride his bike past your house." Nonna was quiet for a minute. Then she spoke again. "The swine flu hit his town hard that year and his whole family died. Within a week, your Nonno was an orphan. He decided that he would try to make his way to America instead of going to live in an orphanage and having to work in the slaughterhouses or on a farm. He sold all the shoes his poppa was working on and rode his bike to my house the night before he left. He was so brave, your Nonno. Fourteen years old, he was. He sold his bike and left early one morning and snuck on board a

278

steamer from Gaeta. He ate bread that he stole from the kitchen late at night. They finally caught him and the captain gave him a beating, but then he let him work until they got to America and he gave him ten dollars, which was a lot of money then." Nonna paused and sipped her wine. She had tears in her eyes and the smile had not stopped playing on her lips.

"Giuseppe had faked his papers and told the Immigration officer he was eighteen, when he was really only fourteen. They sent him to the house where the owner of the textile mill lived and he started work the next morning."

"Dear Lord," I said softly, "I never thought about this until now, but he was the age our Petey is. I can't imagine Petey suddenly having no family and having to make his way to an entire new country." I shuddered to think. It gave me a different perspective on Zippie and why he was so gruff.

Nonna continued with her story; "Giuseppe would write me all the time. Every week I would get mail from him, but back then it was airmail and it took weeks to get it to me. He was working in the mills in Chester and he had moved in with Hank Kroyczek's family. They treated him nice, and he was safe. He would always say in his letters; "I'm sending for you one day. Wait for me." He would ask me about other boys in my town and I would always play like I had suitors, but the truth was I was in love with Giuseppe. If he hadn't sent for me, I might have joined the Convent!" Nonna laughed at this, more to herself than to us.

She kept going, I was surprised at how much she felt like talking tonight. "My Poppa, he tells Giuseppe that he won't send me alone to America, so if he wants to marry me, he has to pay to get us all over there. Me, my Poppa, my Momma and one of my sisters. The other sister and my brother wanted to stay behind. Giuseppe worked for almost four

279

years to save enough money to move us all over to Philadelphia. He worked in the mills all day and drove a garbage truck at night. That's where he realized how much money could be made in trash."

My dad was crying. I wouldn't have noticed, because I was so captivated by Nonna's story, but I heard him sniffle and then he blew his nose into his hanky. He caught my eye and I winked at him, letting him know it was okay. I could tell he had never heard these stories either and he was missing his dad...maybe for the first time in his entire life.   "We got off the boat on a Tuesday afternoon, and that Saturday Giuseppe came to our house to serenade me." A little heritage lesson is necessary here. In the Old Country, when a boy was proposing to his girlfriend, he would go to her house and sing to her. Sometimes he hired a few musicians to help him, but usually because they were poor, the boy didn't have the money and he'd play guitar and "serenade" his bride-to-be and her family. Then the parents would open the doors and have a party in their courtyard and all the neighbors would come and bring food and presents. We still do it, although a modified version, back in Philly when we get engaged. Angie and I had a wonderful serenade at her folk's house the Wednesday before our wedding.

My grandmother continued, "Giuseppe sang to me and my Poppa opened the door and we had a little party in the back yard. We were so poor back then...we didn't have nothin' but we were in love and Giuseppe was such a hard worker. So the following Saturday, just ten days after we landed in America, I married your Nonno, at the same church your Poppa married your Momma and where you and Angie got married. I was sixteen by then and he was eighteen. We were just kids, but we were so in love.

My mom was crying like a baby now. She has a very close relationship with her mother-in-law and now I knew why. They were kindred spirits. We sat there in silence for a little longer and then headed in the house, and got ready for bed. I had learned a whole lot about Zippie tonight, and it was something special. I guess everybody has a story.

A Weekend with the Fellas

By the start our second summer in Virginia, we'd really settled in. The place felt like home. Tommy had a really good crew, and he was doing great with the renovation business. The kids were doing well in school and in sports. I had been awarded a charter for a Son's of Italy chapter here in Forest and I got that started. We met at a nice cigar shop in Wyndhurst, a little hamlet about two miles from my house. It was nice having some paisan to hang with. I was making some great friends in the neighborhood. The guys in Forest weren't exactly like the guys in South Philly, but they were a good bunch of fellas. We did a lot of stuff together. They loved my big, professional sized pool table and they had a blast out at the hunting camp. But the thing they seemed to love the most – besides eating all the authentic Italian cooking they could- was fishing. We fished at Smith Mountain Lake quite a bit, and I was a minor celebrity after disclosing to them one day, that Mike Iocanelli, the B.A.S.S. pro, was my second cousin. I was surprised how important that made me. Back in Philly it wasn't as big a deal as it was down here. This was Bass country and Cousin Mike was a rock star.

One evening early in that second summer, I was sitting on the deck with Angie and watching the sunset. I thought maybe I needed to do something special with the guys in the neighborhood. "Anj," I began, "I think I should take a couple of the neighbor men fishing on the big boat. Just a weekend getaway for the boys." Angie thought that would be a nice thing. "Why don't you do it the week after Independence Day? I'll be taking the kids to my folks for the week anyway." "Yeah, that's a thought." I said. "I'll call them tomorrow." Another couple of minutes later, Emmy came outside wanting to catch lightning bugs so we spent the next twenty minutes trapping them and keeping them in a mayonnaise jar to use as a nightlight.

The next morning I got on the phone and called my neighbors. I planned a nice weekend deep-sea trip with three of the guys who lived closest. I invited Hank Milledge, Tommy Erickson, and Phil Lowery. I also invited my cousin George to come down and go out with us. George loved deep-sea fishing and we always looked for a chance to take an excursion. I invited Tommy Fallone, too. I wanted the locals to get to know him a little better. Someday, his past would inevitably come to light, and I wanted them to see ahead of time, what a great guy he actually is.

We decided to go out the weekend after Independence Day. The drive to Hampton would be less snarled with vacationers, and the Gulf Stream would be a little closer to the coast by then. Even so, we would be going out about eighty miles in order to find the really big game fish. Everybody was in, and cleared their calendars for that weekend.

Everybody except Phil. He made a stream of excuses when I asked him about going with us. I had already decided to try a little harder with Phil, and I'd walked over to his house one early summer evening with a small paper bag full of tomatoes from my garden. Gladys answered the door and seemed a bit nervous. I understood completely. The way Phil likes to play it off like he rules the roost over there, I imagine she has to toe the line when one of the neighborhood men shows up at the door.

I handed her the tomatoes and she looked at them like they were my kids' poopy diapers, from ten years ago. I don't know what it is with Phil and his wife and their aversion to my tomatoes – or maybe to any tomatoes- but it wouldn't fly in Philly.

"Phil here?' I asked Gladys. She stammered a bit. "Y-yes he is, Joe," I waited for a very long, uncomfortable minute. Finally, when it was apparent that she thought I was simply asking his location, and didn't need to actually talk to him, I asked her, "Well, can I speak to Phil, Gladys? I need to ask him something important."

Gladys snapped out of her fog and called down to the basement. "Pheeel!" she said, in her distinct drawl, "Pheel git up here!" Phil walked up the steps talking about how he was busy fixing the TV again. He stepped through the door holding an actual cathode ray tube from a TV. The last thing I watched on a TV with cathode tubes was Nixon resigning, when I was about five. Phil stopped in his tracks when he saw me. For whatever reason, since almost the very day I moved into this neighborhood, Phil Lowery has treated me like he owes me money. Every time he sees me.   "W-well hey there, Joe. Uh...what brings you over?" he stumbled. "Well, Phil I brought you some tomatoes. The early spring has me with a harvest already if you can believe that. Last week of June and I have tomatoes. Nice huh?" Phil looked at the bag in his wife's hand like it contained severed heads. *Tomatoes!* I thought, *These people just don't understand...* "Well thank you neighbor," Phil said, rather uneasily, "We sure do appreciate this." I got to the point right away. "Phil, listen, the rest of the guys are going on that deep sea fishing trip in two weeks. I was hoping to change your mind and get you to go with us. I know you said you had things planned that weekend. What with the Pork Rind Festival and all." That was the excuse he gave us. Over in Galax there was something he called a "Pork Rind Festival" and he went every year.

Gee...I must have missed that one in Conde Naste Traveler.

Phil sputtered, "Well Joe, Y-ya know I'd love to go out there with you boys but I gotta go to the Festival. My cousin Jim-Bob has a vending booth there and he sells some of the best pork rind you'll ever have. He depends on me to help him with the sales that weekend. So let me get this straight, Phil. You'd rather spend the weekend in Galax, Virginia selling pork rind. I thought to myself. You'd rather be dishing out the fried skin of a pig than fishing off the coast of Virginia with three of your friends on a fiftyfour foot Hatteras? My inner voice was so loud by this point that I thought, for just a second, that I had actually said it.

I snapped to attention. "Well Phil," I said, "If you don't want to go along, I guess that's okay. But it will be a fun weekend and the boys sure would love to have you. It's so peaceful out there. We go out about eighty miles and it's just so quiet at night. Nobody around. Nothing to disturb you. It's really relaxing. I hope you'll reconsider."

I turned to leave and noticed Gladys was staring at me slack-jawed. I might never understand these two. To be very honest, I was getting tired of trying.

Gone Fishin'

"Hurry up and shut that dang door, Gladys" I told her. She was standing there gawking at Don Mezilli walking back to his house. "What's wrong with you Gladys?" I asked, "Every time that man comes over here, or you see him outside, you get glassy -eyed and lose your composure. You got a crush on him or something?" Gladys looked at me like she wanted to kill me. Kill me slowly.

"Phillip Lowery. I am a Christian woman." She snarled. "It's just that, he seems so very nice and sometimes I imagine him doing those terrible things you say he's done and it's very perplexin'" I was losing my wife again. Just when I convinced her he was a mafia, she goes and gets all girly on me and wants to see the good in him. "There ain't no good in him!" I said, not meaning to say it out loud. Gladys seemed startled. "Huh?" she barked.

"Nothin'...nevermind" I said.

"Gladys, something bad is gonna happen on that boat, I just know it. There's a reason he is taking the local boys out there along with his hit-man Tommy, and his cousin from Philly. There's trouble brewing. He's gonna consolidate his power and stake his claim." Gladys looked at me as if I had a third eye. "Consolidate his power?" she whined. "Who has any power around here that he'd need to feel like consolidating? Hank Milledge? He's sixty years old. Erickson? Maybe Erickson, he's almost as obsessed with the mob as you are Phil. Is he after Timmy Peppers and his backhoe?" I was getting downright steamed. Gladys was heckling me in my own house. I didn't cotton to it a bit. "The man only understands power, Gladys," I said, trying to be reasonable. "He needs to be the alpha dog no matter where he is. He's got the mindset of a Mafia and that'll never change. Living in Virginia ain't gonna change that part of him." I shouldn't have to explain this to her. Gladys isn't stupid. Well she's a little stupid, but not that stupid. She's not stupid like a dumb old dog; she just isn't wise to the ways of the world. Especially not to a ruthless killer like Joe Mezilli.

"Why don't you go on the fishing trip with the boys, Phil? You could check him out at close range. Unless everyone in the neighborhood is in on it, he can't be killing you out there, he'd have to kill everyone else too. You really think he's planning on killing four people out at sea? How would he do that, Phil?" She was heading for a giant tangent...a thought-vacuum that was about to swallow her mind for a good three hours and unless I threw up a roadblock, she'd be wrecked in a ditch in just a minute or so. "Gladys, I am not going on that deep sea fishing trip with them boys. You want me wearing a pair of cement slippers and sleeping with the seven fishes like those poor souls he tried to kill on Christmas Eve? Huh?" I was really shocked that she wanted me to go with them. "You're trying to get rid of me Gladys, is that what this is about?" She looked away with a scowl on her face.

"Gladys, why in God's name did you invite him in here?' I asked her incredulously. "You might as well petition the governor of California to let old Charles Manson move in with us, while you're at it." I was furious. I felt my face go flush and my lips quiver. "That man is a cold-blooded killer and you never know when he is going to strike and you just let him waltz in here with his paper bag full of tomatoes." I had to sit down. My blood pressure was skyrocketing again. "I'm sorry Phil," Gladys said, "He seldom comes over here, and he just showed up and knocked on the door. I didn't check to see who it was before I opened it and then when I did, I was so stunned..." Gladys was starting to ramble and make even less sense than she usually does. I felt kind of bad for her. Just for a second. "It's okay Gladys," I offered, "He's smooth like that. You just promise me that you won't ever let him in here again. You hear?" Gladys timidly gave me her word.

Now I had this to worry about. I was starting to get tired of saving the neighbors from old Lucky Luciano over there and not being appreciated for it. Heck, nobody but Tim Peppers believed me, even after almost a year of gathering evidence against him. What more did they want? I nearly had pictures of him burying them burlap body bags in his garden. I done heard him setting up the murder of his own mother and father and grandmother, and only my quick thinking and my shellfish allergy saved those folks. I sent the sheriff over there, and he gets bought-off with food and money. Heck, Timmy Peppers was in the middle of eating one of them "special recipe" tomato sandwiches when I reminded him about what was in those body bags. The survival of this entire town is entirely on my shoulders and I can't find one person as smart as I am to help me expose this gangster.

I thought about it long and hard. I guess I was going to have to go on this fishing trip with the rest of them numbskulls if I wanted to have any neighbors left by Labor Day. If I don't go along and remain vigilant, old Mezilli will kill them all and dump them in the Atlantic. I called over to Joe's house. When he answered I found my throat tightening up a little. I didn't realize the man frightened me like he did. I wasn't scared like a girl would be scared...I was nervous-scared. Like a wild animal that senses he is in a life or death battle. "Alert" is what I believe it's called. "Hello Joe." I said, matter-of-factly. "I was thinking," I continued, "I could use some time with the other fellas on the street. I haven't been fishing on the ocean in a mighty long time. If there's still room for me, I'd like to go along, if that's okay."

"Why Phil that would be wonderful!" Mezilli said. He seemed just a little too happy about me going, or so it seemed. That made me suspicious. But I swallowed hard and got the details from him and circled the date on my calendar. Joe told me not to worry about food or drinks; he was bringing all that and just let him know what it was I wanted. "Bring your Dramamine," He said, "In case you get seasick." I was going to remind him I was a Navy man, but I didn't want to reveal to him that I was military trained. If I was ever going to expose this criminal, I would have to thwart one of his evil plans right as it happened. To do that, I have to remain sharp. I thanked him and hung up. I had about two weeks to get prepared for the trip.

I was worried about him supplying the food...that made me suspicious. What if he drugged us all before he shot us and dumped us overboard wrapped in chains? How would I ever be able to stay alert and awake if he did something like that? That remark he'd made about me bringing my Dramamine...that stuff makes you drowsy. Sure, I thought, bring your Dramamine Phil. It'll make it easier to cap you and fit you with cement shoes. The more I thought about what it was he was up to, the angrier it made me. He must have finally realized that we're not so stupid down here. That's what it is! He wants to kill us because we're going to figure out that he's really one of them mafias and then we'll stop him from setting up his own family. He done figured out that I'm wise to them Yankee, Mafia tricks.

I was really mad now.

I called Peppers the next day and asked him for his little voice recorder that he carried in his truck. Tim Peppers has the worst memory in the entire free world. If he went to the bathroom, he'd forget whether he was supposed to stand or sit. So he carried this voice recorder with him. He bought it at the Radio Shack at the mall. Darndest thing I've ever seen. It has no tape or nothing. I don't know how it records your voice, or on what, but it sure as heck does, by God. It's real high tech and it hurts my head trying to figure it out. But it's small and it fits in your pocket, and that was all that mattered at the moment.

Peppers asked me what it was for. "I'm going fishing with Don Barzini across the street next month, Timmy. I want this recorder to gather evidence." I told him. "Evidence for what?" he asked me. Now, he was on the phone, but I swear to you I could hear his mouth hanging open. "Evidence for the killin' Peppers! Dear God, son, don't you understand anything?"

"Phil," Peppers said softly, "What am I not understanding? Isn't this just a fishing trip?" I wanted to smack my head with the phone. "Peppers," I said, "If you watched the Sopranos like I do, you'd know more about the way these mafias think and do business." I explained to him about the time they took Big Pussy out on the boat and shot him for being a rat. Then they stuck him in a body bag and weighed it down with chains and dumped him overboard. "That's what he plans to do with us, Peppers. Me, Erickson, and Hank Milledge. He's bringing that hit man Tommy with him; you know the one he grew up with who has his own crew? The one who drove Mezilli's family down here for the Christmas Eve whackin'? He's coming along. And he even sent for his cousin George. He's probably a hit man too. He figures it'll probably take all three of them to handle us country boys.

"Phil, Erickson is Swedish, ain't he, from Minnesota?" Peppers asked timidly. "I know that!" I barked, "But dangit, he's been here so long now, that he's learned from me and Milledge." "Learned what?" Peppers asked me. *Why, Lord...why?* I thought, *Why am I the only smart man in Forest?* "Peppers!" I yelled, "Who taught Erickson how to shoot? And who taught him to actually use all the tools on a Swiss Army knife? I did!" I was incredulous. "I turned that man from a wimpy little insurance salesman, to a rugged outdoorsman!"

Peppers didn't have much to say after that. "I'll bring that recorder over the week before you go fishing, Phil." He said. "Remind me ahead of time, so I don't forget." He was quiet after that. I tried explaining to him how these mobsters think. I told him about how Don Corleone was a seemingly nice guy unless business was involved. I told him how Tony Soprano loved his family, and animals, but was a sociopath. I guess it didn't get through to old Peppers, because after a long period of silence —where I thought he was actually absorbing some of my insight- he said, "Phil...What, uh...well what if you're wrong about Joe?"   It was too much for me. I just said goodbye and went to the kitchen and ate an Alka-Seltzer. Yeah, I ate one. It was a trick I learned in the Navy. Let that ol' tablet dissolve in your mouth and the medicine goes to work twice as fast. Besides...the fizzing tickles my brain. I kinda like the way that feels.

Bocce and La Birra

Fourth of July was a lot more fun in Forest than it had been in Philly. Not that it wasn't fun back home. It always was. But Virginia lets you have fireworks, so you aren't dependent on the municipalities. Now, given our proximity to the ball park, we always got to see the fireworks that the Phillies shot off on Fourth of July weekend. Either that or we were at the beach and we saw the fireworks at Atlantic City or Wildwood, or Ocean City, Maryland.

But Forest, Virginia lets you have your very own. Heck you could buy them everywhere. The first year we were here, my boys and I had a raucous Roman Candle war in the back yard. Then, at dusk, we launched fireworks for about two hours. We'd hosted a pool party, and all the neighbors were there. Even the Lowery's came over. Poor Milledge's dog wound up stuck in my hedges after he took off running when the fireworks started to explode. His collar got caught in one of the low-lying ewes and he sat there yelping, with his hind legs in the air.

I let my boys help me light the fuses and they got a big kick out of all the exploding and displays. Pop and I never got to do that because fireworks are outlawed in Philly. It was a heck of an evening. I had the laptop out with the Phillies game playing over the internet. I might live in Virginia now, but I'm a Philly boy at heart, and if you're going to have a cookout on July Fourth, you have to have the Phillies in the background.

I was explaining this to Milledge and Erickson and to the newest neighbor, Charlie Bransford. Bransford was a retired FBI agent who had worked out of Washington DC. He moved here to Forest after retirement and taught some criminal justice classes at the college. He made Tommy nervous. He always wondered if Charlie somehow knew about his history. Anyway, I was telling the boys about how summer cookouts required a transistor radio in the background, with the greatest play-by-play voices in the history of baseball painting the picture.

For the next thirty minutes or so, we went back and forth arguing who those voices belonged to. Milledge had grown up listening to the Braves broadcast and Skip Carey. Or he caught the Yankees on days when you could get the radio skip from New York. "Swede" Erickson said he'd grown up listening to Ernie Harwell's broadcasts of the Tigers. "Even in Minnesold-ah" he'd explained in his thick accent, "We heard Ernie Harwell, don't-cha-know?"

It was a great discussion. The kind of thing women have no appreciation for, but men will talk about for hours. Of course my loyalties were with Harry Kalas and Richie Ashburn. I started telling the boys about how my dad didn't have much time to take me to games when I was a kid, with the responsibilities of the trucks and all. But we'd sit on the front porch almost every evening listening to them on the radio. Tommy smiled as he sipped his beer. "I remember that," he said wistfully. "Your Nonna too," he said, "She loved the games as much as any of the men on the block.

That made me smile. Tommy was right. Sometimes I had to explain the same things to her ten times a night, but Nonna loved her Phillies, and she loved Harry Kalas. Everyone loved Harry. "Ooh that Harry Kalas!" She'd say to my grandfather as they sat on the porch listening to the radio. "He's so handsome! And that voice! He's Greek you know Giuseppe...he's almost one of us!"

My grandfather would get red-faced, stand up, wave his hand at her dismissively, mumble something in Italian, and go inside to grab the bottle of vodka.

Sitting there in my big back yard in Virginia, listening to the Phillies and cooking burgers with my neighbors, it was about as perfect as it could be. *Next year,* I thought to myself, *I'm bringing Nonna down here for the Fourth.* Independence Day was actually on a Saturday this year. The Monday after, I called the neighborhood boys and reviewed our plans. "You guys are all ready?" I asked each guy. They all said they were and they were excited about the trip. I felt badly that Bransford wasn't going with us. He'd only recently moved in, and the wife had a long honey-do list he was still attending to, "I'll catch the next one." he said. I called my cousin George and reminded him that he'd fly down on Wednesday, and I'd pick him up in Roanoke. We'd be going out on Thursday afternoon and coming back Sunday morning.

That week was busy. Anj had already planned to take the kids to her parent's house in New Jersey for the week. They left on Monday, and I spent the rest of the week cooking, buying supplies, checking weather charts and fishing reports, and having the trucks detailed. George called me on Tuesday and we talked for a long time. It was going to be good to see me, he'd said. We'd missed each other. Georgie is my closest male cousin and more like a brother than anything else.

I picked George up in Roanoke at 7:30 AM and we spent the day running errands and getting ready. We were in the garage late into Wednesday evening, loading the trucks and getting ready. Mostly we were just talking about the old days. The plan was that Tommy would drive my Tundra with one or two of the boys, and I would drive Angie's Escalade

293

with everyone else. We'd split the supplies between the two vehicles. Lowery came sauntering over after dinner on Wednesday. George and I were talking to Charlie Bransford in the garage. In between packing the trucks, I was teaching him to play Bocce on the court I'd built beside the garage. Charlie was enjoying the new game and we were laughing at him trying to curse in his limited Italian. It turns out that Charlie had been stationed in Anzio while he was in the Navy, before he'd joined the Bureau, and he'd really fallen in love with the place, and he'd learned a dozen or so of the more colorful Italian words.

Phil came over in stealth mode. That's what I had come to call it when he was trying to be sneaky. He likes to think he gets there magically so he can overhear a few seconds of your conversation before you know he's there. He slinks in the shadows created by the setting sun and he is certain nobody sees him until he materializes in the front of the garage like he just got beamed there by Scotty from Star Trek. The problem for old Phil is that he isn't a small man. He's not tall, but he is wide. He has a gut like a small, hillbilly Buddha. Heck, the shadow of his belly weighs thirty pounds. There is no place where the darkness is sufficient enough to hide him completely, but he doesn't realize that.

The other problem he faces —and it's one that literally makes me ill- is that he wears Aqua Velva. Lots of it. When I was a little kid, we had an insurance man in the neighborhood, Mr. Catallano, and he all but bathed in the stuff. He'd come calling on my mom and dad, and she'd have to open the windows and air the place out afterward. Well, Phil likes it at least as much as Mr. Catallano ever did. I can smell Phil coming almost before he crosses the street. There are times when even my dogs will leave the garage after a while, because you simply can't breathe.

Phil is a little old-school and he insists on shaking hands every single time he sees you. "Howdy neighbor" he'll say, and then he'll stick his hand out. Now, I'm not a serial hand-shaker anyway. But Phil slathers on the Aqua Velva with those hands, and he touches up the coverage throughout the day. If you forget this fact, and shake hands with him, you wind up smelling like Aqua Velva yourself.

Then it gets in your hair, on your clothes, hell I've got a pair of shoes that I had to replace the laces on, because they smelled so strong of that drugstore cologne that they stunk up my closet. The way I'd broken him of the habit was one of my all-time best fables. It's a story that bears retelling.

After about a month living in the neighborhood, I had to do the unthinkable. I had to lie. Phil came over one evening while I was tinkering with the 'Vette, and, as usual, Phil stuck his hand out. I'd been dreading this day, but I had decided that if he was going to pursue this ridiculous handshake business, I would have to concoct a story to make him stop. So when he arrived in my garage that night -three minutes after his scent had already set up camp- and reached out his hand, I put my plan in motion. I looked at his hand, and then I looked at Phil. I cocked my head to one side and stepped backwards. I reached under my sweatshirt and pulled out my gold Italian Horn necklace. (I never did wear one of those because they fit the "Goombah" stereotype too much, but I had one for this occasion.) I made my voice sound really nervous and said, "Maddonn...Phil. Nobody told you it's the worst kind of Sicilian curse to shake hands more than ten times with the same person?"

Phil stopped dead in his tracks and looked at his hand. "Wha?" he gasped. "Yeah Phil," I continued, "It's called *La Stunod a Mano*." "What's 'at mean?" he drawled.

295

"It means The Deadly Hand and it's one of the worst curses in all of Southern Italy." They say if you shake someone's hand more than ten times, a day of eternity vanishes from your soul." *The Deadly Hand?* I thought to myself, *I crack myself up sometimes.* This was especially funny to me because *La Stunod a Mano* actually means "Stupid Hand." I knew this, but Phil did not. I know that Phil goes around misusing Italian words he picks up from me and I couldn't wait until this one got back to me.

The only thing worse than my lying to Phil, was the beauty of how seriously he took that incredibly baseless story. The next time he came over, he stuck out his hand to me automatically. I looked at his hand and shot him the maloik. He snapped that hand back like he was feeding sticky buns to alligators. "Oh yeah," he mumbled, "The Deadly Hand." Eventually he stopped offering a handshake altogether. That was funny enough, but what was really great was that Tommy told me that from the first time Phil and he met, Phil would mumble a number when they shook hands. Tommy thought he was OCD. "That fajoot across the street, Lowery. What is he, Rainman?" he asked me. I told him what I did about the handshake and Tommy laughed until he was literally crying. Apparently, Phil now makes mental notes of number of times he shakes anyone's hand. Madonn!

Anyway, I smelled old Phil coming, while me and Bransford, and my cousin George were playing Bocce. I looked at George and laughed. I'd told him about the whole "Deadly Hand" thing on the ride from the airport. We were talking about how different it is down here and how some people think certain things because I'm Italian. "Georgie," I said, "I could make up almost anything and tell them it's an Italian thing, and they'd buy it. Some of them would, anyway." Then I told him about Lowery and the "Deadly Hand." George and I laughed ourselves simple.

So I already knew he was in my garage before he poked his head out the door to where my Bocce court was. I looked up and muttered "Phil's here." to nobody in particular. About five seconds later he poked his head out the door. "Howdy neighbor!" he said, cheerful for a change. George started laughing before Phil even made it over to him. He remembered Mr. Catallano from the old neighborhood. Mr. Catallano had all the Mezilli's under his umbrella, and Georgie's mom and dad bought insurance from him as well. I knew better than even look at my cousin right now, or we'd both morph into unrepentant teenagers, laughing at this overly-perfumed man.

Now, my cousin George is a very funny guy, and one of the quicker wits in my family. To avoid shaking Phil's hand, and subsequently smelling like Aqua Velva for the rest of the night, just before I made the introduction between him and Phil, George excused himself to go to the bathroom. He emerged a few minutes later with a grin on his face. "Yo Cuz!" He said with a wink, "No soap in the john? Just like the washroom at the landfill, right?" George said this while wiping his hands on his jeans in a very animated fashion. Without missing a beat, he walked over to Phil and stuck out his hand. "I'm his cousin George, from Philly. It's nice to meet you." I thought Lowery was going to pass out right there. He looked at Georges allegedly unwashed hand for a long second, probably imagining the germs leaping off at him, then jerked his hand back and started talking really fast, hoping George wouldn't notice. *My Cuz...*I thought, *That's the Mezilli wit right there.*

By the end of the night, I had Phil thoroughly confused about the rules of Bocce. The balls all reeked of Aqua Velva, and

297

he'd had one too many beers. He started telling Italian jokes. That was a big mistake. But not in the way you'd think. See, nobody loves a good "Dago" joke more than an Italian, and my cousin George and I, especially love them. But Lowery didn't know that, so when he fired off the first one, George shot me a knowing look and we acted like it offended us.

I thought that would end it, but Lowery kept throwing back *La Birra* and before you know it, he was making more really bad Italian jokes. I've heard them all, and some of them are really very funny. Apparently Phil has only heard the really bad ones. After the initial few jokes, it was harder and harder to feign offense. But we did it masterfully.

George was so good at it that at one point he had Phil slobbering an apology and begging to be forgiven. George and I had spent a lot of time together, busting other guy's chops. We did it well and we could play it straight like pros. Once, when Lowery decided to tell a mafia joke, George looked at me coyly and then walked over to Phil. He leaned in real close and whispered, "The Mezilli family doesn't joke about the Mafia." Then he looked at me without any facial expressions at all and said "Right Cuz?"
"Omerta" I muttered, as I rolled my next shot on the Bocce court.

It was all I could do not to fall over in fits right there. Poor Phil looked like he'd wet himself. If it wasn't so funny, it would be pathetic. What was pathetic is that Phil only had maybe three beers. I don't drink that often so I don't keep much beer around. He and Bransford killed the partial six-pack that I'd had in my fridge. Georgie and I drank iced tea. It was funnier watching Phil getting drunk, than drinking anything ourselves anyway.

I leaned over to George at one point and whispered, "He's going to be a lot of fun on the ride to the boat in the morning!" George laughed out loud at that. "You need to hit every bump on the way," he said, "Make him pay dearly for these bad Dago jokes. He's gonna be seasick two hours before we leave the docks." Phil finally wobbled home around 10PM. I wasn't envious of the hangover he'd have in the morning, and to be honest, I wouldn't have been surprised if he'd missed the trip altogether.

Bransford was another story. He drank maybe one beer and then watched Phil embarrass himself. Bransford is an observer. Doubtless from all those years in the FBI. He was slightly suspicious of all of us when he first moved to the neighborhood, but a few cookouts and some of Angie's linguine with white clam sauce put his mind at ease. The biggest problem was with Tommy. When he'd heard that Charlie Bransford was a former FBI agent, he wouldn't come around the house if Charlie was here. I asked him what he was worried about. "Just old habits I guess, Joe." he said, softly. There was sadness behind his eyes. "To be honest, even though nobody here knows about my past, I feel like I have it painted on my forehead. I re-live that one stupid moment over and over and over. When somebody who once worked for the Feds is around, it reminds me even more. Like one day he's gonna stand up at a cookout and announce to everyone that I'm a convicted felon and that I robbed an ATM at the Sands. It's embarrassing, you know?"

I couldn't pretend to understand what Tommy was feeling, so I did what I knew to do. I gave him a little punch in the arm and took him inside to get something to eat. Angie's cooking can cure just about anything.

But that night in my garage, Bransford wasn't keying in on Tommy. In fact, he hadn't met him yet. Instead, Charlie waited until Phil weaved his way home and then he sat down on a stool near my workbench. He looked at me straight on and said, "You, my friend, have a problem." I had absolutely no idea what he meant by that. I asked him, "What are you talking about, Chollie?" Bransford loved that I called him that. "Chollie" is the nickname of former Phillies manager Charlie Manuel. Bransford is a baseball junkie and he instantly gravitated toward me giving him that nickname. He leaned in closer on one elbow and looked at George and me.

"That man is scared to death of you, that's what I'm talking about!" I almost dropped my bottle of water. "What?" I said in disbelief. "What the heck are you talking about Chollie?" Bransford started explaining in criminal psychology terms. He noticed that Phil was visibly uncomfortable and nervous around me and even more so around George, he presumed it was because he'd never met him. "He's afraid of you being Italian, pal. It's as simple as that." I looked at George and started to laugh. "This is a joke, right? Cuz...you in on this?" George shook his head. He was as interested in this tale as I now was. "Explain this to me Chollie, please."

Bransford started talking about nervous ticks and "tells" like poker players notice. He talked about how alcohol loosens the tongue and often removes inhibitors. "People say things when they're tipsy, Joe. You can tell a lot by what a guy says when he's had a few. Those jokes he was telling, did you notice anything about the content?" I paused a second. "No, just bad Italian jokes. Same bad Italian jokes I've heard my whole life." I answered. It was actually my cousin George who'd notice the pattern. Georgie spoke up, "At first they were just run of the mill Italian jokes, Cuz. Then every joke became about the mafia."

"Ding ding ding!" Bransford yelped. "We have a winner!" He took a swig of his water. "The man thinks you might be in the mafia somehow, buddy. Plain and simple." I almost spit out my tea. "What!" I gasped, coughing as I tried to speak. "Yeah...he thinks you're in the mob. He was nervous when he walked in here, I could see that plain as day. And he's known you how long now? You ever heard the phrase 'True words are spoken in jest'? Well that's why he kept making mafia jokes at your expense. He wanted to see your reaction. He was actually "joking" about his perception of you." "Oh hell..." I frowned. "You're not kidding? This is what's troubling this guy?"

Charlie winked and said, "You betcha," Then he continued, "You know...what you do with this information is entirely up to you. Nobody is going to know about this conversation." Charlie smiled mischievously. "Hmmm...This could be fun..." my voice trailed off. I'd already begun thinking of how to use this to break old Phil of his nosiness once and for all. But for now...there was a fishing trip to get underway.

Peppers and Eggs

Thursday morning we all met at my garage. All except Phil. Apparently I was right and he was feeling the pain of his three-beer-binge in my garage the night before. I gathered up everyone else, loaded the trucks and was ready to ship out before finally calling him. I figured I'd give him every chance to show up on his own and salvage his pride before giving him a warning shot across his bow. But when 8:30 AM rolled around, and still no Phil, I knew I had to call him.

Phil came slithering across the street at 8:45. I had already told the other guys what happened, knowing they would be riding Phil the entire trip to Hampton. I was going to enjoy this. We'd been here almost two years now and I had —as of yet- not seen how the locals broke each other's balls. This would be a learning experience for me.   Phil crawled into the Escalade wearing his safety sunglasses. The kind with screens on the outside edges to prevent anything from blowing into the corners of your eyes. They were hideous, but apparently Phil had worn them since his days at the foundry, and —being the tightwad that he was- he kept them. The boys were ruthless. Milledge opened a can of Vienna sausages and stuck it under Phil's nose. "You ate yet?" he said with a snicker. Phil groaned a little. Erickson had brought some Lutefisk, which is an abominable use of cod if you ask me. He offered Phil some of the slimy, white, shoe-leathery looking fish and Phil started to look a little green.

Then they started in on him about how he ever got Gladys to let him come over to my garage long enough to drink three beers in the first place. Were they the first three beers he'd ever drank in his life? "Phil ain't had a beer since Prohibition!" Milledge said with a laugh. They were having a good time at Phil's expense and doing a good job of humbling him. But the best was yet to come. In one of the greatest single moments of ball-breaking I have ever witnessed, Hank Milledge leaned over and dropped an Alka Seltzer in Phil's coffee cup. Phil was spitting and howling and I thought he was going to take a swing at Hank right there. I looked at George in the passenger's seat and we burst out laughing. That Milledge, he's a funny guy. I thought.

I turned my head and scowled at Phil, "Don't make me come back there," I joked. I'd forgotten the conversation I'd had with Chollie Bransford the night before. Phil went white. Oh yeah, I thought, Phil is afraid of the big mean Italian. I figured I'd cut him some slack. "Phil," I said, "I have just the thing you need." I handed them a big cardboard box. "Boys," I said, "This is the finest breakfast sandwich you will ever eat. My cousin George and I got up early and made you all some peppers and egg sandwiches. I get these rolls flown down from Philly once a week. You can't get 'em here. Dig in!" George and I took one each and then Milledge grabbed one. Phil looked a little unsure until I told him it was the sure cure for his headache and the way his stomach felt. He slowly unwrapped one of the sandwiches and took a bite.

Now, very little makes me happier than seeing someone taste authentic Italian food for the first time. I'm not talking about those psuedo-cannolis at Olive Garden, or some Ragu poured over Angel Hair. I'm talking about the real deal. The stuff we ate in my house growing up. Like peppers and eggs. Or tomatoes and tripe.

Phil was very uneasy eating my cooking, but the pure wonder of a peppers-and-eggs sandwich on a real Amorosso roll overwhelmed him. Phil was smiling and telling everyone how he'd never had something like this for breakfast.
It was the most talking he'd done in a long time, which, as it turns out, was a little disconcerting. Because Phil talks with his mouth full and he smacks his lips like a dog eating peanut butter. The sounds emanating from the back seat were almost enough to make me lose my appetite. I handed my big thermos to Phil and he refilled his coffee cup. I watched him in the rearview to see his face when he tasted real strong coffee, the way Italians drink it. That was priceless. Maybe drinking some coffee would stop the garbage disposal sounds coming from his face.

My cousin George was riding shotgun with me. Phil and Hank Milledge were in the back. Erickson decided to ride along with Tommy in my Tundra. He apparently had a long list of woodworking projects to complete and wanted to pick

Tommy's brain. Somewhere about halfway to Hampton, my cousin George decided it was time to toy with Phil. Out of nowhere, he looks at me and says, rather loudly, "You'll never guess who I ran into at the Bocce club in Ridley last week." I glanced at him quickly; he was wearing a Cheshire-cat grin. This is gonna be good. I thought to myself.

"Who Cuz?" I asked, trying not to smile. This was a setup, that much I knew. Not knowing where this story was going was almost like having the gag played on me, along with Phil. George leaned over and pretended to not want Phil and Hank to hear him, but spoke loudly anyway. "Rennie Prima Donna!" He said triumphantly.

Oh man! I knew what was coming. This was brilliant! I thought to myself, Why hadn't I thought of this? I feigned surprise. I knew full well George hadn't seen Rennie Prima Donna. Rennie retired to Sarasota about five years ago. But the story that was about to unfold was a classic in the annals of the Mezilli family, and it was perfect fodder for Phil's apparent obsession with the idea that because I was Italian, I was somehow in the mob. In retrospect, maybe too perfect.

"Rennie Prima Donna" was my Uncle Tony's best friend in the Cement Finishers Union. They'd apprenticed together, and when Uncle Tony became local President, Rennie was his Secretary. His real name is Lorenzo Anthony Priemontese. You pronounce it "Pree-mon-teeze," (although his sister Susanna liked to pronounce it "Preemon-tay-zee" because she thought it sounded regal that way) Of course in South Philly, everybody gets a nickname and it's usually some sort of modification of your last name. Priemontese was almost too easy to modify into "Prima Donna" but that's just what it became. Rennie loved it.

He and my Uncle Tony were the same age, right to the day. They were both born September 7, 1939. They met in

St. Rose of Lima Elementary School in the first grade and became best friends immediately. They did everything together, right up to, and including, the famous, "Body Bag Incident, of 1979." The beautiful thing was that George had concocted a brilliant way to retell that story in front of Phil Lowery while not telling the story to Phil directly. George basically set up old Phil to eavesdrop as we discussed it. It was amazing. It happened like this...

I looked at George in mock surprise, just catching his subtle wink. "You saw Rennie Prima Donna? After all these years?" George answered in a not-so-hushed tone, "Yep, Lorenzo Anthony Priemontese, right there in the flesh at the Bocce club." George was getting warmed up now, he continued, "He was looking dapper too. People always said he got made after that whole body bag thing. Uncle Gook never said anything about it, but how else do you explain him witnessing that, and not ending up dead himself?"

George paused and looked over his shoulder at Phil, who quickly bit off another piece of his peppers-and-eggs. He acted like he was looking out the window, but I'd been watching him in the rear-view...he was eavesdropping. George quickly leaned over against his window, acting as if he didn't want to be overheard and giving the impression that this whole conversation was a secret. You have to play this sort of thing right, or it's not going to work. George was baiting the trap, but you can't have the bait actually look like bait, you know?

A few minutes later, George leaned back over and whispered loudly, "Cuz, you think that stuff really happened? Them burying that guy for Nicky Bruno and all? All that concrete? You think Uncle Tony was just shining us because we were little boys back then, or do you believe him?" This was the defining moment. I looked at George and with a really serious tone I said, "I heard from someone who was there, that every word is true. It happened just like Uncle Gook said it did. Only..." I paused here to make the bait simply irresistible to Phil.

"...I heard the guy was still alive when they buried him in the concrete!" I said this in mock disbelief. George let out a low, soft whistle. "Get out!" he said, "Still alive? Who told you this?" George was trying not to laugh. I could hear it in his voice. Now it was a contest between us. Tell this story loud enough for Phil to hear it and get caught up in it, but act like we didn't realize he was listening. The only difficult thing was not laughing at each other.

I continued with my version of the story. "You remember Mosquito Johnny Damonico?" I asked. George chuckled, "The little gimp-legged kid who used to run behind the mosquito truck breathing that fog every night in the summer?" I smiled, "Yeah, the one with the really cute sister, whose..." George interrupted me and completed the story. "...whose pigtails I cut off with the hedge trimmers, because she wouldn't kiss me at the community pool!" George laughed, "Yeah, I remember her. Her name was Margo, or something like that. She had bucked teeth like a little blonde haired gopher. We always teased her because she was a blonde. She was the only blonde in Little Italy." George was really having fun with this. So was I. Now came the good part. I glanced in the rear view mirror and saw Hank Milledge sleeping with his head resting against the window and his mouth open. He was snoring pretty loudly and this made Phil have to lean forward to hear us better. That's what he was doing at the moment, pretending to be texting on his cell phone. Phil never textmessages. He still has an old phone with a number pad instead of a QWERTY keyboard, and he can never figure out how to switch between numbers and letters. He tried texting me directions once to a high school football game his nephew was playing in. All I got was a bunch of cryptic gibberish that looked like an Ottendorf Cipher. Either that or the combination for his high school gym locker.   I leaned over toward George, which made it easier for Phil to eavesdrop. "Well Mosquito Johnny works as a bartender at Pagliacci's on weekends, and he overheard Jimmy-the-Bean Valente telling another guy that they were the ones who put him there. They said he had nicked the poor box at Nicky Bruno's church and Nicky had him clipped for that." George feigned shock. In truth, there is no one named "Nicky Bruno" running any mob in Philly. "Jimmy-the-Bean" was an accountant for John Wannamaker's department stores. That's how he got his nick name, he was a bean counter. Mosquito Johnny was a hairdresser and later -after a chop and a snip- became "Jasmine Dipolito." But Phil Lowery didn't know any of this.

I continued with my tale. "So Jimmy tells this guy that they had this poor slob whacked over the head with a blackjack right in front of his parents. Apparently he was unmarried, and still lived at home. They threw him in the trunk of a Town Car and took him to the old cement factory in Camden. They stuffed him in a body bag and left him in there overnight, pondering his fate." George played up this point perfectly. "Oh Maddonn! Cuz! They left this fajoot lying in there all night knowing what was coming? And Uncle Tony was in on this? Our uncle?" He said. I glanced at George and had to bite my cheek to stop myself from laughing. He sounded so sincere, like he was really shocked that our uncle could be a part of something like this. I pressed on.

"Well somewhere along the way, the message got garbled. Nicky Bruno only wanted to scare this guy into giving the money back and promising never to do it again. So they took him to the jobsite at One Penn Center the next day, but the guy who had the order to not kill him wasn't on the job. He was in Atlantic City, collecting on some debts. So since nobody wanted to disobey an order, and nobody wanted to cross Nicky Bruno and make a judgment call in the field, they just dumped him in the pit and poured two trucks of cement on him." George whispered, "Get out!" "Yeah, Cuz." I continued, "I heard that the next day, an envelope stuffed with about fifty grand shows up at this guy's parent's house with a note; "Don't ask no questions" was all it said. That was the last anybody heard of that guy. George let out a low whistle and feigned a shudder. Phil started coughing and choking on his peppers and eggs.

Fish on the line! I thought. I looked at George. We got him Cuz I said with my eyes. The truth about the story was this; My Uncle was in the pit the first day they poured concrete in One Penn Center, which was the first real skyscraper in Philly. There has always been a story that on the first day of the pour, before one pound of cement was dumped in the hole; they ordered every man out of the pit and off the jobsite. Once they were cleared out, two Lincoln Town Cars rolled in and about six goombahs got out and threw a still very-much-alive, wriggling body in a body bag into the pit and dumped twenty yards of concrete on him. My uncle would neither confirm nor deny that he was there that day and if it actually happened, thus perpetuating the aura of mystery that he enjoyed. Nobody knows how much of this tale was fact, but again, Phil Lowery didn't know this. That's what he gets for eavesdropping. And for making assumptions about me, simply because I'm Italian. Phil was quiet as a church mouse the rest of the trip to the docks. It's not like he's a talker to begin with, but he didn't say a word until we rolled up to the boat and got out.   "There she is, boys!" I said proudly. "The *Emily-A*. FiftyFour feet of fish-stalking beauty! Marlin have nightmares about the sound of her engines and Tuna run from her wake!" I said, sounding like a pirate bragging about his ship. We parked the trucks by the slip and off-loaded all the supplies. "She'll sleep ten, so there is plenty of room. Make yourselves at home, boys!" I said, joyously. The guys were in awe of my boat. Hadn't I told you? I thought. Didn't I say she is a gem? I love this boat.

At one point, Phil started wobbling and I thought he was going to pass out. I figured he was still feeling the beers from the night before. It happened when Tommy Fallone and I had backed my Tundra dockside next to my boat, so we could offload the three huge plastic zippered bags. Each was about six feet long and made of thick Kevlar. It took four of us to get it on them boat and down into the hold below decks. Phil went white and when I came up from below, Erickson was fanning him with a newspaper and giving him a bottle of water. "Take it easy Phil," he said, "Just sit there until you come to your senses." I was startled. "What happened? Phil, are you okay?" Phil was white as a sheet. He shook his head and insisted that he was fine. I was hesitant to go out with him feeling woozy but I chalked it up to remnants of his hangover from the night before. "You're dehydrated, pal" I said, "Drink a couple of bottles of water right away and go lay down. We'll be almost three hours getting out to the canyon. Take a little nap." Phil agreed and Erickson helped him into the stateroom.

We did a little walk-through with the guys. I explained where the emergency items were. We parked the trucks in the overnight lot at the marina and we shipped out. The big Detroit Diesels roared to life and I backed her out of her slip, spun her about, and pointed her toward the mouth of the harbor, and the Atlantic just beyond. We were off. Me, my new neighbors, my cousin, and one of my best friends from the old neighborhood. It was going to be a great couple of days.

14

Chumming For Seagulls

We were heading out to open water. George sat up in the fly bridge with me and we talked for a long time about home, and our family, and how we had missed each other. Before long, Milledge joined us up on the fly bridge as well. "This is a beautiful boat, Joe. Really beautiful!" He said, against the noise of the wind. "How is Phil?" I yelled above the background noise. "Sound asleep." Hank told me. We laughed at poor Phil's misfortune and enjoyed the beautiful late morning sun.

It was a gorgeous mid-summer day with a soft swell and zero clouds. The Gulf Stream was about seventy-five miles offshore by now and getting closer each week. I'd heard they were taking Tuna and Marlin in Baltimore Canyon and shark in the shallower water on the way out. Since we got a late start that first day, I figured we'd try for shark, to give the boys a taste of big game fish right away.

It was about 2pm when I blasted the horn and called "All hands on deck!" The guys were excited as I told them the plan. "Listen boys," I began. To get you guys in the spirit of the day, so to speak, we're going to go for shark this afternoon. We can hit them on the way out to the canyon, and then we can go for big game fish in the morning. But first things first...we have to decide the pecking order here, so we're going to do a little game of "Rock-Paper-Scissors" to decide who gets the chairs first and who does the job of first mate.

The guys played for a few minutes until we had an order penciled in. My cousin was first in the fighting chairs, along with Milledge. Erickson and Phil Lowery had the lowest score, so they had deckhand duty. "Okay, Phil, Swede and Tommy come with me. George, you show Hank how to put together a shark rig."

313

I took Phil and Swede Erickson and Tommy down below decks to the lower storage hold. I started to position two of us at each end of one of the silver plastic bags we'd loaded before we left the dock. Phil reached for the wrong bag and I quickly told him, "No Phil! Not that one! You don't wanna touch that bag! Grab this one." Phil went white again and dropped to one knee. "You okay pal?" I asked him. Phil shook his head like he was shaking cobwebs. "Yeah...yeah I guess so." He said meekly. "Okay, then let's get this thing up on deck." I said.

We lugged the heavy bag up on the deck and dragged it to the transom. "Open it up for me, Phil." I said, offhandedly. Phil went white again. I thought he was going to pass out. "Geez Phil," I said, "You really are wiped out from those three beers. Are you going to be okay?" Phil was struggling to speak and staring at the big bag. I stepped past him and reached for the zipper. "Okay fellas...this is where it gets messy." I said. Phil plopped down in the fighting chair on the left side. "Yeah, you just rest for a second, Phil. Put a hat on your head, the sun will beat you up." I started to unzip the bag and thought for just a second I heard Phil whimper.

"He was a fine specimen for his age." I said. I didn't see when Phil went to the railing but I heard him start to throw up. "Chumming for seagulls?" I asked him. I hate being such a smartass sometimes. "Okay boys, help me get this drag line tied to this guy." I stepped back from the bag and Tommy and I pulled one of the two deer from inside. They were large, old bucks that I'd shot at my camp that past winter and kept in a deep freezer for this purpose. "Deer carcass will raise sharks in no time." I said emphatically. We tied a long line –about a thousand feet- to the antlers of the first buck. Tommy wrapped the other buck inside the bag and George helped him take him back below to the hold.

I shifted the boat into neutral and had Erickson help me lift the deer out onto the transom platform. "One, two, THREE!" The deer carcass hit the water with a loud splash. I went back to the helm and slipped her back in gear and we pulled away from the floating deer. I noticed Phil looking at the carcass in amazement. "Just a deer?" he muttered to himself, barely loud enough for me to have heard. "Yeah Phil, we trail a deer carcass in the chum slick when going for shark. It drives them wild. What'd you think it was?" At first I said this in all seriousness, because I couldn't imagine what else he could have thought we were dragging behind this boat. Then I remembered what Bransford told me about Phil's suspicions, and then I realized how the deer were wrapped in what essentially looked like a body bag. Poor old Phil must have thought I was getting rid of evidence. I filed this away and thought about having some fun with it later.

I looked back at Phil and Tommy and said "Okay boys, get that chum slick started." The fun was about to begin. Phil was shoveling the chum like a pro. He still looked a little pale, but I have to say, he handled the fish guts quite well. Erickson was just as adept at slicking the waters. Before long, George spotted a few fins and within a few more minutes, we'd raised five big sharks.

The deck became a madhouse of activity. They don't call it a feeding frenzy for nothing. We had stirred up about a half dozen very large and very hungry Great Whites and a couple of Tiger sharks. I had hoped for a Hammerhead or two, because they are so rare and I wanted the fellas to see one up close, but it didn't happen on this trip. We each took turns in the fighting chairs and by evening, we'd caught enough sharks that we were all pretty worn out from the battles. It was time for dinner.

We cleaned up the gear and hosed off the deck and I went inside to the galley to get the food ready. It was a perfect evening, as far as the ocean was concerned. The swell was very gradual and the boat barely moved at all. We feasted and laughed and told bad jokes and even old Phil started to relax a bit. Now, any time a group of men gather on a boat, eventually they will start reciting lines from "Jaws." The sun was just about set when we broke into the first lines of the unofficial contest.

It got pretty raucous and then, miracle of miracles, old Phil Lowery absolutely nailed a Captain Quint impersonation. I mean nailed it. If I closed my eyes, I would have thought Robert Shaw had been on deck with us. We were all in amazement at Phil's ability and ended the night singing "Show Me The Way To Go Home" and joking around about Phil's "Gladys" tattoo actually saying "U.S.S. Indianapolis." It was a lot of fun and we hated to see it end.

"Okay boys," I said, "I hate to break up the party, but we're going to set up a five mile chum slick in the morning, before we drop even one teaser in the water. That means an early wake-up. Breakfast is at six. I'll wake you. The guys had, by this point, already staked out their bunks. I decided to sleep on the deck, under the stars. On nice nights like this one was, there is nothing better than sitting under the stars, more stars than you can ever see in the city, and feeling the wonder of it all. The ocean is so big, and the sky is even bigger. George and I sat up for a long time, pointing out the shooting stars as we saw them, and talking about family, and old times.

Sunrise is awe inspiring out at sea. I stood there, up on the fly bridge, (which is about fifteen feet in the air) taking it in for a few minutes before waking the guys. Most of them were stirring already anyway. We still had about an hour's journey to get to the canyon. I didn't take us all the way out there the previous evening, because once you hit the Continental Shelf, two things happen. One: You are too deep to anchor which presents a problem because, two: The Gulf Stream is a fairly well-moving current and you'll end up a hundred miles off course by the time you wake up in the morning. We'd fished the sharks in relatively shallow water about twenty five miles from the rim of the shelf and the Washington Canyon. But the big game fish are in the deeper water, and they come up in the Gulf Stream, so we had to ride the last twenty five miles out to the deep, blue water.

I fired up the engines while George made breakfast for us all. Cuz is a great cook and he did me proud. I like to eat light in the mornings, so I had a biscotti and a couple of cups of coffee. George makes the best coffee I have ever had. Other than Angie of course.

We were about twenty minutes form the edge of the canyons and I let the GPS steer while I got the chum out from the holds. I buy it at the bait shop at the docks in fifty-five gallon drums. It is basically the garbage fish that commercial fisherman can't sell for food, plus the remnants from the processing plants. It stinks badly, but that's the point, the smellier the stuff is, the better it works on attracting game fish. This batch we had on board was as fermented and ripe as I'd ever had. I felt bad for the guys who would be rotating the chum duties throughout the morning.

Phil had done his turn the afternoon before, so he was first in the fighting chair, alongside Erickson. I took George and Tommy down below and we brought up the other silver Kevlar bag. The second deer carcass was inside and we tied the rope to his head and threw him over. He sat there bobbing, just off the transom, for a moment and it was a bit eerie. One eye was sticking up above the water and I turned

317

to Phil and said, "He's looking at you, Phil, which means you'll catch the first fish!" Phil smiled weakly, but I could tell it unnerved him to see that lone deer-eye staring at him. Within minutes, the buck was a few hundred yards off our stern, but Phil kept watching him, like Tom Hanks watching Wilson, the Volleyball, drift away from his raft.

About forty-five minutes into the chum slick, I called down from the fly bridge, "Two sails off the port stern!" George and Tommy jumped into action. We'd had teasers in the water in the middle of the chum. Teasers are lures with no hooks. The game fish will hit them and the job of the mate is to reel them fast enough the make the fish miss, but slow enough to make the fish keep trying to hit it. At the right time, the fish will find the rigged baitfish and hit it instead and then he's hooked.

George and Tommy really know how to work a teaser and in less than ten minutes after I spotted the first marlin, George called out "Fish on! Fish on Chair number one!" "I'll be darned" I thought, "Phil did hook the first fish!" Phil was seated in chair number one. The Swede jumped out of chair number two, and did as Tommy told him, reeling his line out of the water as fast as he could. Only one man can fight a fish at a time. The teasers were out and the fun began. I slipped the boat into neutral and called down to my cousin, telling him to basically run the deck. I had to stay up on the bridge to drive the boat and watch for other fish.

George took up position next to Phil and gave him instruction about when to set the hook and how to fight the fish. "Lower the rod, Phil...wait...wait...NOW! Pull back Phil!" Phil yanked back for all he was worth and if he hadn't been strapped in, he might have pulled himself right out of the chair. The rod groaned under the force of the big blue marlin Phil had just hooked. The big fish was running about

318

ten feet below the surface and I could see him shake his head wildly. He was about seven hundred feet off the stern. He shook and thrashed and then I saw him getting ready to run.

George was yelling at Phil to keep the line tight. Phil did a pretty good job at first but he made the mistake of dropping the rod for just a second and that little bit of slack was all the big fish needed. He managed to turn his head and that was that. Now that he was facing away from the boat, he started to run...fast. He stripped away about five hundred feet of line in less than a minute. Phil was panicky but George calmed him down. "It's okay, Phil, it's just going to take longer to boat him now. He won't turn his head back toward the boat until you wear him down." Phil settled into the chair and George talked him through the next two hours. When to reel, when to relax. About two and a half hours after hooking the giant, the fish slowed down and turned his head back toward the boat. I knew what was coming next.

"He's turned Georgie!" I yelled. "He's getting ready to sound!" Once a game fish has turned his head back toward his pursuer, he has one or two more tricks left. He knows this is a battle to the death now, (or so he thinks...we actually catch and release marlin) so he gets very feisty. His next trick is to sound; to dive deep and try to hide from his pursuer. The marlin was getting ready go deep. He turned and ran back at the boat, this took the pressure off his head and gave him a chance to relax and rest a bit. He was running with the strain of the line instead of against it. He covered about two hundred feet in just a few seconds and down he went. The big rod bent into a hard "C" and Phil's eyes got big. "Let the drag tire him out, Phil!" George told him. Phil sat back and George tightened the drag a click or two and the fish was pulling against the reel.

This was where I came in. I slipped the boat into gear and slowly pulled forward. Now he was pulling against the Emily A as well. So long as I didn't move her too quickly, the fish would tired and surface. Ten minutes later and I saw him shimmering in the sunlight about three feet down, about three hundred feet off the stern. "He's up, Cuz! Getting ready to jump!" George knelt by Phil's right ear. "When he jumps, Phil, you drop the rod tip. Leave it down until you see the splash and he is back in the water. If you pull back while he's in the air, he'll spit that hook out!" George was good at this.

Phil did as he was told and the big monster jumped about fifteen seconds later. He was beautiful! About seven feet of blue marlin, probably four hundred pounds or more. As soon as he splashed down, Phil pulled back and within another twenty minutes we boated him. Actually, we got him to the side, snapped a bunch of pictures and pulled a scale with a pair of pliers. We tagged him and cut the line away from the hook. The hook would dissolve in a week or so and he'd be fighting someone else soon.

Phil was ecstatic. He'd never caught anything this big and he talked more than any time since I'd met him. "Ya'll see that feesh?!" He said gleefully. "That was the biggest feesh I ever caught!" Phil was happy. Which was good because now that he caught himself a fish, it was someone else's turn in the chair and he was back on chum duty.

He didn't seem to mind it a bit. Catching the first fish of the day seemed to really rejuvenate Phil, and he was chumming and talking up a storm.

Every time someone would hook up with a fish, Phil would cheer and hoot and holler. By the end of the first day, Phil's marlin was still the biggest. He was having a good time and so were the other boys. By evening, we'd boated four fish; two marlin, a tuna, and a Mahi Mahi. The Mahi stayed on board and we filleted it right there and had grilled Mahi for dinner.

We had a serious card game going after dinner and George decided to pump Phil a little more with the mob stories from back in the old neighborhood. He told him stories about people even I'd forgotten about. People like "Bobby Knuckles" who lived around the corner from Georgie's parents.

Bobby was probably the stupidest man in Little Italy. Tragically he was also the only guy in the neighborhood with a patch of grass in his backyard, which —in turn- required him to own, and actually use a lawnmower. I'd be kind and say Bobby wasn't very bright, but I'd be lying by omission. Bobby Knuckles was *really* stupid. He had this beat-up old lawnmower that his old man had gotten from saving S and H Green Stamps. He cut the back yard with it each week, even though he could have done the whole job with a weed-whacker in less than ten minutes. He was constantly running over stuff with the mower back there. His dog's bones, his kid's baseball gloves. Honest-to-God, he ran over his kid's glove. How did he not see that?

Anyway, he had this little row of hedges along the back of his yard that separated it from the service alley. They were ewes, or something. I just remember them being low and ugly. So Bobby Knuckles decides they need to be trimmed; only he doesn't have hedge trimmers. Neither did anyone else on the block, because they all had fences in their back yards and not hideous bushes. So since he can't borrow hedge clippers from anybody, Bobby Knuckles decides to use the lawnmower. He fired the thing up, and stood in front of it and lifted it up to use it as a hedge trimmer. Yeah, no kidding, he was going to trim hedges by holding a lawn mower over them and lowering it down.   Well, as you can imagine, this was an insanely stupid idea, but then, Bobby Knuckles was pretty darned stupid. The stunod lost his footing while holding the lawnmower under the base. Then he lost his fingers down to the second knuckle on both hands. His wife Marie was running around trying to bandage his hands and collect the fingers from the bushes he was trimming. Their big slobbery dog, "Rocky" had one of them in his mouth like a bone, and Marie almost got bitten trying to pry it loose.

She managed to get his hands bandaged and got the fingers bagged up and put on ice. Getting an ambulance to their house through the double-parked locals on 12th street was another battle. They finally got there, and by that time the crowd had gathered. Mrs. Begnetti was peeping through her blinds and Father Franco was on the steps trying to calm Marie. Somehow the surgeons at Thomas Jefferson found a way to reattach all but one of his fingers...the one his big stupid dog had gnawed on. The surgery left his knuckles enlarged and grotesque and they only bent about halfway, and so he got his nickname... "Bobby Knuckles." Now, Bobby Knuckles was a bag man for Lito DiStefano who was, in turn, a middle reliever for one of the crime families in Philly. We called them "middle relievers" because they weren't very far up the food chain. They weren't Captains or Capos, just guys who had risen a step above the run-of-the-mill grunts who did the bidding of the bosses. Guys like Bobby. Bobby was a collector. He went out every Monday with a list of guys who owed money to Lito and he shook them down for what they owed, plus his own fees for not breaking their thumbs. Sometimes he went ahead and broke their thumbs and then charged them a fee not to "make it a leg next time."
Mostly he just scared people, because the grotesque scars from the reattachment of his fingers, plus that one missing

digit, made him a pretty scary guy. He was scary in the way that really dumb guys are scary. He was a mouth breather. He stood there staring at you when you talked to him with his mouth hanging open and you could hear him breathing like a scuba diver. We all figured it was because he was too stupid to blow his nose. The people in the neighborhood eventually lost their fear of him, mostly since we were all smart enough to not get in bed with Lito or his goons. The couple of times anyone on the block got in trouble with gambling debts, me or Pop would pay it off quietly and have the guy work Saturdays on the trucks until he paid it back. So Bobby Knuckles plied his trade elsewhere, and on the block he was just one of the neighbors...albeit a creepy one.

Anyway, my cousin George was regaling Phil and the other guys with tales from Little Italy and funny stories about our family. The boys were eating it up. Old Phil was asking a lot of questions about the mob. Did we know the Scarfos or the Testas or the Brunos? *Really?* I thought to myself. *The Testas? Angelo Bruno?* I'm forty-four years old, for God's sake. Those guys were killed in the mob wars when I was like, twelve. Plus I'm not Sicilian and most of the mob guys were. Phil was really getting on my nerves now with the mob innuendo.

We played cards and told jokes until almost midnight. The boys all decided to get some sleep and George and I went out on deck to chit chat before turning in. I planned on sleeping on deck again and so I told the other guys "goodnight." George and I stayed awake for a while talking and planning the next day's fishing. Before turning in, I remembered a little chore I needed to take care of. "Cuz," I said to George," Can you come up and help me with something before you turn in?" "Sure thing," George said, setting down his beer. I turned to the rest of the guys and

323

said "Fellas, chow is 4AM. Lines in the water at five. So get some sleep."

About an hour later, Georgie and I walked up on deck and around to the side entry to the engineering room. The storage deck is next to the engine compartment on my boat and you can get to it without cutting through the staterooms if you need to. "Cuz, I have that one nasty deer down there and I just remembered it's still in the bag. We need to dump it in the drink before it stinks the boat up something awful." One of the four deer carcasses I brought along was actually a big old buck that I had hit with my old pickup, on the road out by my hunting camp and I found him dead by my barn the next morning. It was too cold to bury him because the ground had frozen and so I stuck him in a Kevlar bag and placed him in the old freezer I had out there, intending to bury him in the spring. I had forgotten about him and we had a power outage over the winter and he'd gone bad in there. Then when the power came on, he froze again so I had no idea he was spoiled.

I thought I would just bring him along for an extra carcass in case we needed it. That was a bad move because he thawed out on the drive to the boat and he stunk to high heavens. The Kevlar kept it under control but I knew it was bad. So I decided to dump him in the ocean.

George and I walked down the three steps to the engineering area and I opened the locker where the two remaining deer carcasses were stored in the silver Tyvek bags. "It's the bigger of the two, George," I said, pointing to the bag on top. George grabbed one end and I grabbed the other. We wrestled the bag through the doorway and around the very tight turn near the bow end of the stateroom. You have to be careful walking along the galley-way because it's only about a foot wide. George and I worked our way along the catwalk toward the stern of the boat so we could lay the bag down, open it up and remove the deer.

"Cuz this thing is heavy, and he stinks like a sewer!" George said. "How much did he weigh?" "I don't know Cuz," I said, "I hit him with the truck out by the hunting camp last winter. He didn't die right away so I shot him to end his misery. But he was an old man I know that. I guess he's what...two-hundred pounds?" George huffed and puffed, "Oh he's every bit of that." He said. "I can lift about a hundred and fifty by myself so he's all of two hundred and then some." At one point I slipped a bit and banged against the stateroom window, but I didn't think anyone was awake. We managed to get the bag to the stern behind the fighting chairs of the boat and I started to unzip it. The stench was unbearable.

"Cuz," I said in resignation, "I'm not even going to try to save this bag. This thing stinks to high heaven. Let's just throw him overboard," George and I slip the bag over the transom and watched it bobbing in the moonlight. We waited. And waited. Finally George said, "Cuz he's not going to sink. You didn't gut him did you?" "No," I said, "I wasn't going to eat him, he was road kill. Why bother?" George chuckled, "Well not that it matters, but with his guts still inside, the gas has built up and he's going to keep floating like that. I guess that's okay, but I wouldn't want someone finding this bag drifting and opening it up. Plus, unless you want to go another 25 miles away, his floating in the water will kill the fishing for us tomorrow" "That's a good point," I said, "I'll take care of this. I went into the stateroom quietly and grabbed my .45 out of my duffle bag.   Back out on deck I got up on the transom while George held a spot light on the deer in the Kevlar bag. "I hope I don't wake the fellas," I said. I fired at the bodybag, BAM! BAM! BAM! Three good

325

shots with the .45 should do it. I thought to myself. George and I waited on the transom watching the silver Kevlar bag. "Well if hitting him with the truck didn't do it, three shots from a forty-five sure did!" George said with a laugh. "I just hope he sinks, so the crabs can eat him." I answered. George and I watched for a few more minutes and finally the silver bag sank below the surface of the moonlit Atlantic Ocean. "I guess the boys were pooped and slept through that." I told George, "Okay Cuz, I'm heading to bed." Georgie and I washed our hands and I climbed up to the bridge to get some sleep. We had another full day of fishing in the morning and I was anxious to get some more fish on the line.

Things That Go Bump In The Night

Below decks in the stateroom, Phil Lowery snapped the blinds closed quickly. The darkness hid his fear, and the pale whiteness of his features as the blood drained from his face. "Milledge!" he hissed at his friend sleeping in the bunk next to his. "Milledge wake up!" Phil pushed and prodded his friend until he awoke. "Huh?" Hank Milledge grumbled, "What's that you say Phil?" Lowery was trembling in the darkness. "Hank I seen 'em! I seen 'em just whack a man and throw him overboard!" Hank
Milledge sat up in his bunk and rubbed his eyes. "Phil what the heck are you talking about? Who?"
"Mezilli!" He spit out, "Old Joe and his goon cousin just dumped a body overboard. They even shot the poor bastard so he'd sink! I just seen the whole thing!"
"Phil, calm down. Tell me what you're talking about." "I seen the whole thing, Hank. They went down to the hold and

they got that other body bag...the one Joe very specifically told me not to touch yesterday. They were toting it to the stern and one of them banged the window right over my bunk. It woke me up, and so I looked out the window to see what the racket was. I heard them talking. Mezilli killed this poor bastard out at that hunting camp he owns. He ran him over with his truck, Hank! The heartless sombitch called him "Road kill!" Road kill, Hank! How evil can a man be when he runs another man over and just calls him road kill?"

Phil was on a roll now and if I didn't reel him in he'd be off on a tangent from now until Christmas. But there was something different this time. Phil usually had the facts all wrong or he'd seen something that really wasn't there. This time it seemed different. He was very matter-of-fact and to be honest...very believable. He continued; "Him and his cousin were talking about running this poor man down out at the hunting camp. If you ask me, I think it must be that "Crusher" fella I heard him talkin' on the phone about with some other mobster up in Philadelphia. Remember? I told ya, this Crusher fella was apparently an old hitman and he was long in the tooth and he must have worked for Mezilli at one time but he was employed by the current mob boss up there now." Phil was shaking and I gave him a little glass of water to help him get his bearings.

Phil continued; "I told ya, about eight months ago I was returning that leaf blower I borrowed and I overheard him saying how this fella "The Crusher" was old and ready to retire. He was apparently a very dependable hitman for the Mezilli mob but his time had come. The new boss in Philly called Joe and asked him if he wanted to do the honors or if he just wanted them to do it back there and cut him up in a scrap yard. Honest to God, Hank! They was gonna cut the man in pieces in a scrap yard! Anyway Mezilli told him to have him shipped down to his hunting camp and he would take care of him out there. I guess the poor fella got there last winter and maybe he tried making a run for it and your buddy Don Corleone must've run him down with his truck." Phil was nearly hyperventilating now. He was near hysteria, but his story was fascinating and I was listening intently. He went on; "I reckon he stuffed him in that other body bag and brought him out here with them three deer to disguise it. Him and his cousin just dumped him overboard and shot him so he'd sink! I told you! Didn't I tell you? He's a mafia!"

Phil was beside himself now. A strange mixture of pride and fear. Pride in the fact that he was right all along and now he'd finally gotten proof. Fear in the way you fear the beautiful girl saying "yes" to your request for a date. "You got her now, big-boy, whatcha gonna do with her?" I had to admit; for the first time since Joe had moved to our neighborhood and Phil had begun this crazy witch hunt of his, I was beginning to believe him. Something about the way he told this story was different from the others. He had facts in order and he'd actually seen and heard something for once. Up until now it had been blurry pictures of rolled up burlap or my dog pissing on him. "Phil," I said quietly, "You just get some sleep and tomorrow we'll check some things out on the sly." Phil looked at me puzzled. "You mean you finally believe me?" He asked. "Well I believe something has you mighty worked up right now, Phil. We'll start there. Now go to sleep." I replied. I had to admit, Phil really had me thinking.

When we woke up the next day, Phil leaned over to me and, with a strange, satisfied smile, said "I have proof!" "What?" I asked, "Proof," He said, "I have proof of what I heard last night!" Phil was smug when he said this but we walked to the front of the boat and Phil pretended to be taking pictures with his cell phone. When he was convinced nobody could hear us talking, he reached into his pocket and pulled out a tiny micro recorder. "Hey that's Timmy Pepper's recorder!" I said. Peppers used that thing a hundred times at my house while he was cutting my lawn. I'd recognize it anywhere.

Phil panicked. "SHHH!" he whispered, "Hank shut the hell up! You want Mezilli to hear us?" I looked around; the guys were all on the far end of the boat, with the cabin between us, a distance of over fifty feet. On top of that, we were out at sea and the noise of the breeze was drowning out any conversation farther than five feet away. But I know how Phil is about secrecy and spyin' and such, so I played along. "Why do you have Pepper's recorder, Phil?" I asked. Phil smiled and pressed

Play. "You just give a listen." I heard Phil throwing up and Gladys knocking on his bathroom door. "Phil, you alright in there? You better hurry or you'll miss your fishing trip!" Then Phil wiped his mouth and barked at her; "I'm fine!" Fix me a bicarbonate and find my sunglasses." Phil snapped the button and muttered under his breath. He forwarded a little until he stopped at a point in a conversation where Joe was talking to his cousin; something about burying bodies in concrete and their uncle being involved.

"Phil," I said, "They said it was their uncle! Not them. And George even said he wondered of the story was true. This ain't proof of nothin'!"

"It proves they have mafias all through their family!" he hissed angrily. "Dammit man what if that story is true? The man even said he'd heard it verified by someone else. What else do you need...pictures?" Then Phil forwarded it a little more, he stopped once at the place where he was puking over the side of the boat and the seagulls were buzzing his head.

329

"God damn this thing!" He winced. He stopped it again and I heard some muffled voices, a bumping sound, and a splash and then –clear as day- I heard three gunshots. "By god...you did hear gunshots last night!"

Phil straightened up. "You're damned right I did!" Phil was unstoppable now. He had proof and he had someone actually believing him. That was gas and matches if you know Phil. "They dumped that poor Crusher fella overboard, and then they shot him just for good measure!" Phil said triumphantly. "Joe Mezilli is a heartless, clod blooded damn killer...and I told you all along. Now do you believe me?" I didn't want to believe it. I like Joe. But I know what I heard. "I believe I heard gunshots Phil. I believe you heard something more. I think that's enough to check him out.

"Phil I think we should keep this very quiet until we get home tonight. We're seventy miles out at sea. If Joe is a killer, this ain't the place to confront him." Phil agreed. "Listen, Hank," He said, "If he offers you any tequila, you don't drink it, you understand?" I cocked my head like a Labrador puppy. "Phil," I said softly, "Why would he offer me tequila, and what does that have to do with this killin' nonsense?" Phil ran his hand under his ball cap and scratched his head. "Big Pussy," He said. "Now, goddammit Phil!" I yelled at him, "There you are calling me that again! Just because I've never liked tequila doesn't mean you have to call me names. I hate that word!" Phil squinted his eyes and said "No, Hank. Big Pussy. He was a guy on The Sopranos, remember I told ya? He was a mafia! They shot him on a boat just like this one and dumped him overboard in a body bag." "Phil,' I said, "The Sopranos was a TV show. And what does tequila have to do with it?" "It was a TV show based on facts, it was more like a documentary!" Phil snarled, "And they gave Big Pussy tequila before they shot him."

Tequila, I thought. *Stay away from the Tequila.*

As much as I wanted to maintain suspicion of Joe, after we caught us a few more fish, the whole body bag thing was forgotten. At least for me. Hell, I liked Joe. I liked him a lot and he didn't seem intent on harming us. In fact all he really seemed to be worried about was making sure we'd all caught some nice fish and had a good time. I mean none of us had to bring anything. No food, no drinks, he never asked us to chip in for fuel for this beautiful boat, and I know them big ol' Allisons burn up some diesel. No, Joe seemed to really enjoy seeing us having a good time. He was what you'd call gregarious. From what I gather, most all Italians are like that. 'Cept for the ones in the mob.

Anyway, the more I thought about it the more I was ready to dismiss the entire idea of Phil's. I couldn't be sure what was in that bag they threw overboard and I was having too much of a good time to ask my generous host. Maybe Phil was just trying to pin a tail on a myth, as they say. I do know that Phil loves those mob stories. He watched every episode of The Sopranos until he could say all the lines. Same with The Godfather, and Goodfellas and A Bronx Tale, and he's the only man I know who didn't laugh at Analyze This. Not even a smile. I thought that movie was hysterical but he sat there stoned faced in the theater. I asked him; "Phil, this movie is funny. How come you ain't laughin'?" He shot me an icy stare and said; "That's how they win people over to their side; by makin' movies where they's cute and funny. They make you forget they's killers!" "Who, Phil?' I asked, "Who you talking about?" "Them Mafias!" He shot back, "They are secretly behind all those movies and TV shows. It's propaganda for them. They get the average folks to think they ain't dangerous with shows like that. I read about it on the internet."

When Phil gets like this I just let him ramble. If you argue, he only goes on longer. So instead of discussing this with him, I just walked over to the transom and started throwing chum. Which made Phil madder by the minute. But I knew he wasn't about to keep talking about this in front of the other fellas and especially in front of Joe. Phil sat down in the fighting chair when his turn came around again and before long, the scowl was gone from his face. He'd hooked him a Wahoo and after about forty-five minutes he'd boated it. Now, the Wahoo is sort of our official state fish, and "Wahoo-Wa!" is the war cry of the University of Virginia, so old Phil was sittin' tall in the saddle after he boated that baby. "That's two for me, boys!" He gloated. "Ya'll ain't caught me yet!

"Nobody is going to catch you, either, Phil." Joe called down from the bridge, "Time to head back, boys. Lines out. Pack the bait it's Two PM and we need to be dockside by five." The fellas were all smiles and they scurried about securing the gear, but underneath it all, you could tell none of us was really ready to leave. We'd really been enjoying ourselves. Even Phil. Despite apparently witnessing Joe and George disposing of evidence and in spite of the fact that he was thoroughly convinced that Joe was really planning on killing one or all of us out here, he'd had himself a natural ball. I had forgotten most of what we'd talked about until we were in the stateroom on the ride back and he reminded me very quietly about what was on that little recorder. Then my mind started racing again. What if Joe is a mobster? I thought to myself. What if that was a body he dumped overboard last night, and what was it in those burlap rolls in his garden?"

The rest of the ride in became my own personal little storm inside. My feelings for Joe against my longtime friendship with Phil and the loyalty I had for him. Phil is a good man and I put up with his suspicions and his overworked imagination because deep down he is a good friend. So I didn't quite know where I stood on this as the boat pulled back to the dock. The other guys were packing up and walking out onto the dock and I pulled Phil aside. Usually I just go along with him to keep the peace, but tonight I was a little more direct. "Phil..."I said, "You keep this between you and me until we get more evidence." "Evidence?" Phil groused, "I give you a ton of it already and you want more?" But this time I was concrete in my resolve. "Phil, you're my friend, but if your suspicions are even half true, we have to be very careful and get even more evidence. You go around accusing a fella of being in the mob and you'll ruin his life. Now I don't care what you think, but I don't want that on my conscience. So we keep this quiet for now. Am I clear?"

I don't know if I have ever been so direct with Phil before, and I think it took him by surprise. "Ye...yes Hank. I see your point" He said softly, like a defeated little boy. "We'll give that tape another good listen and look at those pictures again before we move on this." "Now you're making sense, Phil" I said. "C'mon, let's get home.

15

Two-Flush Tony And The Loan Shark

So one evening in September of our second year here, I get a call from Mario Sebastianelli from back home. Mario was the guy we put in charge of the neighborhood fund I set up with proceeds from the buyout. He was an accountant, and a lay-minister at St. Monica's church so we figured he was the most experienced, and the most trustworthy. It's worked well for all these years now.

But there was this one time...

Mario called me sometime that third year we were in Virginia. He always sounds very business-like to begin with but this time he sounded just a little edgy. He was never a guy to beat around the bush, which I always liked about him. "Joe," he began, "I have...*we* have, a bit of a problem up here." Now it was not like Mario to ever call me with a need and I knew immediately he was referring to something in the neighborhood, because if he needed anything for himself he could have simply gone to the committee that oversees the fund.

We'd set up a committee of key people within the Little Italy community, who would decide by secret ballot, whether someone would get the financial help they asked for. Most of the time, the committee would do the buying, instead of just handing out cash. When Mrs. Begnetti was short a thousand bucks for a new boiler, they paid the plumber. When Dominic Stubini was trying to open a new hoagie shop on Shunk Street, the committee paid his lease for a year, directly to the landlord. Seldom did they just write a check to a recipient. Oh they did sometimes, like at Christmas, when a single mom didn't have money for gifts for her kids, or the time Juliana Minetti was light on the cost of her daughter's wedding. Jules husband Lou had been a Philly cop and was killed by a drunk driver on his way home from working his second job doing security at the Tower

Theatre. That time, an envelope stuffed with cash just "mysteriously" appeared on her kitchen table while she was at work. "Giving you a boost" is what we
Italians call it.

The rest of the time, the committee functioned pretty much like a non-profit organization. If you had a need, you submitted a letter. Then you had a sit-down at a monthly dinner at St. Monica's parish hall. You never appeared in a suit, before some board like the Inquisition. These were friends helping each other, not First National Bank. The need was discussed and you got your answer that same night. No waiting, no sweating bullets, and nobody else knew about it. Mario invested the money in some very secure mutual funds and he was actually making interest for us faster than gifts were being paid out. The fund was a great success and it bought a ton of goodwill for Waste International in the years after we left.

But that phone call was the one and only time there was ever any problem as far as the operations of the thing. Normally it was simple. We never loaned. Everything was a gift. If you ever got in a position to repay, then we'd take it and invest it and it would be there for the next family in need. But repayment was never expected or required. Except this time. This time, when we finally decided to help, we demanded repayment. We even went so far as to attach a lien to the guy's house because his reputation wasn't good and we needed to be assured we could recoup in case he welched on us.

I was in my garage one Thursday afternoon with my sons Peter and Jack (whom most of the time I called "Giacomo" which is the Italian derivative of the English "Jack") I was doing a tune-up on Angie's Escalade and it's the kind of thing a dad should teach his sons to do as well. Peter and

Jack were my two oldest boys. David would have been there too except he had a science report due the next day and he and Angie were in the house going through his pictures to document the project. He had started a few string bean seeds on a wet paper towel in a Dixie cup as phase one of the project. He and Angie had snapped a picture each morning as the seed germinated and they were editing it into a time lapse movie. The next step would be to transfer the seeds into a small terrarium and actually –with a little help from dad- start a micro garden.

So it was my two oldest boys, Milledge, Lowery, and Tommy Fallone. Tommy had been working on his own home now for about six months. We had formed the partnership we discussed and had flipped two nice little houses out by Perrymont Avenue and bought two tri-plexes for rentals over by the school. Tommy had a new box truck and about twenty thousand dollars' worth of tools and the house he bought had a nice detached garage where he was setting up a sweet workshop. He took one night off each week to come over, eat dinner with us, and hang with my family.

The kids had taken to calling him "Uncle Tommy," which Tommy relished. He figured that by this point, it was useless to think about having kids of his own. I told him not to give up just yet. He'd been on a few dates but mostly, Tommy threw himself into the business we'd began together and was determined to be a success. And he was doing a great job of it so far.

Anyway, my phone rings and I see in the caller ID it's Mario Sebastianelli. I mentioned it to Tommy as I answered. "Yo Mario! Come' Stai?" Mario is a really sweet guy. He's quiet and to the point, but he has a huge, loving heart. He's a natural as a lay minister at St. Monica's. He was in the final year of his study for the priesthood and he met his sister's

339

college roommate at a Christmas party and that was it. He was smitten. It took a few months to deal with the mutual guilt they felt about him leaving the priesthood, but thirty years and six kids later, their service to the church is about as effective as it would have been had he stayed.

So it's Mario on the phone and he's got a prickly situation on his hands. It seems that one of the locals was asking for a loan and not for the most noble of purposes. Mario explained; "Joey, It's Tony Leonetti; he wants to borrow twenty thousand dollars." I almost choked on my Coca-Cola. "Two-Flush Tony Leonetti wants to borrow twenty large?" Tommy was standing next to me and he spit out his beer. Without even hearing the story, Tommy is waving his arms in a very exaggerated "X" and silently mouthing the word "NO!" over and over again. I winked at Tommy and smiled. "Okay Mario, what's his story this time?" I asked.

Now, you'll need to know about Tony Leonetti. "TwoFlush Tony" is a massive, squatty, annoying guy. He has so much hair on his body that he looks like those "Wolf-Boys" who do a high-wire act down in Mexico. The ones you've seen on the cover is the National Enquirer. He has asthma because he is so fat, so he wheezes. He drives big, flashy, black, Lincoln Town Cars and his gut is so big that he has to have the tilt-steering all the way up, like the steering wheel on a semi, because he can't get that belly behind it otherwise.

He has a huge gambling problem and it's gotten him into some serious trouble over the years down at Atlantic City. He has owed some very important people some very large sums of money. There were times when he was so broke that he would come to the shop begging for a few days' work on the trucks. My dad, big-hearted man that he is, always tried to oblige him. The problem is that Tony weighs well over four hundred fifty pounds. He eats in a day what you and I eat in a weekend. There are side effects from being so huge and eating so much. He's had the reputation as a world-class toilet clogger since he was like, nine years old.

That's where he got his name from. "Two-Flush Tony" Leonetti. It's gross, I know. But it's better than what his old man used to call him. When Tony was a boy, his father, who was a pretty gruff guy, called him "Shit-Stick, the King of Uranus."

The story was that Tony's girth produced so much, umm, *byproduct*, that his parents kept a stick in the bathroom so he could break it up before he flushed, and it took two flushes to get it all down. This was a big embarrassment for his father because he was a plumber by trade. He's a plumber and his son can't stop clogging the toilets. It was so bad he had to keep a stick in the bathroom at school, too.

His old man was not the nicest guy, and Tony's older brother was a star athlete and I think the old man just plain didn't like Tony, so he embarrassed him every chance he could. Including calling him "Shit Stick" in front of his friends, and referring to the stick as his scepter. Since none of us could get by calling him that in front of our parents, Skip started calling him "Two-Flush Tony" and it stuck. We'd go into the *Wawa* and Skip would see Tony and he'd say "Yo! Give Two-Flush Tony, a pound of Bologna!"

Tony was one of the guys who never shook his nickname either. They were still calling him "Two-Flush" when I moved down here to Virginia. Tony gets embarrassed and tries telling people who don't know any better that it's his nickname because he is such a great poker player. But one look at the guy and you know why they call him that. I heard he actually broke a toilet at Harrah's Casino in Chester last year.

Anyway, Mario started telling me about Tony needing money because he owes a lot of dough down in AC. My gut reaction is that he also owes some bookies. Because owing on a tab you got comped in a casino is not a matter of life and death. Owing the private bookies down there...that's another story. Tony is apparently into some recognizable names, and for a lot of money. Almost twenty grand, and with the vig these people add, it's growing every week.

My initial reaction was to turn him down flat. "Mario," I said, "The money isn't there for that purpose. I worked hard in my family business and not so guys like Two-Flush Tony Leonetti could borrow from this thing of ours to pay off the local Gambino guys." Mario agreed entirely, but then his big, almost-a-priest heart would kick in and he went to bat for old Two-Flush. "Joey," he reasoned, "He's got kids, and a house. If he doesn't pay soon you know what those guys will do to him. He has a good job. Maybe we can get him some help and get him to stop." I thought about it some. Then I asked Mario; "Tony has had collection issues in the past. He isn't a good payer. Why should I trust him this time?" Mario rattled off a list of Tony's qualities. He had to repeat himself to make the list sound impressive, because Tony doesn't have that many. And I'm a guy who sees the best in almost everyone. "Joey," Mario said, "I'd be willing to personally guarantee it." Now I knew Mario could cover it if he had to. He might not have that kind of cash on him but he could pull it together in a jam.

I told Mario I would think about it and call him in the morning. I hung up and took a swig from my Coke. Tommy asked me what was going on. I gave him the rundown, and I had to fill-in the details for Milledge and Lowery, including how Tony got his nickname. This, in turn, made my sons both giggle like mad and start running around saying "Two-

Flush Tony." So I hashed it out there in the garage. I didn't tell Hank and Phil about the community fund. I didn't want to come off as pretentious. I just said that Mario handles some financial affairs for me and that Tony wanted to borrow money. I figured they'd never meet the man so what do I care if I tell them about his gambling issues?

After about thirty minutes, I decided I'd go through with the deal but with some conditions. I called Mario back. "Mario..."I began, "I talked it over with Tommy, and some other fellas. I think I might go ahead with this, but there are some conditions involved. First, despite our usual policy, this will be a loan. He is going to repay and with vig. He's not going to work it off by doing jobs around the neighborhood. No more of that. He will repay in cash, with interest. You set the vig aside and return it to him once he's paid off, but you do NOT tell him about that." "Mario agreed, "How much vig, Joe?" he asked. "We don't want to take his head off, how about one percent a month? That sounds fair, right?" Mario agreed with that as well. "Two more items Mario," I continued, "One; you attach a lien on his house. If he welches, you at least have protection. And two...you tell Tony I want him to sit down with my Old Man and talk about this loan face to face. I want Pop to look him in the eye before we loan him twenty large." Mario agreed with this as well. "Okay Joe. I'll see him tomorrow, and I'll pass this along. I think he'll go for it." I laughed at this, "Of course he'll go for it. If he doesn't pay those guys, they'll give him his own deep-sea diver suit. Those guys don't play." I said my goodbyes and hung up.   Milledge and Lowery were staring at me sort of wide mouthed. Milledge asked me, "You do that a lot, Joe...loan money?" Lowery elbowed him so hard I thought I heard ribs cracking. "Hank!" he hissed. But I didn't mind. "Yeah sometimes," I answered, still not wanting to let them

343

know about the fund. "If there's a need." Tommy piped in; "Two Flush want's to borrow money, huh? What, he owes the mob again?" I smiled at Tommy. "Yeah. He apparently got himself into a few big time poker games that are overseen by the Bengiviengo Family. Now he's into them for twenty large and they charge him about three points a week. He's so afraid that he won't even go home at night anymore for fear they'll blow up his car right in front of his kids. Mario wants us to basically buy Tony's debt from them and let him repay the fund with interest."

I was curious what Tommy's take would be, since he had his own run-in with the seamy side of things in his lifetime. "You know how I feel about forgiveness and second chances, Cuz," He said, "But Two-Flush Tony is a habitual offender where stuff like this is concerned. If you compare this to my situation, Tony is Nicky Bowties. No character." Tommy was right in a lot of ways, but I was sort of hamstrung on this. "I hear ya, Tommy." I said, "But he's got kids and Mario wants to personally back it. So I think we'll take the risk. Besides, he has to go and ask permission from the Old Man. That, in itself might cure him of his ills." Tommy got a kick out of that.

While we were still discussing Two-Flush Tony Leonetti and his gambling addictions, my cell phone rang again. This time it was local. I answered and the voice on the line identified himself as Jim Hodge. I had been expecting his call. I ran into someone in the Co-Op who saw us working on one of the new investment properties. They said they knew a guy who needed some work done, and asked me if we did construction work for anyone besides our own projects. I was in a hurry, and I didn't have any of Tommy's cards with me so I gave them my cell number and told them to call. The guy called me the next day and said his friend Jim was needing some work done and couldn't get a decent bid from anybody locally. I thought that was odd, since there were a lot of guys out there and they were always looking to take on a job or two extra.

Anyway, we're standing in the garage and my phone rings and it's this Jim Hodge guy. He introduced himself and asked me if I do concrete. "Do we do concrete?" I said with a laugh. "Well," I said, "I have a lot of experience with concrete Jim, but I'm not actually in that end of the business. Tommy Fallone does all my concrete work for me. In fact Tommy does all my jobs. He runs a full crew and they are all very good at their work. Some of these guys have been in the business for generations. How about if I give Tommy your number and have him call you, and you just contract this job with him directly, fair enough?" Hodge agreed and we hung up.

I turned to Hank and Phil. "Either of you guys know a man named Jim Hodge?" I asked? Milledge perked up and said that he knew about him. "Yeah, I know who he is. He owns a septic tank service. Honeydippers we call 'em. He ain't the kind of fella you want to do business with Joe. Unless you make him pay you in cash." This was intriguing. "Yeah?" I asked, "It's funny, I got a bad feeling talking to the guy, just felt like I was dealing with a weasel, you know?" Hank chuckled, "Calling Jim Hodge a weasel is an understatement." He said. "Here's the thing..." Hank sat his beer on the workbench, and a slight grin came over his face as he told me the story. "Hodge was a very successful businessman at one point. He's a smart guy, and resourceful He owned a huge, nationwide title company. He was doing title work for every major mortgage lender and most of the real estate franchises. He was worth millions! But he was a greedy, unethical bastard and it finally caught up with him when the mortgage industry collapsed a few years ago. They did some digging and he had even been ripping off his own employees. They were doing illegal title recording, writing titles on properties that had liens on them that he ignored. Why, he was as crooked as a barrel of fish hooks." Hank said that with a snicker and I have to admit, the phrase made me laugh. "I'll have to remember that one." I said. "So what happened to him?" I asked.

Hank continued; "He lost everything as far as the business is concerned. I heard he had over two thousand folks working for him and they all wound up without jobs too. Like most shrewd men who do things crooked, he took care of himself just fine. He kept his house, but the government seized his assets. He couldn't restart his business, because he is still under investigation, so he did the only thing he could do. His daddy had been a septic tank serviceman and a good one too. They had one truck, and old Hodge took it out of mothballs and started servicing septic tanks."

Phil piped in with his dark commentary; "He went from shittin' on everybody else to sucking everybody else's shit. It's poetic irony if you ask me." I was going to correct Phil about the poetic irony thing, but I thought it might only serve to strain the already edgy relationship we have. Hank picked the story back up from here. "He's just about the most miserable man alive now." Hank said. "He ain't but about five feet six to begin with, so you got that Napoleon thing going on. But now he spends his days sucking out septic tanks and smelling like turds, and half the time he gets it on himself 'cause he never had to actually work for a livin' before and he doesn't really know how to use the machinery. You know how folks always say there are certain people who fall in a pile of poop and come out smelling like a rose? Well old Jim Hodge just went from roses to poop, and if you ask me, it serves him right."

My son Petey looked at me and laughed, and said; "Gee dad, maybe you should introduce Jim Hodge to Two-Flush Tony. He got the giggles after that and I said, "Okay you two, let's get back to work on your mom's truck. "Hank, Phil, thanks for the information." Turning to Tommy I said, "Cuz he's your job if you want it. You have the crew for concrete work, not me. But if it sounds like you might want to get paid in cash before you start.

Hank and Phil looked at each other for a minute and then we went back to gapping the spark plugs on Angie's truck. I looked at my boys, who were still cracking up about Tony Leonetti and said; "You two think you can hold it together long enough to help me finish this, or is Two-Flush gonna keep you laughing the rest of the night?" This made them laugh even harder as they got up on the stools to lean in and help me work on the truck. Petey looked at Jack and said "Maybe this Hodge guy could put his poop sucker on Two-Flush-Tony's big butt and see if he can clog that too!"
This began a fresh wave of giggles and laughter and I have to admit, I laughed too.

Milledge and Lowery were silent from that point on. But being busy with the car, I hardly noticed. We finished installing the new plugs and wires and I crawled under the truck with my boys to teach them how to change oil. I guess the neighbors thought this was a good time to head out, so they said their goodbyes and disappeared into the evening. Once we got done with the oil, the boys and I washed our hands and I said it was time to test it out. I tossed the key to Pete and told him to "Start her up." His eyes went wide. "Yeah, go ahead. You don't pump the gas or anything, just turn the key and she'll start." Petey jumped in the driver's seat and adjusted it to his liking. He did just like I told him and the Escalade fired on the first turn. "She sounds perfect, boys!" I said. I shut the hood and walked to the open driver's side door. "Okay Pete, now back her out, slowly." A huge grin enveloped Petey's face. "Really Dad?" "Yeah sure," I smiled back at him, "Just go slow. Put your foot on the brake and pull the selector down to "R." Pete did just as I told him. "Good, now take your foot off the brake and just let the engine idle back it out. No need to touch the gas pedal yet." Pete was smiling so much I think his face hurt. He very carefully creaped the big SUV out of the garage and stopped when he had cleared the doors. "Excellent!" I yelled. "Now, put the selector back in "P" and set the parking brake, then turn the key off when you're done. Petey did it like he'd done it before and he got down out of the truck looking like he was six inches taller.

"Dad that was awesome!" He exclaimed, "Uncle Tommy, did you see that?" Petey was beside himself. Tommy looked at me with a smile and winked, and told Petey, "When your dad and I were your age, your grandfather would take us to the yard where the garbage trucks were stored and let us practice driving The Crusher around. We had a blast, your dad and me." I laughed out loud at that. "Wow, I forgot about that. We would all do that. You, me, Skip, Dominucce, and Mark. I remember Uncle Tony coming by once and warning us not to get too good at it or the Old Man would make us all work for him. Tommy laughed, "Yeah. You remember the time we took turns working the compactor and the hydraulic hose blew out?" I smiled at that. "Yeah, I remember that. Zippie got so pissed at the broken hose and my father was afraid to tell him that it was us boys down there playing around with the Crusher so he told him that he had done it. Zippie made him pay for that out of his own pocket." Tommy got stone faced. "You never told me that. "Yeah," I said, a little somber, "Zippie could be a giant jerk sometimes." I'd forgotten how my dad ran interference for me that day. It made me appreciate him a little more.

I turned to my sons; "Okay you two, wash your hands and get inside. We're done out here." The boys responded with a predictable "Aww dad..." but I stood my ground. I did throw them one bone though. "I think we need a project car to work on, so I can teach you how to work on all the other aspects of a car. How about we go looking for something next week?" The boys were gleeful and raced off toward the bathroom to wash their hands, and then into the house to get ready for bed. *Wow,* I thought, *I'm talking about buying a car for the boys already. Time just races by.*

I was glad all over again for the blessing of this buyout. Not many dads get to spend the time I do with my kids. I'm a blessed man.

Phil Makes His Case

"You heard it yourself this time, Hank!" I whispered to Milledge as we walked into my garage. "You heard it!" I was poking my finger in Hank's chest just a little bit. "You heard that man talking about loan sharking and mobsters owing money!" Hank scratched his head. "Now hold on there, Phil," he said, "We don't know that was a loan sharking call. What if old Joe just loans people money from the goodness of his heart?" I couldn't believe Hank still doubted the evidence. "Hank," I continued, "He said he was charging him 'vig', nobody calls it that unless they're in the mob!" "Well now how do you know that, Phil?" he asked me. "Because I heard it on the Sopranos!" I wasn't even gonna argue with him this time. "Come on, Hank," I said, "We're going inside and I'll prove it too you."

We walked inside my house and Gladys met us at the door. "Well isn't that nice," Gladys said as I walked in, "You got some nice tomatoes from Joe, and early in the season too. That's such a sweet thing." "Don't you even think about touching these tomatoes, Gladys!" I barked, "They're poisoned and you know it. That man has no shame I tell you, no shame!' Gladys looked at me wide-eyed. "Phil, what the heck are you going on about?" she asked. I didn't feel like repeating the conversation I had with Hank, an hour later for Gladys, so I grabbed her arm.

"Gladys, do you know what your sweet, lovable Joe Mezilli is into? He's a loan shark! We just heard him on the phone, probably with one of his goons. He was talking about some poor sucker they were thinking about loaning money too. Whoever the poor guy was, they had already loaned him money before. You'd think he'd of learned his lesson!" "Phil," Gladys said, kind of irritated, "What the heck are you talking about?" "Gladys," I said, "Let me tell you what happened. What I heard him say with my own ears. And what Hank here heard with me"

I checked out through the blinds to see where he was. After what I heard, he might be trying to kill me right this very moment. "Gladys I was returning his chainsaw sharpener..." "The one you borrowed last November, Phil?" Gladys interrupted. Always letting the air out of my balloon, I don't know why. "Yes Gladys," I hissed, "that one."

"Anyway, Hank and I walked it over to his garage 'cause I seen him inside there on the phone. He talks on the phone in the garage a lot, I noticed that." "Maybe it's just that you're a nosy Nate and you always go over there when you see him on the phone." Gladys said with a smirk. "Why are you always against me on this, Gladys?" I asked, "I'm trying to save this town and you're doggin' my every step."   Gladys crossed her arms and sat back in the couch. "As I was sayin'" I began, purposefully, "I was over there with Hank, and Joe was working on his wife's big old Escalade with two of his boys, teaching them to tune up a car. So we chit-chatted for a while and then his phone rang and I heard him say that he was considering a loan to some guy who had 'collections issues'. Joe didn't want to do it, and neither did his buddy Tommy, he was there too. Anyways he calls the guy back and agrees to the loan but he has to pay interest and he has to go visit with Joe's father...the kingpin of the family. They're gonna put a lien on his house, and they're gonna hit the poor man up for extra points because he's a risk. That's what they call the interest you pay a loan shark, Gladys. They call it points." I paused, "Points," I said again for emphasis, then turning to Hank I said; "And 'vig'"

Gladys sat with her mouth hanging slightly open. I could tell that she didn't believe me. "He's not a loan shark, Phil." she said emphatically. "Oh yeah?" I asked her, "How do you know that? You heard what I just told you. How can he not be a loan shark?" Gladys stood up and walked toward the kitchen. "Because the man is worth about forty million dollars, Phil. Why would he be concerned with making a few thousand dollars off of some loan shark deal when he already has that much?" Gladys was very smug when she told me this. I instantly wondered how she'd found out this much information. "How do you know this, Gladys? Who told you?"

Gladys sat down at the kitchen table and I sat across from her. "Because I went on the internet and looked it up." she said, rubbing it in like a child on the playground. "What do you mean you looked it up?" I asked. "Simple," she says,

351

speaking between sips of her coffee, "I did some research on him. Found out some interesting things too." She was smiling coyly, like she enjoyed playing me for a fool. She knew I was reaching my limits. "I went on the internet and I researched his name. That's all Phil. It wasn't hard. There were some newspaper articles about him and his family business. How he made his money and all. He's a very nice man, by all accounts."

"By all accounts?" I asked incredulously. "Gladys, didn't you see the part in The Godfather where they had a newspaper reporter on their payroll and they floated the story about the cop that Michael Corleone killed being mixed up in the mob? Those people have their own PR firms, just about." None of that sunk in. Gladys paid it no mind. "All I know," she continued –sounding annoyed at me for doubting her- "is that his family was involved in the waste management business and he sold out to a big conglomerate and a year or two later they moved down here. See Phil, he had a completely legitimate business." I had to sit down. The kitchen was spinning. My head felt light. I saw stars. I looked at Gladys, who was blurry around the edges, and said "Gladys, did you hear what you just said?" She sipped her coffee and shrugged. "No, Phil, what'd I say?" "Gladys, don't you know that 'waste management' is the code word for being in the mob? Don't you remember that Tony Soprano fella was in 'waste management'? They all say they're in 'waste management' Gladys. It's their cover story."

Gladys slurped her coffee. I hate when she does that. Forty-four years of marriage and she still does it, and I still hate it. It usually means she ain't listening to me. I stood up and went to the living room. I got my box set of The Sopranos and popped in the episode where Tony loans Hirsh some money. He charges him interest. He calls it "vig" plain as day. "Come on in here, the both of you!" I called out to Hank and Gladys. They dutifully walked into the living room and I played the scene where he talks about the interest. "There! You see!" I said, looking at Hank. "He called it 'Vig'" Hank leaned back in the chair. "Phil all that means is he uses the word. Maybe he watched The Sopranos too." Hank was trying to get Joe off the hook again. "Or maybe," I replied, "It means Joe is in the mob!"   "Gladys,'" I barked, "Look at the box for season one. Read the description." Inside the case for the first season, there was a sheet that showed the plot line for each episode. "It's right here in the very first episode, Gladys. Right there, read it." She read the line I pointed to quietly, she was mutterin' it but her lips was movin' I saw her eyes get wide when she got to the part that said that Tony was the boss of a Waste Management company but that it was a front for the mob. She dropped the paper on the table.   "Phil!" she gasped, "You really think he's in the mob?" For a fleeting moment I felt sorry for Gladys. Then I remembered I'm married to her. "Yes Gladys," I said triumphantly, "The man. Is in. The mob." Gladys 'hand trembled as she placed her cup on the table. "Well...what're we gonna do?" she said meekly. "I'm working on a plan Gladys. But you gotta keep this quiet. I can't expose this man if he finds out we're onto him." I should have known better. Gladys can't keep a secret at all. I thought maybe the gravity of this situation would work to keep her quiet, I found out later that I was wrong. Very wrong. She'd called her cousin Stan, our Sherriff, the very next morning and Stan called me to tell me to "mind my own damned business!" *This town's safety is my business, Stan.* I thought, *and if you won't take care of this mobster...dammit man I will!*

16

Old Hit-Men

Never Die

So by now I knew Phil was suspicious that I was in the mob. But I had no idea that he'd been spreading this rumor around town. I figured it was just him. Him and maybe Larry Erickson. After what Bransford told me, there was no more mistaking it or wondering. Phil was the guy behind the innuendo, this much I knew for sure. We just had no idea how far he'd taken it. That we'd find out after the FBI came knocking at my door. But that part comes later. At this point, I just thought it was one nosy neighbor and his obsession. Of course, Larry (whose real name is "Lars") "The Swede" Erickson didn't help matters any, with his ridiculous hints about the mob every friggin' time he talked to me. I know he was mostly playing, but it perpetuated the whole mess and I really hated it. I also hated how he would always shift into that terrible, phony Sopranos impersonation whenever he talked to me, especially if we were around other people.

We'd walk into the grocery store and there he'd be with his wife Madge. Madge. It's 2014 for God's sake and your only fifty-two years old. Your mom thought it was a good idea to name you after the Palmolive lady? But whenever Anj and I would see Swede and his wife out somewhere, he'd come sauntering up with a gate that was supposed to be Italian somehow, and start motioning with his hands as he talked. I wanted to put him in a straitjacket. He'd move around like Steve Martin in "My Blue Heaven" and talk in that nasally, Minnesotan-turned-New-Yorker accent he tries pulling off.

Then he'd say, "Yo!" He has no idea how badly I wanted to smash him with a casaba melon when he did that. Why? I'll tell you why. Because people from New York don't say "Yo!" they say "How-ya-doon?" as a greeting. "Yo!" is a uniquely Philadelphia thing, and for him to try walking and talking like a New York crime boss and open his mouth and say "Yo!" was enough to make me want to scream.

Another thing, he was always talking about "Arranging a meeting" and "Talking to this guy about this thing." Listen, Lars, this isn't "Analyze This" here. I thought, I'm not in the frickin' mob, and I frickin' hate it when you act like I am! Now, I have to admit, this mistaken identity thing had a few nice perks. The locals who bought into it started giving up their choice parking spots at the baseball stadium, and I got discounts on my gardening equipment at the Co-op. Heck they even tipped real heavy at my daughter's lemonade stand. But I was sick of it now and I had decided to turn it around on Phil, and Larry the Swede. I wasn't sure how I was going to do it yet, but I figured the opportunity would present itself eventually.

I was right. It happened that third summer we were in Forest. It didn't happen the way I would have planned it either. As it turns out, it happened better than I could have imagined, as most great gags do. It started with a phone call from the Old Man.

Pop called me one evening in May, late in that third spring after we moved to Forest. He'd gotten a phone call from Richard Green over at the Waste International office...our old building. Green was direct, as he always is, Pop said. He said he was sorry but the edict had come down from the corporate headquarters that our old iconic trash truck, the one Nonno had bought from the township, the one we called The Crusher, had to be removed from the property. They wanted to spruce up the building, and make it more like the main corporate center...blah, blah, blah. The fact is, The Crusher was built in 1947 and he was just an old dinosaur. Pop called me on a Tuesday and told me all about the conversation he'd had. I told him I'd take care of it. The following evening I called Richard Green, just as he would be leaving his office. I was out in my garage as always, and sure enough, like clockwork, here comes Phil Lowery. He had the Swede with him too. I was annoyed at first. But then just as the both of them walked into the garage −reeking of Phil's Aqua Velva as always- the words I was about to say suddenly became like gold. Pure. Gold.

Richard Green picked up just as Phil was moseying out of his garage. "Joe!" Green said joyously. "This is a nice surprise." he continued. "How on Earth are you?" "Oh you know, Richard, doing well. Still haven't come close to the bottom of that check you wrote me. Life is pretty good." Green chuckled readily at that. "Rub it in pal, rub it in." I returned fire right away "Look, don't play poor with me. You know as well as I do that you didn't overpay. How's your jump shot there, Eddie Gottlieb?" Green laughed. "You don't forget a thing, do you?"

Just as I was ready to get to the meat of the conversation, Phil and the Swede walked into the garage. They were careful and timid, but oddly, far more at ease than they used to be. I guess three years and I still hadn't whacked them, counted for something. Sheesh.

Then it hit me. This conversation could be full of double entendre if I allowed it to be. And as soon as I saw Swede carrying himself like some goombah with a nervous tic, I decided it was going to work. The fun began.

"Listen Richard, we need to talk about The Crusher." I motioned to Phil and the Swede to grab something from the fridge and gave them the "give me a minute" sign, knowing full well that they'd see that as a signal that they needed to eavesdrop. Phil and the Swede grabbed a couple of Cokes and started pretending to play darts. Nobody plays darts that badly. Neither of them could have hit an Oldsmobile with a handful of marbles if they were sitting inside it.

I let them think I didn't know they were listening, and continued my shadowy conversation. "I understand The Crusher has become a problem for you." I said, barely able to control my laughter already. These guys were in for a real treat. If their imagination had me in the mob, I was going to cement the deal tonight...pardon the pun.

Green said "Yeah, it's becoming an eyesore and management wants it gone." Now...neither of these two yokels heard this, of course. That made it beautiful.

"Well, he belongs to you now, that was part of what you bought when you took over our waste management business." Green agreed with me. "I know it, Joe. But I also know what the truck meant to your family and just as a courtesy I wanted to offer it to you before we just had it scrapped." Richard Green is a really good guy. This phone call proved it once again.

I continued, "The Crusher served my family well, Richard," I continued, "In his prime, there was never a job he couldn't do for us or a load he couldn't haul." I said this with my back to both of my guests, but I could see their faces in the window pane in front of me. "The Mezilli family built our business on his back...especially his ability to get rid of the bigger pieces of trash with ease. And he never broke down. Never. He never missed a pick-up, or a big disposal. I think he deserves to go out with respect." I heard Phil Lowery joking on the Coke he was sipping. I had to play this right. I turned to Lowery and The Swede and excused myself for a moment. I walked outside the garage and meandered over to the side where the open window would allow them to hear every word in assumed anonymity. I continued my conversation with Richard Green.

"Richard, here's what I think we need to do. Either you can just take the old guy out to a scrap yard somewhere and have him cut into pieces, and the final bit of Mezilli family history is stripped from the waste management industry forever, or I can send a guy up there to get him and bring him down here and take care of it from this end." From outside my garage I heard a low whimper...it sounded like The Swede.

Richard Green was always a great guy to deal with and he knew what it was I was saying. I also appreciated that he thought enough of me to give me first rights to The Crusher, instead of just having it chopped to bits in a salvage yard somewhere. It was nice of him to call me. I told him as much.

"Richard, I really appreciate your letting me know about this and giving me the option of handling him myself. That means a lot. I have some great memories with The Crusher, and it's very first-class of you to show me this respect." "Well," Green said, "you just tell me what you want to do and we'll do it. Personally, it's a really cool garbage truck and I wish we'd just leave it right here. But Corporate is Corporate. You know how that works."

"Yep," I answered, "I understand. Sometimes the new guys have no appreciation for what the old guys did. I tell you what. I'll make a call to one of my people up there and arrange to have him brought down here. He needs a good final resting place. Maybe out at my hunting camp. Nobody will see him out there and nobody will notice. That's better than him becoming part of a scrap heap someplace in South Philly. I'll call you in a day or two when the arrangements are made."

"Thanks Joe," Green answered. "I feel better knowing that your family will still have The Crusher. He really represents you guys. I'll wait to hear from you." I thanked Richard

Green and then said, just for effect for my eavesdropping neighbors, "Listen, do me a favor. Don't tell anybody back there about this. The old guy was very popular and a fixture in the neighborhood. If word gets out that it's then end of the line for him, they might not be happy. We'll do this quietly. Save you a lot of bad feelings on the block."

Green appreciated it and we hung up. I walked back into the garage casually, only to see Lowery, and The Swede practically running over to Phil's house. This is going to be good! I thought. I just didn't realize how good. In another year, I'd realize just how far my misdirection had gone.

Half a Pound of Gabagool

I decided that if I was going to turn this thing around on Phil and the Swede, I was going to really play it up, and in the process, fix their ridiculous misconceptions about Italian people. Looking back, I think I got a little too indignant. People love Italians. I can't blame them, being Italian myself, and all. They love mob stories, not for the crime, but for the tradition, loyalty, sarcasm, wit and sheer humor of most Italians. We love our families, and who doesn't like that, right? We're a jovial people, even when we're being smart aleks, and I think that's what people like, and it's what they're drawn to. I mean, take away the crime, and who wouldn't want to be a Corleone? As long as you're not Fredo, I mean.

But at the moment, Phil and the Swede were just on my nerves. As time passed, they'd begun asking me more questions about the mob, about this gangster, or that Don. I'd usually answer them with a smart-mouth retort. "How the heck would I know anything about Joey Bananas?" I'd bark. "He ran the Gambino's in New York. I'm from Philly and I was in Waste Management." Phil would stare at me with his mouth hanging slightly open. Then he would inevitably say, "Right. But you knew Joey Bananas, right?" That's why I finally decided to just give in and play the role for a while and hopefully make it blow up in their faces. If I couldn't convince them straight-up that I wasn't connected, then maybe I could use it for my own benefit in the neighborhood, while I figured out a way to set them straight once and for all. Sometimes, I have to admit, it was fun. Like when the topic of speaking Italian was broached.   Now, here's what you need to know about my grasp of the mother tongue. I have none. My grandfather refused to teach the language to my father and my uncles. He spoke it around the house, and I heard him talking to my grandmother in Italian...or to his brothers. But he never taught us Italian. He used to say, "We are 'medicone' (his modification of "American") now. We speak-ah the English." Nobody argued this point with Giuseppe. In fact, nobody argued much with Giuseppe at all.

I tried explaining this early on to my new neighbors. But they didn't believe me, or they didn't want to believe me. Either way, every once in a while they'd ask me how to say something in Italian. Then I'd hear them speaking "Itanglish" whenever they were around me. Let me explain what Itanglish is. If you ask a Hispanic American to speak Spanish, you might get what they call "Spanglish." It's not really Spanish, it's what their mothers and fathers heard from their immigrant parents as they grew up. They were actually hearing Spanish-speaking parents trying to learn English as they went, and using a mix of both. It becomes a tongue all its own.

Well, Italian's have done this for generations too. There are words that the average American uses regularly and they think they are using Italian words when they aren't. Not exactly. For example, like every Italian-American in the country, I frequently use the exclamatory; "Madonn!" For years I had absolutely no idea what I was saying. I just grew up hearing my parents and grandparents and every other adult in the neighborhood say this whenever they were frustrated, aggravated, frightened, or experiencing any number of unnamed emotions. I didn't find out until I was in my thirties, that this is actually an "Americanized" version of a short, one-word prayer to the Virgin Mary for assistance. The Italians were saying "Madonna!" which is one of the

Latin forms of Mary's name. Well, filter it through three or four generations of broken English, sputtered Italian, and background noise and you end up with "Madonn!" You see how it works?

There are lots of words like that. Mozzerella is actually pronounced "Molts-ah-lella" but my family called it "Moots-ah-dell" since...heck they still pronounce it that way. Riccota cheese is "riggot," etc. Oh and while we're on the subject; it's Gravy and Macaroni, not Pasta and Sauce. Anyway, it was this whole mispronunciation thing that gave rise to one of the funniest tricks I have played on a neighbor since I moved here. I'd already begun hearing Phil and Hank and The Swede tripping over their tongues trying to say "Maddonn!" and it usually ended up sounding like "Malone." I'd try helping them, and they'd butcher it even more. So I let it ride and got a laugh out of it at their expense. They'd throw in the occasional "Capisce" or something else they heard on TV, but I let it go.

One particular summer evening, I decided to have some fun. We were grilling in the back yard with a few families from our church in Lynchburg, and my neighbors. As usual, people were asking me questions about being Italian, the mob, St. Joseph's Table, Seven Fishes, and which Olive Oil brand I prefer. And then someone asked me if I had a preference for deli meats since I moved here.   It was a guy named Chris and he lived out in Alta Vista. He is a really nice guy and I liked him right away. One of the things I liked in particular was that, while he was very fascinated by The Sopranos, it wasn't the crime that he was enthralled by. Chris was genuinely interested in Italian history, tradition, and, especially, food. We'd had him and his family over several times, and each time, he was simply blown away by some authentic dish Anj or myself would prepare. The real

365

test came when he sampled some of my tomatoes and tripe without being persuaded. He liked it. He even took some home with him, which impressed the heck out of me, I have to tell you.

After that, I tried educating him as much as I could. It was a lot of fun imparting my limited knowledge of the homeland to a civilian. One day, though, he made the mistake of using some bad Itanglish and it set up a wonderful joke. Here's what happened. Chris had apparently seen those episodes of The Sopranos where Tony reveals his love for "Gabagool." Chris had stumbled across a recipe and it called for "Gabagool" and so he called me up one day. "Hey Philly..." he began. Now, a little background is necessary here; Chris had taken to calling me "Philly Joe Mezilli" when we first were introduced, and eventually it just got shortened to "Philly." I absolutely loved it. For two reasons, one, they have the most unimaginative nicknames here. Back home, your nickname is usually a mangle of your last name or a descriptive of your face or body or hair color or something very personal. Here, they just call you "Bubba" or "Hoss." It's never personal and therefore it's not endearing. The other thing was I really liked being associated with my hometown. I like Forest, but Philly lives in my soul.

Anyway, that day at our cookout, Chris asked me where to get some good "Gabagool." Now, I have to admit, I knew exactly what he was talking about because I watched The Sopranos too. It's not actually called "Gabagool" it's "Capacola." The beauty here is that I knew this, but Chris did not. As it turns out, I had, by this point, discovered a really nice butcher shop in Lynchburg and where they sold all the deli meat brands we had back home. Wanting to make a nice sandwich now and then, I started buying all our deli meat there. The owner was a little Italian guy named Mickey, from

South Jersey. He'd retired to Lynchburg to be near his grandkids, and he opened the butcher shop as a way to stay busy. We hit it off right away, and he always gave me a big box stuffed with pork neck bones. I make my red gravy (what you civilians call "spaghetti sauce") with neck bones and it was hard to find them in the grocery stores here unless they were smoked, which ruins the taste. Mickey hooked me up. He was a real Goombah that way.

So Chris asks me where he can get the "Gabagool" and I tell him "Go to the Trieste butcher store on Rivermont Avenue. Tell Mickey you are a friend of mine and tell him to slice it the way he slices it for me. He'll take care of you." Now, Mickey really knows how to slice deli meat. You have to slice it paper thin. It's a texture thing and he gets it. That's how it's done back home.

Well, one afternoon I'm watering the tomatoes and Chris calls me on the cell. "Philly," he says, "I'm over here at the Trieste and I can't find any Gabagool. Are you sure they have it here?" It was all I could do to keep a straight face. "Yeah, Chris," I answered. They usually have both kinds. Is Mickey around?" Chris answered, "Yeah he's right here." "Well," I said, "ask him if he has hot and wet, or dry and sweet. He'll know which one to give you." I listened over the phone as Chris asked, "Do you have hot and wet or dry and sweet?"

Next thing I heard was Mickey barking at Chris from behind the deli counter; "You want Capacola! There ain't no such thing as Gabagool! What the hell is Gabagool?" Oh let me guess...you're another one of those god damn Sopranos fans! Listen Uncle June, it's CAP-A-COLA, is that simple enough for you? This ain't Satriale's Pork Store!" There was silence for the longest five seconds of my life, and then I hear Mickey break out in hysterical laughter. By now I'm splitting my sides. Chris gets back on the phone and sheepishly says,

"You son of a bitch! You knew all along, didn't you?" I burst out laughing. "Yeah pal, of course I knew. Listen, tell Mickey you want dry, sweet Cappy for that recipe you're working on. Tell him to slice it the way I like it and to take care of you. I promise, no more jokes." Chris has a great sense of humor and he was laughing at himself by this point.

Chris asked for a quarter pound of sweet, dry capacola and Mickey gave him a pound. He didn't even charge him for it. "You're a friend of Joe Mezilli's and you gave me one hell of a laugh today, kid. It's on the house." Chris loved that part. The whole thing gave me a wonderful idea. Anyway, Like I said, everyone seemed to insist that I teach them Italian, even though I told them repeatedly that I didn't speak the language. After this "Great Gabagool Incident" I realized that they wouldn't know the difference anyway. I mean, Chris was ordering "Gabagool" because he'd heard it on The Sopranos. I figured I'd have some fun.   From that day on, every once in a while I'd work some Italian sounding gibberish into a conversation. One mid-summer day we were all hanging out in the garage, tuning on my Corvette and listening to a Phillies ball game on the radio, and just enjoying the cool of the evening. I took a look at the guys and figured this was a good scenario to try out my new game. There was a close play at home plate and the ump called the base runner out. I yelled at the radio, "That fazzadeetch!" I followed it up with "It's that Ted Barrett, the home plate umpire. He hates the
Phillies...always has. He's such a mezzavoibal!"

The guys all looked at me as if they knew what I meant. None of them did, of course, because I made those words up right there on the spot. But the look on their faces was priceless. They *wanted* those words to be real Italian. It was fun. The more I worked these phony Italian words into our daily conversation, the more I would hear them using them on their own. It became one of the funniest gags I had ever been a part of. Even Lowery started doing it. I heard him cursing at his used-up old leaf blower one Saturday afternoon. He pulled and pulled and couldn't get it to start. He finally threw it on the ground and yelled, "You fazzadeetch!" I laughed until I cried.

We had some families over for a swim one Sunday afternoon and I was cooking on the grille. Nothing fancy, burgers, dogs, some brats, and I had a nice pan of Italian sausages in gravy with peppers and onions on the side warmer. There were four families over including the Lowerys and the Milledges. I carried the tray over to the table and made a couple of sausage and pepper sandwiches and handed one each to Hank and Phil. "Here ya go boys, try these and tell me you're old buddy Joe doesn't know how to make the best Andra-botchelle in Virginia!"   Both of them stared at the sandwiches hungrily. Milledge snagged one right away and took a huge bite. Lowery was his usual hesitant self. Milledge was smiling and red gravy was dribbling down his chin. "This is amazing, Joe!" He said between bites. "Whatddya call this again?" I shot Angie a quick, knowing glance and answered him; "Andra-botchelle" Milledge wiped his mouth and asked me earnestly, "Say it again, slower..." I had no problem teaching my buddy some farcical Italian. Glad to do it. "You pronounce it, Ahn-dray-bow-tchell-ay, Hank. It means "Sweet loin of the pig." I looked across at Angie who was standing behind Milledge. She silently mouthed the words *Andrea Bocelli?* to me. I nodded my head ever-soslightly so only she noticed. She quickly buried her face in a napkin and pretended to sneeze. She walked to the other side of the pool and I watched her laughing hysterically. It was all I could do to keep it together after that.

Milledge said it over again about five times until he was sure he'd mastered it. "Hey Joe, is that the word for all sausage, or just this sausage here, the way you prepared it?" he asked me. "Oh it's pretty much what you'd call any sausage, Hank. This is special sausage, but you'd call any sausage by that." Hank smiled and said it again, "Andrabotchelle! I like the sound of that!" "Look at you!" I said with a light slap on his back, "You're becoming a real paisan."

About a week later, a couple of us men went to breakfast at the Cracker Barrel over by the college and Hank actually ordered the "Big Country Breakfast" and told the waitress he wanted extra "Andra-botchelle." I choked on my coffee as he explained to the young girl, "Why Miss, it means 'Sweet Loin of The Pig!' Yep..." he said with a wink in my direction, "That's real Eye-Talian!"

This was working better than I'd hoped. Sadly...that was what caused the problems with the FBI.

(Meanwhile in D.C.)

Harvey Robertson sat alone at his desk, late on a Friday night. The office lights had long been extinguished, and Harvey sat under the glow of his desk lamp and his computer monitor. His eyes grew blurry as he perused page after page of information from a file that was worn and weathered on the edges. The paper had long ago taken a yellowish hue and the font was classic typewriter.

Robertson took a sip from a cold cup of coffee and reviewed his own notes on a case that has haunted him for more than thirty years. A missing person. An assumed mob hit. A classic burial at a construction site. He'd worked the case from the day it opened. He remembered interviewing the forlorn parents. He was the only agent who believed their tale from the beginning.

In the middle of his investigation, they'd gone silent. Clammed up. Word in the neighborhood was they were instructed to have nothing more to say to the FBI and so Robertson struck out on his own. Unwilling to let the case be classified as "unsolved," he worked every lead, followed every rumor, chased down every possible witness. But the names that kept being spoken all but assured that he was not going to get any information. Nicky Bruno, "No-Neck" Scarzone, Sam Colubriale. These were heavy hitters in the South Philly mob world and nobody...*nobody*, was going to speak if these men said not to. His frustration grew over the years.

Robertson had built a decent career with the bureau, but in his heart he knew he'd never really accomplished what he'd come here to do. He wanted a big case, a blockbuster. Something that made the headlines. This one case might have been that, except it went as cold as ice on him and never came back to life. Thirty years had passed and Harvey had worked hundreds of cases. None of them spurred his passion and so none of them saw his best efforts. He was mailing it in, and somewhere deep in his heart he'd known that. This one case...this one *damned* case, and this one damned missing guy. He just never got his bearings after seeing his superiors reclassify it despite his protestations. He'd begged them not to close it. He'd always had a hunch that he was close, he told them. But they grew weary of the file and they over ruled him and shut the door.

Harvey's wife had left him about ten years ago. She too grew weary of the hollowness behind his eyes that spoke of the obsession he still had with this old, weathered file, stuffed full of leads that never materialized, and witnesses that had suddenly forgotten everything they claimed to have seen. When she could no longer take it, she left. Harvey barely noticed. His work had been his mistress and now he could devote his full affections to all her enticing curves.

Earlier in the week, a young agent who was working the tip lines, and whom Harvey had befriended because he'd gone through training with the man's father, brought Harvey a thumb drive. It was late in the day, almost quitting time. The agent walked up to Harvey and slipped him the drive discreetly, so no one else would see. "You need to have this," was all he said. The young agent never even slowed down, he simply handed the small drive to Harvey and kept walking.

Instinctively, Robertson put the drive in his pocket. Whatever it was that was on this file was so secret that he didn't risk opening it while his coworkers were still in their offices. He would wait until they were all gone. He'd gone to the cafeteria and grabbed a bite to eat and waited. Around 6:30PM, he knew the office would be empty. Agents had families and they were gone to them. Gone to smiling faces, and kids, and hot meals and four bedroom, two-story colonials in nice neighborhoods. Harvey went back to his desk.

He slid the drive into the port on his laptop and opened the file. "Anonymous Tips compiled from Forest, Virginia." It read. "Topic: Possible mob activity." Harvey Robertson stayed until almost midnight that first night, reading the tips and taking notes. Then he clicked on an MP3 file that said "Voice recorder." And his world changed.

He listened to a lot of unintelligible garbage for the first seven minutes or so. He was about to write this entire thing off when he heard three male voices talking about what sounded like mob activity. He was listening rather absentmindedly, when he heard a name that shot through him like a lightning bolt. *Rennie Priemontese.* He sat up with a start, running his mouse over the start button for the voice recording, he played it again, to make sure he'd heard what he thought he'd heard. *Rennie Priemontese.* Robertson was certain he recognized that name, but he couldn't remember where. He said it over and over to himself...

By midnight he was exhausted and couldn't keep his eyes open. He walked the four blocks to his tiny, cramped apartment over the ratty liquor store near the building where he worked. His wife Sue took the house in the divorce and he never saw any reason to buy another one. His apartment was immaculate and organized in the fashion of a man with OCD. Robertson was detail obsessed and it showed in his life, and in his personal quarters. Tired, he crawled into bed and fell asleep.

At 4:47AM, Harvey Robertson sat up in bed, sweating profusely and saying the name out loud. The name that was haunting him. The Moriarity to his Sherlock Holmes.
"Rennie Priemontese!" He said it again and the memories rushed back to his brain like an avalanche. Priemontese had been the business manager for the cement finisher's local in Philly. He was rumored to have been in that pit, the day that poor bastard was buried alive in the concrete. He was

alleged to have information about the case. Robertson had tried interviewing him once but he wouldn't talk and eventually, he moved to Florida.

This was the name he'd heard on the voice recording in the anonymous tips file that the young agent had laid on his desk.

At precisely 8:01 AM, Harvey Robertson was rapping on the wire mesh cage that surrounded the evidence room at Quantico's FBI headquarters. He'd called ahead and called in a favor or two and gotten his pal Teddy Sinclair to dig up the evidence box from the case that had haunted him all these years. Teddy knew he was taking a risk giving this box to his friend, but he owed Harvey. They'd grown up together and when he'd run into some bad luck, Harvey had put the word in and gotten Teddy this clerk's job.

Teddy hurriedly handed the big cardboard box to Robertson, saying nothing. Robertson grunted a quick "Thanks Ted." And spun on his heels and was gone in a flash. The box stayed in the trunk of Robertson's car all week, and he brought in as much of the contents as he could slip into his briefcase each day until the entire file was secreted in his desk. That's how he came to be sitting here tonight, on a Friday night, when his fellow agents were home with families or out with friends. Harvey Robertson was busy revisiting a case that had haunted him for half his life. All these years later, and now, finally, he had clues.

He'd read, and re-read every note, listened to every call to the tip line until finally he knew this was his big chance. He found a number where he could reach the anonymous tipster and wrote it on a slip of paper that he tucked into his wallet. He carefully placed the files back in his bottom desk drawer and locked them up tightly. Then he walked outside into the late evening cool and dialed the number from his personal cell phone. From his home in Forest, Virginia, Phil Lowery answered...

17

Today I Settled

All

Family Business

All good things must come to an end. That's how the old saying goes. Had I known I was alleged to be the "Accidental Mobster" I would have milked it a bit. I don't know if it was a good thing or not...menz ah menz. I guess it could have had its good and it's bad. It would be fun getting good parking and special seats at restaurants, but to be quite honest, I got that back home, and not because I was mistaken for a Don. It was because I was a good employer, a good neighbor and a good friend. I like to think maybe I was a good man as well. But here in Virginia, without me knowing it, the rumor mill had churned up too much trouble for me and I decided it was time to end this game. Especially after the FBI came knocking. Yeah...the FBI.

It's not like I'll ever forget the date. It was December First. We'd been in Forest for a little over three years. I was putting up Christmas lights. Actually, I was putting up *more* Christmas lights. I typically put our lights out over Thanksgiving weekend and I had already done that, but it felt like we needed more. Like I said, I really get into Christmas.

So I was in the front yard driving stakes into the ground to tie-down the giant inflatable "Winter Warlock" I'd had made. I had it made because I already have every available Christmas decoration on my lawn. I also have an enormous inflatable Eagles player that I put up on Sundays during the football season and leave up after Thanksgiving. The kids put a big Santa hat on it and we string some lights from its huge, broad shoulders. I always liked "Santa Claus is Coming to Town" and I wondered why there were no "Winter Warlock" Christmas decorations. So I found the name of a company who makes inflatable promotional merchandise, did some digging about the licensing, and had a fifteen foot inflatable made. It even plays "Put One Foot In front of the Other." I love the thing.

So I was out on the lawn making a spot for it, hoping to get it done before the kids came home from school that afternoon, when three dark blue Ford Crown Victoria pull up and out pop seven very obvious government agents. I thought maybe it was another check on Tommy, so I wasn't startled. Honestly...I haven't done anything wrong so I wouldn't get nervous anyway. I stood up and stretched my back and walked over to the guy who looked like he was in charge. This time he didn't smile or appear casual. When the Feds had come to check out Tommy's address change a couple of years before, they were very nice, very cordial and very pleasant. These guys were serious. That was my first clue.

I stuck my hand out anyway and all I got in response was the flash of an FBI I.D. (They don't actually carry a "badge") and a sour look. "Joseph Mezilli?" He said gruffly. "Yeah, I'm Joe Mezilli. Something I can do for you?" He identified himself as Agent Robertson. He rattled off the names of the other agents with him, but it's not like I was writing them down or anything. There was one woman. An attractive woman named Martina Eversen who instantly went to my door. Now I was pissed. "Excuse me, Cuz...is there some reason you're here and some reason this lady thinks she can just walk into my home?"

Agent Robertson took the typical "bad cop" approach. "Mr. Mezilli we don't have a warrant but we could obtain one directly if that becomes necessary." Now he was threatening me. I don't enjoy that. It ranks up there with trying to pressure me. The last time someone pressured me, the selling price of my garbage company went up over fifty percent. There's a reason a man lives his life the right way, it's so that in times like this, he can be bold. I was getting pissed and I could feel my blood pressure going up. "Well now what would you obtain a warrant for, exactly, Agent Robertson? Too many Christmas lights?" Just as I said this, Angie came out of the house. "Joe...what's going on Baby?" Angie was scared. Now I was hot. Turning to Robertson I got a little closer and probably a little menacing. I'm six-feet-four. He is about five-feet ten. "Listen, Agent Robertson, now you've upset my wife. You have precious few seconds remaining to tell me what the hell you are doing here or this can get ugly."

Robertson's hand went to his hip, under his trench coat, but he didn't bring it out. "Are you threatening me, Mr. Mezilli? Because I am a federal agent and that is a crime, sir." "Two things Cuz," I answered, "One; It's no more a crime than showing up here and harassing me without any reason, and Two; It's not a threat. It's a guarantee. You understand me?" I stepped back a bit when Anj grabbed my arm. "Now, you want to tell me what you're doing here?"

Agent Eversen came over and tried to defuse the situation. I didn't know whether she was simply being the "good cop" or she had picked up on Agent Robertson's asshole hormone working overtime and decided it was a good idea to stop this before it became some sort of "Ruby Ridge" thing. Agent Eversen got between us and tried to make some peace. Instantly I knew this was a bluff. If there was a real reason for them being here, I had already given Harry Hairshirt over there a reason to take me down. He was blowing holes in me in his imagination...I could tell that from his eyes. But he didn't move on me so I figured this was a fact-finding mission. My first guess was someone back home was in some trouble and this was a climb up their family tree, so-to-speak. But I instantly dismissed that idea.

It wasn't anything like that at all. It couldn't have been because I would have already heard about it long before the FBI showed up.

Agent Robertson, red faced and seething, stepped away and walked over toward his car. Another agent, a very Italian looking guy named DiMeolo walked over and stuck out his hand. "You'll have to excuse my partner," he said. "He's had a bad couple of days, what with the way the Redskins are playing and all." I looked at Angie and said, "You see this? This is the nice Italian guy here to gain our confidence after his jerk partner has thrown a scare into me." Angie laughed at this. Agent Eversen looked at Anj and said coyly; "Something funny. Mrs. Mezilli?" Oh God. She went after my wife. You think I can be a hardass? Try messing with my beautiful, sweet, loving wife where her family is concerned. *You just poked the bear, lady.* I thought to myself.

Angie took a step towards her and stuck her finger right in her face and said "Yeah! I think it's really funny that you think you scared my husband. The only thing that scares this man is me when I'm pregnant or his grandmother when she shoots him the maloik. Now you've played your game enough, what the hell are you doing here?"

Eversen took a step back. Literally. It was like Angie used "the force" or something because she looked like she'd been pushed. Maybe it was that terrible "naked-from-thewaste-down" feeling they got when they realized their bluff didn't work. But whatever it was they suddenly decided that the pressure and bluster wasn't going to be productive. They turned into humans.

"We have some things we need to talk to you about, Joe," offered agent DiMeolo, "The front yard isn't the place to do it. Can we come in?" "All friggin' seven of you?" I asked. DiMeolo got a slight grin on his face. "No...no that's a good point. Give me a minute." He walked over to the car where agent Robertson was leaning. I'd been watching him the whole time. He was working on his fourth stick of nicotine gum since I stood him down. DiMeolo discussed something with him for a brief minute and then they both came over to where we were standing. "We'll send a couple of these guys home, Joe," DiMeolo said, "Maybe we don't need this much presence." I looked at Angie. She was still visibly shaken. She was still visibly pissed, too. I glanced over and saw Lowery looking out his window, smiling. He didn't even try to hide himself this time. I did something I hadn't done in about thirty years...I flipped him off. His face slid into a quick frown and he closed the blinds.   "Yeah," I said to DiMeolo, "Yeah, we can go inside."   So Agent Robertson, Eversen, DiMeolo, and two other of their crew came in and we sat down in the kitchen. "Youse want some coffee?" I asked. Angie shot me a quick look. "If any of you want coffee, there is a Dunkin' Donuts out on Timberlake Drive, our friend Joe Randa owns it. Mention our name and you get a free donut, but you aren't getting any of mine. Why don't you get to the point of your intrusion so we can get on about our day?" Angie was angrier than I'd allowed for. "You heard the lady," I said. "You have five minutes. Then I call my attorney."

Agent Robertson had just started to speak when his Italian compatriot interrupted. "Harvey," he said to Robertson, "Let me go first, huh?" Robertson looked a little angry at this but he took a step back. DiMeolo smiled. "May we sit down, Joe?" He asked. "Yeah, you can sit in your car when you leave. Sitting in my living room is reserved for friends. Now get to it. You're down to four minutes." DiMeolo actually smiled a little at that. I could hear the distinctive Philly accent in his voice, so I asked him; "Where you from Cuz? I know that accent anywhere." He smiled.

381

"Sixteenth and Oregon." He said, half apologizing. "I worked my way through college at Chickie's and Pete's."   "Okay so you're paisan. We speak the same language. So cut the crap and tell me what's going on." "Mob involvement, Joe." He said plain as day. "What?" Angie and I both said this simultaneously. "Mob involvement," he repeated. "We've received several...actually many, anonymous tips that you were involved in mob activities. Now normally we tend to just file these things away as someone with a vivid imagination, but when we get that many of them we have to at least sniff around. So we did. Now we're here to ask you some questions."

I was shocked. I was angry. "Mob activities?" I said. "Do you know my reputation...my family's reputation? Do you know how I ran my business and how hard I worked to avoid any sort of involvement with those people? I was probably the only guy in Philly who wasn't in bed with the mob. That's why Waste International specifically targeted my business for buyout. Did you know that?"

Agent DiMeolo agreed. "Joe we did our homework before we came here. We know all those things and they're all true. But we kept getting tips. Now in fairness, you do know some people with mob ties. We cross-matched your name against our "known active" list and there were a few hits." "Oh yeah?" I said, "Like who?"   "Well," DiMeolo replied, "Anthony Leonetti for one." "Two Flush Tony Leonetti? He's in the mob?" I asked. "Not exactly," Agent DiMeolo continued. "But he has serious gambling debts with some of the mob families in Atlantic City, and you did just loan him the money to pay those debts off, and I understand you're getting some vig on top of it. That makes you a direct contact Joe."

"First of all, I didn't pay those debts. That money came from a neighborhood fund we set up as part of our selling out to Waste International. We paid off Tony's debt to keep his family from not having a father anymore. He is paying the loan back with interest and it's not going to me. It goes to the fund, same with the interest he's paying."
DiMeolo apparently knew this but it still made me somehow suspicious.

"Well Joe, you do have a convicted bank robber here working for you. Thomas Fallone. He tried to steal and ATM back in 1989. That is a federal crime. "You didn't think I knew about Tommy?" I answered, "He's one of my best friends. I know Tommy since childhood on Shunk Street. Me and my dad made his bail so he could get out before his trial. I hired him down here and I bankrolled his construction business. Tommy needed a second chance and I was happy to give it to him. As far as I know, being a friend isn't a crime either, Paisan. Again...cut the crap and let's get down to business."

I was getting pissed now and I think DiMeolo knew it. "I'm calling a friend to come down here. Give me a minute." I got Charlie Bransford on the phone. "Chollie" I said, "How fast can you be at my house?" "I'm at your front door right now Joe..." With that, Charlie Bransford walked in my living room. "Joe!" he said as soon as he walked in. "I looked out my window and saw the Crown Vics. They're easy to spot when you've spent half your life in one." Then he stopped in his tracks and looked at the men in my living room. "Well, well, well, look who it is. Good Morning, Harvey." Agent Robertson went white and he started biting his cheek. Joe looked at me and a smile slowly crept across his face. "Joe I don't know what's going on here, but if Agent Robertson is involved, the facts are probably wrong." Charlie wasn't smiling when he said that and he shot Robertson a look like a big brother would when he caught his little brother in a lie.

Charlie introduced himself to DiMeolo and showed him his credentials. "I can vouch for this man, agent DiMeolo. Now what's the problem?" DiMeolo gave him the finer points in a hurry. The entire attitude in the room changed once Charlie showed up and everybody became cordial. Everybody except Agent Robertson, who stood there with his arms crossed, wearing a scowl. We went back to our conversation. "So what else is there Agent DiMeolo?" I asked.

He cleared his throat. "Joe," he began, "Do you know Jimmy Verducci, from back home?" I thought for a minute. "No...no I can't say that I do. Why?" DiMeolo stiffened a bit. "He's a major leaguer with the Porcinilli family. Maybe even a capo. Well about a year ago he went missing. We never had a clue about where he might be, until one of the anonymous calls we got about you. That led us to believe he was here." I cocked my head quizzically. "Like I said, I don't know the guy. So what makes you think he's here?" DiMeolo leaned in a little. "Joe, his nickname is 'The Crusher.' Jimmy, The Crusher, Verducci. Does the name mean anything now?" I thought about it some more. Then the light came on. "Wait..." I said. "Did one of your anonymous phone calls claim I had this Crusher guy out at my hunting camp?"

DiMeolo smiled. He actually looked relieved. "Well you wouldn't ask me that if you really had him out there. So, yes, that's exactly what the informant said. Now please tell me this is some mistaken identity." I laughed. "Okay, first, why don't you guys all have a seat? I think it's safe to drop the boxing gloves." DiMeolo laughed and Eversen smiled at Angie. Robertson was still basically intent on being an ass, but he was outnumbered and he seemed completely intimidated by Chollie being there in my living room.

Angie finally eased up a bit and offered to make some coffee for our guests. *Ice, broken.* I thought. Agent Eversen walked into the kitchen to help Angie while we stayed there in the living room to finish this whole affair. "The Crusher," I began, "Is the first garbage truck our family ever owned. My grandfather bought him from the township back in 1953. He's an old Ford Heavy Duty chassis and they always had a grille on them that looked mean and menacing. Of course, being a trash truck, it crushes everything. So we gave him the nickname, 'The Crusher.'" "So how did it end up out here at your hunting camp?" DiMeolo asked me. "About a year ago I got a phone call from Richard Green. He is the V.P. who did the Waste International deal with me. He said their corporate office wanted The Crusher gone. We had retired him years ago but we parked him on the front lawn of our office complex. He became a monument of sorts. The neighbors loved him. Anyway Green wanted to give me a chance to save him if we wanted to, so I had him shipped down and we parked him out by the hunting camp. I take my boys out there once in a while and let them practice driving a big truck like that, out where nobody can get hurt. I can take you out there to see him if you want."

Robertson spoke up, "I think that might just be a good idea..." he began. Then DiMeolo winked at me and said, "No, no I don't think that's necessary. Who would make up a story like that?" DiMeolo walked over and stuck out his hand. "Mr. Mezilli, we owe you a big apology. We should have simply called you first, sir. The element of surprise wasn't needed here." He said this as he shot a sarcastic look at Robertson. I instantly got the feeling that this was his idea, not

Dimeolo's. "I'm very sorry we upset your afternoon like we did."

Now, I have a long, slow fuse for a temper. But I'm also quick to forgive. I shook his hand and smiled. "It's okay Paisan. You have a job to do and these days you never can tell, right?" I turned and walked into the kitchen. Why don't you guys come in here and have some coffee before you go, huh?" DiMeolo, Robertson, Eversen, Charlie Bransford, and one other agent who never said anything, came in and sat down at our table. We had coffee and broke out some cannoli and by the time they left, we were all on a first name basis. All except Robertson who looked like someone had given him a wedgie.

The FBI agents all left around 2:30, which was good because my kids were going to be home soon and I didn't want them to see this. As we walked out to their waiting cars, I asked DiMeolo -whose name was actually Frank- "Frank can you tell me who the tips came from?" Now, I had a damned good idea but I wanted to be certain.

"They come in anonymously, Joe. Even I don't know" He said. Then he winked, "I bet Agent Bransford could find out for you." "Fair enough." I said, shaking his hand. "You guys be careful out there and Merry Christmas to you." They drove off and as I was heading back to my house, I noticed Lowery staring out his window again. *I know it was you, you ass!* I thought. Just to give him fits, I raised my right hand with the index and pinky fingers extended and gave him the death horns. He closed his curtains in a hurry.

This ends now. I said to myself.

Charlie turned to leave and I stopped him. "Hang on a second Chollie; come inside if you have a minute. I need to talk to you." Charlie agreed and we went back inside and sat at the breakfast bar drinking coffee. "This has really pissed me off." I began, "I know it was Lowery, and you know it too. You nailed it a year ago when we were in my garage that night. But I had no idea he had taken it this far. This could have really gotten out of hand." Charlie agreed, "Yeah I was thinking the same thing when I walked in and saw Harvey Robertson was here." "You know Robertson?" I asked. "Yeah, we have a history." Charlie replied. "I worked with him for about a year or so up in Quantico. I was getting some specialized forensic training and he was sort of desk-bound.

He got his start in the Trenton, New Jersey office and then moved to Philadelphia for a time. He was a terrible field agent and they moved him to HQ just to get him off the live cases. Harvey was known for working from presupposition and ignoring the facts that didn't fit his narrative." Charlie took a sip of his coffee and continued.

"Robertson is past retirement age but he hangs on. They moved him back out to the field in the hopes that the activity would push him to wanting to hang them up. He just stays on stubbornly. He acts like the lead agent in every investigation but he really isn't. You probably picked that up today. DiMeolo was really the guy in charge." "Yeah," I said with a smirk, "Robertson started off calling the shots but DiMeolo stepped in and steered us away from the rocks.

Charlie continued, "Well if it was entirely Robertson's call, he might have come here with a tactical team and kicked your door in. That's no joke either; he's that sort of an asshole. I also wouldn't be surprised that if he was in charge, your lines would have been tapped and your house bugged." I sat up, startled by what he was saying. "What? Are you serious?" "Serious as a heart attack. I'd say the odds are sixty-forty against it, because I think DiMeolo was running this case. But you never know" Charlie responded. "I'll call DiMeolo tomorrow and ask him for a tech clearance on your house. I still have enough clout to get something like that done. If there's anything here, they'll tell me. I'm doubtful though. Robertson wasn't calling the ball on this one. DiMeolo doesn't strike me as the type who would get special permission to get a tech warrant on something as flimsy as anonymous phone tips. But Robertson would have. That jackass would have staked out his own mother in the bathroom at Macy's if he had a suspicion. He's gung ho."

Angie took a sip of her coffee and asked Charlie something a lot more important. "Chollie, how far do you think this goes? I mean if Phil Lowery was such a slave to his vivid imagination that he called the FBI so many times, who else did he tell?" I smiled at Anj. I was thinking the same thing myself. "Good point, Babe." I said, "How do we know the entire town doesn't suspect us? You know what a busybody Phil is, who knows how far this has gone." Charlie scratched his head and smiled at us. "Well," he said, "You can either go door to door and tell each and every fix this with every single person in town, or you can just assume that Charlie hasn't gone too far afield with this and just deal with him for now."

What do you suggest, Charlie?" I asked. "I'd just keep an eye out for people treating you differently and let it go from there. I never suspected you, and I was in the FBI for twenty-seven years. From what I've seen since I moved here, only a handful of folks even give Lowery any credence anyway. I wouldn't worry about it much. Besides that, Phil isn't a guy to waste words on the locals if he thinks the big fish will believe him. That's why he went to the FBI instead of spreading a rumor around town...so he'd be the hero when they kicked your door in."

Charlie is a smart guy and Angie and I decided to just let it go for now. But I was definitely going to have it out with

Phil. Charlie stood to leave. "Thanks for coming over Pal," I said to him. "You probably saved us from a very ugly scenario." Charlie put his hand on my shoulder. "Joey Trucks" he said with a laugh," "My neighbor, the accidental mobster." I closed the door behind him and turned to Angie. "I'm going over there right now..."

Dealing With a Rat

One time when I was a kid, my dad had heard some rumblings about our family being "connected." Some neighbor was jealous of the dividend our hard work was paying and he decided to just spread a rumor. It pissed the Old Man off to no end and he went straight to the source. It was one of the few times I ever saw my dad really, enraged. He could get mad, God knows he could. But I never saw my dad look like he was going to lose control other than two or three times. He was not very pleasant with that guy.

Once I remember was when the unions tried forcing themselves on our shop. They harassed our guys so much, even damaging our trucks, so that my father actually went to the local president's house with a baseball bat. He never even knocked. He just walked in and poked the guy in his chest with the bat and said "Listen Lou, if you show up at my place again with your goons and your pamphlets, I'm going to come back here and I'll go through you," then he turned to Lou Gentile's big, fat son Robert "and I'll go through you," then he looked at his wife "and I'll go through you, and anybody else in your god-damned house until I figure out who is bothering my guys. Capisce, paisan?" My old man said Lou peed his pants right there in his own kitchen.

I wasn't carrying a bat, and I wasn't out to make Phil Lowery's dam burst. But I was hot. I knocked on Phil's door and Gladys answered. As soon as she saw me she went white as a sheet. "Hello Gladys" I said, "Where is your husband?" I was going to just walk in his house but I knew Phil was a gun owner, and I didn't trust him not to actually take a shot. I also didn't think Gladys had the slightest clue what Phil had done so I tried to remain calm and not show my anger towards her. Gladys' knees buckled a bit and she stepped back from the door. "Pheel!" she yelled, never taking her eyes off of me. "Pheel get up here now!"

Phil trudged up the steps from his basement. I imagine he was down there trying to adapt a baby monitor into a bugging device so he could spy on me. He opened the basement door and as soon as he saw my face he went limp. I thought he was going to cry. He swallowed hard and tried sticking his hand out. "W...well hello neighbor!" He offered. "What brings you over here to..." I wasn't in the mood for Phil's crap. "Don't give me that country-boy charm, pal. You know damn well what you did. The FBI was just at my house, Phil. The Mother-F... the FBI! In my home!" I had almost blown the fuse. I hadn't uttered the "F" word in over thirty years. It was one of those things I had decided on early in life, that I would distance myself a bit from the regular Joe's in the neighborhood. It was part of being a success and part of being a Mezilli. You work to earn respect, and then you work to keep respect. Just now...that was as close as I'd come to launching an F Bomb in more than half my life.

"Do you know how hard it is to scare my wife, Phil? My Angie? Well the FBI will do the job. They'll scare pretty much anybody. If my kids had been home, I'd already be beating the shit out of you, are we clear about this?" I thought Phil was going to have a heart attack. He grabbed his chest and started licking his lips. And then he did the one thing that would cement my never respecting him again. He lied.

"Now hold on there, Joe..." He whimpered, "What on earth are you talking about? The FBI you say?" I was getting hotter by the second. "Don't you bullshit me, you bastard, I saw you looking out the window while they were there interrogating me and my wife. In my home! I saw you again

391

when we walked out. You know damned well you're the one who was calling them anonymously. You were in my garage that day when I took the call from Richard Green about The Crusher. The Crusher is a garbage truck, Phil...a garbage truck! You called the FBI to my home because you are a shitty eaves-dropper with too active an imagination and nothing interesting going on in your entire miserable life!" I was seething. The more I thought about what he'd done and the more I thought about what could have gone wrong this morning with seven armed federal agents in my house, the more pissed off I got.

"Phil, I've tried to be your friend. I've put up with your avoiding us and never being quite the neighbor to us that everyone else was. I'm done. Today you insulted me, and you never, ever insult an Italian man's honor. You insulted mine, and my father's, and my grandfather's. We worked hard to make our business something great and you looked at my success as some sort of mob connection. I am *not* in the god damned mob!"

I was on a roll. Then, in a moment of brilliance, I decided to have a laugh at Phil's expense. I made up a couple more Itanglish words just to give him something to stew over for a few weeks. "Phil..." I barked at him, "You are a *sfinginue!*" I tried not to smile because it would have ruined the moment. "You're a *sfinginue* and you have a lot of trouble coming because of this day!" I paused for effect, then I raised my hand, extended my index and pinky and growled; "Noddafingah!" I spun on my heels and walked out the door. *Sfinginue,* I said to myself. *If that isn't a word, it needs to be.* Oh and in case you're wondering, I borrowed "Noddafingah" from "Old Man Parker," the dad in *A Christmas Story.*

There's No Escaping This Thing of Ours

I walked back to the house. Angie had left to go get the kids from school. I was glad they hadn't been there to see the events of the morning. I sat down in my recliner and just stared out the window. *Oh Crap!* I thought to myself, *in the morning's excitement I never got the Winter Warlock put out on the yard.* I had wanted to get it out there and inflated before the kids got home. *Oh well,* I thought, *I guess I'll do it tomorrow.*

I was too upset to get to it today and I wanted to get rid of this bad mood before the kids got home. But I was too angry. I kept thinking about what Phil had done. The things he'd implied. The dangerous game he'd played all because he's just a suspicious old man with a vivid imagination and an obsession with the mob. I was literally shaking. It hurt. My family worked so hard to stay away from that mafia stuff. We never liked those images of mobster Italians to begin with. There was a reason I never wore the silk suits and got my hair sculpted and wore pinky rings. I earned every penny I made honestly, and I didn't want to be looked at as one of those guys. Hell, I had some of them as friends back home, but I made sure there was a clear line between us, and nobody crossed it.

It felt like none of that mattered. I was Italian, I was in the Waste Management business, and I had a ton of money. That, and I was very different from my neighbors. That's all he needed to believe the lie.

But for all my efforts, I apparently couldn't convince one guy, one very loudmouthed, opinionated guy, that all those things he thought were me being in the mob, were simply me being Italian. *This is what happens when you eavesdrop.* I said to myself. *A sixty seven year old man should know better.*

Angie and the kids came home a few minutes later. I smiled just hearing them pull up the drive. The boys opened the door for their mom and sister, like I'd taught them. They were straight "A" students at a private Christian Academy. They weren't A.J. frickin' Soprano. I was getting angry all over again. I decided to just stop thinking about it. It was done. Phil was put in his place and as far as I was concerned, it was over.

Angie got the kids a snack and made sure they changed their clothes and put their books in their bedrooms. Petey wanted to throw a football for a few minutes before it got dark. Before long, I had a serious game of "Delco RoughTouch" going in my front yard. The boys called a few of the neighbor kids and Uncle Tommy Fallone came over to join in. Afterwards, I made my sons instant neighborhood heroes by telling them –in front of their friends- how my uncle Tony, their great uncle, had played Rough Touch with the great Vince "Invincible" Papale. The neighbor kids had seen the movie and knew exactly who I was talking about. My sons were strutting like peacocks.

Later, after dinner, I was talking with Angie and Tommy in the living room about the events of the day. Tommy got pretty angry and was ready to go over to have a few words with Phil on his own. "It's okay Paisan," I said to him. "I think I scared him enough." Tommy sat down and opened a beer. "It's done." I sighed, "I think I nipped Phil in the bud today. I don't think there will be any repercussions anymore. And I don't think this went any farther than Phil and maybe Lars Erickson. So we'll let it go."

We talked a few minutes longer, when there came a knock on the front door. I opened it to find two of the neighbor boys

we had been playing football with just a couple of hours before. Sam McGrew and Micah Lawson.
Nice kids, both of them were Jack's classmates.

"Well boys," I said, "The kids are in for the night, they'll see you tomorrow in school." Sam shuffled his feet and sheepishly said he was actually here to see me. "Me?" I wondered, "Well what can I do for you, Sam?" Sam and Micah came into the living room and began their tale. "Last week I loaned Micah my bicycle," Sam began, "He brought it back a day later and the back tire had a leak. It didn't have a leak before." I was baffled. "So, how can I help with this, Sam?" I asked. "Well my dad said to come here and ask your opinion. He said you have lots of experience settling problems and it's a sign of respect to ask you."

In the background I heard Angie snicker. *Oh my God,* I thought, *I'm the friggin Godfather.* I stood up and walked them to the front door. "Sam, this is for your dad to settle, not me." I said. But poor Sam looked distraught. I got the impression that if I sent him home without settling this dispute and giving my blessing, his father would be worried about starting his car the next morning. So I looked at them both and asked; "How old was the tire when it started leaking?" Sam answered; "About two years." "Good" I said, "So it was getting old already, and you can't say Micah actually caused the leak?" Micah smiled and said "See! I told you Sam!" "Not so fast!" I said to Micah, "You still popped his tire. So here's what I want you to do. Tomorrow after school you both come here and help me and the boys finish putting up the rest of our Christmas lights. Then after that you stay for dinner. Then, we go into the garage and I'll show you how to patch a tube on a bicycle, like we did when I was a kid. Deal?" The boys smiled. I smiled. Problem solved. I waved goodbye and closed the door.

395

Turning to Angie and Tommy I sighed. Angie said; "You handled that well, *Don Mezilli*." I paused for a moment, slumped my shoulders, and in a bad Pacino voice, smiled, and said; "Just when I thought I was out, they *pull me back in!*"

Across the street, Phil Lowery's cell phone rang. Phil sat in his kitchen in the dark, smoking his pipe. He answered on the second ring, as he'd been instructed. "This is Elliot Ness." Said the voice on the other end of the line. Phil squinted into the darkness, set his pipe down and said, "This is Preparation H" using the code name given him by the agent. "I figured you'd be callin,' what the hell happened over there? I thought this was it!" The voice was mysterious; "Your neighbor is better at this than I thought. He's got friends. But this isn't over. No sir. This is *not* over…"

The End

Love it? PLEASE, leave me a brief review at Amazon.com
Oh and stay tuned…Joey *will* be back!